THEY MET IN A TAVERN

THEY MET IN A TAVERN

a novel

Elijah Menchaca

CamCat
Books

CamCat Publishing, LLC
Brentwood, Tennessee 37027
camcatpublishing.com

© 2021 by Elijah Menchaca

Hardcover ISBN 9780744303834
Paperback ISBN 9780744303643
Large-Print Paperback ISBN 9780744303476
eBook ISBN 9780744303469
Audiobook ISBN 9780744303315

Library of Congress Control Number: 2021936570

Cover and book design by Maryann Appel

5   3   1   2   4

To my Wings, who makes me feel like I can fly.

THE
CONTRACT

As the crackling fireplace kept away the last chills of the dying winter, the Handler made a show of examining a stack of papers in front of the client. He'd already read them, had aides read them, and read the aides' notes on them before this meeting started. He'd kept his job as long as he had by being thorough. But for some reason, clients never believed it unless they saw him doing it.

The Handler didn't mind; showmanship was his favorite part of the job.

"Well, it would seem everything is in order," the Handler stated, straightening out the stack of papers. "I'm certain we can make all the necessary arrangements to move forward with your contract."

Silas shifted uncomfortably in his seat on the other side of the Handler's desk. He probably thought he did a good job of hiding it, but the man may as well have been proclaiming his emotions in song. The poor soldier—and even without any heraldry, his posture gave him away as one—was almost adorably lost in the unfamiliar territory of criminal enterprise. All the more reason to make him feel at ease with whatever pageantry and pleasantries were necessary.

"Thank you," Silas said. "And you can keep my name out of this?"

"All contractors will conduct their business through us," the Handler assured with a sweeping wave. "Your hands will be clean right up until the targets are handed off to you."

"Good."

"There is one minor problem I'd like to address now," the Handler said.

"What?"

"There are a few names on the list you provided . . ." The Handler leafed through the papers until he found the one in question and plucked it from the stack. With a dry quill he pointed to the offending names. "These five here. I would advise you to *double* the reward for each of them."

The client frowned, and the Handler knew he felt like he was being conned. The Handler took no offense. It was only natural for someone of the client's background to distrust someone like the Handler. They were from opposing worlds. And, even if they weren't, it was an obscene amount of money they were discussing.

"Why?"

"I advise this purely out of a desire to ensure satisfactory results," the Handler said. "Simply put, if you want to capture the Starbreakers, you're going to need the best. And the best won't bite for what you're offering."

Silas's frown deepened as he stared at the names. The Handler waited patiently for him to see sense.

"I thought they were failures."

The Handler chuckled softly. It wasn't an inaccurate assessment. But it wasn't the full picture either. He wondered where Silas must have been from, to not understand who they were dealing with. Or maybe he was younger than he looked.

"The Starbreakers toppled the tower of the Hegemony when they were children. They've slain things from other worlds and found some of the Old World's greatest marvels," the Handler said matter-of-factly. "Even *now*, anything less than the very best won't be enough to touch them."

Silas continued to stare at the list and the five offending names. Brass. Phoenix. Snow. Church. Angel. Securing other names from the list would be beneficial. But these five could be the key to everything.

"You have a deal."

2

BRASS

B rass woke up lying naked on the floor of what was either an expensive inn or a pretentious brothel. His first thought was that the place had incredibly lush carpeting in its rooms. His second thought was that his head hurt. A lot. But that was nothing new, and, if he could find his things, easily fixable.

He just had to wait for the room to stop spinning.

Slowly, fighting his hangover's protests, he sat up and blinked. Thick curtains pulled shut over the windows were blocking the early-morning sun, leaving the room dimly lit. There was an excess of red velvet in the room's decor, which told him most of what he needed to know about where he was and what he'd gotten up to last night.

The bed, which he seemed to have missed by a few feet last night, was occupied by a woman with smooth caramel skin and flowing dark hair that spread out over the sheets and obscured her face. Somewhere, deep in the back of his mind, fighting to be heard over a stabbing pain in his temples, alarm bells were going off. He gingerly searched for her wrist under the sheets. When he found it and felt a pulse, what little concern he had evaporated, and he returned to looking for his things.

Finding them was easier said than done. Besides the bedroom the suite had a bathroom, a kitchenette, and a living room, and absolutely all of it was a mess. Dozens of room-service trays were strewn about, stacked with half-eaten plates of cold food and empty bottles. That wasn't even touching the unconscious strangers scattered in every room with about as much dignity as Brass had woken up with. Actually, slightly more, given that most of them seemed to have managed to collapse onto a piece of furniture instead of the floor. There were six people in the suite, and Brass had absolutely no memory of meeting any of them. Brass wouldn't have had a problem with that, except their clothes thrown all over the suite made it harder to find his.

It took about ten minutes of stumbling and searching before Brass finally spotted his pants and belt in the kitchenette, draped over the back of a chair. He took about two steps forward before he tripped over his own feet and fell face-first onto the floor.

"Oops," he muttered. Rather than repeating the incident, he opted to crawl the rest of the way.

From the floor, Brass rummaged through his pockets until he found a small pouch and a book of matches. He made his way to the nightstand, which was the closest flat surface he could find. From the pouch he took a generous pinch of specially blended herbs, deposited them in a neat pile on the nightstand, and lit a match.

The blend burned, releasing blue-gray smoke into Brass's face. The smoke smelled like blueberries and driftwood. Brass breathed it in for a few minutes, feeling his headache evaporate with every breath. He sighed in relief, then sniffed again. The smell had changed. Now it just smelled like burning wood as the smoldering herbs scorched the nightstand.

"Shit!"

Brass frantically slapped the still burning herbs until the flames were out, stinging his hands in the process. As the herbs finished their work, the last traces of distracting pain receded from his skull, paving the way for a sudden rush of stark clarity to take its place.

"Probably shouldn't have done that on the table."

Feeling significantly better, Brass grabbed his pants off the chair and tugged them up to his waist. He found his vest shortly after and slipped that on as well. But he could only find one of his boots.

That's irritating.

Single boot in hand, Brass toured the living room again with freshly sobered senses. Most of the men and women there wore makeup that gave them away as escorts or dancers, and the skimpy clothing Brass found lying around backed up that guess. But one woman didn't fit the look at all. Her haircut was too sensible, and out of everyone in the room, she was the only one still wearing anything, even if it was just her underwear and a blanket.

Brass made a mental note to take another crack at finding a blend that could help with memory blackouts. He went back to the bedroom. Without a splitting hangover sucking up his attention span, something about the woman he'd found when he first woke up was making him uneasy. Trying not to wake her up, Brass brushed some of her hair out of the way so he could get a better look at her face.

"Fuu—"

In the bed was none other than Diane Recpina, one of the princesses of the City of Orm. On a hunch, Brass peered from the bedroom to take another look at the other woman who didn't fit the bill of an escort and tried to picture her holding a tablet and quill. It was easy to do.

He still wasn't entirely sure what had happened, but he was fairly certain he was going to be in very big trouble soon. Foreign princesses were pretty high up on the list of things he wasn't supposed to sleep with.

As if to punctuate that thought, a knock came from the door.

"Who is it?" Brass asked, hurriedly tucking the princess in.

"Brass?" a gruff voice came from the other side of the door.

The alarm bells came back when he heard his name. Someone knew he was here, which meant they probably knew who else was here.

"Ah, one second!" Brass called out, rounding up spare blankets and towels from the floor as he drafted a perfectly innocent explanation for the scene his visitors were about to walk in on.

He ran around the room, throwing the towels and blankets to cover up the escorts, all the while trying to keep an eye out for his other boot. There was a second, more impatient knock at the door.

"Be with you in a moment!" Brass yelled back.

The search for his boot was getting him nowhere, so he gave up on it and made a beeline for the door just as the person on the other side knocked again. Brass could practically hear how many seconds of patience his caller had left. He combed his hands through his hair, threw his single boot off to the side, and opened the door.

"How can I help you?" he asked with a smile.

Brass was expecting Iandran royal guards, here to collect the princess— dark hair, steel rapiers, colorful robes, and engraved breastplates. The two men waiting outside were not that. Their skin was tanned from time spent in the sun but still unmistakably white. They wore rough traveler's cloaks over piecemeal leathers.

Instead of rapiers, they were holding shortswords.

These men were not here for the princess.

"Sorry, wrong room," Brass apologized, slamming the door in their faces while they were still staring at him. Before he could reach the bolt to lock the door, it exploded open, and both men charged in.

Brass threw himself just out of reach of the men's first swings and hit the floor. Without thinking, he rolled away until he collided with a chair, which he immediately hurled at the intruders to buy time.

Brass sprang to his feet just as one of them got closer. Luckily, their swordplay was pathetic. Unarmed, Brass swatted aside the first stab that came his way, and as the second guy came in, Brass grabbed his offending wrist and redirected his attack into his friend's arm.

The attacker snarled, "Watch it!"

"Yeah!" Brass agreed, pointing to the guy he had used as a weapon. "Watch it, Greg!"

"What?" one of the men asked.

"Well," Brass explained as he dodged another stab from one of the intruders, "you gentlemen neglected to introduce yourselves, even though you know my name. So, until you learn your manners," Brass warned, pointing at the two men, "you're Greg, and you're Wallace."

Wallace circled around, trying to get behind him. At the same time, Greg lunged at him again. Brass twisted on his heel and in one motion dodged the stab while kicking the man behind him in the stomach.

"Shut up!" Greg roared, charging again.

Brass sidestepped his attack and jabbed Greg in the eyes with his fingers. While he was distracted, Brass took his sword. With a burst of speed, and a quick turn to the side, he jammed the stolen weapon into Wallace's shoulder. Just as quickly, he pulled the blade free and opened the man's throat.

One down.

Greg tackled him to the ground, and Brass lost the sword. The two of them struggled, with Greg getting solid hits in as they tumbled across the floor. Their roll came to a stop near the door, Brass on the ground, Greg's hands around his neck.

"Bastard," Greg spat, getting blood on Brass's face. "You're gonna pay for that."

Out of the corner of his eye, lying on the floor underneath a small end table, Brass spotted his boot. He was confused, thinking he'd thrown it somewhere else, until he realized it was the one he'd been looking for all morning. Brass tried to laugh, but all that came out was a strangled gargle.

"Save your breath for the devils, you sack of shit," Greg said, squeezing harder.

Brass strained every muscle in his throat as he reached for his boot. Feeling on the cusp of passing out, he managed to croak, "What's your shoe size?"

Feeling along the heel of his boot, Brass found the small, concealed button and pressed it, deploying a blade from the toe end. He grabbed the boot and jammed it into the side of Greg's head. The tension around Brass's neck disappeared, and Greg collapsed. Brass coughed and wheezed underneath the man's bulk before shoving him off. He staggered to his feet as stillness took the room. The only sounds were occasional mutters from the escorts as they blissfully slept on, too deep into their drug- and drink-induced morning comas to have even noticed the racket.

"No, no, I'm fine, don't get up on my account."

Hearing the sound of a door creaking, Brass whirled around, still brandishing his boot.

Princess Diane stood in the bedroom doorway, clutching a sheet around herself, a look of utter horror on her face. Brass looked around the room, at the two bodies, and at the blood that was soaking into the carpet.

"Well. Good morning." Brass greeted her breathlessly. "Would you like to get breakfast?"

The princess screamed.

3
OLD HABITS

Arman walked the streets of the Pale, grateful that not too many people were out this early in the morning. It had been a long time since he'd come to this part of Olwin, and his rumpled old coat made him stick out enough on its own without him also looking like a lost tourist. The Pale was the playground of the city's richest citizens, full of high-end clubs and restaurants that generally didn't see real business until later in the day. His memory wasn't the problem—his mental map was out of date. There was a music hall where the theater used to be, Nathan's Bakery was completely gone, and somebody had the brilliant idea to rename some of the streets. Strangest to him was the new tenant housing building that looked like it had been converted from an old hotel. People didn't live in the Pale, except for a few business owners with rooms above their establishments. Well, not the last time he'd been here anyway.

Finally he found his way to the place he was looking for. The Crimson Lilac was a large three-story inn painted dark brown with red accents. On a second-story dining balcony, a few guests were enjoying a light breakfast. It was a higher-end establishment with a reputation for "expanded hospitality." Exactly the sort of place he would have expected to find Brass.

He stepped through the front doors and was greeted by an extravagant interior. Expensive woodwork, fine paintings, bright red carpet. The lobby was a simple space, mostly built to exhibit art and sculptures. But there was a front desk and an inviting lounge visible just a room over that was currently almost empty. Like the rest of the Pale, it was the kind of place that didn't really come alive until the sun went down.

The woman at the front desk was absorbed in a book and didn't greet him.

Arman approached her.

"Excuse me?"

She looked up, quickly closing her book as she straightened her posture, brightened her eyes, and flashed a wide, apologetic smile. He always had a hard time telling real smiles from the professional ones.

"How can I help you?"

"I'm looking for someone who might have stayed here last night," Arman explained. "A man named Brass?"

"I'm . . . afraid I can't give out guest information."

Arman had expected the rebuttal, but he hadn't expected the delivery. The woman said it like a question. She sounded surprised. No, not surprised. Confused maybe.

"If you'd like, I can . . . take a message for him, when or if he comes here." The woman blinked, reading from a mental script as her mind worked. "Is this Brass someone . . . important?"

"Not exactly."

Not in the way most people were important anyway. Arman was sure now that Brass was somewhere in this place. It was just a matter of figuring out where. He could try to convince the woman to tell him, but he wasn't really sure how. Or he could try getting a look at the hotel's books somehow. That could get complicated, but it would involve less talking.

He missed having an invisibility belt.

He realized he was overthinking the issue just as a piercing scream from upstairs interrupted his thoughts.

"I think that's him."

The woman's disapproval of him going up the stairs was written on her face, but she didn't say anything out loud. On the way up, he tried to prepare himself. It had been years since he'd seen Brass, and the last time they'd spoken, things had ended . . . poorly. He told himself he could handle this. He wasn't trying to make amends or hold a conversation. It was just a job.

He got lucky when he reached the top of the stairs. There was only one room along the hall with its door open.

Arman cautiously made his way to it.

"Brass?"

He peeked in. He didn't see anyone, but there were signs of a struggle. Furniture overturned. Objects scattered. He was starting to get worried.

"Brass, you in here?"

Arman took another step, and a sword point was at his throat. It was a thin, shining rapier with an ornately swept handle. Wielding it was a wiry man with short, dark curls, finely groomed facial hair, and brown eyes that were accented with just a hint of eyeliner. He was wearing pants, an open vest, and nothing else, exposing a chest of scars and more than a few tattoos.

"Brass?"

Brass blinked, smiled, and sheathed his rapier. "Phoenix? Seven hells, what are you doing here?"

Brass dragged Arman into a hug, which Arman stiffly accepted without returning. He hadn't known exactly what to expect, but it hadn't been this. It was like their last meeting, and the last seven years, had never happened.

He gave it a second before gently pushing Brass off of him.

"The castellan called in a favor," Arman explained. *Focus on the job.* "Apparently, an Iandran princess went missing last week, and you know where she is."

"Oh," Brass said, disappointed. "Yeah, she's over there."

Arman followed Brass's gesture into the next room. There was the princess, wearing a robe, clutching a cup of coffee, staring at a pair of dead bodies on the living-room floor.

"Son of a—purple, Brass! What did you do?"

"Okay, I know this looks bad, but it's really not," Brass defended. "These two guys—wait a minute. Son of a *purple*?"

Arman blinked, trying to think of the simplest way to explain himself. "Uh. I'm trying to watch my language, so I've been . . . using substitutes?"

"Why?"

"There was this whole thing with my parents about how kids are sponges or something," Arman said. "I'm trying to make sure one of my daughter's first words isn't an expletive."

"You have a daughter now?"

"Oh saints." He hadn't meant to tell Brass that. Or anything about himself. *Too late now.* "Uh, yeah. Seven months."

"Phoenix! Congratulations!"

Brass pulled Arman in for another hug, tighter this time. Once again, Arman mostly stood there, though this time, he tried to half-heartedly return the embrace with one arm. At least until it went on for too long.

"Brass."

"Hm?"

"What happened here?"

"Oh. Right. Them." Brass turned his attention to Greg and Wallace. "Weirdest thing. They came knocking on the door asking for me, I answered, and then they barged in and tried to kill me. And well, you know how that goes."

"What was the scream?"

Brass pointed back at the princess, who was now staring at the two of them, and Arman remembered the whole reason he was here. He cleared his throat.

"Apologies for all of this, Princess Recpina," Arman said in Iandran. *"My name is Arman Meshar. The university and the castellan asked me to bring you back to school."*

As soon as she heard her native tongue, the princess fixated on Arman. What he said almost didn't matter. Just hearing it lent him an air of familiarity and safety she was desperate for. In Iandran she asked, *"Those men. Who are they? What's going on?"*

"The authorities will handle this. Please, go get your things."

The princess hesitated, still distracted by the bodies. She slowly nodded and left the room, holding her head. Arman recognized the signs of a hangover.

Brass cocked his head.

"Well, you would have been useful when I was trying to make conversation."

As soon as the princess was out of the room, Arman glared daggers at Brass, who looked offended.

"What?"

"You took a foreign dignitary's daughter to a sex hotel, got her drunk, and then killed two people in front of her!"

"I didn't do it in front of her. I think. She was just sort of there once it was over. I'm fine by the way, thank you for asking."

A mouse-like voice interrupted them, this time speaking in Corsan. "Hello? Is someone there?"

Another woman walked into the room wearing a dazed expression and a shirt too large to be hers while clutching a blanket around her.

"Her staffer too?"

"That wasn't my call. She wouldn't leave her side."

The woman peered past them and shrieked. "Are those . . .?"

"I'm with the city watch," Arman interrupted. "You and the princess are leaving. Go get your things."

The woman seemed a little confused, and shaken, but she quickly nodded and walked away in a hurry. The sound of her and the princess talking in panicked whispers filtered in from the next room. Arman dragged his hand over his face.

"This is a mess, Brass."

"I think I've made worse."

"That doesn't make this okay!"

Sooner or later, security would arrive. Then it would be the watch's turn, and all this would get back to the castellan, who would expect answers. Arman figured he might as well get them while he was there.

"Who were these guys?" Arman asked.

"I don't know," Brass said. "Forgot to introduce themselves before they started stabbing. Killers today: no manners."

Arman ignored Brass, crouching down to look at the bodies. It would be a few minutes before the princess and her attaché would be ready to leave, and he was curious. They were men used to lean living, by the look of them. Dressed for a fight.

On a hunch, he removed the bracer off one to get a look at his forearm. As expected, there was a tattoo. It was a pair of crossed pikes, circled and entwined by chains.

"Freelancers. Not a company I recognize though."

A cross between mercenaries and treasure hunters, freelancers roamed the world, braving its dangers for a chance at fortune and glory. They almost always worked in groups, and more often than not, those groups dissolved or got killed long before they ever made anything of themselves. And now two more had learned just how common that fate was.

Arman stood up. "Looks like you pissed someone off enough for them to hire glintchasers over it."

"Not particularly good ones either," Brass lamented. "I think I'm insulted."

Another man walked into the room. He was tall, easily a head above Arman and Brass, with gray skin and pointed ears—but no tusks—and human eyes. A half-orc. He had his thumbs hooked in his belt and a questioning scowl. Arman recognized security when he saw it.

The princess and her attendant emerged from the other room, fully clothed.

"I hope you get this sorted out," Arman offered to Brass. "I'm gonna go."

"What? Just like that, you're gonna leave me?" Brass asked. "Someone wants me dead, and I don't know who. It's a big mystery. That's like, your thing."

"No."

"C'mon. We haven't seen each other in years. Help me out with this," Brass pleaded. "It'll be just like old times."

"That is the problem," Arman said. "I don't do this anymore, Brass."

"Oh, come on. You got something better to do?"

"Yes. It's called an actual life," Arman said. "I have a family, Brass."

"So, what? I'm just supposed to figure this out on my own?"

"Yes," Arman stressed, before softening. "I'm sorry."

Arman motioned for the princess and her attendant to follow him. The half-orc moved to stand in his way.

"I'm working for the castellan to get these women home safely," Arman said. "It's really not worth the trouble trying to get in the way of that. Besides, I just got here. You want to know what's going on, talk to him."

Brass stared at Arman, jaw slack. He mouthed the words *"You bastard."* Arman ignored him. The half-orc thought it over and stepped out of Arman's way.

"Thank you." Arman let the princess and her attendant go first so he could say good-bye to Brass. "Good luck. With whatever this is."

"Phoenix, you're an asshole," Brass retorted as the half-orc eyed him down.

Arman just shrugged and walked out the door.

"I hope your kid's first word is *cunt!*"

4
THE CASTELLAN

The carriage ride across town was a quiet one. The princess and her attendant said nothing and avoided eye contact with Arman. He was a man of deep brown complexion, with near black hair and a closely shorn, slightly ragged beard. He was modestly built, but his eyes and mouth easily settled into a frown, as if it was the expression his face was the most comfortable making.

Even still, the women stole glances at him, and Arman recognized the look in their eyes. It was a very particular breed of trust, the kind people only gave when they were scared and needed someone to latch on to. After what they'd seen this morning, that look didn't surprise Arman. In lieu of conversation, Arman watched the city go by on the cart ride. It wasn't just the Pale. Most of Olwin was foreign to him now. The streets were more crowded. Distinct fashion trends stood out against each other as natives and immigrants rubbed shoulders with one another. Even without the differences in clothing, it was easy to tell the natives from the newcomers. Locals couldn't stop staring at new arrivals, but the foreigners were just trying to keep their heads down.

When Arman and the women arrived at the castellan's keep, things grew loud as guards hounded them with questions. They then were swept in through the gates in a hurry once the guards realized who Diane was, lest anyone on the streets recognize the princess and swarm the keep. A member of the guard ran to get the castellan while a member of the city watch Arman knew came to escort the princess.

"Kaitlyn?"

"Arman! I heard Elizabeth talked you into leaving the house," Kaitlyn said. A relieved smile spread across her face as she looked the princess over. "Thanks for helping out with this."

"I owed Harbin a favor," Arman said. He realized that probably wasn't an appropriate response, then amended, "I mean, you're welcome."

Kaitlyn ordered a few men to break off and escort the princess away, and Arman noticed new livery of crossed swords decorating Kaitlyn's left arm instead of the single sword she'd had the last time he saw her. She'd gotten a promotion.

He smiled but thought better of saying anything. No need to hold her up while she had a job to do.

"Her Corsan's a little choppy," Arman warned her. "Probably best to find someone who speaks Iandran."

"Right," she said hesitantly. "No one in the watch speaks Iandran."

"Oh."

Without a solution to offer her, Arman opted to give a curt, apologetic nod and take his leave before anyone could ask for his help. The castellan would be expecting a debrief from him.

When Arman got to the castellan's office, he did his best to give Harbin a quick summary of things. He explained how he found Brass, where they were; mentioned the men who attacked. The castellan took it about as well as could be expected.

Harbin was about fifteen years Arman's senior, and he'd been the king's man in Olwin since before Arman had ever set foot in the city. His hairline was receding, and he was putting on weight, but he still went out of his way to maintain a neat shave and a clean presentation. He was never a particularly reserved man, especially when he was getting bad news. Right now, his round face was bright red.

"The Lilac?"

"Afraid so."

"Of fucking course they were there," he muttered. "I'll have a cleric give them a once-over before we get them back to the university. Last thing I need is a foreign princess with a social disease."

Arman agreed. "Probably a good call."

"I'll get someone out to the Pale to look into those men as well, but there's not gonna be much to find. Always manage to clean things up before we get out there," Harbin mused.

"Brass can probably handle himself, if it's just gonna be more trouble than it's worth."

"I don't give a glint about him. He can die in a pit, and I'll toast to the day he does. I care that someone thinks they can put a hit on a man in my city." Harbin considered what he'd just said and amended. "Ah, sorry. I know he was your friend."

"You don't have to apologize," Arman said. "Brass is Brass."

"Of all the places he could have turned up," Harbin grunted. He was still fuming but decided that was enough anger to expend on this. He had to save some energy for whatever else the day had in store for him. "Well. Brought you in to do a job, and you did it."

Harbin started shifting through his keys, but Arman held up a hand.

"I don't need money, Harbin. This was just a favor."

Harbin stopped just as he seemed to find the right key. "Right. Guess you wouldn't then. Well, I'll walk you out."

The two of them walked through the keep's halls toward the exit. The place had started its life as a fort, guarding a smattering of houses, and had been built up, one brick and beam at a time. Very little had actually been torn down in all that time. Just repurposed. The walls were left as a monument to the building's history, changing subtly in color or composition from one hall to the next.

Along the way, they passed the training yard, where a few squads were going through crossbow drills.

"Archers are looking good," Arman noted.

"They know what the Lady'll do to them if she comes back from leave and thinks they slipped up," Harbin replied with a smirk. "How many more favors do I have from you?"

"Actually, I'm pretty sure this last one made us even."

"Well, suppose I paid you for this one like it were a job and called in the favor for something else?"

Arman stopped. "You know, if I wanted to work for the watch, I would have asked for a job."

"It's not just a normal job."

"No."

"You haven't even heard it."

"Don't need to."

Arman resumed walking toward the exit, a bit quicker now. Harbin matched his pace.

"A week ago, we got word of an explosion going off in the Crest Ward. Blew a hole in a townhouse and set two other places on fire. Brigades did fuck all to put it out. They had to get a cleric to make it rain."

Briefly, Arman wondered which church Harbin had called, but he decided it wasn't worth asking. Instead he asked, "Why me?"

"That townhouse that went up? It's still smoldering."

Arman unconsciously slowed his pace. "A week later?"

"We figure it's arcane, but that's all any of my people can make of it. I've got a lot of good people. Good heads on their shoulders. But they know fuck all about magic."

"The king could send a mage," Arman reminded.

"Sent for one. They're months out," Harbin dismissed. "Meanwhile, whatever son of a bitch did it is still loose, in my city. Or maybe he died in the blast. I don't know, because no one I've got can tell me what the hell's happened."

"And you think I can?"

"Who else?"

They came to another stop at the door that would lead outside to the gates. Arman did his best to keep a neutral expression while he mentally sifted through theories. Could have been arcane. Could be chemical. There was always demonism, but in practice, that was almost never the answer. He wouldn't know for sure without getting a better look.

That had to have been exactly what Harbin was banking on.

"I'll think it over."

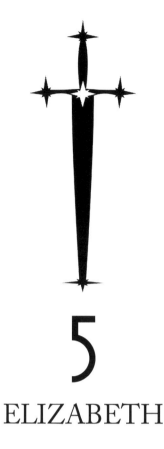

5

ELIZABETH

While Arman technically lived on Olwin's lands, he didn't live in the city proper. As the great bread basket of the kingdom, the country-side surrounding the city was filled with countless farms and the occasional homestead. Akers was one such place. A collection of about two dozen squat houses and sheds with a single inn thrown in to welcome travelers, give people a place to talk, and let locals get out of the house without making the trip all the way into the city. It was a quiet place where people tended not to poke into each other's business without good reason. Arman liked that the most about it.

It was still afternoon when Arman made it back from the keep. Most of the people in Akers were still working on their farms, but there were a few people who spotted Arman and waved or said hello. Quiet didn't mean deserted. But he'd learned that living completely alone was unhealthy, even for him.

The whole of Akers occupied the slope of a large hill, with Arman's house near the top. It was certainly one of the bigger buildings of the bunch, only really matched by the inn, but it still wasn't much. It technically had two stories, but the second story was only half the size of the first. It certainly didn't look worth the fortune that had been sunk into it.

Arman got to the door. Instead of keys, he just grabbed the handle and waited. After a second, he heard the locks click, and he went inside.

The savory smell of fresh-baked bread wrapped around him as he shut the door behind him. A smile broke out on his face. Elizabeth was home.

He found her seated at her desk in their shared study, croissant in hand, another on a plate, book propped in front of her. She was a petite woman but with a toned physique. Her chestnut hair was tied back and out of her way. She kept saying she needed to just cut it.

Arman greeted her. "Those smell good."

"They are good," Elizabeth confirmed, smiling but not looking up from her book. "And they are mine."

"Really? Even this one?" Arman reached for the plate, only for Elizabeth to pull it out of reach, still without looking.

"Even that one. I didn't put nuts in these, which means they are not for you."

Arman feigned a hurt expression. Elizabeth didn't notice.

"You said you didn't know when you'd be back and to not wait up. So, I made food for me," Elizabeth said. "If you are hungry, you may feed yourself."

She finally looked up from her book at him, and her rosy cheeks brightened as she smiled. Arman felt like a set of weights fell off him. She ran her hand across his face, pulled him close, and gave him a peck on the cheek.

"Welcome home."

"How's Robyn?" Arman asked.

"Sleeping. Finally." Elizabeth sighed. She shot him a sly look. "Looking forward to her father making up for all of the shifts he's missed."

Arman laughed. There was no real sense of dread. He liked taking care of Robyn. Mostly. Cleaning up after her was a hell all its own, but the chest naps more than made up for it.

"Sorry I missed so many."

"It's fine."

Elizabeth gave Arman a comforting pat. "How did the search for Brass pan out?"

"Found him and the missing princess," Arman said. "It wasn't that hard, but I get why the watch couldn't find him. I only knew where to look because I know him."

"How is he?"

Arman was surprised by the question. "Well, he hasn't changed at all. So there's that. Still dresses like he sprinted through a closet and threw on whatever he got snagged on."

"Does he still make those herbs you can burn to cure hangovers?"

"Why? Are you planning on getting drunk soon?"

"Unfortunately not," Elizabeth said, smirking. "But being prepared never hurt anyone."

"Who told you that?" Arman asked, already knowing the answer.

Elizabeth shrugged as her smirk only grew bigger. "Some bookworm glintchaser from the coast."

Arman rolled his eyes, but the smile didn't leave his face.

He wrapped his arms around Elizabeth, and she grabbed his arm with a free hand.

"How did Harbin take it?"

"Well, when he found out where they'd been, he was . . . thoroughly perturbed," Arman said. "But he didn't put a warrant out for Brass's arrest, at least. I think he was just glad to have the whole thing sorted. He was happy with my turnaround."

"*He* wasn't pulling double duty with a baby waiting for you to get back."

Arman cocked his head. "You said you were fine with me going."

"I was," Elizabeth said, patting his arm. "Really, I'm glad you took it. You needed it."

"Why did I need it?"

"You just did."

Arman sighed, accepting this. It actually got him thinking again, about Harbin's other job. The explosion in the Crest Ward. The fire that was still smoldering. Just remembering it racked his brain with questions.

"Well then, what if I took another one?"

"Hmm?"

"What if . . . I took another job from Harbin?"

Elizabeth very gently but very deliberately lifted Arman's arms off of her and turned her chair so she was facing him. Arman instantly suspected he'd done something wrong but couldn't read her face well enough to know for sure. Either she was intrigued or she was upset.

"What kind of job?" she asked.

That was encouragement enough to keep talking, even if he still couldn't quite get a read on her, so Arman recounted all the details that Harbin had given him, plus a bit of conjecture on his part. He got so caught up in it, he forgot to ask Elizabeth whether or not she was upset with him for bringing it up in the first place. When he finished, he realized he'd paced to the other side of the room without even noticing. Nervous energy raced along his nerves, fresh from thinking out a problem in a dozen directions at once. It surprised him. He could have sworn he'd felt tired a second ago.

Finally remembering his initial worry, he tried to read Elizabeth's face. She wasn't overtly frowning or glaring. He wasn't entirely sure though, until she asked him a question.

"What do you think happened?"

"I'm honestly not sure," Arman said. "Off the top of my head, there are too many possibilities. I'd have to get an actual look at everything, run it through detection and identification, see what comes up. And even then—" She was smiling at him. "What?"

Her smile wasn't big, but it was unmistakable, and now Arman was uncertain all over again.

But this time, he knew he'd done something right. He just wasn't sure what.

"Nothing," Elizabeth said. "You've just got your thinking look on your face. It's kind of adorable."

Arman took the compliment, and it took him a second to remember what they were actually talking about. "So. What do you think?"

Elizabeth leaned back in her chair, folding her hands. Her thumb traced across her fingers a couple times before she answered.

"I think . . . I haven't seen you this curious about something in a long time," she said. "And I think Harbin wouldn't have asked if he didn't need you."

"So I should do it?"

"I don't know," she said. "But I know you want to."

Almost reflexively, Arman started to deny it and apologize, but Elizabeth stopped him.

"It's okay." Her voice carried a softness with it that instantly quieted him. All the energy he'd been feeling settled down at once, and suddenly she was the only thing in the world.

Arman hadn't even understood that he'd been asking for permission more than advice, but Elizabeth had. Of course she had. He missed and misinterpreted signals from people all the time. But Elizabeth heard every breath, watched every movement of the eyes, and seemed to read it all perfectly.

"What about Robyn?" he asked.

"We'll be okay," she assured him. "You help Harbin sort that mess out."

An infant's cry broke the comfortable silence between the two, and a look of pity crossed Elizabeth's face as she pointed Arman down the hall.

"After you sort out that."

6
A DEAL

The half-orc was stronger than he looked, and considering what he looked like, that was saying something. Brass had tried to get up twice since being sat down in an office and told to wait. Both times the half-orc sat him back down with arms like worked stone. Brass decided not to press his luck with a third attempt.

The door to the office opened, and in came a person of androgynous features, short-cropped blond hair, and shrewd gray eyes. Their clothes looked like they were expensive at one point in time and were clearly not being worn to impress anyone: simple in style, muted in color, but expertly tailored and made with imported material. As a side effect of his lifestyle, Brass was prone to forgetting a lot of faces. But never this one, and as soon as he realized who it was, his eyes lit up, and he forgot all about the mess he'd made.

"Vera? Are you running the Lilac now?"

Vera's lips pressed into a thin line, and their eyes narrowed as they slowly sat down across from Brass. "For the last five years."

For the second time that day, Brass was struck with the realization of just how long it had been since he'd seen most of his friends. It felt like just yesterday that Vera was an escort landing a new gig in the fancy hotel they'd once been kicked out of.

Where did the time go?

That aside, there was a concerning edge to Vera's voice, and Brass quickly realized this was not going to be a simple, happy reunion. Still, he knew Vera. He could salvage this.

"That's great! Really, congratulations. If anybody could take over this place, it would be you."

"Brass."

"Hm?"

"Shut up."

"Oh."

Vera rubbed their temples while Brass checked on the half-orc again, just to see if he'd maybe wandered and created an opening. He hadn't.

"Do you have any idea how big of a mess you've made?"

"Well—"

Vera held up a finger. "No. This is the part where you listen."

The half-orc standing next to Brass tightened his grip on his shoulder to emphasize the point, but it was overkill. Brass knew better than to go against Vera. The list of people on Vera's bad side who were still alive was a short one. Then again, it had been a few years. It could be blank by now.

"You killed two people in my hotel, scared my staff half to death over it, and if the blood and bodies weren't enough, you brought the watch. They're poking around, asking questions, and throwing around words like 'interference of justice.' The amount of glint I'm going to lose over this is obscene."

"How much can you lose dealing with the watch?" Brass asked.

"After bribes, favors, and cleanup?" Vera looked Brass over, confirming a suspicion of theirs. "More than *you* can afford."

"I feel offended."

"Don't play at dignity," Vera scolded. "You haven't been flush in years."

"Well," Brass tried to think of the best way to downplay the fact that Vera was right. "I mean, we all go through rough patches. But glintchasing's got glint right there in the name. Give me a few months, I can get you what you lost on this little incident and then some."

"Just a few months?" Vera asked, a mocking edge in their words.

"Two at the most," Brass said. He racked his brain to figure out how he was supposed to actually pull that off. "You know, there's a shipping group in Sasel that's got a piracy problem. I can catch a boat that way, clean things up, and be back with the reward money before tax season."

"You're going to pay me back with a castellan's bounty? That a half dozen companies are probably already chasing?"

"Well, when you put it like that, I can see the flaws in the idea, but the principle's not a bad one," Brass defended. "I can find a gig somewhere and make what you need in no time."

"But not now?"

Brass glanced around for a possible escape route. The half-orc loomed behind him, perfectly positioned between Brass and both the window and the door. "No, not right now. But I promise you, let me go, and you'll get your money."

Vera leaned over the table, at once shocked and impressed that Brass would admit that he couldn't pay them back. Their jaw was slack, even as the corners of their mouth curled upward.

"Brass. When, in all my life, have I taken promises as payment?"

"Once, right now? For an old friend?"

Vera blinked, stared, and then finally laughed so hard, their eyes started to tear up. "Avelina spare your heart, I forgot how much I liked you."

Brass felt a wave of relief. *Still got it.*

"Kratz?" They turned their attention to the half-orc. "Don't kill him. Just break a few bones and take an arm. Maybe dump him at a church if you're not too tired afterward. Leave the face alone though."

Brass's smile dropped. "Pardon?"

"What can I say?" Vera shrugged. "I liked you more when you had money."

Kratz lifted Brass out of his chair and began dragging him out of the room. Brass dug his heels in to pull back but only succeeded in scuffing the carpet as he was dragged out.

"Vera. Can't we talk about this?"

"Nobody's going to hire a glintchaser without a company, Brass."

Kratz reached the threshold of the office door, and Brass braced his legs against the doorframe to try and hold the half-orc back. It was undignified, but it bought him a few seconds while the hulk of a man debated whether or not to just break Brass's legs now.

"What if he was willing to work for free?" Brass asked.

That managed to catch Vera's attention, if only because it confused them. They snapped their fingers, and the half-orc stopped trying to drag Brass out. After a nod from Vera, Kratz released Brass but still stood, ready to grab the glintchaser if he tried anything.

"What?" Vera asked.

"I'm not going to pretend you're not right. It's hard to find good work as a solo act," Brass admitted. "But you know me. You know what I'm good at and how good I am at it. There has got to be some problem that you have that you know I could fix. Whatever it is, I can take care of it, free of charge. That's the services of the best of the best, immense market value, for the low, low price of not having Tall, Gray, and Handsome rip off my limbs."

"The best of the best?"

"You have another way to describe the Starbreakers?"

"I've heard a few choice ways over the years," Vera said. "And you're not the Starbreakers. You're not even my favorite out of the five."

"I can . . . Wait." Brass paused. "Which one of us was your favorite?"

"The cleric."

"Church?"

Vera shrugged. "He's cute and he doesn't cause trouble. Unlike someone I know."

Brass waved a hand dismissively. As much as he wanted to object, he had more pressing concerns. Like not getting his limbs broken. "Fine, I'm one-fifth of the best. The point is, if I am good for nothing else, I am good for two things. A good time and getting you out of a jam."

Vera considered Brass, who answered with a knowing look. That look. Like he knew exactly what they wanted and knew he could deliver it.

They shook their head. Brass was trouble. Maybe even more now that he didn't have a company keeping him in check. But dammit if he couldn't sell himself.

"Well. Now that you mention it, there is one other pain in my ass that you might be able to deal with."

Brass eagerly took his seat again. "Tell me all about it."

7

THE INVESTIGATION

The Crest Ward was where idle money lived in Olwin. The people who called it home were well-off merchants, forgotten scions of old houses, and particularly fortunate retirees. They had plenty of money but not much interest in doing anything with it other than living comfortably and ensuring they wouldn't have to cross paths with any wayward newcomers from the north.

The homes were all well-made; uniquely commissioned and constructed. Most had multiple floors, with the tallest building being the local church, which came in at a full four stories.

Fences were common here, but to Arman's eyes they seemed more decorative than practical.

It wouldn't have been hard to find the town house even without directions given to him by Harbin. All he had to do was follow the smell of smoke.

When he got to the street corner, he found more or less the scene he'd expected. There was a space between two houses that was little more than a smoldering pile of ash and rubble encased in the charred remains of a wooden frame.

Edges of wood here and there still glowed an angry orange. It looked like it had been on fire less than an hour ago.

A few members of the watch were waiting at the wreckage, stationed to make sure nobody touched the place who wasn't supposed to. It was their best attempt at preserving evidence they couldn't move.

Some of the watch shifted uncomfortably as Arman approached. He wasn't carrying any sort of weapon, but he was wearing a set of reinforced dark leathers, and walking armored in the city carried enough implication of trouble on its own.

"It's all right, he's with us."

The watch visibly relaxed as Kaitlyn trotted over. Most of the watch were used to dealing with thieves, drunks, and the occasional murderer. Dealing with magic had them on edge.

"Harbin told me you might be coming," Kaitlyn said.

Arman hadn't said yes to the job until this morning. He didn't know whether or not to be offended that Harbin had just assumed he'd say yes.

Kaitlyn gestured to the ruins. "Welcome to . . . *this*. Haven't really touched anything in there. Whole place is like an oven."

Arman nodded. He'd come prepared for that.

Without looking, Arman traced a quick pattern across the arcane glyphs that were etched into his armor's bracer. The glyphs lit up in response to his touch, creating a trail of light in sync with the path of his fingers until he finished the sequence, and the enchantment woven into his armor responded. The stitching and seams began to glow sky blue, and

Arman felt a refreshing, cool sensation radiate from it. Instantly the heat became more bearable.

"What was that?" Kaitlyn asked.

"Fire resistance enchantment."

"Ah. Don't suppose you've got more of them?"

"Just the one suit."

"Well." Kaitlyn looked around as if trying to spot some way for her or her team to be useful. "We'll make sure nobody gets in your way then. Hope you can figure this one out."

"Right."

There was still some smoke curling off of the ruins in places as he carefully stepped through the remains of a door frame. It wasn't enough to be a real issue, but he still didn't want to breathe it in if he didn't have to. He fished into a pouch on his belt, producing a breather he'd packed from the drawer full of them in his basement. It was a small metal cylinder with a mouthpiece attached to the side that used extra-dimensional pockets of gas to let him breathe normally when that might otherwise be a problem. He'd made his first ones to explore a shipwreck ages ago. These days he mostly used them as an alternative to properly ventilating his workshop.

Breather in his mouth, Arman set to work. He counted three bodies half buried in the charred remains of the house. Judging from bone structure, he made out one male and two females. Scraps of armor hung around the male's arms. A warped metal circlet had fused to the skull of one of the women. The other woman's skull had horns protruding from it. A hellborn.

Between the unnaturally persistent fire and the hellborn, Arman came up with his first theory to test. He reached into one of the pouches on his belt and pulled out a golden rod etched with a pattern of thorny vines and open eyes. At over a foot long, it had no business being able to fit in the fist-sized pouch on his belt, but that was the wonder of enchanted pocket space.

The device was an old find, pulled from the tomb of a defunct order of knights dedicated to hunting demons. When activated, it emitted a glow that turned blood red in the presence of demons or their handiwork.

Arman grabbed the rod in two hands and twisted until it clicked. Slowly, the rod began to give off a soft glow, but its color remained white.

It's never demons, Arman mused, putting the rod away.

Eliminating demonism left divinity or arcana. So, Arman pulled down his goggles over his head and tapped the side of the lenses. The world became bathed in orange, and Arman looked around for anything glowing white.

Nothing did, which meant divine influence was out.

He tapped the lenses again, changing everything from orange to blue. And suddenly the wreckage around him lit up. His clothes and armor were all glowing bright white under the filter, and the remains of the town house also gave off a faint white glow.

We have a winner.

Beyond the magic residue the fire had left behind, Arman caught sight of another, much brighter glowing shape in the floor of the house with the unmistakable outline of a trapdoor.

Still looking directly at where they'd revealed the location of the trapdoor, Arman switched the goggles off and saw only a pile of ash and burnt wood. Buried. He immediately started sifting through the rubble, feeling the heat even through his enchanted gloves.

Hot cinders and soot kicked up and into his face as he excavated, stinging his skin.

Standing a safe distance from the smoke and heat but still keeping an eye on things, Kaitlyn raised an eyebrow. "Got something?" she asked.

Arman briefly took the rebreather out of his mouth to speak. After breathing clean air from it for so long, the air of the wreckage tasted especially acrid.

"Trapdoor. Basement maybe."

He finished clearing the debris to reveal a simple metal trapdoor with a ring handle. He tugged, but the door didn't budge. For a second he thought it was locked. Then he remembered he'd been able to see it with his goggles.

Arman had over a dozen enchantments prepared, some to protect him, some to provide him information, and all of them handcrafted and woven into the armor by him. There was no set like it in all of Corsar, maybe in all the world. And that was because there was no one else in Corsar who knew how to enchant armor.

He traced a new pattern on his bracer, triggering its identification spell. A wizard might spend weeks learning to cast a spell from memory. Arman built it into his glove and then let it do the work when he needed it. The differences were lost on most people, even ones like Kaitlyn, who had seen him and other mages in action. To them, magic was magic. As long as hands were waved and glowing lights appeared, Arman was as much a mage as someone from the Academy.

Strands of light extended from the fingertips of Arman's gloves, tracing across the trapdoor in a grid pattern and occasionally glowing even brighter as they passed over the anchor points of the door's magic. When the identification spell finished its work, the strands vanished, and glowing text written in Arcania materialized in the air front of him, telling him everything it had learned. There was an arcane seal placed on the trapdoor, identical to the one Arman had on his house.

At the touch of the right person, the seal would suspend itself and allow the door to be opened. To anyone else, it was almost impossible to budge.

Since he didn't bring any explosives, he was going to have to be gentler about this. Arman reached into his belt again, this time drawing out three small wooden counters about the size of checkers pieces. Dispelling discs. Enough to break most ongoing spells entirely and suppress more permanent magics for a short period of time.

He placed them in a triangle, stepped back, and traced a corresponding pattern on his bracer. With a bright flash and a sound like cymbals crashing, the three discs dissolved into a shower of crimson embers.

When Arman tried the door again, it opened, revealing a steep stairwell that led into a stone corridor. Underneath his goggles, the door still glowed, but much more faintly now that the enchantment was broken. He had about five minutes before the seal reactivated.

"I'll be right back."

The corridor was pitch-black, so Arman produced a lightstone from his belt. In the Old World, lightstone had been mined and used to create magical light sources of all kinds. Lightstone was still used now, but outside of recycling it from Old World ruins, nobody knew where to find more of it.

The stone responded to Arman's mental command, casting white light into the basement. The far end of the hall opened up into a massive training room, where Arman noted the presence of practice dummies and targets, weights, wooden training weapons, and a dirt fighting pit.

There was one other room, which was smaller and packed with shelves of weathered books, jars containing scrap materials, and vials of just about every color of fluid. A desk was covered in papers and ink stains. An old workbench against one wall was covered in candles, scrawlings, burnt materials, and jars of glittering dust.

To the right people, the contents of this room were worth the kind of money that changed lives. The fact that they were here, spread out and kept organized for use rather than packed away in preparation to be sold, gave Arman another piece of information to work with. He was in the home of a fellow arcane practitioner.

Then he spotted it. The sparking wand that told him exactly who had been living in this house and who'd owned it. Mounted above the doorway to the training room was a shining black-and-gold rotella shield engraved with the face of a dragon.

This was the home of the Golden Shield, a freelance company employed by the Academy's Office of Requisitions to find and reclaim Old World artifacts. They got the job four years ago, after the Academy put out the call for auditions, and they submitted the Shield of the Sun Dragon as theirs.

They were good. Emphasis, it seemed, on *were*.

For the first time in years, Arman regretted not being more connected to the local gossip. He didn't know how many members the Shield had or if any of their members matched the remains he'd found. They could all be dead, or there could be someone left alive who could tell him what happened.

As he got closer to the shield above the door to see if it was the real thing, his foot kicked something in the dark. Metal scratched against stone as whatever it was clattered across the floor. At first glance, it looked like a helmet whose faceplate mimicked the look of a human face. But the jaw was hinged. And while the eyes were dark, the helmet wasn't hollow.

It was the head of an autostruct.

Arman didn't know much about autostructs. They were sentient beings of metal, wood, and magic, created rather than born. Allegedly they ran off of the same design behind arcane intelligences, but Arman had seen one in person only once, and it had tried to kill him before he could get the chance to study it.

He crouched down, poking the head with a finger. For a moment, there was no response, and Arman wondered if the magic he was reading was just residual. Then, just as the disappointment was beginning to set in, the head's eyes lit up like two glowing golden orbs, and Arman nearly fell backward.

"Halt."

The head spoke with a hollow, tinny voice. Metal shutters closed and opened over its glowing eyes, and Arman's curiosity immediately fired up. It blinked. Why did a metal construct with arcane eyes need to blink?

"State your name and intent, or I will be forced to deploy counter-measures."

Arman was almost too entranced by the thing to pay attention to what it was saying. As the head spoke, the movements of its jaw made it rock from side to side on the floor, threatening to topple its balance.

"Easy," Arman urged, putting his hands up to show he was unarmed. "My name is Arman. I'm investigating what happened to this place for the castellan."

There was a pause from the autostruct and a soft whirring sound from its temples.

"You do not appear to be lying."

"I'm not."

"Arman?" Kaitlyn's voice just made its way down to the basement. "You okay down there?"

"Yeah!" he shouted back up the stairs. "I found something!"

No sooner had the words left his mouth than Arman watched the basement trapdoor pull itself shut, followed by a subtle flash of light along its edges that signaled the seal reactivating.

The color drained from Arman's face as he stared at the trapdoor. After trying to will the door back open with sheer dread didn't work, he scrambled up the stairs and shoved at the trapdoor with everything he had, but it didn't budge.

And he was out of dispel discs.

"F—fishing line," Arman almost cursed, as he realized his own stupidity.

He should have just propped the door open.

He rammed the door again in frustration, only to lose his footing on the steep stairs and tumble backward. And the door still didn't even so much as shift.

Aside from some bruises, the only thing injured was his pride. But he was trapped.

Arman let out a long sigh as he stood up, more annoyed with himself than anything. This was going to complicate things. He could call for help, but the only ones around who might hear were Kaitlyn and the other watch members, and they couldn't open the seal on the door. Not without siege equipment anyway.

The tiny clink of the autostruct's metal eyelids reminded Arman of the construct's presence. It was staring at him.

"Do you have something to say?" he asked.

"What is the current status of the Golden Shield?"

Arman thought back to the three blackened bodies in the mess above ground and weighed the odds going off of everything he knew. He sighed. "Probably dead."

The head blinked. For a moment, it just stared. Not even at Arman. It just stared. It almost looked sad.

"That is counterproductive," it eventually said.

Arman briefly forgot he was trapped in the basement, his curiosity overtaking his thoughts.

"Who are you?"

"I am Gamma, autostruct chronicler for the Academy, member of the Golden Shield."

Arman thought he detected a hint of pride in the autostruct's monotone. Thoughts of his current predicament were pushed to the back of his mind as he began to appreciate the unique opportunity in front of him. This wasn't just an autostruct to study. The construct had been a member of the Golden Shield. He might have an eyewitness on his hands.

"What happened here?"

"Unknown," the head replied. "I have been separated from the Golden Shield and rendered inactive for an unknown period of time."

"Okay. What's the last thing you remember?"

"I formulated an answer to your question: 'What is the last thing that you remember?'"

It was Arman's turn to blink. He wondered if all autostructs were like this or if this was just the damage and decapitation at work.

"No. I mean, what's the last thing you remember from before you reactivated."

"There was an explosion."

"I—" Arman stopped himself. If you ask bad questions, you get bad answers. "What caused the explosion?"

"I am not permitted to answer."

Arman folded his arms. "Why not?"

"Parameter Three: preserve the secrets of the Academy."

Now they were getting somewhere. For a sentence meant to hide information, it told him a lot.

"What are your parameters?"

"Parameter One: complete the mission," the head stated. "Parameter Two: protect the Golden Shield. Parameter Three: preserve the secrets of the Academy. Parameter Four: comply with local laws. Parameter Five . . ."

It kept going, listing off rules, mandates, and exceptions. The longer it went on, the greater Arman's understanding grew. Its rules all boiled down to, essentially, causing as little trouble as possible while completing its assignments. And not betraying the Academy.

Arman always wondered how an institution as rigid as the Academy would ever be okay with employing glintchasers. Having unquestionably loyal eyes and ears in the company they employed was exactly the sort of thing they would do.

It made him wonder how the Golden Shield felt about the autostruct. His old company wouldn't have stood for it.

Well, Brass might have tried to fuck it.

Regardless, he knew what to say now. "Tell me everything you can about the immediate circumstances that led to the explosion that rendered you inactive."

The autostruct blinked.

"You're required to comply with local laws," Arman reminded it. "I'm working on behalf of the castellan. That makes me auxiliary law enforcement. You have to answer."

After a final moment of hesitation, the autostruct's forehead split open, revealing a shimmering, blue lens that flickered to life.

8

THE
GOLDEN SHIELD

A robin flew into the open window of the sitting room in the Golden Shield's town house, coming to rest on the back of a chair. It gave a friendly chirp to the only other creature in the room: Gamma.

The autostruct stood a full seven feet tall with broad shoulders and a body of polished dark wood and silver metals.

He examined the bird. It was energetic and seemed to be eyeing him with familiarity.

In an instant, the robin's eyes bulged and changed colors. Its chest swelled as its feathers retreated and shrank. Its wings stretched out and then grew in size. In a moment, the robin was gone, replaced by a raven-haired young woman with bronze-toned skin. She was dressed in a sleeveless blue tunic decorated with druidic symbols. A silver circlet with small, ornamental antlers held her hair back.

The shapeshifter plopped into the chair with a relaxed sigh.

"Hey Gamma," Antlers said. "Have you seen King and Showboat? I've been looking for them all morning."

"They went to the basement for training," Gamma explained. "They requested privacy."

"Oh," Antlers said before fully processing the words. "Privacy" meant something very specific in the Golden Shield. "Ohh."

Antlers kept her curiosity constrained for all of five seconds. "How long have they been down there?"

"Two hours, thirty-five minutes, six seconds."

Antlers marveled at the time, wondering how much of it had been spent actually training and how much had been devoted to privacy. The sound of the basement door opening and closing came from downstairs.

Showboat wandered into the sitting room. The Golden Shield's resident scholar had snow white skin, silver hair, and ram-like horns that started in her forehead and curled back and around the sides of her head. Her eyes were solid red without pupils or irises. She wore a black cape and vest over a simple white shirt, pants, and traveler's boots. A saint's pendant hung around her neck. Hellborn were rare as a rule. It was even rarer to find one with any sort of connection to the church.

Gamma noted a slight flush of pink in Showboat's normally white face, a sign of recent physical exertion.

"How was training?" Antlers asked.

"Training was fine," Showboat responded. "Is the relic secured for transport?"

"It is," Gamma answered. He gestured to the room's central table where a closed carrying case that contained the relic in question rested. Meanwhile, Antlers was not one to be distracted so easily. She was prepared to press the previous conversation, when movement near the window drew her attention.

"What was that?"

"What was what?" Showboat asked.

Antlers approached the window, curious. She leaned out of it, looking for what had caught her eye.

Too late, she saw a man scaling the side of the town house. Before she could call out a warning to her friends, the man reached up, grabbed her head, and yanked it down onto the windowsill.

In one motion the man used Antlers as leverage and pulled himself into the sitting room before shoving her aside, dazed and bleeding from the forehead. He had two short, curved blades already drawn. The man was lithe, a mask obscuring the lower half of his face. Most of what he wore consisted of simple traveler's clothes, but he carried an array of weapons on his person, and his arms sported light armor.

Gamma took in Antlers's sudden injury, the intruder's posture, and his array of blades and determined him to be a threat. Showboat would make a similar assessment in a moment, but she processed information more slowly than Gamma, and the intruder was faster than she was.

A throwing blade struck Showboat in the abdomen. The point of entry and disruption in breathing indicated her lung had been punctured. The injury would impair if not eliminate her ability to use prayers, and Antlers was still recovering. For the time being, Gamma was alone.

Gamma's forearm split down its length to allow a two-pronged metal wand to extend out from it. Frost formed along the length of the prongs before a beam of bright blue energy shot forward, striking the intruder in the side. It didn't incapacitate the intruder, but it slowed his movements and bought the others precious time.

Before Gamma could fire again, a second masked figure somersaulted into the sitting room from the window. Physical features indicated a woman, and her drawn daggers indicated another threat. New calculations had to be made. A single intruder was one matter, but the second introduced an uncertainty in the enemy's number. Gamma couldn't cover both intruders and the room's points of entry.

Fortunately, Antlers finally recovered enough to join the fray, leaping forward. Her muscles rippled as her face flattened and whiskers protruded from her cheeks. A moment later, Antlers was gone, replaced by a mountain lion that pounced at the intruders.

What followed was a tight melee, as Antlers in her lioness form darted between the intruders, claws crossing with their blades as Gamma did his best to provide covering fire. Showboat finally managed to gasp out the words of a prayer, healing her injury. But no sooner had she done so when the male intruder winded her again with a quick, precise strike to her stomach.

Antlers turned and tried to pounce on him, but the female intruder lunged for her. When Gamma fired, throwing blades answered his shots. Every move made by one side was countered by the other. Even with the Shield's numbers advantage, the intruders were simply too fast to overwhelm.

As Antlers was forced back by the woman, Gamma surged forward, grabbed the assailant by the back of her neck, and slammed her bodily into the table. The woman noiselessly took the impact before twisting in Gamma's grip and attempting to lock his arm in a grapple. It was a skillful attempt, but the raw strength of Gamma's artificial form overpowered it, leaving the woman yanking in vain.

That was when she switched tactics, released her hold, and, before Gamma's eyes, blinked out of existence.

In the same instant, Gamma registered a blade being driven through the back of his neck. He turned around just in time for the woman, who had somehow appeared behind him, to drive her other dagger through the front of his neck. Gamma had countermeasures he could have deployed, but his mind remained fixated on how she had managed to disappear.

He took only a fraction of a second to process the technique, ruling out invisibility and illusion, before settling on some form of short-range teleportation. That fraction of a second was all the woman needed.

Gripping her daggers, the woman pulled and twisted in one motion, neatly separating Gamma's head from his body. Because everything that sustained his consciousness was built into his head, this did not kill Gamma, but it robbed him of his body and effectively removed him from the battle as his head rolled across the floor.

Unable to assist, he could only watch as Antlers and Showboat fought a losing battle for their lives. Antlers's fur was matted with her blood, while Showboat struggled to stand. Her attempts to heal them were stopped as, midway through a prayer, the female intruder covered her mouth, and ice spread across the scholar's face. All that came through the ice were Showboat's muffled screams before a knife was driven into her back.

Antlers roared, fighting as only a cornered animal could, but she was not enough. With every failed pounce, the intruders added to her wounds.

The sitting room doors burst open as King stormed in, only partially armored but with a sword in hand. His umber-brown face was contorted into a look of rage that only intensified when he saw Showboat lying bleeding on the floor, and he lunged. Two against one, King dueled with the intruders in a whirlwind of steel and held his own against both opponents.

Antlers found an opening in the melee and finally landed on one of the intruders, pinning them to the floor as they tried desperately to hold back her fangs. King forced the other back toward the table, trying to pin them down before taking a heavy downward swing. His opponent sidestepped the blow, and King's sword instead cleaved straight through the carrying case on the table that contained the relic.

Bright red light poured out from the case. All heads turned to look at it. For a moment, the case glowed bright orange. Then fire engulfed them all. All vision became obscured, and Gamma felt himself lifted up and launched from the room by the shockwave as an impact occurred, then another. At some point, as the entire house was engulfed in a roaring conflagration, Gamma felt himself tumble down the stairs into the basement, and everything went black.

9

PHOENIX

Arman stroked his chin as the imagery from Gamma's projector ceased. The lens retreated back into his forehead, clicking shut. The members of the Golden Shield matched the description of the bodies he'd found. But that meant the bodies of both of the assassins were missing.

He could understand the watch missing two bodies. The heat of the wreckage would have made it impossible for them to do a thorough search. But he had protection.

He'd poured through the debris while trying to figure out the layout of the place. He occasionally missed things, but never something that obvious. *File it under questions for later.*

"What was the artifact in the case?" Arman asked.

"I am not permitted to say."

Of course not.

He didn't necessarily need Gamma to answer. Just knowing that it existed and that it caused the explosion was plenty of information. He was pretty sure it was already enough to satisfy Harbin. But if he was lucky, he might find some trace of it left behind.

He just had to open the seal and get back upstairs to look. But the trapdoor would only open for members of the Golden Shield.

"Hey, Gamma, I need another favor."

"Do you have further questions?"

"Not exactly."

Arman picked the construct head up off of the floor and climbed the stairs to the sealed trapdoor. He pressed Gamma's head to the door and smirked when he felt the click of the seal releasing.

"As I understand the concepts, you have violated my dignity and autonomy," Gamma complained.

"I had to get out somehow."

With Gamma tucked under his arm, Arman returned to the world above. This time he propped the trapdoor open with a burnt hunk of wood. Investigating the wreckage and questioning Gamma had taken nearly an hour. The late-afternoon sky had given way to the first stars of dusk, leaving the whole place cast in its own smoldering glow.

"Is this all that is left?"

Arman was caught off guard by the question from Gamma. He'd delivered it in the same monotone he did everything, and his face betrayed no emotion. Arman wondered if the construct could feel. What was it thinking, seeing its company dead and their home in cinders?

"Uh." He tried to think of a gentler answer and came up with nothing. "Yeah."

The construct remained silent.

"I'm sorry."

"You do not shoulder fault for these circumstances," Gamma said.

Arman struggled to explain. "I mean, I'm sad that this happened to you, and I . . . sympathize."

"I am an autostruct," Gamma replied.

Arman tried to think of something else to say but again didn't come up with anything worth saying.

"You are a freelancer," Gamma stated, breaking the silence and pulling Arman from his thoughts.

"What?"

"You are conducting an investigation on behalf of the castellan, but lack a formal watchman's uniform or a knight's heraldry, indicating your services were requested as a supplement to the castellan's needs. Freelancers routinely respond to requests for aid made by local governance," Gamma observed. "Your ability to circumvent the door seal to enter the basement, as well as your interest in the relic and ability to remain in an environment of hazardous temperatures, indicate both familiarity with and access to magical equipment. Such knowledge and access is in short supply, constrained primarily to students and faculty of the Academy, knights of the crown, and freelancers. You bear no royal seal, and you do not work for the Academy."

"I used to be a freelancer," Arman said. "I stopped."

"Was your company also killed?"

"Not exactly," Arman said.

This time it was the sound of footsteps that pulled him back to reality. Kaitlyn was making her way through the wreckage, already sweating profusely.

"Hey!" she yelled. "Where have you been?"

Arman didn't look her in the eye. "I . . . got stuck downstairs."

"What?"

"It's not important. Isn't this whole place too hot for you?"

Kaitlyn panted. "Just about. But I left to take a piss, and when I came back, the rest of the detail was gone. Did you see where they went?" The blank look on Arman's face answered her question. "Of course you didn't. Avelina's ass, where did they go?"

Behind them, two young men approached. They weren't watch members, but both of them were armed . . . and armored. One wore a chain shirt over a gambeson and casually carried a war hammer at his side. The other had a pair of clubs in his hand with a long chain connecting them. The men looked to be in their early twenties at most.

When they were still some distance away, the one with the hammer greeted them: "Evening. Which one of you is Phoenix?"

"Technically me," Arman answered. "I didn't expect Harbin to send anybody else."

The two exchanged glances.

Kaitlyn figured out what was going on before Arman did and reached for her sword. Gamma clued him in. "Arman. Eye movement patterns and body language indicate violent intentions and additional assailants positioned at unknown vantage points."

"Guilty as charged," the man with the hammer said.

As both men came toward them, instincts Arman forgot he had came crashing back. His body felt lighter. His heart raced. Every nerve in his body hummed, ready to fire. His thoughts, always so scattered between what he was doing, ideas for inventions, and his family, now worked in unison to give his surroundings clarity. There were no distractions. No uncertainties. Just information and a single goal to achieve—survival.

Arman the family man was gone. In his place stood the freelancer, Phoenix.

Reflexively, he shifted his weight to his back foot and reached to where his wand should have been on his belt, only to grope empty air. He hadn't carried it since he'd retired, and he'd packed for an investigation, not a fight.

No wand was a significant handicap. Kaitlyn was armed and ready, but she was already looking exhausted from the heat. The longer she stayed, the more likely she was to become a liability. Better get her clear and let her run or call for backup.

There were more opponents nearby, if Gamma was on the money. Maybe they weren't protected from the heat, maybe they were. Easier and safer to assume the worst. The two he could see were young and hungry but inexperienced. He'd fought their kind. Been their kind.

The one with the chain let one of the two clubs drop and dragged it along the ground.

"They're here for me," Phoenix said to Kaitlyn. "Get out of here."

"Better listen to him," the one with the hammer said. "Before you end up like your friends."

The words drew their attention to the traces of blood on the men's weapons, and Kaitlyn's face hardened.

Phoenix saw a way to save her. "There are members of the watch bleeding in the street right now. They need you more than I do. Now go."

It was a cheap shot. But if Kaitlyn thought there was a chance any of the watch were still breathing, she would leave Phoenix to help them.

Sure enough, after staring at him and weighing her options, Kaitlyn backed away, keeping her eyes trained on the men as she retreated. Phoenix stepped in front of her to make sure the men didn't pursue, but they only seemed interested in him.

He was unarmed, but he had his belt. Nothing in it was made to be used in a fight, but that wasn't anything his imagination couldn't solve. He had his armor, which would buy time. He had a few devices he'd figured would have been useful. And he had a hunk of sentient metal tucked under his arm. It would have to be enough.

Phoenix dropped Gamma, took a step back, and punted the construct into the man with the hammer. Then he tried to run.

Unfortunately, the man with the chain reacted faster, swinging his weapon like a whip. The weapon wrapped around Phoenix's neck before he could react. An electric shock coursed down the chain, into his neck, and through his body. Every muscle tensed and his body shuddered. The man yanked on the chain, pulling it taut and bringing Phoenix to his knees.

Barely able to move, Phoenix just managed to trace a pattern on his bracer. The light emanating from the seams in his armor changed from light blue to bright yellow. Instantly, the pain from the chain diminished to an uncomfortable sensation of pins and needles, and the air became swelteringly hot.

Phoenix pulled the chain off his neck. The man holding the other end yanked again, trying to pull it from his grasp, but Phoenix held on. The man with the hammer charged in, and Phoenix drove the club end of the chain into the man's stomach. The man jerked back from the shock, and Phoenix used the opportunity to run.

He spotted Gamma's head lying ahead of him and scooped it up off the ground. Immediately, he regretted it. Gamma's metal head had gotten extremely hot after lying in the still smoldering wreck of the townhouse, and with his armor no longer set to resist heat, Phoenix's hands were burned.

He dropped Gamma again and resorted to kicking him ahead of him as they escaped.

"Sorry about this!" Phoenix yelled to the construct.

"Behind you!" Gamma called out as he rolled down the street.

Phoenix whirled around in time to see a hammer crashing down on him. He brought his arms up to protect his head and turned away, taking the hit on his shoulder. He felt something pop.

Phoenix staggered, taking another blow to his ribs as he did. Without the enchanted armor, his ribs would have broken. Even with it, he couldn't take too many more of those before something important gave.

He mentally rummaged through his equipment until he thought of something he could use. He reached into a pouch on his belt and pulled out a pair of silver wristbands. Before his opponent could wind up for another swing with his hammer, Phoenix rushed in close. The man retreated into a defensive stance, one Phoenix would have had no chance of getting through to land a hit. But he wasn't trying to hit the man.

Instead he touched one of the wristbands to the man's raised arm, letting it wrap around his wrist. As soon as the first band was secure, Phoenix tossed the other onto the man's ankle. A deep hum came from the two bands, and with overwhelming force, they pulled themselves toward each other. The man went from standing tall to collapsed onto the floor, his right wrist pinned to his left ankle.

Phoenix didn't have time to rest, as the man with the chain came in swinging. Every hit left him feeling like parts of his body were falling asleep, but he ignored it and kept running. A loud clink sounded off to his right, and Phoenix spotted a crossbow bolt embedded in a house's stone fence. Gamma was right about there being more than just the two. An archer drawing a bead on him complicated things.

It was after sundown. There were no crowds to get lost in. He would've hopped fences, but he doubted he could make it with the pain in his shoulder. Losing his attackers was rapidly becoming less and less of an option. He had to take them out.

Still running, Phoenix dug his rebreather out of his pocket. There were a lot of different gases and liquids needed to make it function. And some of them were flammable.

Phoenix clutched the rebreather in his mouth and pulled an engraving tool from his belt. Using the tool like a pick, he punctured the side of the rebreather. A sharp hiss tore through the air as a jet of liquid and gas shot from the it. Phoenix jerked to a stop and turned to aim the jet at his assailant. Gas streaming from the rebreather, he pulled his endless match from his belt. Closing his eyes, he lit the match, and held it up to the puncture.

The jet of gas turned into a line of flames that poured over the man with the chain. He cried out in pain, dropping mid-stride as the fire washed over him. Phoenix kept the flames on him for a second longer, then he spat the breather out with as much force as he could before the pressure of the escaping gases waned and the flames caused the whole thing to explode in his mouth.

The man with the chain was in agony, screaming and disoriented but not down. Gritting his teeth, Phoenix charged the man while he was still on the ground and kicked him in the head as hard as he could. The man crumpled. Phoenix kicked him again for good measure.

Phoenix was more winded from the sprint than he'd expected. He was out of shape.

His shoulder felt dislocated. After taking a second to survey his surroundings, he spotted a building corner that would serve his purpose. He took a second to brace himself and slammed his shoulder to try to knock it back into place.

It did not work.

Pain shot through his shoulder, and before he could even finish screaming, more pain shot up from his thigh. He stared down, seeing a crossbow bolt jutting out of his leg. It hadn't gone deep, but it managed to punch through the armor.

He was tired. Bleeding from his head, his lip, and now his leg. Several parts of his body felt numb. Before he could think of his next move, another bolt struck him in the chest. The armor held this time, but the force of the impact overcame his already compromised balance and knocked him onto his back.

Lying on the ground, he made eye contact with Gamma, who had rolled to a stop in the middle of the street not far from him.

"Bolts are originating from the rooftop due west of our position," Gamma warned. "Previous bolts loosed indicate only one archer."

Phoenix looked in the direction Gamma indicated and finally managed to spot the archer, silhouetted on a rooftop against the backdrop of the dusky sky, loading their crossbow.

Knowing where the shots were coming from helped.

Growling as the muscles in his injured leg protested, Phoenix stood, scooped up Gamma, and hobbled for cover. He rounded a corner and pressed himself flat against the wall just as a crossbow bolt whizzed through the space his head had occupied a second earlier. He choked down the knot of panic that formed in his throat as he stared at the bolt, lodged in a nearby wall. There wasn't time to think about how close that had been.

He'd broken his line of sight. That was good. That meant he was almost clear. He plotted out a path through the streets of the Crest Ward, careful to keep buildings between him and where he estimated the archer's position was.

He had to account for the fact that they would be moving, trying to get an angle, but he could work that out in his head as he ran.

He made it to a thoroughfare that, during the day, would have been packed with people. In the evening, there was still one building that cast a bright glow from its windows. The sounds of drinks and conversations filtered out from its partially open door.

A tavern. A place full of witnesses, and maybe even off-duty watch members. He would be safe from his pursuers, whoever they were, at least long enough for him to catch his breath and maybe try to do something about his shoulder.

"Don't move."

Phoenix complied with the woman's voice, which came from behind him. The voice was laced with aggression, impatience, and the unmistakable air of victory. He didn't turn around, but he could imagine the crossbow pointed at his back right now.

He may have overestimated his ability to predict his enemy's movements. His fingers stung from burns. The numbness from the electric club had spread to all the wrong places. The pain everywhere else was getting harder to ignore. But he wasn't out of tricks just yet. The archer had made the mistake of getting too close.

"Drop the head, and put your hands in the air."

Phoenix complied with the first half, letting Gamma hit the ground again with a clank. At the same time, he pulled his lightstone from his belt, transferred it to his left hand, and raised his one good arm into the air.

"Can't really get the other one up," Phoenix said. "Your buddy did a number on my shoulder."

"I don't care," came the terse retort. "Both hands behind your head, now."

Phoenix let out an overly dramatic sigh and made a big show of slowly lowering his one good arm down, as if preparing to forcibly raise his bad arm.

"All right," he said. He stared down at the crossbow bolt in his thigh. This was going to hurt. "Both hands."

In one motion, Phoenix yanked the crossbow bolt from his leg and stabbed it into the light stone, shattering it like glass. At the same time, he squeezed his eyes shut. As it broke, the stone let out a dazzling flash that Phoenix's body did little to block.

Behind him, the woman cursed as she was blinded. Phoenix turned on his heel, took two steps toward the woman, and stabbed her in the stomach with her own bolt. She gasped, staring at him as her vision slowly returned to her. There was shock and pain in her eyes. Phoenix ignored it, twisted the bolt, and stabbed again—higher this time. The woman dropped to the ground.

Phoenix heard voices coming from the tavern.

"What was that?"

"It came from outside!"

"Who's that?"

"Saints, he killed her!"

"Someone get the watch!"

Arman let out an exhausted sigh. He dropped the crossbow bolt and got down on his knees. He placed the hand he could still raise on his head. In a few seconds, people had swarmed him.

With the fight over, he felt suddenly heavier. Slower. And tired. He wondered if Kaitlyn was okay. If she'd found any members of the watch. He wondered how long this mess was going to keep him from getting home. If Elizabeth was all right. Who these people were, why they'd attacked, if there were more. And as more of the watch arrived to haul him to the nearest jail, one thought loomed in his mind above everything else.

Harbin is going to love this.

10
HOME

W hen Arman didn't come home that night, Elizabeth started to regret encouraging him to take the job. First the search for Brass, and now this. She missed having someone around to split parenting duties with. And sleep. She also missed sleep.

Robyn slept through enough of the night now that Elizabeth was at least maintaining a grip on her sanity, but some mornings, it didn't feel like it. When she was greeted by the first rays of morning sun and hungry cries from the nursery, she felt like no time at all had passed since she'd closed her eyes.

The day stretched out in front of her like a long march, and she missed her bed before she'd even gotten out of it.

But mercy came just a few hours later when, in the middle of Robyn's morning playtime, Elizabeth picked up on someone at the door. His gait was off of its usual rhythm, but she still recognized Arman before she even caught sight of him. The front door unlocking only confirmed it was him.

"Oh, *now* you're back," Elizabeth called out as she went to meet him. "What took you so—"

She stopped when she came around the corner and saw the state Arman was in. His armor and clothes were scuffed, dirty, and stained with blood. He had bandages around his forehead and leg. One of his arms hung stiff and awkward. His lip was scabbed from where he'd bitten it and drawn blood, and his nose and eye were bruised. Tucked under one arm was the inactive head of an autostruct. Elizabeth stared, jaw slack. For a moment, she wasn't sure where to start.

". . . the head?"

"It's a long story."

Elizabeth helped Arman wince his way out of his coat and sat him down in the living room. When Robyn saw him, she immediately stopped playing with her toys. She didn't cry, but she did stare, point, and make garbled noises.

He started to explain what had happened, but Elizabeth cut him off almost immediately.

"What's wrong with your arm?"

"Uh. Shoulder. I think it's dislocated."

Elizabeth closed the distance between them, and Arman immediately grew wary. He turned, trying to keep his shoulder away from her. Elizabeth rolled her eyes.

"I just want to take a look."

Arman hesitantly lowered his guard, allowing her to examine his shoulder. He winced when she felt it, but her touch was disarmingly gentle, and before long, he relaxed in her hands. As soon as he did, she grabbed his wrist, braced her leg on his, and pulled.

Arman yelled, startling Robyn. Now she was crying, but his shoulder was back where it was supposed to be.

"What was that for?"

"You're welcome."

"You're welcome?"

"Can you move your arm now?"

Arman stopped yelling and tested his arm. It still hurt; didn't have the full range of motion that it should. But it felt infinitely better.

". . . yes."

"Good," Elizabeth said. Her attention turned to their crying child. "Give me a minute. Then you can explain."

It took only a few minutes to take care of Robyn, and when Elizabeth came back, she had a bandage roll in her hand and stalks of lavender tucked under her arm. She silenced his protests with a look before he could form them and started stripping the purple flowers off of the ends of the stalks, collecting them in her hand.

She reached out with her self, letting the flow of her own being touch the life still in the petals and bulbs, and willed that life into her palm. In response, the flowers dissolved into her skin, leaving a faint purple color and a tingling warmth. She ran her hand across the wound in Arman's leg, slowly and carefully. Where she touched, the same sensation in her skin spread across Arman's, and the wound rapidly began to shrink and close.

She repeated the process, one injury at a time, mending every scrape and bruise she could see. What her magic didn't completely heal, she wiped clean and bandaged. This wasn't the first time she'd done this for him. But it had been a long time since he'd been this bad.

"Start talking."

He told her what had happened the night before, starting with arriving at the scene of the fire and ending with Kaitlyn bailing him out of jail on behalf of a very angry Harbin. She did her best to stay calm during the story, even as tough as it was to hear that people tried to kill him. She kept her face neutral, but her fingers twitched the way they always did when she was anxious.

When he was done recounting the details, Elizabeth had to take a breath. Every fiber of her screamed to get up, go out, and do something, but she restrained herself. Folding her hands to keep her fingers still, she asked, "But why you?"

"I don't know. Maybe they were trying to cover up what happened to the Shield and knew I was looking into it. Or maybe . . ."

For some reason, in that moment Arman thought of Brass, back at the Lilac, attacked by a pair of swords for hire.

"What?"

"I mean . . . the Golden Shield last week, Brass two days ago, and me yesterday makes three different attacks on freelancers in the city. What if it's connected?"

Elizabeth raised an eyebrow. "What if it is?"

"If it is . . ." Arman frowned, thinking.

Three attacks on freelancers in a short span of time, with no obvious personal motivation. That almost always meant a sword-for-hire job. If the attacks were connected, if someone was targeting freelancers and money was involved, one attack was not going to be the end of it. People were going to keep coming after them until either someone finished the job or the person doing the hiring decided to pull it.

Harbin had good people in the watch, and now with confirmation that their errand squad had been killed, the Academy would be stepping in too. He should have been fine with that. Just yesterday, he was trying to wash his hands of the castellan's business and go back to his quiet life in his quiet home. But something within him rebelled. A switch had been flipped somewhere in his mind, and gears that had gone years without turning were active and refusing to go dormant again. How could he leave this to someone else—someone whose priorities were completely different from his?

The worst part was how little he knew about what was going on. How personal was this? How focused on him? How dangerous were the people involved? He didn't know anything.

He hated not knowing things.

"I can't just do nothing," he said.

"So, what's the plan?"

"Do some digging, ask around. Figure out what exactly is causing all this," Arman said. He ran his fingers through his hair. "I've got almost nothing to go on right now. If I can get a sense of what we're dealing with, I can figure out what to do about it. Maybe I'm just seeing something that isn't there. Maybe it's small or doesn't actually involve me, and Harbin can handle it. But maybe—"

He stopped, but they both knew what he meant. Maybe they should handle this personally. It would be exactly what Harbin wouldn't want him to do. Exactly what he would have done without a second thought when he was younger. When he was Phoenix.

Elizabeth raised an eyebrow.

"I thought you were done being a freelancer."

"I am."

"You're talking like one."

She was right, and he knew she was right. The line of thinking he was using only ended one way. Running around, facing down criminals, and pointedly ignoring any authority figure that might want him to stop and let them handle things. Dangerous. But effective. And on his terms. The memory of his fight from the night before came back, and all the feelings that had come with it. Not just the fear. But the clarity.

He'd forgotten how simple and straightforward things had been as a freelancer. Nothing to worry about but the very solvable problem in front of him.

"Just for this. And only until we figure out if Harbin can handle it," he said.

Elizabeth wasn't sure she believed that. Neither was Arman.

"Where do we start?"

Arman drummed his fingers. "One of the assassins who attacked me is still alive, but Harbin would never let me near him. The guys who came after Brass are dead. And whoever hit the Golden Shield are in the wind. So . . . I was thinking . . . Clocktower."

"They'll kill you on sight."

"Only if I go as *me*."

Elizabeth's eyes lit up as she parsed his implication. If Clocktower would kill him on sight, there were really only two options: not be seen at all or not look like himself at all.

"Planning on going alone?"

"Not exactly." Arman shrugged. "I mean, I'm not sure."

Elizabeth felt a twinge of disappointment when he didn't ask her to come. Already her heart rate had increased just thinking about an undercover mission in enemy territory.

"What do you mean?"

"I was . . . thinking of asking Brass for help."

"Really?"

"Really." Arman almost couldn't believe he was saying it either. "He's still in town, he can find Clocktower faster than I can, he can talk anything out of anybody, and . . . if things go sideways, he is good in a fight."

"You think he'll say yes?"

"I don't know. A part of me hopes he doesn't."

"Well, if he says no . . ."

"I'll manage on my own."

Elizabeth frowned. Arman noticed and realized he'd upset her. But he wasn't sure how, and he didn't know how to fix it.

She could see him struggling, mentally playing back his own words looking for where he'd tripped up, and gave him an out. "Where do I fit into this plan?"

"I need you here. Someone has to keep an eye on the house and make sure nobody's tracked down where we live. And keep Robyn safe if they have."

She hated how good he could be at making sense. Her fingers were twitching even more now, but she nodded. "Okay."

She was still upset, Arman was sure of it. Even if he wasn't sure exactly why, he wanted to make her feel better. He took her hand, and in doing so, felt the twitch of her fingers against his palm. Even unsure of the source, he knew what the tic meant. He squeezed her hand tight and met her emerald gaze. His way to focus her attention and slow her down.

"We'll figure something out."

In seconds, the twitching of her fingers stopped. A small smile appeared on Elizabeth's face. "You're smart, and I'm stubborn."

She rested her head on his shoulder and breathed. There was still a whirlwind in her stomach, but it was calmer now. For one quiet moment they stood holding each other. Then she nudged him with her forehead.

"One more thing."

"What?"

"What are you planning on doing with that?"

Elizabeth pointed at Gamma's severed head, which currently sat on their dining table, staring back at them with dark, lifeless eyes.

"Oh. Right."

PROFESSIONALS

B rass adjusted the amount of chest his shirt left exposed, attempting to walk the fine line between socially acceptable and obvious trull. It was a delicate balance, and he'd spent the last hour trying to perfect it. Just the right amount of makeup on his eyes and cheeks. A dash of perfume. An eye-catching dark purple suit. Cuffed boots with pointed toes and two-inch heels.

He turned away from the mirror, presenting himself to his date. "What do you think?"

Her name was Ruby. Well, her working name anyway. They weren't really on a real name basis. She stared at him, arms folded, a look of amused disbelief on her face.

"I think this is the weirdest thing a client's ever asked for."

Ruby was an escort from the Lilac. Instead of the normal provocative clothing the Lilac dressed their escorts in, she was wearing an outfit Brass had provided for her. Mostly black, accented by a pure white coat and minimalist silver jewelry.

Brass broke out in a smile. "Love that honesty. I meant, how do I look?"

Ruby looked him up and down for a moment. "Like an expensive whore."

"Perfect."

Brass grabbed the wrist-pocket he'd set out on the nightstand. It was a segmented silver bracelet with two blue gems embedded into one of the segments. After taking a moment to make sure it was secure on his wrist, he picked up the nail he'd made that afternoon, lit it, and took a long drag. After a few hits, he could feel a shielding fog starting to creep over his brain.

"What is that?" Ruby asked, not recognizing the smell of the smoke.

Brass blinked, then realized she was talking to him. "A precautionary blend I came up with. If this thing's got any kind of charm up its sleeve, it's not going to work on me."

She eyed the nail with renewed interest. "You plan on sharing that?"

"Nope," he said, putting it out. "Dulls reaction time, and we can't risk ruining your performance."

"So what if it tries to mess with *my* head?" she asked. She was trying to come off as annoyed, but she was talking a little faster now. A twinge of fear in her dry demeanor.

"Killer's been targeting trulls," he said simply. "You're not the trull tonight, remember?"

Ruby sighed, twirling her hair around her fingers. "Maybe I should charge double for this."

"Someone tries to kill me, I'll make it triple," Brass offered.

Like any man or woman in her profession, Ruby had learned to mask her feelings. But everyone had their tell. When she was scared, her eyes started jittering like an animal looking for predators. When Brass noticed, his cocky smile dropped. He took her hand in his, surprising her. It took him a moment to find his words through the fog in his mind.

"Nothing is going to happen to you tonight," he promised her.

For a moment, Ruby's facade dropped. Not completely, but enough for him to know she believed him. She composed herself, hardening her exterior.

"Well, are we doing this or what?" she asked.

Brass's smile returned, and he offered Ruby his arm. Together they left the Lilac, taking a ride in a covered carriage. Their destination was Gargan's, an upscale tavern in the Pale famous for its fine food and extreme discretion.

According to Vera, someone, or something, was killing escorts in the Pale. Mostly men, but at least one woman. The story was that they'd get hired, or lured off, and then they'd turn up a few days later dead in a gutter.

The watch wasn't looking too deeply into things, as per the usual arrangement in the Pale. The watch had enough problems to worry about in the Stays, and when some of the extra services businesses in the Pale provided their clientele were less than legal, it was usually more cost efficient for owners to wave the watch off and sort things out themselves.

Vera had an investigator looking into it. They'd managed to figure out that the culprit was some kind of shapechanger operating out of Gargan's. But then the investigator ended up dead in a gutter too.

Brass and Ruby arrived a few hours before sunset and were ushered inside by a well-dressed serving boy. The boy took one look at the two of them, and Brass knew he was coming to the exact conclusion about their relationship that Brass wanted him to. All that time spent in the mirror had paid off.

Despite the fact that the sun was still up and shining outside, the interior of Gargan's was kept dim with thick curtains and minimal lights.

Except for the foyer where guests waited to be seated, the entire place was absent of natural light. Unlike most places in the Pale, which used lightstone, Gargan's used oil lamps. It gave the place a warm, natural glow that magical light fixtures always struggled to imitate. It was the flicker of the flames that did it.

Lightstone's glow was just too constant and clean to give the right atmosphere.

Ruby was asked where she'd like to sit and, with a glance at Brass, if she'd be needing a room this evening. She played her role perfectly, requesting a room like she was speaking a secret code. When someone came to take their order, she ordered for the both of them. A genuine smile began to spread across her face. She was enjoying the role reversal.

Brass was doubly glad for how well she took to it. The drugs had dulled his normally silver tongue. The weight of the deception was on her, and she was carrying it marvelously.

He was staring, and she noticed. "Did I fuck something up?"

"What? No. No . . . not at all," he said. He searched for the right words as memories of another face and another time drifted into his head. "It's just . . . been a while since I've met somebody so good at this."

"So, what happens now?" she asked.

"We . . . keep an eye out for anyone staring at me instead of you."

They went through all the motions of having dinner. Brass passed the time by asking Ruby about herself. Occasionally, with less speed and flair than he could have managed sober, he told stories about himself that weren't true. It proved surprisingly hard to make her laugh, and he embraced the challenge.

By the time they were done with dinner, Brass had narrowed it down to one of two people. There was a woman, maybe in her early twenties, who they'd caught staring at Brass and biting her lip more than once. And there was a man, maybe a few years older than Brass, who was sitting with a group.

He was watching the both of them, but Brass couldn't tell if it was jealousy or hunger in his eyes.

———————————

Ruby paid for the food and drinks with money Brass had given her and led Brass upstairs to the room that had been reserved for them. The plan was to spend some time in the room, then for Ruby to leave first. Ideally it would signal to the killer that she was done with Brass, and he was free and alone.

There was no real plan for this part, outside of just waiting for enough time to pass to sell the story that Ruby had gotten her money's worth on her expensive whore. About an hour of killing time later, Ruby collected herself, gave Brass a kiss for good luck, and took her leave.

Brass gave it a few minutes, passing the time by idly playing with his shirt laces and thinking about tits, before he finally got bored and decided he'd probably given it long enough.

He was surprised to find Ruby standing just outside the door, ready to walk back in.

"Good, I caught you," she said.

"Forget something?" Brass asked.

Ruby looked him over. He was fully dressed, but the look on her face suggested she wished he wasn't. With one hand on his chest, she pushed him back into the room. Brass raised an eyebrow and smirked but said nothing as she guided him toward the bed and shut the door behind her.

"I changed my mind about leaving," she said.

The backs of his legs hit the edge of the bed, but he resisted falling back into it for a moment.

"Round two's going to cost extra," he said.

"Money's no object," she assured him breathlessly.

Brass cocked his head. "Is that so?

With a flick of his wrist, Brass activated his wrist-pocket. The gems on the bracelet gave a flash of bright light, and a gleaming swept-hilt rapier materialized in Brass's hand. Before Ruby could react, he tumbled backward over the bed, swiping with the blade as he went, and came up on the other side with sword extended.

"Yikes, that was slow," he said, more to himself than her. "Might have taken too many hits earlier."

"Ruby" wailed, clutching the stump of her wrist. On the floor, the severed hand's skin was rapidly changing color as it grew in size, and the joints of the fingers swelled and contorted. When she glowered at Brass, her eyes were black.

"Evening. Since you're clearly not Ruby, allow me to introduce myself," Brass said in greeting. "I'm Brass, and you must be the one killing hookers in their spare time."

The shapechanger snarled at him as its skin quivered, and Ruby's appearance melted away. Its skin darkened and sagged, becoming a deep, leathery, bluish green. Joints began to look gnarled as the whole body elongated and took on a far bonier appearance. Smooth red hair turned frizzy and silver, rapidly growing out into thick sideburns. The feminine figure gave way to almost unfeasibly broad shoulders and a hairy barrel chest, largely exposed as tailored clothing turned into tattered rags. Unless he'd accidentally mixed a hallucinogen into his blend from earlier, Brass was pretty sure he was dealing with an ocre. That explained the "murdering people's companionship" routine. If there was one thing ocres hated more than anything, it was people getting laid.

"Huh," Brass mused. "You know, I was kind of expecting a demon, but I guess it really never is them."

"How did you know?" the ocre asked in a voice that sounded like it gargled steel scraps.

"Well, for one thing," Brass said, slowly moving to cut off the ocre's escape out the door, "there was no round one. For another, your breath—"

He never finished the sentence, because the creature lunged for him, grabbing him by the throat. The ocre's bony appearance belied an iron grip and lightning speed. It lifted Brass off his feet, examining him. A snort came from its nostrils as it took in Brass's scent—taking in his life story from the thousands of smells no human nose could hope to notice that clung to his skin—and the creature's lips curled at the stench. Foreign sands, lingering magic, and the blood of countless slain creatures, to say nothing of the dozens and dozens of lovers. Only one kind of human could be so steeped in such an amalgam of smells.

"Glintchaser," it growled.

"Guilty," Brass choked out with a welcoming grin on his face.

It snarled and heaved, throwing Brass into the wall hard enough to crack the wooden paneling.

"All right, fair enough." He coughed. "Final warning then. Come along quietly, or I'll—"

The ocre tackled him into the wall. This time, the boards splintered apart behind him, giving way to open air. Monster and man fell out of the hole in the building and through the air, tangled around each other in a shower of wooden planks and dirt insulation. Outside, heads immediately turned to see what all the fuss was about. Brass and the ocre hit the ground, splitting apart on impact and tumbling away from each other. The monster landed in a crouch, fingers digging into the pavement, ready to pounce. Brass ended up on his back, waiting for the world to stop spinning.

"Ow."

The crowd began to part around them, but few people ran outright, instead sticking around to watch what looked like it would make for a good show. Very few people in the Pale had ever learned proper self-preservation. No one even shouted for the watch. Brass rolled his eyes as he caught his breath.

The ocre was furious now. Letting out a roar like a wild animal, it charged. Brass was still getting to his feet, and the drugs were slowing him down more than he'd expected. He braced for impact, but just before the creature got within striking distance, there was a sound like glass shattering underwater, and its head whipped to the side, struck by a barely visible force.

Brass took the opportunity to get in a thrust with his sword, drawing blood and forcing the creature back.

From out of the crowd of onlookers, Arman stepped forward. In one hand, he carried a metal wand just over a foot long with a rotating cylinder built into it just above the handle. The tip of the wand crackled with bright white energy.

"Phoenix?" Brass said. "We've got to stop meeting like this."

"Look out!" he yelled.

Brass reacted too late and got knocked across the pavement again, skidding to a halt at the feet of a visibly concerned elderly woman in a fur coat. While Brass assured her everything was under control, Arman aimed his wand and fired off another blast that struck the creature in the chest. It recoiled from the pain, retreating from both of them.

The sound of reinforcements coming could be heard over the din of the crowd. Someone's private security, or maybe even the watch. They were seconds away. The ocre looked around frantically, like a cornered animal. Its eyes locked on the two glintchasers that stood in its way, and it extended a bony finger at them.

"Serve me," it crooned, beckoning them forward with its finger.

Brass felt a dull pressure in his forehead but little else. The blend did its job perfectly. He was too high to be charmed. Next to him, Arman lowered his wand, and his eyes glazed over. Brass stared at him, annoyed.

"You've got to be kidding me."

Arman pointed his wand at Brass. Brass turned his sword on Arman.

"Oh, it's been a minute since we've done this," Brass said, bracing himself for a fight. He knew firsthand how much pain that wand could dish out.

"That's quite enough," a new voice announced.

Hundreds of glowing blue threads lashed out from the crowd. They wrapped around Arman. They wrapped around his wand. They wrapped around Brass and the ocre and streetlamps. Then, they all pulled taut. Arman, Brass, and the ocre were all lifted off the ground as the threads pulled tight around them. Wherever they touched the threads, their bodies tingled.

The ocre thrashed and wailed, which only made the threads bite into its flesh more, enough to draw blood. Brass remained motionless, knowing better. Arman was still, staring off into space with a stupefied look on his face.

Three heavily armed individuals bearing the insignia of the Seven Gates of Sasel marched forward. Knights, royally sanctioned protectors of Corsar and from the order that protected the kingdom's capital city no less. Leading them was a pale, beige-skinned woman with short, dark blue hair and matching eyes. She was adorned in flowing robes with glyphs stitched into the trim that glowed the same bright blue as the threads holding everyone in place. Each thread originated from the fingers of her right hand, which was currently clenched in a fist.

"Well, if it isn't the Starbreakers," the woman said. "I thought you broke up."

"Ink," Brass said in greeting. "Long time no see."

12
HISTORY

Ink unclenched her fist, and the threads around Brass and Arman loosened until they were gently deposited onto the ground. The threads around the ocre held, and the knights with Ink moved to encircle it and begin the process of manacling the creature.

"For the record, I had that under control," Brass stated, pointing at the ocre with his sword.

"I'm sure you did," Ink said.

With a flourish and a flash of light, Brass returned his sword to the wrist-pocket. "So. To what do we owe the pleasure?"

"I could ask you the same thing," Ink said, glancing at the ocre. "Care to explain?"

The knights had managed to secure a pair of manacles on the ocre, but it was still struggling, even as the threads of Ink's spell bit into its flesh with every thrash.

"I'm working," Brass said.

"Me too," she retorted. She looked at Arman. "And you?"

Arman said nothing, still staring into space. After a moment, Ink realized what was the matter. A smile curled across her face as she savored the moment before she finally snapped her fingers, and the charm on Arman's mind was dispelled.

"Brass, be careful," he said, before taking in his surroundings with confusion. After a moment, he growled. "It charmed me."

"Like a brunette in a backless dress," Brass confirmed.

Arman rubbed the back of his neck. He hated when that happened. Out of the corner of his eye, he noticed the blue-haired wizard and, though he didn't want to, acknowledged her.

"Ink."

"Phoenix."

"The Academy sent you."

"Word travels fast."

"You could say that," Arman said. "I was the one who found out about the Shield."

"Wait, what about a shield?" Brass asked.

He was ignored.

"Well, thank you for doing the groundwork. The Academy will be taking over from here, obviously," Ink stated.

With the ocre subdued, Ink had become the focus of the onlookers. Lightstone, potions; these were fairly common in the Pale. But spellcasting on this level was beyond what most people had ever seen, or that some even thought possible. For the people here, this was a once-in-a-lifetime spectacle.

"Official business. Move along," Ink told the crowd. Some of them glanced at each other. Few actually left.

Ink grew impatient. Her eyes crackled with blue energy, and her voice boomed with supernatural volume. "NOW."

The crowd dispersed in a hurry.

She turned to Brass. "I'll take the ocre off your hands as well. Unless that's a problem?"

"It's all yours," Brass said. "This one was on the house anyway."

"Well, boys, love to stay and chat, but I'm late for a meeting with the castellan," Ink said. "We should catch up some time, though. It's been too long."

She lowered her hand, and the threads extending from it vanished. The ocre, who by now was in chains many times over, hit the ground and immediately began wriggling and thrashing, to no avail. The knights hauled the creature to its feet and began leading it away.

Ink followed them, blowing Arman and Brass a kiss as she left. "Good seeing you!"

Brass watched her go. "Well, first you, then Ink. This has been a day."

"Yeah," Arman agreed. He tried to think of something to say. This was only his second time talking to Brass in seven years. The last time, a few days ago, Brass had started the conversation, and Arman had ended up telling him in so many words that he wanted nothing to do with him. He wasn't sure how to turn around and ask for help.

Agonizing over his first sentence, Arman didn't realize Brass was already walking away.

"Well, I'll just get out of your hair now."

"Brass, wait."

"Can't. Busy."

"Brass, this is about those guys who attacked you."

Brass kept walking. Arman followed.

"This is important!"

Brass spun on his heel. Arman was impressed at how he managed that with the kind of boots he was wearing.

"Maybe I'm doing something important too," Brass retorted.

"Brass, I'm serious."

"So am I. It's called an actual life," Brass said, turning back around with an exaggerated wave good-bye. "Good luck with whatever your thing is."

"I deserved that."

"Deserved what?" Brass paused. He glanced over his shoulder but thought better of it. "Ah, never mind. Build a dick and fuck yourself with it."

Arman growled in frustration. He had one shot left to try and convince Brass. If it didn't work, he'd visit Clocktower by himself.

"Brass, I need your help."

Brass stopped dead in his tracks. He didn't just look over his shoulder. He made a show of it, bending backwards and revealing a coy expression. Arman immediately regretted this.

"Oh?" Brass twirled around to face him again. "You need *my* help? Whatever would a respectable family man like yourself need the help of a glintchaser for?"

"I told you, it's about the people who attacked you," Arman said. "Two days ago, I was attacked."

"Ohh, I *see*," Brass said, drawing out each word. "When *I'm* attacked, I can go fuck myself. But when it happens to *you*, I should drop whatever I'm doing to come lend a hand."

"It's not like that!" It was, but that wasn't the sort of thing to admit while asking for help. "A week before people came after you, the Golden Shield was attacked in their home, right here in Olwin. I think it's all connected. I think someone is targeting freelancers."

"I thought you didn't do this anymore," Brass said. "Aren't you too good for this sinful world now . . . or something?"

"Brass. Please," Arman begged. "One job. That's all I need your help for."

Brass pursed his lips, thinking. Arman suspected he'd already made up his mind and was just drawing this out to fuck with him now.

"I will help you," Brass declared, "on one condition."

"What do you want?"

"You help me first. I've got a job of my own."

"What is it?"

"Finding a trull. What's yours?"

Arman almost wanted to give Brass a chance to renegotiate. "I need to get into Clocktower."

"Oh." Brass's mouth held the O shape, and his eyebrows shot up. "Well that's way bigger than mine."

13

CLOCKTOWER

The next day, Arman met Brass back in the Lilac's lobby. Arman dug into a pouch on his belt and produced a leather wristband that incorporated an engraved metal disk in its center that gave off a soft white glow. He handed it to Brass.

"As fast on the delivery as ever," Brass said, putting the wristband on. He started fiddling with it, tapping the disc, squeezing its edges, tugging on the band. "How do I turn it on?"

Phoenix grabbed Brass's wrist and ran his finger around the edge of the disc. A white ring of energy materialized around Brass's head and passed over him from head to toe. As it did, his entire appearance changed. His bright purple jacket became a dull gray. The fabric took on a coarse, worn-out appearance. The rest of his clothes underwent a similar roughing up. His face changed entirely, and his tan skin tone shifted to a pale one. His hair darkened and straightened, and a small goatee appeared on his chin.

"I still say we should have gone practical," Brass stated, staring down at himself. "Illusions always feel weird."

"It literally feels like nothing."

"That's the problem," Brass said. "Did you give me a hat?"

"No."

"Well." Brass copied Arman's earlier movement, running his finger around the edge of the wristband's disc. A white ring passed over him again. He looked exactly the same as before, except now he was sporting a stovepipe hat.

"Brass, it's an illusion. The hat'll give you away."

"You are no fun," Brass said, but he complied. He activated the wristband again, removing the hat from his illusory disguise.

"Thank you," Arman said. "And stop messing with it. It's only got a few charges."

He traced a pattern on his bracer, triggering the disguise spell on himself as well.

The two of them took a walk into the Stays, one of the parts of Olwin built up by the massive influx of settlers from the north. Olwin had always had a cobbled together air to it, but the Stays in particular looked and felt like an entirely different city had been haphazardly stitched onto it. Everything was smaller here. Taverns in the Stays were barely the size of houses in the Crest. Narrow roads were made to feel even narrower by the rivers of bodies that choked them. Even the people, so many of them comprised of the recently displaced, seemed to try to make themselves as small as possible.

Finding Clocktower's hideouts and picking the best one to drop in on had taken up most of Brass's evening. What started with seducing a waiter from Gargan's to get their bloodsmoke supplier had sort of spiraled out of control and ended with paying someone twenty glint to throw eggs at a city watch station while he peeked at their files. But in the end, he'd gotten what they needed. He'd also gotten charged with trespassing and escaping custody, but he didn't tell Arman that part.

"And you're sure this is the right place?" Arman asked.

"Have a little faith," Brass said. "When have I ever let you down?"

"Constantly."

"I meant when it counted."

Once.

Arman did his best not to think about that. Those memories wouldn't be of any use to them right now.

They came to a stop outside a squat earth-brick building with large windows that exposed its bright interior of chairs and mirrors. Displays showing off various bottles and cases sat in the window. Above the door hung a sign that read, "Clean-Cut Looks," above an engraving of scissors and a razor.

"We're here," Brass announced, waltzing inside.

The shop's large windows allowed light to pour inside from every direction, and the floor was almost spotlessly swept. Most of the chairs were empty, save for one where a man was receiving a shave. The barber was a tall man with a sizable paunch, receding hair, and a thick mustache.

"Afraid it's just me today, sirs." He greeted them without looking up from his work. "Something I could do for you?"

"Actually, I'm in need of a close shave," Brass said, making a show of scratching his ear as he did.

The barber looked up now. Brass had caught his attention. "Going for the Iandran style?"

"Whatever makes the missus happy," Brass answered.

The barber nodded, an unspoken test passed. "Be right with you."

When the barber was finished and his lone customer was gone, he led Arman and Brass to a set of cellar doors in the back of the shop. He opened them, revealing a set of stairs that went down much farther than they would have had to if this were a normal cellar. At the bottom, Arman could just make out a long corridor that winded off into darkness.

"Thank you very much, good sir," Brass said, leading the way down.

The barber closed the door behind them, leaving them in total darkness. Arman produced a lightstone from his belt, illuminating the stairwell in faint white light. Wordlessly, they descended the stairs.

It was cold in the passageway and dark except for the light emanating from the lightstone. The stench of dirt and old wood hung in the air, which was uncomfortably still. Why was it, Arman wondered, that nobody these days seemed to know how to properly ventilate an underground tunnel for decent airflow? Then, in a moment of self-awareness, Arman realized the fact that he was thinking about tunnel ventilation at a time like this was probably why his wife called him easily distracted.

"This brings back memories," Brass said, smiling.

"Wandering around in the dark, trying to get ourselves killed?"

"Sneaking into the bad guys' house, finding secrets, saving lives," Brass said. "I mean, we're saving our lives this time, but same idea. I guess it's also different without everybody else here."

"Brass." Arman stopped walking. "I'm just here to make sure that Harbin and the watch can handle this."

"Oh, I know," Brass said with a wave of his hand. "But what's the plan when they can't?"

The corridor ended at a wooden door. Orange light seeped out through the crack between it and the floor. A muffled hum of music came from the other side; as did the smell of pipe smoke. Brass raised his eyebrows and gave a tight-lipped smile.

He opened the door, and the corridor was flooded with light. Inside was a spacious room with a vaulted ceiling and glass chandelier light bathing the whole interior in an orange tinge that filtered through the subtle haze of smoke in the air. Wooden booths and tables filled most of the space, save for a bar counter at the far end and an aisle in the center that led to a thrust stage.

Most of the seating in the room was filled by men and women dressed for a scrape, with the odd person dressed in finery mixed in every so often. Onstage, front and center, was a woman draped in a trailing scarlet dress, singing a song of heartbreak while the band behind her strummed out a melancholic accompaniment.

A doorman with curly red hair and a scraggly chin moved to intercept them. He kept his hands behind his back, but his posture sent a message that they weren't to come any farther. "Something I can do for you gentlemen?"

"Winston?" Brass said, recognizing the man.

"I know you?"

Brass realized his error too late; he'd forgotten he was disguised right now. Arman really wanted to hit him now, but Brass recovered. "No, but your reputation precedes you! Who hasn't heard of the Firechin of Faithwater?"

"What?" Winston asked in disbelief, even as he broke out in a smile. "No, they're not still telling that story. Are they?"

"Well, I've heard it," Brass said. "Never expected to see you here."

"Place is full of surprises," Winston said. "Sorry, what were you here for again?"

"Ah, just looking for work," Brass said. "I understand this is the kind of place where we could be pointed in the right direction."

The doorman looked them over and seemed impressed. "You're in the right place. Find yourselves a seat. The Dial will take you when he's ready."

"Perfect," Brass said.

"What did you say your name was?"

"Pardon my manners, I forgot to give it," Brass said. "You can call me Copper, and this is my associate . . . Shaft."

Arman suppressed the urge to punch Brass in the face. It wouldn't have been worth it to try, even if it didn't risk blowing their cover.

Brass was always quicker than he was.

"Shaft, huh?" Winston asked, giving Arman another once-over.

"I can assure you, it's a name well earned," Brass stated, before giving Arman an encouraging slap on the ass. "Come on, let's find a table."

Once they sat down, out of anyone else's earshot, Arman glowered at Brass. "What was that?"

"You're going to have to be more specific."

"Shaft?"

"All part of the ruse. No one'll suspect the well-endowed gay hitman of being Clocktower enemy number one. Well, number twenty-three, realistically. They've got a lot of enemies," Brass said.

"You couldn't think of a better name, could you?"

"I blanked like a university kid on an entrance exam," Brass said. "But hey. It's not an entirely inaccurate name."

Arman cocked his head. He wasn't sure he wanted an explanation of what Brass meant.

"What are you talking about?"

Brass smirked. "Snow used to tell me everything."

"Oh saints."

"Very respectable, by the sounds of things."

"Please stop." This was not happening. He was not discussing the size of his penis with his ex-companion in the middle of an undercover operation.

Brass chuckled but eventually seemed to settle down. He turned his eyes to the stage, taken in by the slow swaying of the singer's hips and the raw sadness she projected through her voice. The lyrics only made the performance even more haunting. It was a song about loneliness, self-loathing, and desperation to be someone else.

He'd never heard it before, but with one performance, the woman managed to make him feel like he'd remember every word for the rest of his life.

"You hear from her lately?" Brass asked abruptly. His voice shrank, taking on a wistful quality.

"Who?"

"Snow."

Arman was silent for a moment. "Not since Relgen. You?"

"Once, right after everything went down," Brass said. "These days it's just rumors and word of mouth. A dead noble here, guy freezing to death in summer there . . ."

"Oh."

Arman tried to come up with something else to say, but he couldn't figure out what the appropriate response was. It had taken him months to be able to talk to even Elizabeth about how the Starbreakers had ended. Still, the city's name left him uncomfortable. He couldn't read Brass. Couldn't tell what he needed to hear.

A gruff voice broke their silence. "I don't think I recognize either of you two."

A tall, broad-shouldered man in dark clothes loomed over their table. He had fair skin, bleached blond hair, and calloused hands. The predatory smile on his face made Arman want to reach for his wand. The man was flanked on either side by brick houses of men dressed in chain mail with shortswords on their belts.

Brass immediately stood up, and Arman followed suit.

"You must be the Dial," Brass said. "Copper, pleasure to meet you."

"Sit," the man said.

They obeyed, but Brass cocked his head for a moment at the Dial's brusqueness.

Both of the Dial's bodyguards remained standing.

"Winston tells me that you're looking for work," the Dial said, eyeing them both.

"That we are." Brass nodded. "A rather specific kind actually."

"What specific kind is that?"

"Well, my partner and I are rather experienced swords for hire," Brass said. "Got our start as glintchasers, but castellan bounties weren't cutting it, and digging up old tombs and ruins always felt wrong. So we transitioned."

The Dial nodded his understanding, his eyes flitting between the two of them.

"We heard there was a contract out on a bunch of freelancers worth looking into," Arman said, cutting to the chase. "We figured this would be the place to get the details on that."

"That is not one of ours," the Dial said. "But I have heard of it. It's a large list. Different pay for the different names on it."

"What names?" Arman asked.

"I have someone who can tell you," the Dial said.

Without needing to be prompted, one of the Dial's men left. Of course he didn't know himself, Arman thought. Remembering details was a thinking man's role. This Dial was a brute. The crime lord continued to stare at both of them, eyes narrowing occasionally.

"A warning," the Dial said. "You are not the first to ask about this contract. You will have competitors."

"I like a little competition," Brass said.

"Yes," the Dial said. The corner of his mouth twitched as he nodded again. He'd made up his mind about them. He gestured to the stage.

"Have you enjoyed tonight's performance?"

"She's phenomenal," Brass said.

"She's Antemer," the Dial said, like he was hungry and talking about an expertly cooked meal. "Iandrans invented the stage, but Antemer were born to it. They're a dishonest people by nature. Perfect for the illusion of performance."

Alarm bells rang in Arman's head. The Dial's choice of words worried him, but he couldn't be certain he wasn't imagining it. It took a sharp and practiced eye to see through illusions. No. It had to be a coincidence.

"She came to me not too long ago," the Dial said. He sounded particularly proud about that. "I knew at once there was something magical about her."

"She's certainly talented," Arman said, trying to maintain his cool. "Probably could have been an opera singer."

"Are you a patron of the operas?" the Dial asked.

Arman instantly regretted opening his mouth. Brass was so much better at this than he was.

"I stayed in Iandra when I was younger." Arman could never come up with a fake story on the spot, so he figured his best bet was just cherry picking the truth. "There were a lot of operas."

"I never had the chance to attend an Iandran production. But their reputation precedes them." The Dial stood. "I have others I must meet with. But please, enjoy a drink with my compliments."

"On the wife's tab, sir?" one of the Dial's enforcers asked.

"She won't mind the expense," he said, eliciting a knowing nod in response.

The exchange reminded Arman of Brass's conversation with the barber. Brass kicked him under the table in a warning that confirmed his worst suspicions. They were made. He'd underestimated the Dial. And overestimated himself.

The Dial was leaving the table. His man wasn't. As he walked, he gave small subtle signals that Arman never would have seen if he didn't already have an idea of what was happening. A nod to one person, a handshake and whisper to another, and the entire atmosphere shifted. People got out of their seats. Someone walked onstage to escort the singer off. Both Arman and Brass started counting just how many other people were in the room.

Maybe it was because he was with Brass or because he'd actually brought his wand this time but old instincts came to Arman even easier than they had last time, like they'd never left. The focus as everything that wasn't right in front of him fell out of his mind. The unambiguity that turned the threat of death into a puzzle and everything around him into pieces of a solution. Two of them. Too many enemies. Six already standing with easy paths straight toward them. Only one exit. Unobstructed, but not for long.

Brass made a move for the door, and Phoenix was right behind him. They weren't quick enough.

A line of men formed in front of the only exit. People were beginning to draw weapons. Phoenix cursed himself for not keeping a better eye on the exit or coming prepared with an alternate escape route. He really was out of practice.

"I've heard stories of the glintchasers who set the Clock back by decades," the Dial said from a table where he now sat, watching the rest of the hideout encircle them. "I never imagined they'd be so foolish as to come here. Or think they could fool me with parlor tricks."

The first of the lot stepped forward, eager to be the first to draw blood. "This is for what you did back—"

The woman never finished her sentence. In a single motion, Brass activated his wrist-pocket to summon his rapier and swung. The woman gurgled as a line of red appeared on her throat and started to leak profusely. She collapsed, and the rest of the crowd was stunned to stillness. They had never seen a person move that fast.

"I'm Brass, by the way," Brass told the woman as she twitched on the floor. "Sorry for doing that out of order, but you didn't leave me much time."

He threw his arms open wide, swinging his rapier out as he did. Everyone near the sword took an instinctive step back. Their fear would last maybe another second before turning to revenge, Brass knew, unless he could distract them.

"Well. Who wants to go next?" Brass asked.

The challenge threw them off balance. It put the idea in their minds, if only for an instant, that they would have to fight him one at a time. It wouldn't take long at all for them to realize they could just rush them. Even he wasn't sure he could take that many dirks coming at once.

"Anyone? Come on, step up, we haven't got all day!" His mouth was moving faster than his mind now. He trusted it to catch up before he got himself killed.

Phoenix watched, tense, but dared not get in Brass's way.

The crowd parted as one man shoved his way through. He stood a head above anyone else in the room, and he was clad in heavy plate armor. His face was crisscrossed with scars, and one of his ears was a mangled mess. He had a sword only slightly shorter than Brass was tall in hand, dragging the tip across the floor. Scratched all along the surface of the blade were tick marks. Brass couldn't count how many.

"Just one?" Brass declared, pointing with his sword. The challenger approached no farther, eyeing Brass's blade. Brass knew he was being sized up. But now he had a plan. "I guess the rest of you must know what my partner is carrying."

Phoenix hesitated, but only for a second. He remembered this play. It had been a very long time since he'd enchanted something this fast. He reached into the belt pouch that carried his spare parts, and produced a small stone sphere. At the same time, he quickly traced his fingers across it in a series of rapid patterns. By the time he held the stone up to the crowd around them, it was emitting a pulsing red glow while angry-looking glyphs slowly moved across its surface.

"Shaft!" Brass shouted. "For the uneducated in the room, tell them what they've won!"

"This is a class-four fire sphere," Phoenix warned, making sure to show it to everyone surrounding them, "with a dead man activation glyph."

"In Corsan for the slow folks in the back!"

"If this thing leaves my hand, it'll explode in a fireball that'll take out this entire block and everyone in it."

"You heard the man! The entire block!" Brass said. "I commend you all for good instincts, seeing as if any of you had been stupid enough to take another step forward, we would have been forced to incinerate us all. Show of hands, who wants to be incinerated?"

No one raised their hand.

"Now, this is what's going to happen," Brass said. "We're going to walk out of here. You're going to give us a thirty-second head start—"

"Sixty seconds," Phoenix interrupted.

"A forty-five-second head start," Brass said. "And then you can all do your darndest to catch us. Or you can pack up your little operation before the watch, who are already on their way, get here."

Brass and Phoenix both began inching toward the exit while everyone looked on, unsure of what to do. It didn't matter if they actually stuck to the terms Brass had laid out. If they got out of the room and into the passageway, they could bottleneck the crowd and even the odds.

They got to the line of men blocking the door without anyone making a move against them. Brass gestured with his sword for the men to get out of their way. Hesitantly, they began to move.

"The king's man doesn't work with glintchasers," the man with the enormous sword said. He pointed at the stone in Arman's hand. "And that is a rock."

"Well, I encourage you to test that theory," Brass said.

Brass grabbed the rock out of Phoenix's hand and threw it at the man. Everyone else in the room flinched, expecting a ball of fire. Instead the rock simply smacked the man in the eye and clattered to the floor. While everyone was still in shock, Brass attacked, and in the space of a breath, killed two men guarding the door. Phoenix drew his wand from his belt.

The cylinder in the base of the wand spun, cycled through its chambers, and clicked into position. The light at the tip of the wand changed from white to red an instant before a jet of flame spewed forward, engulfing part of the crowd. It didn't destroy the entire block, but it threw the ranks of the enemies closest to them into chaos. Now with an opening to the exit, Phoenix and Brass sprinted out, while curses and crossbow bolts followed them.

They reached the stairs, a chorus of footsteps behind them. Phoenix sent out another jet of flame from the wand, covering their retreat as they ascended the stairs.

Brass shoved open the cellar doors at the top of the staircase and slammed them shut the moment Phoenix was clear. Phoenix aimed his wand at the doors, but before he could do anything, crackling blue threads of energy materialized around the handles of the cellar doors, wrapping around them and pulling tight. The doors jostled as people on the other side tried to open them, but the threads held firm, and the doors stayed shut.

"For someone supposedly retired, you get into a lot of trouble," Ink said, standing at the far end of the alleyway with a smirk on her face.

14

INK

"Can we not do this here?" Phoenix asked as the cellar doors shuddered again.

"Obviously," Ink said, rolling her eyes. "Let's go for a ride."

Ink spread her hands out, and a circle of iridescent glyphs appeared on the cobblestone where they were standing. A shiver went down Phoenix's spine as a slick feeling slowly encased him. Brass looked down at the glyphs, then at himself. He could feel it too, like being submerged in cold oil. Everything around them took on a shimmering, fractal appearance. Colors around them changed. Images blurred. The sound of thousands of glasses shattering drowned out all noise. Then, all at once, everything returned to normal, only now, they were standing in the lobby of the Crimson Lilac.

The woman at the front desk yelped, nearly dropping her book.

The only evidence of the teleport was the faint smell of ozone and the churning in their stomachs. The cellar doors and Clocktower were on the other side of the city. They were in the clear. A tension Phoenix hadn't realized he was feeling relaxed, and the need to *be* Phoenix faded away with it.

Arman did his best to steady himself. Brass doubled over.

"Teleporting," Brass said. "That's a sensation I forgot I hated."

If the teleport affected Ink, she didn't show it as she smiled and waited for Brass and Arman to recover. She was watching them both expectantly. The woman at the desk was staring at all of them as if she wasn't sure they were real.

"Not that we don't appreciate the assistance," Arman said, trying to be diplomatic, "but what do you want?"

"I said we should catch up, didn't I?"

"I didn't think you were serious," Arman said. "How did you find us?"

As soon as he asked it, he felt stupid. She could have teleported them anywhere, but she'd picked the Lilac. She knew they'd been here last night. The smile on her face only confirmed it for him. She'd scried on them.

"We should talk," Ink said. "Drinks are on me."

Arman could still feel his heart pounding from the incident with Clocktower. He wanted to sit down and process everything that had just happened. He didn't want to deal with Ink and whatever it was she wanted, and she wanted something. But there was really only one way to get rid of her.

"Fine," Arman said.

The three of them sat down in the Lilac's bar and ordered drinks. Arman made a point of ordering the most expensive whisky the bar sold. He didn't drink it. He knew it wouldn't hurt Ink's coin purse, not with the Academy's money behind her, but it was the principle that mattered to him.

"What do you want?" Arman asked again.

"Has he gotten meaner?" Ink asked Brass.

"You know, I thought that exact thing, but I didn't know if I was misremembering so I didn't say anything."

Arman briefly reconsidered not drinking.

"Misremember? So the gang really did split up after Relgen," Ink said. "I didn't believe it when I heard it."

"Well, things happen, people change, you move on," Brass said, looking at Arman. There was no judgment in Brass's eyes. If anything, there was concern. Brass had a vague sense of where to draw the line when talking about the old days. Ink wouldn't. "You understand. You're not still with the Cord after all."

"No, I'm not," Ink said. She let out a forlorn sigh. "I do miss that bunch sometimes. But I'd gone as far as they could take me."

"Which brought you here," Arman said, hoping to steer things back to her actual reason for being here. He thanked the saints it worked.

"That it did," Ink said, turning on her seat to face her whole body toward him now. "I came to ask you some questions about the Golden Shield."

"I already told Harbin everything I know."

"Harbin's a wheelwright out of his depth," Ink said dismissively. "I need to hear this from someone who half knows what they're talking about."

His fingers curled, but he stopped himself short of making a fist. Ink lived to get a rise out of people, and he didn't want to give her the satisfaction.

Arman had spent most of his life as the smartest person in the room and feeling isolated for it. People's eyes glazed over when he talked too much or too in-depth about his projects.

Getting excited about a historical discovery only made him realize how much of an outlier he was for knowing the Old World's history of succession. Things other people were amazed by were mundane, basic principles of study to him. It all just made his existing problems of understanding people even worse.

Ink was in the same boat as he was, separated from other people by how much she knew. But she reveled in it. Looked down on anyone who couldn't match her. Of course she didn't value Harbin's version of events. Harbin hadn't studied arcane theory and Old World scholarship for fifteen years. What did he know?

"Okay," he said, doing his best to keep his voice level.

"The Golden Shield?"

"Two assailants attacked them. An artifact was damaged in the fight and caused an explosion that killed all of them." Arman knew for a fact Harbin would have told her this already.

"The assailants?" Ink asked.

"Couldn't find their bodies," Arman said flatly.

"Incinerated in the blast?"

"Not likely. Three other bodies survived, including one from the epicenter."

"So someone recovered their bodies," Ink said. Not a question. She'd already come to a conclusion. *Maybe the wrong one*, Arman thought.

"Or they survived," Arman said.

"Survived an explosion that destroyed a whole house?"

"It's not impossible," Arman said. "Fire resistance. Teleportation. Dumb luck."

Ink leaned back, observing Arman with a much more reserved smile than her usual one. Much as she enjoyed dismantling blatantly wrong ideas, Arman had convinced her of the possibility. She was impressed. It wasn't often someone else thought of something she didn't think was wrong.

"The artifact that was destroyed," she changed the subject. "What was it?"

"You tell me," Arman said. "The Shield worked for you."

"They worked for the Academy," Ink said.

"Since when are you modest?" Arman asked. "There aren't too many people in the Academy who don't answer to the High Inquisitive."

Ink chuckled, running her hand along the glyphs on the sleeves of her robes. "Well done. I forgot you could read Arcania. You don't seem to be doing too bad for yourself either."

Arman's smile dropped. He'd meant it as a power move, showing how much he knew about Ink and her work. He hadn't expected her turning it on him. She looked very deliberately at his hand. At his wedding ring.

"So, which of those poor girls did you finally pick? Or did you convince them to share?"

His legs shook. Stupid. He'd brought Ink's life into this, and now she was bringing in his.

Should have known better.

"Are you here about the Shield or me?" Arman asked.

"Both, actually."

His heart rate picked up. That wasn't the answer she was supposed to give. Ink's smile got bigger again. He'd done a terrible job of hiding his discomfort.

"What happened to the artifact?" Ink asked.

"Destroyed."

"What about the head?"

"The what?" Brass stopped drinking Arman's whisky to interject for the first time.

"Gamma's still with me," Arman said. "I've been trying to repair him."

"That construct is Academy property," Ink said.

"Well right now, he's the Academy's paperweight," Arman said. "Damage from the blast rendered him inert. I can fix him. Besides, I already told you everything he told me."

"It has more information," Ink said. "Information it won't tell you."

"Well he's not going to tell you either," Arman said. "Unless I can get him working again."

Ink narrowed her eyes. "You know, Harbin thinks you're retired."

"I am."

"You're not acting like it."

Brass was actively paying attention to their conversation now as he sipped Arman's drink. He wasn't sure how Arman would react to Ink pushing that button, but he was anxious to see.

Arman breathed.

"I'm just trying to keep the people I care about safe," Arman said. "The Golden Shield weren't the only ones attacked. Their assailants aren't the only ones out there."

"Fair enough," Ink said.

She stood up and placed a coin pouch on the counter. Arman could tell at a glance she'd overpaid.

"Deliver the construct's head to the castellan as soon as it's functional," Ink said. "If you get in the way of my investigation, I will haul you and anyone else I feel like into a cell in Oblivion and lose the key."

She waved her hand, causing the teleportation glyphs to appear under her feet once again. The air started to fracture and shimmer around her.

"That's a promise from the High Inquisitive of the Academy."

With a shattering sound, the air undistorted itself, and Ink was gone, leaving behind the faint smell of ozone. Brass waved his hand to clear the smell.

"Well, she's as much of a delight as ever," Brass said as he counted out the money needed to pay for drinks from Ink's coin pouch and pocketed the rest. "You know, they say power corrupts, but what does it do when the person's already a bastard?"

Arman grabbed his drink, which was half gone already thanks to Brass, and downed the rest in one go.

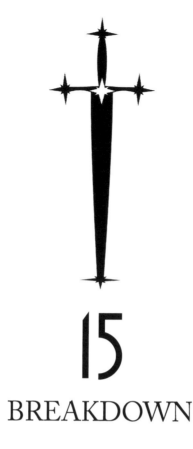

15

BREAKDOWN

Arman's whole body was shaking, and his heart hammered in his chest as everything played over in his mind, from walking down into Clocktower's hideout to Ink's exit. The more it played, the more idiotic he felt. Amateur mistakes.

Stupid decisions. Stupid.

And Elizabeth. And Robyn. If he'd made even one more mistake, they'd have never seen him again.

"Are you feeling okay?"

"No, Brass." Arman ran his hands through his hair. "No, I am not feeling okay."

"Well, they sell a few fixes for that here," Brass offered.

"You might want to stick to the drinks though. Don't think your wife would appreciate it if you—"

Arman punched Brass in the face.

"This isn't funny, Brass!" Arman shouted. Heat was building in his face and chest. His heart pounded, and he had to stand up.

"Clearly not, since you opted to talk about it with a right cross," Brass rubbed his jaw. Brass had taken far worse hits, but from Arman, it was a surprise.

"Saints know how many people are after us, and who knows who else. We don't know, because we tried to find out and we fucked it up. I almost died! I almost left Elizabeth a widow and Robyn without a father, and we didn't even get anything out of it! And now I've got Ink and the entire Academy breathing down my neck. This whole mess gets worse every day, and I have no idea how to fix it!"

He sat back down. Yelling had vented some of the heat building up in him, but his legs were shaking again. Again, everything that happened replayed in his mind as he frantically tried to figure out what he could have done, should have done, differently. He couldn't afford mistakes. Mistakes were how people died.

Brass put a hand on Arman's shoulder.

"Phoenix, you were right." His voice was gentle but firm.

Something about hearing his old freelancer name refocused Arman. He started breathing slower. Started processing what Brass had said. "About what?"

Brass looked him in the eye. "The attacks being connected was just a theory. But the Dial said it himself. It's all one contract. You were right."

"What does that change?" Arman asked.

"How should I know? You're the one who usually does this deduction business," Brass said.

Arman glowered. This was supposed to be making him feel better?

"That's not the point though," Brass said. "The point is it wasn't for nothing. It's never for nothing. We'll find another way, figure out what's going on, and save everyone. It's what we do."

He made it sound so simple. Maybe it was because back in the old days, it *was* that simple, and Brass was still living in those days. Arman could use a little bit of that right now. A little bit of the old him.

"We?" Arman asked.

"You thought I was going to botch one job and hang you out to dry?" Brass said. "Rule number one of freelancing: you look out for your company. Besides, that whole Clocktower mess was the most fun I've had with my clothes on in years."

Arman laughed. It was an exhausted, terrified laugh. But it wasn't without comfort. Brass was still Brass. In its own way, that was a relief.

"I'm sorry I punched you," Arman said apologetically.

"Oh, that was a punch?" Brass said. "I thought you were tenderly caressing my face. I was very flattered."

Arman crossed his arms. He felt a little better. Maybe it was Brass. Maybe it was the alcohol. Probably a bit of both.

Brass saw some of the tension release and flashed a knowing smirk. "So. It's Elizabeth?"

For a moment, Arman wondered how Brass knew who he was married to but then remembered he'd blurted out her name during his meltdown. He really was doing a terrible job keeping his personal life personal today.

"Yeah," Arman admitted. "I was banned from Sasel. I couldn't face my family . . . I didn't know where else to go. I just knew I shouldn't be alone. And she put me back together."

"That's sweet."

"Why do you say that with a smirk on your face?"

"It's nothing. Angel just owes me twenty glint."

"You made a bet on me and Elizabeth?"

"Don't act surprised, we bet on all of your relationships back then. And Church always lost, poor bastard."

"Of course you did," Arman muttered, running his hands through his hair. He thought he'd be more annoyed, and yet, he found the thought of his companions doing something like that oddly comforting. His heartbeat steadied even more, and he sighed. "Well. Clocktower's a bust, and that was our best shot at figuring out where the contract came from."

"Best shot isn't the same thing as only shot," Brass said. "We'll think of something. Or something will fall in our laps. It'll work out."

"That's not a plan."

Brass shrugged. "That's because I'm moral support. Plans are your thing."

Arman sighed, rubbing his temples. "Right. Well. I suppose I'll try and think of something."

Brass had a point. Clocktower wasn't the only option. There was at least one person in Harbin's custody who knew about the contract, assuming they'd found the assailant he'd left tied up back at the Golden Shield's house. Three if the Academy wanted to drop the glint on a couple resurrections. There were other organizations that could be tracked down that might know something. Maybe there were other freelancers who'd been attacked who knew more about what was going on.

Arman stood up.

"Where are you going?"

"Home," Arman said. "Until I can find us another lead, I might as well work on getting Ink off my back about her construct. And I miss my family. I'll be in touch."

Brass rolled his eyes but smiled. "All right, well, off you go then. Swear at baby for me. And tell Wings I said hi."

Arman got up to leave and then stopped at the door, debating whether or not to say something. "Brass?"

"Hmm?"

"Thank you."

Brass looked surprised for a moment, then smiled. He gave his old companion a knowing nod. "My pleasure."

16
CARP'S

By the time Arman made it back to Akers, the late-afternoon sun was on its last legs. The long walk had given him time to calm down, think, panic, and then calm down again. Knowing he could count on Brass was a small relief, but there was still a lot to deal with.

On the way home, he stopped by the inn. It had been a while since he'd checked in on the appliances he'd built for them, and if he didn't do it now, he was going to put it off for another week. And after the mess he'd dealt with, he could use a simpler task to settle himself.

Carp's Inn was the center of Akers: the place where everyone in the small homestead gathered after a long day's work and where travelers were welcomed into town. It was a wide building, but short for something that had rooms upstairs. Most of the tables were wood, but the counters were polished stone. Walls were decorated with pieces of old farming equipment and artisan's tools donated by the different families. Everyone in Akers had a piece of something in the inn.

Behind the counter was one of Arman's contributions—a slab of dark gray stone where a cooking stove should have been. Pots and pans rested on it, and where they were placed, bright orange arcane glyphs appeared, heating them.

It was busy and warm when Arman walked in, and the smell of stewed beef and chili wafted through the place. There was no table or booth where there weren't at least two people sitting. No one sat alone in this place. Clanks and clatters of mugs and cutlery punctuated the chatter that filled the room.

An older man with a dark complexion and graying hair walked by Arman, carrying a platter of empty tankards on one hand. "Arman!"

"Hey, Ferris," said Arman.

"Carp's out back getting something from the chiller," said Ferris. "Go ahead and sit down by the bar. He'll find you."

"Thanks," Arman nodded and sat down. A few minutes passed, during which Arman kept himself busy by taking some spare odds and ends from his belt pouches and tinkering with them.

"*Are you making me a new marvel?*" a man's laughing voice drew Arman back to reality. There was only one person in Akers who spoke Gypic with a voice like that.

Carp was an older Gypic man with rich brown skin, dark hair, and chocolate eyes. He was a hairy fellow with a thick beard and hair across his forearms that his rolled-up sleeves showed off. His clothes had been white once, but years of wear and work in the inn had tinted them a slight yellow-brown color.

He hugged Arman, almost lifting him out of his chair. Arman returned the embrace, even if he couldn't match Carp's strength.

Carp spoke Corsan, but he preferred the languages of his homeland and early travels and indulged in them whenever he could. Besides Carp's husband, Arman was the only person Carp could converse with in it.

"*Just some trinket,*" Arman said.

"*I suppose I can make do with what you've already done,*" Carp said, finally releasing him. "*It's been a while since I've seen you. How's your beautiful family?*"

"*Happy and healthy, thanks,*" Arman said. "*I was headed back to them, but I wanted to make sure things were good here.*"

Carp nodded enthusiastically. "*The stove works perfectly. I never get tired of watching newcomers touch it for the first time. No matter how many times you show them, they're always sure it will burn them.*" He poked Arman in the chest. "*A man traveling for his master saw it and wanted to buy it. I told him if he wanted one, he would have to speak to you.*"

Arman got worried for a moment. "*You didn't tell him where to find me, did you?*"

"*Of course not,*" Carp assured him. "*I told him, 'If you want one, you must speak with the man who made this one.' When he wanted to know who made it, I told him only that I would pass along his message.*"

Arman relaxed. *Good man, Carp.*

"*If you sold these creations, you could be the richest man in Corsar,*" Carp said, for not the first time.

"I *don't need the money,*" Arman replied.

"*So you always say,*" Carp said. "*But everyone needs money eventually.*"

"*How's the chiller?*" Arman asked, changing the subject.

"*Oh, right. That is something you could take a look at,*" Carp said. "*Just this morning, something went wrong with it.*"

Arman raised an eyebrow. "*Did it stop working?*"

"*It worked too well!*" Carp said in amazement. "*I went to pull ingredients from it this morning, and everything was frozen solid.*"

Arman was genuinely surprised and intrigued by this.

The stove and chilling cabinet were experiments of his. When he'd first built them, it had been hard to maintain the enchantment on them. Power inefficiencies, mostly. But he'd cleared those up. His last few checkups had mostly been to clean them while he worked out the best way to enchant them to sustain and maintain themselves.

A surge in effect was new. His mind started concocting possible causes. An accidental cascading effect that increased the power of the enchantment over time. Something destabilizing the flow of energy between planes. Some damn sorcerer sneezing.

"*I'll take a look,*" Arman said.

Carp led Arman out back behind the inn, where the chiller was kept. As soon as they stepped outside, the temperature dropped considerably. That was Arman's first clue that something was off. The chiller's interior was supposed to be cold. Not the area around it.

The chiller was an oversized pantry about the size of a small shed, its back, a maze of tubing and tanks. At the moment, the grass around it was covered in frost. Arman could see his own breath while standing next to it.

Carp left him to it.

Arman set his armor to resist the cold, just as a precaution, and then started by examining everything. One thing became readily apparent. The enchantment was surging. Its effects were being amplified by something. But he couldn't find the cause.

"Phoenix." An icy voice spoke out.

Arman turned around as slowly as he could. A woman sat on the roof of Carp's inn, staring down at him. Her skin was white, tinged blue. She had long black hair, most of it tied back but some of it free, framing her face and her bright blue eyes. She wore a mix of black and dark blue leather armor.

As soon as Arman saw her, he knew why the chiller was acting up.

It was Snow.

17
SMALL
BEGINNINGS

Crackling silver smoke obscured the floor as Phoenix entered the tiny church of the town of Aenerwin. He couldn't see his boots, but he still heard his footsteps against the hard wooden floor. And yet, his feet felt wet and they tingled. There were no candles or lanterns lit inside. The only light came from the soft white glow emanating from the smoke itself.

Somewhere in the back of his mind, there was a part of him screaming to run. He was a glorified librarian with a secondhand crossbow on a research trip, and what was happening to Aenerwin was so thoroughly beyond him, it wasn't even funny. Of the four glintchasers he'd recruited, none of them had signed up to fight a mad cult bent on sacrificing the town to their dark god. But curiosity and adrenaline drove him forward.

He'd come to Aenerwin to dig through the nearby Old World ruins, making stops in every tavern along the way to look for help until he finally caught a break with four glintchasers about his age, all willing to work with his incredibly limited budget. He'd only had to pay Snow and Brass. The timid cleric and the angry girl following him around, who gave their names as Church and Angel, were willing to work for free.

Apparently the very ruin Phoenix had wanted to explore was luring too many people to their deaths.

Church wanted it cleared out, and for whatever reason, Angel was willing to follow him.

But then they'd learned what was going on in Aenerwin. It wasn't what any of them had come to do, but someone had to do something, and after learning what they were all capable of, the five of them were just confident enough to try. But now that confidence was faltering.

Sending the others to deal with the rest of the cult while he handled the leader had seemed like a much better plan before Phoenix actually saw the inside of the church the leader was holed up in.

The nave's wooden pews were full of dozens of people, all sitting motionless in their seats, eyes blank as they craned their necks to look up at the ceiling. All Phoenix saw when he looked up was more smoke, blanketing the ceiling and flashing like storm clouds.

The cult's leader stood at the front of the room, positioned behind the priest's podium, waiting. Tall, impossibly thin, with stark white hair and a deeply receded widow's peak. Black linen robes hung from his frame and swallowed his legs. A narrow twelve-pointed star was crudely carved into his forehead.

All members of the Cult of Stars marked themselves this way, believing it granted them insight and power. Considering what he was seeing, Phoenix was starting to think they were right about that.

"Hello, child." The man greeted him. His voice was unsettlingly calm, and his silver eyes bored into Phoenix. "I see you and your companions turned down your opportunity to run. Have you come to bear witness then?"

Phoenix looked around again, at the entire town's population sitting in a trance, and at the smoke that enveloped everything else in the church. His finger drifted to his crossbow's trigger.

"To what?"

"To the return of this world to its rightful owners," the cultist said.

"The elves are dead," Phoenix stated.

The man let out a low growl, and the pins and needles Phoenix felt in his boots intensified. In his mind a theory formed on the source of the smoke. Phoenix swore he saw the carving on the cultist's head grow larger.

"The elves are nothing. Pretenders to the throne of creation, whose hubris inflicted the world with the infestation of humanity," the cultist spat. "No. I speak of the true lords of creation. Those born among the stars whose very being governs existence."

Phoenix had read a lot of books in his seventeen short years, but he knew very little about the starborn, beings said to be older than the gods. But even what little he did know told him they weren't something he wanted coming back to the world.

The young glintchaser took aim at the cultist and loosed a crossbow bolt at his chest. Just before it struck, a cloud of smoke burst out from the man's torso, and the bolt vanished into it.

When the smoke dissipated, the man stood unharmed.

Phoenix swallowed.

With a casual expression and complete lack of urgency, the man drifted out from behind the podium and slowly stalked Phoenix, drawing an undulating dagger.

The doors of the church slammed shut of their own accord.

"Very well. Join this place, as a sacrifice to the stars."

Phoenix frantically looked around the room, his heart pounding. He loaded and fired a second bolt, only to meet similar results. His mind raced, taking in everything around him and looking for the best way out of the situation his bravado had gotten himself into.

*"What did you think you would accomplish by coming here, glintchaser?"
the man said mockingly. "Did you think you were a match for me? Or your
companions a match for my own?"*

*He prayed to Avelina, Ellanour, and every other saint he'd ever heard the
name of that he hadn't made a colossal mistake in coming here, relying on a
group of strangers to have his back. He backed away from the cultist and threw
a hunk of recovered lightstone from his pocket as hard as he could. It shattered at
the cultist's feet, producing a dazzling flash that Phoenix used as cover to make
a break for the doors. They didn't budge.*

*An unsettlingly cold hand gripped him by the shoulder, and the cult leader
loomed over him.*

"Any last words?"

*Phoenix dug another crossbow bolt from his bag. He didn't think he could
load it in time, and by now, he wasn't sure shooting the man would work, but at
the very least, he could try stabbing with it. But just as he was bracing to fight for
his life, he caught movement in the shadows of the nave behind the cult leader.*

*Immediate relief surged through him, and his shaky legs steadied. One of his
companions must have gotten inside.*

"Yeah," Phoenix said. "You really should have found better help."

*The cultist paused, raising an eyebrow before letting out a gurgling, choking
sound as a dagger drove through the back of his neck. A moment later, another
was slipped between his ribs. He dropped to the ground, his body scattering the
smoke as he fell. As he lay twitching, the smoke rapidly thinned out, until the last
wisps of it curled away in time with the cultist breathing his last.*

It was over.

"Cutting it kind of close there, don't you think?" Phoenix asked.

*The thief girl from the motley company he'd assembled brushed her dark hair
out of her amber eyes. Her normally white face was flushed pink from exertion.*

*"I worked as fast as I could, all right? You try getting the drop on these guys.
It's like they have eyes in the back of their heads," Snow said, yanking her blades
free and wiping them on her pant leg. "You're welcome, by the way."*

Her voice was as cool and collected as ever, but her eyes were wide with adrenaline. Maybe it was just the fact that she'd saved his life, but Phoenix thought they were the most beautiful eyes he'd ever seen.

"Where's everyone else?"

"Hopefully outside?" Snow called out.

"Yep! Good news!" Brass's voice answered from outside the church. "Angel killed all the bad people! Bad news, our cleric has a weak stomach!"

Snow glanced around the church full of bewildered people, some of whom had noticed the teenagers standing over the freshly killed body and looked concerned. Suddenly self-conscious about the blood on her pants, she took a step toward Phoenix, subtly positioning him between herself and the townspeople.

"Any ideas on what we're supposed to do now?" she asked.

Phoenix tried and failed to gauge the looks on the gathered faces. He'd researched every scrap of information he could find on the Old World's history and possible locations of its greatest treasures. He had read zero books on consoling the recently mind controlled. And yet he felt exhilarated—it was more than just an adrenaline high from looking death in the face. His thoughts were racing, trying to process everything he'd seen the cultist do. There was so much to unpack, so much he'd discovered, and so many more new, unanswered questions.

If this was how being a freelancer always felt, he was beginning to think he could get used to it.

"Well," he said, turning his attention to the townspeople. "How about we start by explaining what just happened to them, and work it out from there?"

"And here I was thinking the hard part of the day was over," she retorted.

"You know, if you and Brass want to run, now's really the time," he offered.

She looked him up and down and smirked.

"Nah," she said. "I think we'll stick around awhile."

18
SNOW

"We need to talk," Snow said.

She slipped off the roof of the inn, landing silently. She looked like she was waiting for him to say something, and after a moment Arman realized it was because his mouth was hanging open.

When he'd tracked down Brass at the Lilac, he'd prepared to run into him. Initiated it, even. This was different.

This paralyzed him.

Say something, damn it.

"Hey."

Snow sighed and hooked her thumbs into her belt. She'd been hoping she could avoid this part. "Hey."

She looked him over. His face had a light dusting of soot, save where his goggles would have been. There were holes in his coat and armor. Those had to be fresh, because he always repaired those whenever he got the chance. That or he'd just gotten sloppy. He did look a little softer than she remembered. Maybe put on a little weight. The beard was definitely more of a mess than it had ever been before.

"So, you're in town," Arman said.

"Yep."

They stood an arm's length apart. Arman could clearly see his breath now, but his armor kept him from feeling the cold. Snow tapped her foot. He wanted to say something. She knew he did. He always wanted to say something.

"Okay, we need to skip this part," Snow said as her patience ran out.

"What part?"

She skipped the explanation and jumped ahead, hoping to shock him into business. "There's a contract out on your head."

"Yeah, I noticed," Arman said. "Little late with the warning there."

He missed the point, so she tried again, more explicit this time. "There's a contract out on your head that *I* heard about."

The way Snow stressed it finally got through to Arman, and he felt stupid for not putting it together the first time she said it. People only told Snow about the biggest, highest-paying jobs. Nothing else was worth her time. If she'd heard of the price on his head, he was in deep, deep shit.

His thoughts started racing, and with it came the pacing. "Why is this happening? Why now?"

"I don't know."

"How much do you know?"

"It's a hit list," Snow said. "Decently long one. A lot of the names on it aren't worth much, but the ones at the top are a small fortune. A bunch of freelancers, mostly. And right now, you're in the top bracket."

"I'm flattered," he said, masking his panic. "Who put it out?"

"I don't know that either," Snow said. "It's all brokers and go-betweens. All I know is whoever they are, they want you alive."

Snow didn't say that like it was good news, and Arman knew it wasn't. Death was quick, and there were countless reasons to want someone dead, especially someone with a career history like his. But alive meant they wanted something from him. And would do whatever it took to get it.

"There are a lot of zeroes attached to you right now," Snow said. "Every dirk in Corsar has their eyes on it. Some of the best of the best."

"And it specifically said alive?"

"Actually, no," Snow said. "Alive or intact body, but there's a pay cut for bringing in a corpse, and it's big enough to cover a resurrection."

Arman gripped his wand—to feel it there, and have a reminder that he wasn't helpless. That he'd dealt with things like this before and he could do so again. There was also the fact that Snow was, at the end of the day, an assassin. And there was a price on his head.

"Are you—"

"No, I'm not after it." She'd been waiting for that one. "It's a big number, but it'd have to be a bit bigger before I went after you."

"Oh?"

"I know how dangerous you can be when you're backed into a corner," Snow said. "Hazard pay."

So much for old times' sake. ". . .thanks."

Arman scratched his chin. "What about Brass?"

"He's on it too, same bracket as you." Snow nodded. "So is Church. And Angel, which is frankly underselling her."

"What about you?"

"People know better than to come after me," Snow said quickly.

It made sense to Arman. Freelancers like Phoenix, like Brass, were useful, dependable, or troublesome, depending on who you asked. But Snow had a different sort of reputation. The kind that made people check over their shoulders before invoking her name.

But that got him thinking about the assassins who'd attacked him and Brass already. Bounty hunters and freelancers they'd never heard of. They were no slouches, but they didn't hold a candle to Snow.

"If there's such a big reward on the table, why haven't I run into any of them yet?" Arman asked.

"They're biding their time," Snow said. "Letting the small fish go first to see what they're dealing with. It's what I'd do in a mess like this."

"Have you told the others?" Arman asked.

A thin layer of frost started to creep across Snow's cheeks. "Church wouldn't listen to me even if I tried. Angel definitely wouldn't."

"And Brass?"

For a moment even Arman could see there was something she was holding back. But she buried it, and it was gone.

"I'd rather not deal with Brass right now."

"What about the Golden Shield?"

"They were on the list. Somebody fucked that one up."

"Any idea who?" Arman asked. Information about the attack on the Shield might help get Ink off his back.

Snow hesitated, and Arman realized she knew. She was just debating whether or not to tell him.

"It was Pitch."

Arman's eyes went wide. Years ago, Pitch had been a member of the Cord of Aenwyn, one of the only companies to ever match the Starbreakers. That is, until Ink got him kicked out for being too difficult to work with. If he was after the contract, things were even worse than he thought. "Oh."

"Yeah," Snow said. "So he's out there. And probably after you or one of the others."

Arman's pacing ground to a halt as the pile of information finally became too much. He leaned against the chiller and slowly slid down the side of it until he was sitting in the frozen dirt. His head spun. This was at least part of what he'd wanted out of Clocktower. But it was more or less the worst case scenario. Whoever was after him was paying top dollar. That was going to attract very dangerous people. And he wasn't the only target. How many were there?

Too many for Harbin.

Snow stayed standing. On some level it felt wrong, dumping all of this on him. But he had to know. Better he found out now, before it was too late. He'd figure out how to deal with it. If he didn't, he'd be dead in a few weeks.

"Sorry." She turned to leave.

"Where are you going?"

She looked up at the sky, trying to avoid looking at him. "I came to warn you. Warning delivered. I've got other things to handle."

"Wait—"

She turned around. Her eyes had turned a pale white. Frost was clinging to her hands and armor now. She'd gone cold on him. "I'm not staying."

Arman felt a hundred sentences get stuck in his throat at once as Snow vanished from sight and reappeared on the roof of the inn. No hand gesture, no arcane glyphs or distortion of the air, just there one moment, gone in the next—a thief's shadow blink. She moved silently across the rooftop, poised to disappear over the other side.

Arman watched her, thinking about how long it had been since he'd seen her. Wondering if he'd ever see her again. Everything he wanted to say fought to be heard, until in the end, nothing came out.

Just before she went over the other side, Snow looked back at him, a hint of blue having crept back into her eyes.

"Good luck."

And without another word, she was gone.

19

CRISIS

Elizabeth stood in the living room, cradling Robyn in her arms. The infant girl peacefully drooled into her shoulder, seemingly asleep, but Elizabeth knew it was a ruse. It had been a full day, and they both needed sleep, but the baby had been fighting it. If Elizabeth tried to put her down in the crib, she would open her eyes and start crying. Elizabeth was done taking chances. She wouldn't stop rocking until she knew for certain that Robyn was asleep.

Fighting off exhaustion, she thought about Arman; somewhere in the city, either looking for Brass or shaking down a den of cutthroats for information, maybe fighting off assassins coming after him as he went.

He had the easy job.

Her fingers twitched as she held Robyn. Logically, she knew what she was doing was important. Vital. But it didn't make her feel any less stuck. Any less useless. She didn't know where Arman was, didn't have a way to check on him. He could be fine. He could be dead. She didn't know, and she couldn't do anything. Her fingers were twitching even more now.

When she heard something approaching the front door, she almost jumped out of her skin before she recognized Arman's footsteps. And someone was with him. Their movements were energetic, almost bouncing. Familiar, but she couldn't quite place it.

Elizabeth opened the door.

Standing outside was a man in a wide-brimmed hat and greasy clothes. He had a paunch and a thick, scraggly beard streaked with white. She gripped the door, but just before she slammed it in the man's face, she recognized the mischievous twinkle in his eye. Once she saw it, it was trivial to spot the light-footed grace of his movements—and the carefully hidden strap on the fake beard.

"Brass?"

Brass pulled off his disguise and threw his arms out as if asking for a hug. "Surprise!"

Her head cocked to the side as Brass twirled the pieces of his disguise victoriously.

"Phoenix said we had to travel in disguise, wanted to do it with illusions, but I insisted I go practical this time! I think it turned out great, what about you?"

Arman came up from behind him, and relief washed over Elizabeth. She had a dozen questions. Where had he been? What happened? Why was Brass here? But before she could ask any of them, Arman walked straight past her into the house.

"Arman?"

Without a word, he continued through the house and down the stairs to the basement. Elizabeth followed him, leaving Brass at the door. She kept calling his name, but couldn't get him to so much as look at her. Robyn woke up and started crying again, and Elizabeth silently cursed her timing. As quickly as she could, she set Robyn down in the nursery and chased after her husband.

She caught up to him in the basement as lightstone in the walls came on, revealing Arman's workshop. It was a cluttered mess spread across two workbenches, multiple shelves of parts and components, and a toolbox as big as he was.

He crossed to the far side of the room to the only wall that didn't have anything on or in front of it and placed his hand on it.

An outline of light traced around his hand. After a moment, the seams of the wall flashed, and part of it spun around, revealing racks of equipment and magical devices he'd built and collected over the years. There were dozens of pieces, none of which she recognized or even knew he still had.

Arman stood for a moment, taking it all in. An anxiousness set into his face as he frantically started taking things off a rack and loading them onto his belt and into his coat pockets. Completely out of patience, she grabbed him.

"Arman!"

He finally looked at her, and she noticed his eyes. They were afraid, they were angry, and they were determined. Her heart started pounding in her chest when she saw that look. Every time she'd seen it before, he'd nearly gotten himself killed.

"Talk to me."

"No."

"What?"

"No." He twisted out of her grip. "Because I have to go, and you need to stay, and if I talk to you, you're going to try to talk me out of it, but you can't because I have been thinking about this from every angle, and this is the only good option."

The more he talked, the faster the words came out and the more erratically his hands shook. He turned back to the rack and resumed cleaning it out.

"What are you talking about?"

The equipment rack was bare now, and he moved to the workbench to start taking apart his wand and replacing some of its parts. "The attacks. Brass, me, the Shield. It is connected, it's worse than we thought, and Harbin cannot handle this. So we have to, so I have to, and you are staying here."

Elizabeth blinked. "No. No, I have been stuck at home by myself for days while you run around. I barely know what you're doing, and I never know if you're okay until you come back, beat half to death or so stressed you won't even look at me. Now talk to me, damn it."

He shook his head and put down his wand. His legs were shaking. "There's a contract out on freelancers, including me and Brass. Pitch is one of the dirks chasing it. And the others are just as bad."

"And what are you going to do?" Elizabeth gestured to the now empty equipment rack and to his wand. "What is the plan here?"

"The plan is, I find whoever put out the contract and cancel it, and you and Robyn stay here with Brass."

"Excuse me?"

"This is why I said no talking." He went back to reassembling his wand. "You're arguing and you're trying to talk me out of it, but I am *not* debating this. The house is shielded from scrying, the doors and windows are sealed, and the property is owned by Elizabeth Meshar, not Phoenix. It is the safest place for you and Robyn to be, and I need you to stay here, and stay safe."

"While you run straight into trouble? Alone?" She tore the wand from his hands before he could stop her.

He grabbed at it, but she held it out of reach. He ran a hand through his hair, his fingers knotting in it as he fought back frustration. She wasn't listening. Of course she wasn't listening. People never listened when he most needed them to.

"Wings." He used her old nickname; the one he'd given her a lifetime ago. It had the desired effect. Her eyes softened.

"I . . . I am not good. At a lot of things," he said. "But this is one thing that I was good at. I have thought about this and thought about this. We can't fix this from here, and it is absolutely not safe for Robyn to come with us. God forbid somebody does track down where I live, you'd be fighting with one hand tied behind your back. So Brass stays, and I go alone. Please, trust me when I say this is the best option for everyone."

His eyes pleaded. He held his hand out for his wand.

She wanted to hit him with it. Wanted to argue. To yell. She was exhausted, frustrated, and terrified, and nothing he'd said had even remotely helped with any of that. But she did trust Arman. Implicitly.

"Will you at least tell me where you're going?"

His gaze fell to the floor, and his shoulders sagged. Even thinking about what he was planning to do weighed on him.

"Harbin shut me out, and Ink won't help. I need somebody who might know something about the contract. So, I'm going to find Church and Angel."

"What?"

"They're targets too."

"You think they'll help?"

Arman didn't look her in the eye. It was an instinct to try and hide the uncertainty on his face. She saw straight through it. From the moment they met, she'd been able to read him like a book.

"I don't know. But they're the best idea I've got."

With a sigh, Elizabeth handed over the wand. He grabbed it, but she didn't let go. Instead she pulled him close, wrapping her arms around him and resting her head on his chest.

"Be careful."

Arman was caught off guard by Elizabeth switching from anger to . . . he wasn't actually sure what, but it wasn't anger anymore. He knew she wasn't okay, and he didn't feel okay either. So he did the only thing he could think to do. He held her, like his sanity depended on it.

"I will."

They stayed that way, steadying each other, until a voice from upstairs brought them back to the rest of the world.

"I hope I'm not interrupting anything, but I believe we have a problem with the baby. I got her to stop crying, but now she smells."

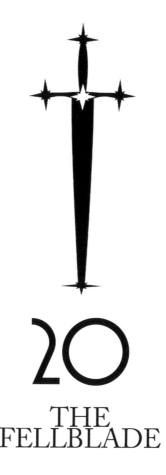

20
THE FELLBLADE

The Fellblade's target was somewhere in the small town of Aenerwin, northwest of Olwin. A cleric, and supposedly a good one at that.

He didn't have much to go on. Just this location, a reputation, and an alias. Glintchasers never used their real names, for lots of reasons, most of them rooted in paranoia and pageantry. That never bothered the Fellblade. He couldn't even remember his own name.

What *did* bother him was how on the nose the clerics always were when it came to their aliases. Bless. Preacher. Bishop.

And now Church.

God botherers had no imagination.

At least it gave him a good place to start looking for the bastard.

The Church of the Guiding Saint was the largest building in Aener-win. Standing four stories tall, the church's belfry could be seen from anywhere else in town. It was also the newest building in the city's center. Its stonework was still pristine. Light from the setting sun reflected off of its stained-glass windows to create a dazzling array of color. The Fellblade could tell what Church had spent all of his glintchasing money on when he'd retired.

A boy in his late teens was out in front of the building on a ladder washing the windows. He spotted the Fellblade as he approached, and a wary look came over him. The Fellblade was used to those kinds of looks.

"Is the priest in?" the Fellblade asked.

"Uh, Brother Michael is mentoring a small group inside," the boy said. "But weekly service is tomorrow."

The Fellblade wasn't really sure what that meant. He couldn't remember the last time he'd gone to church. The actual workings of their operation were a mystery to him. It sounded like there was some kind of priest inside, though, so he kept walking for the doors. The boy didn't stop him.

There was just enough sunlight left outside that there was no need to light any flames inside the church yet. Rows of pews filled the nave; most of them empty. A smattering of people occupied the very front rows, listening intently to a middle-aged man in priest's cloth. He looked to be in his late forties, with a weathered face.

The Fellblade tried to square the man's face with his mental image of Church. It fit closely enough. He certainly looked about the right age the Fellblade pictured for a retired glintchaser.

But he seemed so ordinary. His robes were plain. When he talked to the small gathering of followers in front of him, he didn't use big words or flowery language. Light didn't cascade off of him. If it weren't for the saint's amulet on his belt, the Fellblade might have mistaken him for a cleanly dressed commoner.

Maybe this was just what retirement looked like. No power. No gravitas. No anything. The Fellblade couldn't imagine what would possess someone to choose to end up like this.

The shadows cast by the setting sun clung to the Fellblade, masking his entrance. A familiar cold sensation washed across his skin. It was the touch of the Fell. Serene. Empty. Omnipresent. He wrapped himself in it, until he was, for all intents and purposes, invisible.

The meeting continued for a few minutes, during which the boy from outside came in and began lighting candles and lanterns. They wrapped things up with a prayer to Renalt, and the priest walked everybody to the door, leaving just him, the boy, and the Fellblade. If he attacked now, there would be only one witness. Tempting.

"Brother Michael, do you have time for another chess game?" the boy asked.

Brother Michael chuckled. "I don't think the vicar would like you hearing too many more of those old war stories."

"Stories?" the boy asked, feigning ignorance. "What stories? I was just talking about chess."

"Lies are unbecoming of a cleric," the priest said. His voice was gentle, and amused, but the boy nevertheless looked ashamed.

"Yes, Deacon," he said. After a pause, his nerve returned to him. "But could we play anyway?"

Brother Michael laughed in earnest before nodding. "I think I can squeeze a game in tonight. But I have some last-minute shopping to do first. I'll see you in an hour. Assuming you can finish the rest of your chores."

"Right," the boy said, beaming. He hurried off down a hall, deeper into the church.

An old hand telling his war stories to the altar boys. The Fellblade was even more sure now that he had his man. And even better: now there were no witnesses. The priest walked out of the church into the dusk-cloaked town, and the Fellblade followed.

21

ARNO

At two in the afternoon the next day, the front doors of the church parted, and the streets flooded with the crowd from the weekly service, talking, laughing, and making their way home or back to work. The children would be back in an hour for reading lessons, and in the evening, the church would play host to youth guidance.

But for the moment, the church interior was quiet, and the vicar could relax.

A young man just shy of thirty, Arno had short auburn hair and a clean shaven face. Most days he wore simple clothing, but for services he wore a priest's cloth. The white fabric was a fine material with blue accents, but even it was still far from ornate.

He breathed a sigh of relief as the last person left the nave and the doors shut behind them. It wasn't that he didn't enjoy service, but talking in front of that many people that long was always draining.

"Well said as always, Vicar Arno," Bart said. He was one of the acolytes who worked and lived in the church. A young man, only seventeen, but with a talent for getting along with people regardless of age.

"I just do my best," Arno said. "If it works, that's even better."

Bart nodded his understanding. "Vicar, did you send Brother Michael on an errand?"

Arno frowned, confused. "No, why?"

"We were supposed to play chess last night, but he never showed," Bart said. "And I haven't seen him at all today."

Now Arno was curious. Brother Michael was one of his senior deacons and a sociable man. It wasn't like him to miss a meeting with anyone.

"I'll see if I can find him and let him know he owes you a game," Arno said. "For the time being though, I believe the nave's floor is filthy."

Bart sighed. "I'll get the mop."

Arno smirked, remembering days long gone when he was in Bart's shoes. He'd actually found solace in cleaning duty. A simple, solitary task, where he could just let his mind wander without sacrificing his own usefulness. Not Bart though. The boy had talent, and heart, but the mundane side of a cleric's life was still very much a drag for him.

Arno took his leave, retreating through the stone halls of the church to his private quarters. It was roomy enough but far smaller than the typical vicar's quarters. The furniture was simple wood, most of it secondhand, consisting of a wardrobe, a bed, a desk, and a chair. The smell of incense clung to every piece of it. A generous window allowed light to pour in and warmed the space when the sun shone through. It was his refuge.

He took a seat at his desk and pulled the amulet of Renalt from his belt. It was a silver disc, slightly smaller than his palm, with a sword and shield engraved across the face. Anyone could pray to the saints for guidance or aid. But clerics could ask their saints to grant them the power of the gods. And if their faith and virtues were strong enough, and if they held an appropriate talisman, the saints obliged.

He closed his eyes and recited a prayer. The prayer connected two souls across any distance, let them share their emotional states and, if the person reciting the prayer knew what they were doing, even let them speak to one another. Arno figured it would be the easiest way to find out where Brother Michael was.

But something went wrong.

Arno's soul reached out, but it latched on to nothing, groped blindly for a moment, and retreated. He felt the sensation of a firm, apologetic hand on his shoulder, though he was alone in the room. Arno knew what it meant. Brother Michael was beyond the reach of the prayer. That meant only two possibilities.

Either Brother Michael was in another world altogether, or he was dead.

Now Arno was worried. His grip tightened around the amulet, and he had to make a conscious effort to keep his breathing steady. He began a different prayer, a kind dangerous to an unprepared mind who attempted it. The prayer addressed a saint directly with a question and both allowed and bound them to answer.

Is Michael alive?

The answer came back in the form of a weight that nearly forced the air from Arno's lungs and made his head spin. He could all but see the sorrowful expression on Saint Beneger's face as he gave it, clearly and concisely.

No.

Arno gasped for air and sank deeper into his chair, reeling from the force of the prayer and the news it gave him. He shook his head. It didn't make any sense. He'd talked to Brother Michael only two days ago. He was in perfect health. And if he hadn't been, Michael was more than practiced enough as a cleric to fix that.

Arno tried to reconcile Beneger's answer with his own understanding of the world. He didn't understand how this could have happened, and the prayer he'd used to get this answer wouldn't work again, not so soon after his last use of it. He was left to figure it out on his own.

He had a white-knuckle grip on his amulet now. Maybe there was an accident. Maybe he'd come into contact with some sickness that had worked too quickly for him to counteract. Maybe it was foul play.

He tried to keep that last one out of his mind because he couldn't accept the thought. Aenerwin wasn't the kind of town where people killed each other. Nothing dangerous—not monsters, not bandits, not conquerors or cultists—had come near the town in almost a decade.

There was only one way to know for sure. Arno would have to try and find him. Or whatever was left.

He took another few moments to compose himself. The color had drained from his face, and he didn't want anyone to see him in his current state. In times like this, the church would need someone stalwart to depend on. Not someone who'd turned into a sheet from dread.

When he was sure he had a grip on himself, Arno left his room. The first thing he did was search Brother Michael's quarters. He found them empty, the interior neat, and the bed made. No sign of any struggle or theft. No sign of Michael.

He asked around to find out if anyone had seen him today. Nobody had. His neighbors in the dormitory couldn't recall him coming to bed at any point. Several people asked what was wrong. Arno told them the truth.

Sadness spread through the church as Arno searched. Some asked if there was danger. He told them he wasn't sure, but it wouldn't hurt to send a runner to the watchman to let him know. Better to be prepared for danger and find out there'd been an accident than assume everything was fine and be blindsided.

The last people to see Brother Michael alive said he'd gone to the market around dusk yesterday to make some last-minute purchases before the shops closed, but that was all Arno could find out in the church. He went into town. He asked shopkeepers if Michael had bought anything from them. No one said he had.

Hours passed, until the sun was setting, and Arno still hadn't found Brother Michael. The vicar returned to the church, tired and stressed. Surprisingly, there was someone waiting in the nave who wasn't a cleric. He was a lean beanstalk of a man, dressed in clothes that looked like they used to fit but he'd lost weight. His eyes and cheeks were sunken. A tattoo of some kind peeked from underneath his collar and crept up his neck.

"I'm sorry, youth guidance has been canceled this evening," Arno said. "There was a sign at the door."

"I'm not here for that," the man said. "I'm looking for a man named Church."

Arno's heart skipped a beat, and his blood ran cold at the name. Years of instinct and pain tied to it came flooding back. He reexamined the stranger with new eyes. He'd been distracted, so caught up in thoughts of Michael, that he hadn't noticed what should have been obvious. The man's clothes were accented by armor. Though he kept a casual posture, his weight was on his back foot. His arms were deliberately folded in a way to obscure his hands.

And then there were the eyes.

The man's eyes were black, as if his pupils had swallowed his irises. It was the unmistakable calling card of a soul stained by Fell magic, a dark power matched only by demons, starborn, and black saints.

The man was here to kill.

"There's no one here by that name," Arno said. He didn't think the man would believe him, but he had to try.

"That's not what I heard," the man said, resting his hand on one of the wooden pews. Arno couldn't be sure, but he thought he saw the wood start to rot. He swallowed. "The man who built this place? You're sure he's not here?"

"Whoever you lost, I'm sorry," Arno said apologetically. "But you don't have to do this."

"It's not like that," the man said. "I promise this isn't personal."

The man leaned closer to Arno, who didn't move from his spot. He trailed his fingers along the back of a pew, leaving behind a long, black stain in the wood.

"Then what is this?" Arno asked.

"Business," the man said. He plucked at the edge of the stain he'd left on the pews, and it started to peel off of the wood, taking shape and form as it did. It curved and flattened, developing a sharpness at the edge. A sword made of shadows, whose inky black swallowed the light around it. "I'm going to be rich from this."

Arno gripped his amulet tightly.

The front doors of the church opened. Arno expected more assassins backing the stranger's threats. Instead, in walked a man with brown skin and a short beard. He wore goggles on his head and a deep red coat over black leather armor that glowed at the seams. Arno was stunned, amazed, and even terrified to see the man after so many years.

"Am I interrupting?" Phoenix asked.

The stranger released his grip on the shadowy weapon he had been summoning, and it vanished into wisps of black smoke. At the door, Phoenix pushed aside his coat to reveal the wand holstered at his hip.

"Some other time then," the stranger said.

"Don't move," Phoenix said, drawing his wand and taking aim.

The stranger glared at Phoenix before shooting Arno a warning look. Then, before Arno or Phoenix could react, the man himself evaporated into black smoke . . . and was gone. Phoenix swiveled in all directions, waiting for an attack.

Nothing happened.

He pulled his goggles down and set them to magic detection. No sign of the stranger.

"Sh—shin splints," Phoenix said, just holding back a curse. "He got away."

"Arman?" Arno asked. "What are you doing here?"

Phoenix pulled off his goggles, an apologetic look on his face. He tried and failed to gauge Arno's reaction to his arrival. At the very least, he wasn't yelling at him yet.

"Hey, Church," Phoenix said. "We need to talk."

22
OLD WOUNDS

Arno turned his amulet over in his fingers. Holding it helped subdue the hammering in his chest.

"Why is this happening?" he asked. "Why now?"

Phoenix threw his hands up. "I don't know yet. I was hoping you could help."

"Sorry. This is the first I've heard of it."

Phoenix frowned, turning the question over in his head. This would be so much easier if the only targets were the Starbreakers. Or if he had the full list of targets. Or *any* information to go on.

"So, that man in the nave?" Arno asked.

"My guess is bounty hunter, unless visitors like him are common."

"They're not. Nothing like this has happened here since—"

Phoenix lost interest two words in, but Arno's sudden stop drew his attention. He could see the cleric's mind working. "What?"

"Brother Michael."

Arno explained the disappearance, and Phoenix added the information to the puzzle he was constructing while Arno sank into his chair.

"It's connected," Arno said. "It has to be."

Phoenix nodded. "The dirk probably thought he was you."

"We need to find that bounty hunter."

Phoenix nodded, thinking. "Questioning him might actually be the fastest way to figure out who's behind this, if we can pin him down."

Arno stared at Phoenix, mouth open, but Phoenix wasn't even looking at Arno anymore. "He could hurt somebody else."

"Maybe not," Phoenix mused. "He was here for you, and now he knows what you look like."

"A man is dead!"

Phoenix glanced back at Arno, who was glaring at him. He'd done something wrong. Or maybe Arno had been upset from the moment he'd walked in, and he hadn't noticed until right now. Maybe Arno had never stopped being upset after their last fight.

Arno was even harder to read than most people, and Phoenix was out of practice.

"I'm sorry."

The glare faded, but Phoenix couldn't tell if he'd made things better or worse. Just when he was feeling at the end of his rope, Elizabeth came to save him. The memory of her words buzzed in the back of his mind. *"If you can't tell, ask."*

"Are you mad at me?"

"No." Arno looked Phoenix over. His beard was messier than it had ever been when they were younger, and the beginnings of bags had formed under his eyes, but other than that, he looked exactly like he remembered him from seven years ago, right down to the color of his coat. "I guess I just hoped after all these years, you'd changed."

This was familiar territory; Arno, disappointed in him for reasons he didn't totally understand. He hadn't missed this.

"I don't follow."

Arno sighed as he shoved himself out of his seat. "Maybe it's best we don't go there."

Phoenix could get behind that idea. It saved him the trouble of trying to unpack the years of mixed emotions.

"I should thank you," Arno said, changing the subject. "If you hadn't shown up, I'd still be in the dark about all of this."

"What're you going to do now?"

"I need to warn the town, but beyond that, I'm honestly not sure."

"Oh." Phoenix looked around the office—bedroom with a desk, really. He'd kept all of his old stuff in secret compartments in his basement. He wondered where Arno might keep his. If he'd kept anything. "You know . . . I could always use your help."

"What?"

"This is all happening because somebody is putting up a lot of money to send people after us. If we take them down, there's no money and no contract. Everything goes back to normal. And I could use some backup."

Arno shook his head. "I'm not a freelancer anymore."

"Neither am I." Arno gave him a look even Phoenix could tell was incredulous. "I'm not. I gave it up after Relgen. The same as you."

"So what are you doing now?"

"Fighting back. I couldn't just bury my head in the sand, and I didn't want to just wait for a bunch of dirks to find me."

"Well, while I can appreciate that, *my* place is here."

A knock at the door drew Arno's attention and provided a welcome exit. Bart was standing on the other side, looking on the verge of a breakdown.

He was the same height as Arno, but with the fear in his eyes, he looked small.

"Bart, what—"

"Is it true? Is Brother Michael dead?" Bart asked with a voice that begged for the answer to be "no," and Arno felt his heart break.

He kept his own face calm for the boy's sake. "Yes."

"Why? How?"

Arno placed a firm hand on Bart's shoulder and turned to Phoenix. "Could you give us a moment?"

"Sure," Phoenix said, suddenly feeling very out of place. "I'll be . . . downstairs, I guess."

Phoenix cast one last glance at Arno as the cleric comforted the boy, and felt a twinge of anxiety grab at his heart. Bart was losing his fight against tears. For an instant, he wasn't looking at Arno and Bart. Instead, it was Elizabeth and Robyn. And it wasn't Brother Michael who was dead, but him.

23

CULL

Cull hated investigating. And talking to people. And anything else he wasn't overwhelmingly good at. He prided himself as a man who was good at what he did. Not being good at something, and being reminded of it, stung.

His reputation and appearance were his saving grace. When people saw a man who stood over six feet tall, armed and armored like a heavy infantryman and sporting about as much scar tissue as normal skin, they could easily figure out what kind of man he was and what information would be worth his time. He'd also learned to hang around places where people with information were. Certain taverns in certain neighborhoods would be frequented by people who could use men of his talents. Failing that, people often gave him directions to someplace where he'd be more welcome.

Clocktower's barber-shop hideout had been one such place. It was filled with work offers that he would get without having to say anything and with people who'd done all the investigating for him and knew the things he needed to know. He liked places like that.

That was what made its shutdown so frustrating. The fact that not one but likely two of the high-value targets of his contract had gotten away at the same time only made it worse. The rock thrown at his head was the insult on the injury. So he'd spent a week in taverns of poor repute, waiting for appropriate news to find him of where Clocktower was operating now. Sooner or later, somebody always saw him and recognized that he was the sort of man who could be useful to those in need of directed violence. Some of his colleagues disparaged his methods as too passive. He let results speak for themselves.

And at last, he'd made progress. A woman dressed in a wealthy person's idea of inconspicuous clothing had spotted him in a tavern and none too subtly passed him a location where he was assured he could find people with use for "a man of your disposition."

And so Cull made his way to a gambling den in the south end of Olwin. The coppery stench of bloodsmoke hung thick in the air. Ambient cheers, curses, and prayers filled the place. The ground floor of the establishment was crowded, as men and women were packed tightly around tables to see if their bets paid off.

It didn't take long for one of the den's staff to single him out and make their way toward him. In the mass of energetic faces and fancy outfits, he stuck out for a dozen different reasons.

"Something I can help you with, sir?"

"I'm here for Clocktower."

There was a code to speaking about these kinds of things, Cull was aware. He also didn't care. Codes were annoying to keep track of and he wasn't good at remembering them. The direct approach suited him fine, and anyone who had a problem with it was welcome to confront him about it.

Very few people had.

The man who'd approached Cull laughed. "Think you might be lost, sir. The clocktower is in the Heights, by the Church of Avelina."

"The other Clocktower." Cull took a step closer to the man. They would have been nose-to-nose if Cull didn't loom over him. Cull stared down at the waiter, who was slowly backing away.

"I'm sorry, there's . . . just the one." He tried to keep up the lie. He turned and quickly made his way through the crowds, no doubt to tell someone attached to security about Cull. Good. They'd know to let him in.

Cull remained where he stood in the middle of the den, waiting. A few minutes passed. Someone at a table on his right won big. The scar on the back of his neck itched, which he ignored. A different waiter bumped into Cull without looking, apologized, actually took a look at him, and then apologized more emphatically. Cull gave a grunt in recognition, and the waiter fled.

Finally two men pushed their way through the crowd toward Cull, ready to draw weapons. Cull met their gaze and gave them both the once-over. They were heavyset, one blond, one ginger. Both with enough fat on them that they were probably out of shape. Big but not especially powerful.

He wouldn't need Charnel to deal with them, if it came to that.

Both men halted in their tracks. The blond one recognized him and frantically yanked his partner's hand away from his weapon. Cull waited for them to get on the same page.

The blond one came forward. "Sorry about the confusion, sir. Front staff must not have recognized you."

Cull grunted.

After a moment of waiting for Cull to say something else but getting nothing, the blond guard cleared his throat. "Right. Well. This way."

They led Cull upstairs.

He nearly had to duck his head through the doorway, but after that, Cull felt instant relief at the opening of space. There were far fewer people upstairs. The windows were shuttered, and there were few lanterns lighting the place. There was an almost overpowering smell of lavender coming from burning incense sticks on a table near the door, used to mask the smell of the smoke from downstairs.

The clientele here matched the sort that had frequented the barber's cellar, and Cull spotted the Dial at a table; a woman in a silk dress sat next to him, doing her best to keep a neutral expression. He was playing cards with a man sitting across from him.

The Dial noticed Cull out of the corner of his eye and gave him a nod of recognition that Cull returned before finding somewhere to sit. There were no empty tables, but there was one that had only a pair of men at it, poring over a map.

Cull sat at their table, and instantly they began trying to shield the map with their bodies, but he paid them no mind. A weedy man in a gray formal suit and thick glasses sat down across from him.

"My apologies, but the Dial is occupied," the man said, adjusting the glasses on his face. "What brings you here?"

"I want Brass. And the one he was with," Cull said.

"Brass? Oh! You mean the one from last week!" The man's eyes widened, and he grinned. "Well, you're in luck!"

The man pointed across the room at the Dial's card game. "The Dial himself is currently negotiating a price for their location with that man across from him. If you'd like to wait an hour or—"

Cull stood up and walked to the Dial's table. The Dial's bodyguard saw Cull coming and swallowed hard. Timidly, he moved to get in his way. Cull shoved him aside and sat down at the table. The Dial gave him a measured glare, but Cull only had eyes for the man across from him.

Sitting across from the Dial was an Iandran, going off of the light brown skin, elaborately styled mustache, and massive grin. His clothing was a multicolored mess. No two segments of it were the same. One sleeve striped, another solid. Half his torso red, the other dotted yellow and orange.

"Why, hello there, sir." The multicolored mess greeted him. He turned to the Dial. "Is this a friend of yours?"

"He is an associate," the Dial said. The Dial's steely gaze zeroed in on Cull. "And this is not his table."

Cull was not intimidated by the Dial. The most he could do was order everyone in the bar to attack, and Cull believed he could kill everyone here without issue. But that would burn all bridges with Clocktower. And he would prefer to avoid that.

He decided to act quickly, before the Dial's patience wore thin. "I want Brass," Cull repeated. "And his friend."

"As do I," the Dial said. "I will have the information tonight, and you will know it then."

"He knows," Cull said, pointing an armored finger at the Iandran, who only smiled. "Make him tell you."

"This man has come here to sell information," the Dial said. "I am required to give him the same treatment as any thief or dirk who would come to sell something of worth to Clocktower."

"Then pay him."

"He asks for too much," the Dial said. "We are attempting to come to a fairer price in a way he is comfortable with."

"How much?" Cull asked the man.

The Iandran looked Cull over. "Five thousand crowns, and I will give you his location."

The Dial narrowed his eyes at both of them. Cull, meanwhile, was briefly surprised. It was nearly half what Brass was worth according to the contract.

"As I said previously," the Dial said, "he asks for too much."

"I just know what it's worth. I'm well aware of the price on the man's head," the Iandran said.

"If you know, and you can find him," Cull asked, "why not take him yourself?"

"I have heard many stories of the Starbreakers in Her Lady's City," the Iandran said. "I would never be such a fool as to cross blades with them. I'd much prefer to profit off of the finder's fee."

"You're a coward," Cull said.

"I prefer the term enlightened self-investor," the Iandran said. "It's just good business. Generous pay, fraction of the danger."

"I could make you tell me," Cull said.

The Iandran raised an eyebrow and smiled, as if daring Cull to try something. Then, in the blink of an eye, he had a dagger drawn and pointed at Cull's throat. Cull remained still, surprised. The Iandran's ridiculous outfit had duped him into underestimating him. He hadn't even noticed the man was armed.

"You would not be the first to make such a mistake as to try," the Iandran warned.

"You will lower your weapon, or leave this place," the Dial said. "I will not tolerate a fight among patrons."

"Well, my friend, how would you like to settle this?" the Iandran asked.

Cull stared the man down, considering him. The Iandran had nerves of steel, and he admired that. More than that, finding Brass was about more than money now. The glintchaser had caused him enough trouble to be an irritation. He wanted revenge.

"Six thousand," Cull said. "And you don't tell anyone else for a week."

The Iandran sheathed his blade and extended his hand. "You have a deal."

The Dial frowned as his cruel eyes narrowed into slits. He had half a mind to bar Cull from setting foot in a Clocktower property for the rest of the brute's life for going over his head like this. But there was a larger picture to consider. Dealing with the Iandran would have cost the Dial money.

Now, because of the standard practice of Clocktower receiving a cut of every deal made on their property, he was making six hundred crowns—enough to buy a small tavern. And as long as the glintchasers who'd caused him trouble ended up dead, he didn't really care who did the killing.

With a final glower to warn Cull to not do something like this again, the Dial nodded his approval of the deal and allowed the parties to make the exchange. Dusk was falling by the time Cull stepped outside, bathing the cloudy sky a vibrant orange. Something felt off to him though. With the sun going down and fewer bodies packed together, Cull had expected it to feel cooler outside. Instead, it was just as warm.

The explanation announced himself. "I never took you for a gambling man."

Leaning against the building was a lithe man clad mostly in earth-toned traveler's clothes save for leather armor along his arms. More than a dozen small, crescent-shaped throwing blades were strapped to his arm, and two curved swords hung from his belt.

Cull hadn't seen Pitch when he'd walked out. He distrusted how good Pitch was at going unseen. No one that hard to see coming could be trusted.

"Pitch."

"Whatcha been up to, big guy?" Pitch asked, pushing off the building and sauntering over to him. "Bet everything on a rat race?"

"I was working," Cull said.

"Yeah?" Pitch asked. "Dig up anything worth a damn?"

For a moment, Cull considered keeping the information to himself. He had paid a substantial amount of money for it, and earned the ire of the Dial doing so. But Pitch was another bridge he was not yet prepared to burn down. If the Starbreakers were as dangerous as everyone said they were, he would need help.

"Brass and his friend are in Akers, outside the city."

The cocky smile on Pitch's face vanished, replaced with a look of genuine shock. "Well shit. All I found was a whore."

24

PITCH

Ruby sauntered down the hall of the Lilac, adjusting her hair so it all fell over one shoulder. This was the second time in the same week someone had asked for her personally. She was almost flattered, even though she was mostly just confused by the sudden uptick in attention. Not that she minded, if it meant more work.

She reached the end of the hall and knocked on the door. She cleared her throat and spoke up in a rehearsed, measured voice. "Room service."

The door opened, revealing a lithe man with leather armor strapped to his arms. Ruby did her best to hide her confusion and to avoid staring in a way that wasn't expected of her.

The man didn't look or carry himself like a watchman.

He radiated the same kind of confidence as Brass. The same casual grace in his stance. The same cocksure smirk. Now she was beginning to wonder if she just attracted a certain type.

"Come on in." The man stepped to the side to let her pass.

Ruby walked past him, swaying her hips and avoiding looking at him as he shut the door behind her. She had a mental game of seeing what she could guess about clients based on how they kept their room. When she saw a second, much larger man standing in the corner, dressed in full plate, she got a bit nervous.

"So," she said, turning back around, "what exactly did you have in—"

She stopped as she found herself staring down the blade of a curved sword less than an inch from her face. Pitch's eyes promised nothing good.

"Scream, and I open your throat."

Ruby stared at the blade. Her heart pounded in her chest, and she instinctively began backing away. Pitch matched her pace, keeping the blade just beneath her chin. After a few steps, Ruby backed into Cull, and armored hands gripped her arms like a vice. She tried to pull herself free, to no avail.

Her face felt hot, like she was standing in front of a fire. She was on the verge of hyperventilating, but she summoned courage she didn't know she possessed to stare Pitch down.

"We have people to deal with guests who harass the staff. You're leaving this place with your legs broken."

"You mean the tin swords downstairs?" Pitch asked. His voice matched his mocking smile. His eyes were a bright, fiery orange. Ruby realized the heat she was feeling was coming from him. "Go ahead, call them. Been a while since I've gotten to kill something. Just don't forget what I said about screaming."

The tip of the blade was almost touching her skin. He had another in his off hand.

When she didn't say anything, Pitch nodded in approval.

"Smart move," he said, as if congratulating a dog on performing a trick. "Now, relax. I want some answers to a few questions."

"Go fuck yourself."

Pitch shook his head. He hadn't lowered the sword. "You're not off to a great start. I'm looking for a tavern rat who goes by the name Brass. Curly hair. Stupid shoes. Won't shut up to save his life."

A lump formed in her throat when he mentioned the name. What did this have to do with Brass? How fucked was his life that this lunatic was after him?

"Never met him."

She said it without even thinking about why. Possibly to protect Brass. Then again, she barely knew him. More than anything, she just didn't want to give this asshole satisfaction.

Pitch sighed, disappointed.

Cull maintained his vice grip on Ruby's arms as he held her still. Pitch lowered his blade from Ruby's throat down to her abdomen. The edge of the blade itself began to glow orange. Scalding heat radiated from it that Ruby could feel through the fabric of her clothes.

"You made me do this," Pitch said, casually.

He touched his blade to her.

Ruby's eyes went wide, and she tried to call out, but the pain of the blade made her words escape as soft whispers. Her kicks turned to spasms as her legs gave out from underneath her, and Cull had to hold her up. She was still conscious, but her head reeled from the pain that stabbed at her in pulses timed to her heartbeat. Air stung in the spot the blade had touched.

"Brass. I know you've met him, more than once," Pitch said. "What's he been up to? Did he tell you anything? Is he carrying anything fancy? I know you know something."

Unable to offer a retort, Ruby spat in Pitch's face.

Pitch snarled and slammed the hilt of his other sword into her stomach, knocking the wind out of her.

She started coughing, gasping for breath.

He pointed one of his swords to the door and said to Cull, "Kill whoever tries coming for her. I'll handle this."

Cull considered just leaving. But security was going to be a problem either way now. Might as well handle them. He dropped Ruby and strode out of the room. Ruby, still coughing, tried to stand. Pitch leveled the glowing, hot sword in her face.

"Don't get any ideas," he said.

Out in the hall, Cull walked toward the stairs. Some people were opening their doors, poking their heads out of their rooms. When they noticed Cull and his greatsword, they slammed their doors. Two armed guards came running up the stairs, weapons drawn. They saw Cull and charged him.

Cull didn't have time to evaluate them, so he simply reacted, taking Charnel off his back. He swung once. The first guard let out a gurgle as he was cleaved at the waist. His legs crumpled to the floor, and his torso sailed over Cull's head.

The second guard ground to a halt, his eyes wide in horror. Cull took a step forward and thrust. He punctured the guard's breastplate as if it were made of paper, punching out the other side. The guard let out a gasp. Cull pulled his sword out and swung again, cleaving off the man's head and right shoulder.

Blood was splattered on the walls and on Cull's armor and face and soaked into the carpeting. The red color of the velvet carpet probably could have hidden small splotches of blood. It wouldn't hide this.

Cull swung Charnel one more time to shake off the blood that had accumulated. A faint sizzling sound came from the blade's surface as two more tick marks supernaturally etched themselves into the steel. Two more souls added to its graveyard.

Cull returned the sword to his back. He stood in the center of the gore, waiting for whatever came next.

Back in the room, Pitch was frustrated. Ruby refused to say anything, and his patience was wearing out.

"You know what? You wait right here," Pitch said.

He pulled a throwing blade off his belt. As Ruby grabbed onto a nightstand to try and pull herself back to her feet, Pitch threw the blade. The ends of the crescent bit into the wood of the nightstand, turning the crescent into a shackle that trapped her wrist.

After taking a second to admire his throw, Pitch left the room, leaving Ruby alone. Immediately she started screaming and trying to pry the blade from the nightstand to get loose. She heard shouting from the hall.

Before she could break free, Pitch came back, and he wasn't alone.

He coaxed one of the other girls into the room with his sword. Ruby instantly recognized her: Brandy. She'd started around the same time Ruby had. Normally Brandy had a relaxed, casual air about her. She was good at helping nervous or stressed people unwind. At the moment, she looked terrified.

"You're a tougher nut to crack than I thought," Pitch said. He was congratulating her. "So, let's try this again."

He met Ruby's eyes and held his glowing, hot sword to Brandy's throat. It was hard to make out his pupils now in the bright, burning orange of his eyes. Ruby could feel the heat radiating off of him.

"Brass," Pitch repeated. "Anything you know. Start talking."

"Let her go," Ruby begged. She pulled at the blade that had captured her wrist. It was coming loose but wasn't free yet. She never took her eyes off Pitch.

"Now we're getting somewhere," Pitch said. "You're a smart girl. I know you've got something on him."

"I met him twice. I barely know him," Ruby protested. She was shaking. From fear. From pain. From rage.

"He didn't tell you anything?" Pitch said. "Two nights with a man who never stops talking, and you didn't learn a thing?"

"No!" Ruby said. "I—he left with a friend of his. They were going to the friend's house."

"Yeah, in Akers, I know, what else you got?" Pitch asked, gesturing with his sword for her to keep talking. "What friend?"

"I don't know," Ruby said. "I don't remember. He said his name was . . . he called him—"

Pitch touched the glowing edge of the blade to Brandy, and she screamed. Ruby was panicking now. She pulled on the blade holding her wrist with everything she had. It was almost free.

"You son of a bitch, stop it!" Ruby said.

"What was his name?"

"I—" It finally came to her. "Phoenix!" Ruby said. "His name was Phoenix. That's what Brass called him. Now leave her alone!"

To Ruby's surprise, Pitch did lower his blade away from Brandy. The temperature in the room rapidly started dropping back down to a normal level. The color in his eyes faded to a more natural but still fiery amber.

Brandy scrambled to get away, fleeing the room. Pitch let her go, laughing to himself.

"Avelina's ass. Two for the price of one," he said, sheathing his sword on his hip. He leaned out of the door, calling down the hall. "Hey, Cull, you're never gonna believe this!"

Ruby managed to pull herself free, and now she had a blade in her hands. Pitch's back was to her. He was distracted and exposed. The blade was awkward to hold. She doubted she could stab him with it. But it was well-shaped for throwing.

So she took aim at Pitch's back and let it fly.

Without looking back, Pitch sidestepped, drew a sword, and sliced. The glowing, hot edge of his sword cleaved the throwing blade in two, and Ruby gasped. Pitch turned around, slowly. His eyes were bright orange again.

"Points for effort," Pitch said.

Ruby's chest was heaving. Her face was hot, but this time it wasn't from Pitch. She was furious. Impotent, murderous rage boiled in her veins. She wanted to see him dead. She wanted to be the one to kill him.

Pitch considered her and this place. He was in a good mood at the moment. He wanted to celebrate. And since he'd gotten these new powers, he hadn't gotten to kill anything with them. It was past time to break them in.

Out in the hallway, Cull did not like the look on Pitch's face.

"Well, thanks for the tip," Pitch said to Ruby, who was glaring at him. He touched his hand to the wooden door frame. An instant later, it burst into flames. With a tap of his foot, the carpet caught fire. The flames were all around him, licking at him, washing over him. They didn't so much as singe him.

Cull took a step back from the blaze Pitch had created.

"Time to go," Pitch said.

He made for the stairs, running his hand along the wall and setting it alight as he walked. Cull made his way down and out of the building as quickly as he could. Pitch took his time, indulging in the destruction.

Back in the room, Ruby was trying desperately to beat out the flames with a sheet she'd pulled from the bed. It wasn't working, and the smoke was starting to burn her lungs. The burns Pitch had given her screamed in protest.

Not only was the fire not going out, it was burning hotter and faster than any she'd ever seen. A violent coughing fit took over. The heat was quickly growing unbearable.

Please. Not like this. Ruby had never been especially religious, but at that moment, she prayed to who or whatever would listen. Clerics' prayers made literal miracles happen all the time. Surely something out there could spare one. Pitch had left her for dead. She needed to get out of this. Needed to take away his victory. She couldn't hope to touch him with violence.

But she could live to spite him. *Please let me get out of this.*

She started to feel lightheaded. There was too much smoke. Too much heat. She tried to get the window open, but the metal frame of the pane burned her hands and forced her back. She looked around for something she could use to break it.

It was hard to see.

She dropped low, trying to stay out of the smoke. She hated whatever idiot had chosen thick carpeting. It was terrifyingly good kindling. She coughed again. It was hard to breathe. It was hard to think.

Ruby closed her eyes, starting to collapse. Her last thought before everything went black was one, final, desperate plea to anything that might be listening.

Please, not like this.

She blacked out as the room went up in flames.

Outside, Cull was staring at Pitch, who was watching the Lilac burn. The entire building had caught, turning into a bonfire. People came running out or jumped from windows. Some of them were on fire when they did.

"What was the point of this?" Cull asked.

"Well, I found out who Brass's mystery friend is," Pitch said. "I was wondering who'd be stupid enough to actually let that prick stay at their place. Now I know."

Cull gave a low growl of disapproval. It seemed like a small piece of information for such a colossal mess. Pitch didn't seem to mind.

"You were right," Pitch said. "He is with another target from the list. It's actually a good thing I know it's him now. Last time I tried breaking into a house he lived in, it was a pain in the ass."

"Which target?" Cull asked.

"Phoenix," Pitch said. He smiled a hungry, wolfish grin. Bathed in the firelight of the burning hotel, he looked absolutely monstrous. Of all the assassins Cull had met as a part of this contract, he considered Pitch to be the most dangerous.

Though Cull feared no man, woman, or beast, he was wary of him.

Pitch gave Cull a pat on the arm. "Well, the night's still young. I think I'm gonna go scout out Phoenix's place."

25

THE SAINT

Bart took time to compose himself, and when he did, he had questions. With only a brief hesitation, Arno filled him in on everything. It was a lot to dump on Bart all at once. The young man went through an amplified version of the utter disbelief that Arno had experienced.

Bounty hunters. Fell magic. Murder.

Such dangerous, evil things felt almost impossible in Aenerwin. Arno at the very least had his own worldly experiences to fall back on for understanding. But Bart had only known the small, quiet town.

Every explanation only prompted more questions, which Arno patiently answered, right up until Bart threw one that hit him like a hammer to the chest.

"But if we find Brother Michael, you can bring him back, right?"

Arno had to take a moment to prepare himself. The most coveted of divine powers was not his favorite topic. People had an imagined version of it in their mind, and in desperate times, they clung to it. The reality was almost always disappointing.

"Resurrection is . . . it's not as simple as people imagine," Arno said. "There are a lot of conditions that can affect it. The state of the body. The strength of the soul. And time. The longer someone is dead, the harder it is for them to come back. And after a few days, it's impossible."

"So, we have to look fast then."

Arno could hear Bart trying to hold onto hope. It broke his heart, but he couldn't tell Bart anything less than the truth.

"The killer would have hidden the body to make it as hard to find as possible. If he even left one."

He stopped when he saw Bart's tears. That was enough. Bart understood now. Brother Michael was gone.

Bart was silent for a long time. More tears ran down his face, but he stopped short of breaking down into sobbing this time. Arno got the impression the boy was trying to keep his composure in front of him.

"What about last rites?" Bart eventually asked. "Can we still . . .?"

Arno nodded. "Those will work without a body. Michael's soul will be safe."

It was good news, but if anything, it just made Michael's death more real, and Bart started crying all over again.

"I'm so sorry, Bart," he said. "I wish there was more we could do."

"What about that freelancer who was here? Is he going to help?"

Bart surprised Arno. There was a sudden energetic, almost righteously determined tone in his voice. Arno recognized that voice, that feeling of seeing evil in the world and desperately needing somebody to do something about it.

It's like looking in a mirror, isn't it?

Arno blinked. It was a deep, rugged voice he'd heard inside his head. The voice of an old craftsman. The voice of a saint.

"Vicar?"

"He . . ." Arno started to answer, only to feel the mental voice cut him off.

Think about that one before you answer.

Think about it. That meant he was missing something. Something about Phoenix. Or this situation. He didn't have time to figure out what the voice meant. Bart was already looking at him expectantly.

"I'm not sure yet."

The disappointment on Bart's face was obvious, and Arno felt compelled to add, "But I promise, this will be dealt with, and the people responsible will be punished. Renalt will answer this."

He felt like a priest of Saint Avelina saying things like that. But she was Renalt's most popular saint for a reason, and it had the desired effect. The disappointment left Bart's face as he accepted the promise that Renalt would not leave injustice unaddressed.

The young man would be grieving for some time, Arno knew, and bound to go through all the stages that process brought on. He needed something to ground him, give him focus. And closure.

"Brother Henry is overseeing preparation for Michael's funeral, including his last rites," Arno offered to him. "I'm sure he would appreciate some help."

Bart nodded and collected himself.

"Renalt's strength to you," Arno said.

"And his saint's guidance to you," Bart finished.

Bart left the room, and when Beneger spoke next, Arno heard his voice outside his head: "Strength and guidance. It's all anyone really needs in the world, isn't it? Besides bread and a roof, obviously."

Saint Beneger the Guide was built like a man who'd worked from sunup to sundown every day since adolescence, and he dressed about the same. As soon as Arno saw him, the atmosphere shifted. Light became softer and out of focus. New smells overtook the room—sweat, oil, and sawdust.

"Beneger," Arno greeted. "It's been too long."

"Well, you've been doing just fine on your own," the saint countered. He looked around the room, affectionately patting the walls. "Better than fine, really."

"Did I do something wrong?"

"Not necessarily."

"What is it then?"

Beneger smirked at the anxious edge to Arno's voice. Still so eager to be corrected. "You know better than that. What kind of lesson would it be if I just told you?"

"A quick one."

Beneger gave a loud laugh. "If you're only doing it because someone told you to—"

"You're not really doing it," Arno finished. Imitation was hollow. Understanding was as important as the action.

Beneger gave an approving smile. "So, you have been paying attention. Well, go on then. What is the lesson, oh student of mine?"

Arno noted the sarcasm on the word *student*. The word did feel just a little odd, after so many years teaching. But he would never be too old or too experienced to learn.

Arno tried to figure out what could have piqued Beneger's interest enough to warrant a visit. "Is this about Phoenix?"

"Now what would give you that idea?" Beneger asked in a tone of voice that told Arno it absolutely was.

"You think I should help him?"

"It doesn't matter what I think. What do you think?"

"I think . . ." Arno knew what he thought. The same thing he'd told Phoenix when he'd asked. But clearly there was something wrong about his opinion, otherwise Beneger wouldn't be here.

His instinct was to try to figure out the right thing to say, to figure out whatever it was Beneger was trying to teach him. He fought against the urge. He wasn't going to learn anything by trying to read his saint's mind.

"I think that, especially if there's danger coming, my place is here, in Aenerwin," he said. "The people here need me. And I need them."

Beneger nodded his understanding. "Of course." Arno waited for the rest. Beneger smirked, keeping it to himself for a moment to toy with his cleric's patience. "So you belong here. Where do you suppose Phoenix belongs?"

Arno didn't bother trying to hide his confusion. His first instinct was to say nowhere, but that felt intrinsically wrong. How many times had he stood in the knave and preached that everyone had a place, a calling? How could he even think something so antithetical to everything he believed?

Beneger nodded as he watched Arno's mind begin to work. "You're a sensitive soul, Arno. It serves you well. But it also means you're easily blinded by your feelings. And nothing blinds quite like old pain."

"I'm not—" Arno started to protest, but the words died in his mouth. "And the only person you've lied to in your life is yourself."

Arno stared at the ground, shaking his head. He felt almost embarrassed now, to have served for sixteen years and still need to be reminded of the most basic tenets of his own faith. He knew the real reason he'd refused to help.

Because it was Phoenix. Because the last time they'd all seen each other, they'd watched an entire city die and put the blame on everyone but themselves. And even if Arno didn't feel that way anymore, he remembered a time when he did. When the family he'd known for so long went for each other's throats.

"Go back. Pretend you've never seen the man in your life. Tell me where he belongs."

Arno sighed, closed his eyes, and did his best to replay everything he'd seen of Phoenix since he'd came to Aenerwin. He still looked like a freelancer. But now he was less sure. Was that the truth, or was that just the conclusion he jumped to because he thought he knew Phoenix?

He played it all again in his mind. Every word, every movement he could remember, until he came to the first revelation that should have been obvious. Scared. Phoenix was scared.

That was new.

And something else. Something was off. He hadn't noticed it when he'd been too busy writing everything he saw off as "the same old Phoenix." What was it?

He started over at the beginning. Phoenix showed up, saw the Fellblade, went for his wand—Arno's eyes opened. He almost couldn't believe he'd missed it. Phoenix had been wearing a ring. And the stress that seemed etched into Phoenix's face. He'd seen the exact look on a dozen parents in Aenerwin.

"He has a family," Arno realized.

Beneger didn't say anything. He knew Arno would follow the trail himself now. That singular difference, that irregularity in his mental image of Phoenix was enough to shatter his conception of the man, and for maybe the first time since his old companion had turned up in Aenerwin, Arno was able to look at the situation for what it was. A man was being hunted, driven from his family, and was asking for his help.

Arno understood now. If it had been anyone else, he wouldn't be having this conversation right now. He'd have offered to help even before Phoenix could have asked.

Beneger nodded, as if hearing Arno's thoughts. "You would have gotten it without me, eventually. But it might have been too late. You're a good man, Arno. And whatever you decide, I didn't want you to make a decision unless you knew *why* you were making it."

"I have to help him."

"That's *your* choice," Beneger stressed.

"No choice," Arno corrected. "It's the right thing to do."

26

ALLIANCE

It was well after dark by the time Arno came down to the nave again. He half expected Phoenix to be gone. What he did not expect was to see him in one of the pews, head hanging to the side, asleep.

"Phoenix?"

When he didn't respond, Arno decided to try the direct approach. He said a quick prayer to wake him, and Phoenix shot upright.

"Sorry I kept you," Arno apologized.

"It's fine. I needed the break."

Phoenix rolled his joints out as he felt a ripple of warmth carry through his body, wiping away fatigue and stiffness as it went. It had been a long time since someone had used divine healing on him.

Had it always felt this good, or was he just getting old?

"I can go now, if you want," Phoenix offered.

"I'm coming with you."

Phoenix's surprise did the rest of the job of waking him up. He reexamined Arno, noticing all the things he should have sooner. He was dressed for travel. He had a different amulet on now, hanging from his neck instead of his belt. In its place, he had a sword Phoenix could recognize even in its scabbard.

Zealot, the angel blade. The memory behind their discovery of the sword came back to him, and a smile crossed his lips as he remembered Brass burning his hand trying to use it.

"What changed your mind?"

"I was explaining what was going on to Bart," Arno said. "And he asked if you were here to help. I almost told him no."

"Almost?"

"I know you came here for answers, not to help Aenerwin or even to warn me. But we're both on this list. What you're trying to do helps everyone here, even though that wasn't your intention," Arno said.

Phoenix was surprised at the lack of admonishment in Arno's voice. At least, none that he could hear.

Maybe he imagined it, but there might have been a tint of fondness to his voice.

"On top of that," Arno added, "your timing was insensitive, but your point stands. The target's on me, not Aenerwin. As much as I want to stay here, the best way to protect what I love might actually be to leave it."

"That is . . . a lot more eloquent than I could have put it."

"Well, I'm guessing I've had more practice public speaking than you." Arno let the sentence hang, debating about including the real reason he was helping him instead of the logical excuses he'd come up with to make it easier. In the end, he decided against it. Logic would be good enough for Phoenix anyway.

"So. Together again," Phoenix said. And for just a moment, it felt like the good old days. When they were just a bunch of kids looking for their next adventure.

And then the present came back into focus, as Arno clarified it. "Just for this."

"Right," Phoenix nodded. Bringing back the past wasn't that simple. Bringing back all of it wasn't, anyway. They had bits and pieces of it. Their old gear. Working together. He hoped it was enough. "Well. Get your coat."

"Are we going somewhere cold?"

"No, but the windchill from flying can get pretty harsh."

Arno's reserved smile wavered. "That was a joke, right?"

27

TARGETS

"And that is why your dad is an asshole," Brass told Robyn. The baby took a break from gnawing on the side of Gamma's disembodied head to stare at Brass again. Left alone to watch her while Elizabeth took care of something, Brass had taken the opportunity to do his best to corrupt the child's vocabulary. For her part, Robyn was transfixed by her new playmate, and the strange-tasting new toy he'd given her.

She made a sound that was a cross between a laugh and a gurgle, and Brass nodded.

"Good try. But it's 'asshole.' Remember the consonants."

He stopped when he heard the sound of Elizabeth coming back.

"We'll work on this again later," he whispered, to which Robyn cooed in response.

"I'm back," Elizabeth announced. "Did you have fun with—Brass, where did she get that?"

"What, the head?" He gave an unconvincing shrug. "I haven't the *slightest* idea. What is it, by the way? Phoenix making a metal nanny?"

Elizabeth gently pried the head out of Robyn's grasp and lifted her into her arms. Before Elizabeth could figure out which part of Brass's blatant evasion to address first, Robyn distracted her by squealing in delight, flailing her tiny arms and nearly swatting Elizabeth in the face. The unbridled happiness in her daughter's voice went a long way toward disarming her irritation before it could find a target.

She sighed, deciding it was probably Arman's fault for leaving the head unattended in the office anyway. She gave Brass a grateful look. "Well, thanks for watching her."

Brass shrugged. "Wasn't any trouble at all."

Until recently he'd never actually been this close to a baby. For some reason people didn't trust him around them. It was a damn shame. They were absolutely adorable creatures.

As if on cue, Robyn let out an excited burble. Brass chuckled. "She's beautiful, Wings."

Elizabeth glanced up at Brass, remembering he was there. She smiled. "Thank you."

"You know," Brass said, "I kind of gave Phoenix a bit of a hard time about all of this. Having a life, a kid. But I think I get it now. Sort of, anyway. I actually think I'm going mad with boredom. But for Phoenix, I get the appeal. I get why he wants to protect this."

Elizabeth gave half a laugh. "Yeah. Protect it."

Brass raised an eyebrow. He caught the tinge of sarcasm in her voice. "Still angry?"

"Let's just say I don't appreciate being benched."

Brass shook his head. "You haven't been benched."

"Dirks are hunting my husband, and I have been stuck in this house the entire time. That feels like being benched to me. Meanwhile—" Elizabeth was cut off when Robyn started tugging at her hair, distracting her. "Sweetie, no. No pulling."

After another second she tugged herself free. "Meanwhile, he's off, on his own, up against gods' know what. And he wouldn't even take you."

"Of course he didn't," Brass said. "He doesn't want either of us going anywhere because we've got the most important job in this whole mess. Keeping all of *this* safe. He isn't benching us, he's . . . trusting us."

Elizabeth rolled her eyes. "That wasn't his reasoning at all."

"No it wasn't," Brass agreed. "Really, he's a paranoid mess who can't stand to be around me for longer than a day and probably rightfully thinks that if I was even in the same room as Angel she'd punt me through a wall. I'm just trying to be a good friend. And by the way, staying in one place for more than a day makes me physically ill, so I was being very selfless when I said yes."

Elizabeth actually laughed this time. It felt good to laugh like that. For one, it was a relief just to feel something other than exhaustion and simmering annoyance. But more than that, it gave her a chance to reconsider things.

"He is a mess," Elizabeth agreed. "And you are a good friend."

"I do have my moments, don't I?" Brass asked.

"He thinks so too," Elizabeth said. Brass gave her a look of disbelief. "He does, really. He's just bad at showing it."

"You know, he punched me in the face earlier this week."

"He's *very* bad at showing it."

Now they both laughed. Even Robyn joined in, though she had no idea what they were laughing about.

"Someone has to stay here and take care of Robyn," Elizabeth admitted. "Arman can't nurse, so it might as well be me. But I don't need protecting. He does."

"Well, I guess we can tell him that when he gets back," Brass said.

"Yeah."

". . . on the subject of you not needing protection . . ."

"Mm-hmm?"

"I'd be a terrible friend if I just up and left altogether. I did make a promise after all," Brass said. "But I could really use an afternoon to stretch my legs."

"Go ahead," Elizabeth said. "We'll be fine."

"You're a saint among mortals." Brass stood up and enveloped both Elizabeth and Robyn in a hug. He was smiling like a fool. "I will head out tomorrow and be back before sundown, you won't even know I'm gone."

"Sure . . ." Elizabeth's voice trailed off as she bounced Robyn on her knee. She understood probably better than most what it was like to feel stuck in one place and desperate to get out of it. If she didn't have to force it on someone else, she wouldn't. At the very least she had Robyn. As much of a hassle as the baby could be, just staring into her child's eyes was usually enough to quiet the cyclone of nervous energy in her stomach. Robyn's eyes shone with a curious spark, like she was examining the world and enthralled by every new detail she discovered. It was the same look her father had in his eyes.

Then she heard them. A distance away from the house, rogue footsteps carried on the wind back to her ears, and the hairs on the back of her neck stood on end. Her heart picked up like a hummingbird's, and the green of her eyes swirled and crackled to an even brighter shade as she reached out, feeling the slightest movements in the air around her. For a moment, just at the edge of her senses, she thought she detected someone moving near the house.

But just as quickly as she felt them, they disappeared.

"Everything all right?"

"I don't know. Maybe. Probably," Elizabeth said. "I thought maybe there was somebody outside, but then they weren't."

"You think we're in trouble?"

Elizabeth paused, waiting for whoever she'd felt to come near the house again. But nothing did, and after a while she shook her head. "It was probably just someone on their way home."

28

FIRE AND ICE

Pitch sat on a fence post, spyglass in hand, staring at Phoenix's house. Now that he knew which one it was, he felt stupid for not figuring it out the second he got here. It was far and away the biggest and most expensive-looking.

Of course it would be. He'd never admit it to their faces, but the Starbreakers had been a halfway decent company once upon a time, and freelancing was the kind of work that would make you rich if it didn't get you killed.

There were people inside. A victorious smirk slowly spread across his face when he saw them. He caught sight of Brass first, meandering around the room, running his fingers along furniture, inspecting things left lying around, and being a general nuisance. He didn't see Phoenix anywhere. But he did see someone else. She was a short, brown-haired woman who kept popping in and out to talk to Brass and occasionally tell him to stop touching things. Sometimes she'd be holding a baby.

Pitch tried to work out who she was. She looked familiar, but he couldn't quite place her. The Brass he knew would never pick one woman, let alone raise a kid with her. She acted like the house was hers, and he knew from the whore back in Olwin that this house was Phoenix's. The skin color ruled her out as immediate family. Phoenix was Gypic, and this woman was white. She was Phoenix's wife. Had to be.

There was still no sign of Phoenix. He couldn't see a lot of the house's interior, but this was the only room with the lights on. Either Phoenix was asleep or he was gone.

He'd come here for Brass and Phoenix. But Brass and Phoenix's little family would still get him one payout and the perfect bait to draw out the other. In a way, this was even easier.

Instead of fighting two Starbreakers, he'd only have to deal with one at a time. He collapsed his spyglass. *Wish I still had the mask. Would make a hell of a reveal.*

"Whatever brilliant idea you think you have, it's not."

Pitch's heart jumped. He spun around on instinct. Before he'd even fully recognized the voice, his swords were drawn. His eyes and blades both glowed a bright orange, heat cascading off of him.

Snow stood behind him, unflinching. Her arms were folded, but she had a dagger in hand. The air rapidly shifted from the cool of an early spring evening to an unnatural humidity as her cold clashed with his heat.

"If it isn't the Cold-Blooded Killer herself," Pitch lowered his swords, though he didn't sheathe them. "Was wondering when I'd see you again. Hey, what are you doing here, anyway?"

"Stopping you from embarrassing yourself, apparently," Snow said. She kept her dagger in hand. "What do you think you're doing?"

Pitch pointed one of his swords at himself. "Me? Nothing. I'm just scouting. Cull and I tracked Brass and Phoenix here, so I came out here to get a lay of the land before we go in."

Snow didn't say anything. She just narrowed her eyes at Pitch and waited.

After about a second, he broke.

"All right, you got me," Pitch shrugged. "I was never going back for Cull. I figured I'd take them both down and keep all the money for myself. But since you're already here, I'd be willing to let you in on it."

"I'm not going anywhere near that house," Snow said. "And neither are you."

"Oh come on, this is perfect!" Pitch gestured to the house with a blade. "Phoenix is gone. It's just Brass and a housewife."

"Are you forgetting the last time you tried to break into a house Phoenix lived in?" Snow asked. "Because I'm willing to bet you still have scars."

"Only scar I got that day was from you," Pitch said.

Snow took a step forward. "Back. Off."

Pitch tilted his head. There was an edge to Snow's voice beyond the typical chip on her shoulder. Every muscle had the tension of a loaded spring. Hints of frost crept across her cheeks and fingertips, and her eyes were a paler blue than normal.

His eyes flared up constantly. He left trails of embers almost everywhere he went, and sometimes, he accidentally burned things by touching them. But he'd only had these powers a few days. Snow had years of practice keeping a handle on hers. Something had her on edge enough to make her control waver. He wondered if he could poke her enough to find out.

"That's not gonna happen," Pitch said. "I've got a contract to fulfill and a reputation to uphold."

"You try to go after them in that house, and you can forget about your reputation. Phoenix doesn't live anywhere without turning it into a fortress," Snow said. "You'll be lucky to get out alive."

"I think I can handle Brass, a farm girl, and a baby," Pitch said. "How are you even here anyway?"

Snow shifted her weight to her back foot. "What's that supposed to mean?"

"Well, Cull and I had to do all kinds of investigating to find this place," Pitch said. He omitted the fact that it'd really been mostly Cull. "How'd you find it?"

"Did you really think you or any other dirk was going to find them before I could?" Snow asked.

"All right, so you got here first," Pitch said. "Why haven't you made a move then?"

"Because I'm not an idiot."

Pitch's heart rate picked up, and it was his turn to take a step forward. Her grip on her dagger tightened, but she held her ground. Their eyes locked, fiery orange meeting icy blue.

"You think you're better than me?" Pitch asked.

"I've always been better than you."

"Not anymore."

The air around Pitch's swords shimmered from the heat they gave off. The blades twitched occasionally as he debated taking a swing just to prove a point. Snow didn't budge. That only made him angrier. He wanted her to be afraid of him. But she just stared him down, like she was waiting for something. He wanted to stab her.

That probably wouldn't work, at least not the first time he tried. He could kill her, if it came down to it. He was sure of it. But not without a fight that would give away his presence and give his quarry time to run. And if he botched nabbing Brass like he had bagging the Golden Shield, he might actually have a reputation problem on his hands. The truly aggravating part was that he knew no one would believe him if he tried to spin it as Snow's fault. In the world of contract killing, the word of the Cold-Blooded Killer went much farther than a Cord of Aenwyn washout.

"If you're such an expert on your old company, what's your plan?" Pitch asked.

"Wait them out."

"What?"

"Brass can't stay in one place for too long. Sooner or later, he's going to get stir crazy," Snow said. "He'll leave the house, for food, or booze, or sex. That's when he's vulnerable. Divide and conquer."

Pitch gave Snow the once-over and smiled. With a flourish, he collapsed his swords and returned them to his belt. "All right, you win. That's not a bad plan."

"Great," Snow said. "Now get out of here."

Pitch folded his arms. "What? Why?"

"Because your murder boner is turning you into a literal beacon, and spying on people usually takes subtlety," Snow said. "I can keep an eye on this, and I'm not liable to get bored and fuck everything up."

"I'm subtle."

Neither he nor Snow believed that.

"Go."

"Fine," Pitch said, backing away without taking his eyes off her. "I'll go. But you better not screw me over on this."

"Like you tried to screw over Cull?"

"Exactly. Don't do that."

Snow shook her head, opting not to dignify that with a response. And with that, Pitch disappeared into the night. For a walking torch, he could still manage to go unseen when he wanted, as long as he wasn't too fired up.

Snow let out a long sigh. Droplets of water were forming on her forehead, which confused her for a moment, until she realized she was sweating. She hadn't done that in years, and she wasn't sure what exactly had caused it now: the heat from Pitch or the way her heart was pounding.

That had been too close.

29
COLD FRONT

Elizabeth stepped out through the back door of the house, double-checking that it was shut and locked behind her. True to his word, Brass was gone when she woke up this morning, leaving her alone in the house again. And after feeding Robyn, tiring her out with playtime and putting her down for an afternoon nap, she was left with a quiet moment to herself. She decided that now was the best chance she was going to get to check a suspicion she'd had for the last few days.

The garden she kept behind the house had a scattered collection of bushes, most of which Arman had planted back when they'd first built the house. Some of the leaves had traces of frost along their edges—rapidly melting away in the morning sun but enough to catch Elizabeth's attention.

They were a bit far into spring for the leaves to have frost on them this late in the day. The tiniest of sounds reached her ears. A creaking of wood, almost imperceptible, above and behind her.

She was right.

"You can come out now," she called out without turning around. She knew who it was. She had nothing to fear.

Snow crept back into sight on the roof of the house. She stared down at Elizabeth with ice-blue eyes. "How did you know?"

"Even you make some noise." Elizabeth stared up at her. "Are you just going to sit up there and brood all day?"

Snow hopped off the roof. "Aren't you wondering why I'm here?"

"Actually, I'm mostly wondering why you're hiding," Elizabeth said.

Snow cocked her head slightly. This wasn't how she'd expected to be discovered.

Elizabeth could tell she'd thrown Snow off.

"How long have you known?" Snow asked.

"Saw you skulking around Akers the day before Arman came home and said he'd run into you," Elizabeth said. "Had a feeling you stuck around after you talked to him."

"You didn't say anything to Phoenix?" Snow asked.

"He had a lot going on, and it was just a hunch. I also know things ended bad for . . . all of you. If you didn't want to talk to him or Brass, I wasn't about to drag you into it without a good reason."

Snow was surprised by Elizabeth's consideration. And her trust. "What if I was here for them? I'm an assassin, and there's a price on their heads."

"If you were here for them, we'd have known by now."

Snow didn't say anything, but the look on her face said she didn't disagree with that. "So why talk to me now?"

"Well, Brass is gone, at least for a while," Elizabeth said. "Wanted to know if I was actually alone."

"What's that supposed to mean?"

"Someone was here last night."

Elizabeth carefully scanned Snow's features, waiting for any kind of tell. The assassin almost kept a straight face but her brows furrowed just enough for Elizabeth to know it wasn't a simple twitch. Snow was worried.

"I heard somebody, outside. They were watching the house, I could feel it," Elizabeth said. "But they never came for us. In fact, they left."

Snow's shoulders hunched, and she folded her arms. The blue in her eyes faded ever so slightly. An unconsciously given signal Elizabeth could read like a book. Snow was bringing up her walls. Readying a denial.

"Did you have something to do with that?" Elizabeth asked.

"What?"

"I think last night, someone after the contract finally found out where we lived. I think they were all set to barge in," Elizabeth said. "And I think you stopped them."

Snow looked away, telling Elizabeth everything she needed to know without a word. Instinct told Snow to lie, but by now she knew not much got past Elizabeth. So she tried deflecting instead.

"Does that ever annoy people?"

"Like you wouldn't believe." Elizabeth smirked. "Want to come in?"

"No."

"So, you come all the way out to Akers to warn us, skulk in the bushes to protect us, but you draw the line at coming inside?" Elizabeth raised an eyebrow.

"It's not that," Snow said. "I can't stay here. There's something I have to do."

"Do you need help?"

Snow's jaw hung open, and her head cocked to the side. She wasn't sure if Elizabeth was serious. Elizabeth, to her credit, didn't look like she was joking. Snow rolled her eyes. "You've got your own problems to worry about. Like your kid. And staying alive."

"I meant Brass," Elizabeth said. "Or even Arman."

Snow bristled at the mention of her former companions. "You really want your husband around my kind of company?"

"No," Elizabeth admitted. "But you're helping us. In your own don't-want-to-be-caught-dead-actually-giving-a-shit kind of way."

Snow jabbed a finger at Elizabeth, like she took personal offense at that. "I *don't* give a shit. I'm just balancing the books."

"What's that supposed to mean?"

Snow lowered her finger and her eyes. "Look. You weren't there, most of the time. But there's a lot I owe Ar—Phoenix for. This is me paying that back. That's it."

Elizabeth didn't buy that for a second, but Snow was digging her heels in. She wanted to argue with the assassin, call her out on her real reason for going to all this trouble. But getting the truth out of her wasn't her goal—not anymore. Snow was in exactly the kind of place Elizabeth didn't want Arman to be. Alone. And if she couldn't stop one Starbreaker from isolating themselves, maybe she could stop this one.

"Then why not actually help?" Elizabeth asked. "In the open? Work with us instead of sneaking around trying to do it behind our backs?"

"That is how I help."

"Not just avoiding them?" Elizabeth asked.

"So what if I am?" Snow said. When she glared at Elizabeth, her eyes were bright blue, but they gradually faded to white with every word. "I told Phoenix already. Brass is a pain, Church is a judgmental prick, and I'm pretty sure if Angel and I ever ended up in the same room, we'd try to kill each other. Again." Snow's glare softened. A bit of blue color returned to her eyes. "It doesn't matter anyway. Like I said, I have to go."

"Are you coming back?"

"For your sake, you should hope that I don't," Snow said.

Snow took a few steps toward the bushes, then blinked out of sight. For another second, Elizabeth could still feel her somewhere close by, but then even that sensation vanished. She sighed.

How is it that Brass is the most well-adjusted of them?

30

THE RUSTED
STAR

Glassburrow was a small lakeside town surrounded by forests on three sides. Poles tipped with lightstone were scattered through town, creating islands of light in the otherwise dark evening. On the water, the lone lantern illuminating the small dock was accented by clusters of fireflies patrolling the shore.

Phoenix and Arno came gliding down from the air into the town at top speed, riding an oblong board with a mast and a shimmering triangular sail attached to it. Phoenix gripped handholds along the mast, and Arno gripped Phoenix. The contraption let out a low hum as it coasted along before finally coming to a stop on an empty dirt road in the middle of town. It hovered for a moment a few inches off the ground, then dropped the rest of the way. The pattern of lights rippling across the sail faded, and Phoenix felt the force anchoring his feet to the board release. With shaking legs and white knuckles, Arno let go of Phoenix and staggered off the board. Only Phoenix had been anchored. Arno had spent the last hour hundreds of feet in the air, his grip and balance the only thing separating him from a fall. Then there was the wind chill, which Phoenix had not exaggerated.

Arno wasn't a fan of flying in general, but he despised sky surfers.

"I can't believe you still have that thing," Arno said. His throat still hurt from screaming during the trip.

"Well, it wasn't exactly taking up space," Phoenix said.

With minimal effort, the sail folded against the board, and Phoenix kneeled down. As if his bag were bottomless, Phoenix shoved the entire length of the board into it, and then stood up, slinging his bag over his shoulder like it was still empty.

They walked the streets in silence for a few minutes, scanning the wood slat faces of buildings as they walked past, searching for anything that looked like it was advertising a hot meal and warm bed.

"How do you know she's here?" Arno asked.

"I'm not certain, but . . ." Phoenix paused, debating whether or not to say more. *Might as well come clean.* "I kept tabs on everyone. Or, I tried to, for a while. You never moved from Aenerwin, but I lost Snow in the first week. Brass I could only track retroactively by the chaos he left behind. Angel was . . . I guess a middle ground. She moved around every so often, but she always turned up running an inn, and they've always got similar names. This was the last place I heard about."

"Were you planning on visiting?"

Phoenix didn't answer right away. "No."

"Then why keep up with all of us?"

"I . . . don't know." He'd asked himself that a few times over the years. He told himself it was just a smart idea to keep tabs on people as powerful and dangerous as his old companions. But maybe he had wanted to visit.

Maybe he'd just wanted to know how they were doing after everything had gone wrong and confirm his assumptions that everyone else was doing better than he was. As if that would prove something. "At any rate, it's a good thing I did."

"I suppose so," Arno said.

After some searching, they found a long building with a plethora of windows lining its second floor and a rusted iron sign depicting a constellation of stars hanging from the door. It fit the description they were looking for. Angel's inns always mentioned stars in the name.

"Well," Phoenix said. "Let's see if anybody's home."

The first floor was a wide, open space with tables lining the walls, an impressively stocked bar at the back, and a stage off to the right that was currently empty. The smell of pine wafted off the walls and floor. Aside from a young couple sitting in a corner exchanging hushed words, a lone old man nursing his drink at the bar, and a bartender wiping down glasses, the place was empty.

The bartender was a light-skinned woman with dark, thick curls that she had tied back. Her clothes were well-kept dark linen, but she had a yellowed and stained apron on over them. When Phoenix and Arno walked in, she gave them a nod.

"Sit anywhere. With you in a second."

Arno slid into a seat at the bar and motioned for Phoenix to sit as well. After a moment of hesitation, Phoenix plopped down.

He tried to flag down the bartender. "Excuse me—"

She set the tankard she was cleaning down with a thunk. Phoenix couldn't tell if she was annoyed or just a forceful woman. The uncertainty was enough to silence him.

She wiped her hands and turned her attention to them, no obvious malice on her face. He might have overreacted. "Sorry. It's just me most nights, and I have to clean up the messes everyone else made."

"It's all right," Arno said.

She smiled. "So, you two need a place to stay?"

"Actually, we're looking for someone," Phoenix said.

The bartender glanced around at the three other people in the room. "Well, if you were trying to find them here, I think you missed them."

"Maybe you can help us then," Arno said. "We're looking for the owner. She's an old friend."

The bartender cocked her head at that and gave both Arno and Phoenix another once-over. Her gaze was especially searching around their belts. She shook her head. "You got the wrong place. The owner doesn't have any friends."

"Well, we used to be friends," Arno said. "Seven years ago."

The bartender reached for something under the counter, her eyes narrowing and darting between them. "I think you two should leave before you get hurt."

Arno's brow furrowed. "What?"

"Do you see that window?" the bartender said.

She pointed off to a window that wouldn't have been visible from the front of the inn. It was boarded up.

"That's what happened to the last people who tried to start something here," she said.

Phoenix put it together. They weren't the first people to come here for Angel. But she was also still here. This could be good for them, except for the fact that Angel probably wouldn't talk to them if they got into a fight in her inn.

Arno came to the same conclusion and was already trying to diffuse the situation. "We're not here for trouble, we just want to talk."

The bartender didn't back down. "You need to go."

"But—"

Before Arno could say anything else, another voice called out from the stairs at the far end of the room. "If my bartender told you to leave, you need to listen to her."

A tall, dark-skinned woman descended the stairs. She was dressed in simple, practical clothes, mostly grays and whites, with a splash of red in the sash that made up her belt. Her shirt lacked sleeves, exposing well-muscled arms.

When she saw them, she stopped on the stairs and stared. Phoenix met the gaze, unable and unwilling to speak. Arno gave an awkward wave.

"Thalia, I'm going to need a drink," Angel said, walking the rest of the way down the stairs.

Thalia nodded, grabbing a glass and a crystal-blue bottle while Angel sauntered over to them. She didn't sit down. Thalia handed her the glass, and she threw it back before smacking it down on the bar and glowering at them.

"Get out."

"We were hoping we could talk," Phoenix said. "There's—"

"No."

Phoenix cleared his throat. "Arno?"

"Monica—" Arno began.

"Don't call me that."

Arno swallowed and tried again. "Angel. We don't mean to disturb you. We just want to ask a few questions, and then we can go."

Angel glared like she was debating whether or not to physically throw them out, while Arno offered a pleading look.

She relented, but the glare stayed. "What do you want?"

"Has anyone come after you recently?" Phoenix asked. "Attacks? Threats?"

"Yeah."

"How many?"

"Four guys, depriving villages of their idiots. Came in here, asked for me, jumped me as soon as I came down," Angel said. She pushed her glass toward Thalia for a refill. "Tried using a net."

"Did you get anything out of them?" Phoenix asked.

"Piss, probably."

"Any information about why they came?"

"I didn't really ask questions, just handed their asses to them and told 'em to fuck off." She emptied her glass again. "That was like a week ago."

Phoenix grimaced, disappointed. Was he really the only person inclined to look into being targeted? He admitted he had a bit more context, but even still. Not to mention, now he was out of people he could ask about this. Safely ask, anyway.

"I'm glad you're okay," Arno said. "Was anyone else hurt?"

Angel shook her head. "So, what's this about? Somebody we piss off trying to settle old scores?"

Phoenix raised an eyebrow. They hadn't mentioned anything about anyone else being attacked yet. Angel rolled her eyes as soon as she saw the look on his face.

"For fuck's sake, you're not the only one with a brain. You wouldn't be here asking shit like that unless somebody was after you too. So, what is it?"

"We're still not sure," Phoenix said. "But it's not just about us. Someone's put out a contract on a list of freelancers. We don't know every name on it, but you, me, Arno, and Brass are."

"No Snow, though?" Angel asked. She scoffed. "How's that for a change?"

"The price on our heads is big enough to attract the worst of the worst. Snow heard about it. Pitch is after it."

"Snow's coming for us?" Angel asked, impressed rather than worried. "That is something."

"No, she's not coming for us, it's just a point of ref—" Phoenix stopped himself and groaned. Arno hadn't been able to tell him anything either, but at least he had the decency to feel bad about it. Angel wasn't even taking this seriously. "We've all been targeted, and people are going to keep coming for us unless we can figure out who's behind this and shut them down. Is there anything at all you can remember about the people who attacked you we can use to find out who hired them?"

"No," Angel said flatly. "Are we done here?"

"That was all we wanted to know," Arno said. Phoenix's whole body was tensing up. Best to step in before things went south.

"Great. There's the door."

Just like that, she was done with them. Phoenix was shocked. No, shocked implied surprise. This wasn't even remotely a surprise coming from Angel. He was angry.

"Do you even care that we're trying to help you?" he asked.

"You're trying to help yourself," Angel corrected. "The fact that it would help me at all is an accident."

"We're all targets. This is equally all our problem."

"Actually it's not," Angel said. "I'm fine. I'm not scared of Pitch or any other dirk who thinks they can take me. None of them can, and any idiot stupid enough to try barely counts as exercise. Fuck, I hope Snow comes, so I can beat her ass a second time."

Phoenix glared, and not just because she might have actually had a point. But he wouldn't admit that. Not when she was acting like this anyway.

He wanted to prove her wrong. So he stood up out of his seat, and he went low.

"Right. Because you've never lost to someone you thought you could handle."

Angel's face shifted in an instant as her glass shattered in her hand. Until now, she'd been annoyed. Dismissive more than anything. Now Phoenix had her full, undivided attention. And she was furious.

"Even if this was my problem," Angel said, slow and deliberate, every word carrying the threat of a punch to the face, "how many times did I get hurt over all of your bullshit? Snow's dad. The Library. Sky pirates. Every rich asshat Brass ever pissed off because he couldn't keep it in his fucking pants. I spent seven years fighting all of your battles. You can fight mine for once."

"You're unbelievable," Phoenix said.

"No, what's unbelievable is you having the balls to come back here and ask for my help after everything you did," Angel said.

Without even thinking, Phoenix glanced at Angel's collarbone and spotted the tip of a scar peeking out from under her shirt. A pang of regret flared in his chest as he remembered the day he'd given it to her. And for a moment, he was struck by the need to somehow make it right. But he pushed it down. He couldn't afford to get bogged down in hurt feelings and old grudges. He had to stay focused on the goal. On solving the problem.

"That was years ago," Phoenix protested.

"That's supposed to make it okay?" Angel asked.

Angel closed the distance between them, and Phoenix reached for his wand. Panicking, Arno gripped his amulet and said a prayer to clear both of their minds.

It wasn't much, just a small burst of divine influence to bring their emotions back to a neutral state. But it did the trick. When the prayer was finished, they both let out a sigh and blinked.

Phoenix backed down.

"Coming here was a mistake," he said.

"Yeah. It was," Angel agreed.

Without another word, Phoenix turned to leave. Arno stayed seated. Angel gave him a look and shook her head. "Let me guess. You're not mad, you're disappointed?"

"I . . . just wanted to apologize," Arno said. "If I ever made you feel like you were anything less than a friend. Or that I was anything less than grateful for everything you'd ever done."

Angel's mouth opened, but no words came out. All the heat and tension she'd built up was gone. She wanted to keep being angry. But even without Arno using another prayer, she couldn't be mad at him. Not when he was so damn understanding.

Phoenix had just made it to the door when something burst through the window. At first glance, it looked like a rock. But the texture was wrong. It was milk white, shiny, and covered in glowing engravings. He read them a second too slow. Before he could warn anyone, the stone flashed and everything went white.

31

ANGEL

The front door of the Rusted Star flew off its hinges, and people poured into the tavern dressed in worn armor, brandishing an array of blades and bludgeons. Someone tackled Phoenix, lifted him off of his feet, and slammed him into the floor. The impact dazed him, and he dropped his wand.

With him on the floor, a few of the invaders immediately started raining down blows on him.

Phoenix raised his left arm to shield himself, and a translucent wall of force materialized from his bracer, forming the shape of a round shield. Swords and clubs came down on him but sparked off the barrier. He'd bought himself breathing room, but he had only six seconds before the shield ran out of energy, and maybe only one before his assailants realized they could just kick underneath it.

Angel's eyes recovered before anyone else's, and she dove over the bar, tackling Thalia to the floor. Arno stumbled blindly in the direction of the bar toward the old man's voice, shoved him down, and shielded him with his body. Thalia tried to stand up, but Angel held her down.

The invaders fanned out, descending on everyone in the bar. Using a haphazard mix of ropes and shackles, they started struggling to bind people. Phoenix kicked and thrashed but, being disoriented and disarmed, was overpowered.

Arno fared a bit better. He restored his sight with a prayer, just in time to see two people bearing down on him. With another prayer his skin became as hard as stone. They rained down blows on him with their weapons, trying to beat him to the ground. He kicked the legs out from under one and used another prayer to hold the other in place. As soon as they realized they were dealing with a priest, more of the attackers rushed to Arno.

Surrounded, Arno couldn't stand up, and he didn't have room to draw his sword. Somebody dove onto him and was trying to wrestle his amulet from him. It was a struggle just to hold on to it.

"What's happening?" Thalia yelled. She could hear shouts, Arno's prayers, and the sound of chains, but she couldn't see anything.

"Stay down!" Angel yelled, not that it mattered. She was holding Thalia down so tightly that the bartender couldn't stand up if she wanted to.

One of the attackers came around the bar and made the mistake of trying to go for Thalia. He grabbed her by the hair and pulled, drawing a yelp from her. Angel lunged for him, shoving him off of Thalia, and grabbed him by the throat. She stood up and, with one arm, raised him off the ground and threw him over the bar. He collided with two of his friends, who were still tying up Arno.

Angel's heartbeat was hammering in her ears. Her fingertips felt hot. She tried to fight it, to force it back down. But it was too late. Her eyes turned into orbs of light. Her fists started to glow with a golden aura, and a burning halo materialized above her head. Thalia stared at her, surprised and confused.

"Monica?" she said.

"Stay down," Angel repeated.

She talked through clenched teeth, but her voice still sounded louder than normal. It echoed, as if there were two of her talking at once. Her face contorted into a grimace of barely contained rage. Thalia shrank away from her.

All gazes fell on Angel.

"It's her!" one of them yelled. "Take her!"

With one hand, Angel vaulted over the bar. As she swung her legs over, she kicked a man in the jaw. His head spun, there was a snap, and he crumpled to the floor.

A sword struck her in the face, but it left only a cut on her cheek. She growled and punched the offender in the chest hard enough to dent his breastplate and send him flying across the room. The point of impact she'd left behind was glowing hot.

The whole bar rushed to Angel, leaving Arno, Phoenix, and the other patrons alone. Arno took the opportunity to crawl to his amulet and used a prayer to enhance his strength. With a grunt, he tugged himself free of his bonds. Phoenix rolled onto his side, looking for his wand, but when he saw Angel's current state, he just stared. When she got like this, the minimum safe distance was as far as possible.

One by one, Angel broke everyone who came near her. Faces crunched under her fists. Blades failed to leave more than minor wounds. She caught one sword in her bare hand and heated it until it snapped in two in her grasp. The longer she fought, the brighter she glowed, and the hotter the whole room got. Arno and Phoenix took cover, and the other patrons followed suit. Only Thalia stayed exposed, peeking out from behind the bar to watch the fight.

Angel grabbed a man foolish enough to stand in front of her by the throat and hoisted him into the air. The man screamed as his skin burned on contact with Angel's glowing hands. The only other assailant left standing against her swung with everything they had and managed to bury an axe in Angel's back. She screamed in pain and doubled over, dropping the man she was holding. She actually felt that one.

She let out a roar of anger as she stood back up. Blinding light poured from Angel as she screamed, and everyone standing around her recoiled from a wave of heat that made their skin blister. Two beams of light shot out of Angel's eyes, piercing a man in front of her. Phoenix and Arno had to look away to avoid going blind.

After a second, the light faded, and Angel was back to normal. The man standing in front of her staggered backward and fell. The smell of burnt flesh curled off a gaping hole in his chest.

The last standing assailant backed away from Angel in fear, leaving his axe in her back. Angel whirled around and grabbed him. With a scream, she slammed him into the floor hard enough to break the floorboards.

Angel's shoulders heaved, and her breath came out in ragged pants. Smoke wafted off her. With a grimace, she reached behind herself and pulled the axe head out of her back. It clattered, splashing blood on the floor.

No one said a word. The only sound was Angel's breathing and fearful stammering from the couple and the old man.

"Fucking hells," Angel said.

With one last deep breath, she stood up straight. None of the bodies strewn around the bar so much as twitched.

Phoenix stared at the window Angel hadn't melted a hole in, waiting for another crossbow bolt to come through it. When none did, he stood hesitantly. "Please tell me at least one of these guys is alive," he said.

"Wanna check? Be my guest," Angel said, sweeping an arm out. She winced. "Hey, Church?"

"Yes?" Arno asked.

"If you're sticking around, you mind making sure everybody's all right?"

Arno slowly nodded. Angel seemed satisfied with this and started for the stairs.

"I'm gonna change shirts," she said.

32

AFTERSHOCK

Arno placed the last stone over the last of the bodies and then sank to the ground. The wet remains of dead leaves stuck to the seat of his pants, and a musty scent clung to his clothes. His eyelids were heavy. Blinking felt like it took longer than normal. His breath came out in slow, deep pants.

There was no graveyard in Angel's town. When people died, their bodies were taken out to the surrounding forest to be buried. Normally they dug proper, dirt graves. But there were a lot of bodies, and it had already been a long night. Standing behind him, Angel rubbed the dirt from her palms on her pants. He wouldn't have been able to gather enough rocks for the burials without her.

"Are we done?" she asked.

"Almost," Arno said, forcing himself to stand back up. He clasped his amulet to his chest and closed his eyes. Channeling divine power through prayer took a certain amount of focus. Arno was practiced enough that he didn't normally need to close his eyes. But as tired as he was, and with so many bodies to pray over at once, he needed to block out distractions.

Closing his eyes felt good. Too good. It had only been a few hours since he got the news about Brother Michael, but it felt like days.

He spoke the words of the last rites for the bounty hunters. The fate of souls beyond the veil of death was the realm of divinity, but the prayers would ensure that no one on this side of the veil would be able to tamper with their bodies or souls any further. When he finished the prayer, he felt the wash of Renalt's presence over the graves. It came and went like a warm breeze, and Arno breathed a sigh of relief.

"Whole lot of work for people who attacked us," Angel said.

"They're still people," Arno said, opening his eyes.

Angel sighed and stared down at her boots. It had been a while since they'd had this conversation. She folded her arms.

"I'm not sorry," she said.

She didn't look at Arno when she said it, which was how he knew she was lying. But he figured she wasn't in the mood to be called out on her bluff, so he didn't say anything. He was too tired to get yelled at anyway.

"Okay. Well, I'm done," he said. "Thanks for the help."

"They were in my inn," she said. "Had to do something with them."

"Right."

Arno cast one last look at the cairns that marked the newest burials in this forest. He wondered who they were. If they'd be missed. Angel was already walking away.

The air had a faint, cool dampness to it that was almost relaxing. The ground was wet, and bits of leaves and dirt stuck to their shoes and pants as they walked.

The ground and the trees absorbed most of the sounds of their footsteps. Aside from the occasional chirp of an insect, it was silent.

Arno cleared his throat.

"Sorry about the trouble."

"Why?" Angel gave him a confused look. "They were after me, not you."

"I meant everything else," Arno said. "Phoenix . . . he's just scared. We all are."

"Funny how you're the one apologizing and not him."

"It was never his strong suit."

"Just . . . fix this," she said. "However you two are planning to."

Arno spent the rest of the walk making idle conversation, doing his best to avoid the topic of asking for help. He asked a lot about Angel's inn, since that seemed to be the one topic to which she'd give more than one word in reply.

He was struck by how different talking to Angel felt compared to talking to people in Aenerwin. Back in the town, he was a respected figure. A leader, a voice of wisdom and guidance. Everybody looked up to him and expected him to have the answers. But not Angel. She still treated him like he was just another person, and a slightly annoying one at that. In some ways, it was a relief.

They got back to the inn after a few minutes. The front door was propped up next to the doorway. Furniture had been righted, but debris was still everywhere. Several spots on the floor were wet where blood had been mopped up. Most of those spots were still stained. And there was still the giant hole burned in the wall.

Phoenix was sitting at the bar while Thalia wrung out cleaning rags into a bucket. Besides them, the bar was empty.

"It's done," Angel said. "Thalia, you can go home for the night if you want."

Thalia shook her head. "I'm good to finish my shift."

Angel shrugged and made for the stairs. Something nagged at the back of her mind. A better version of herself, reminding her how late it had gotten and how tired Arno looked. She grimaced but called down, "You guys can stay the night. Not for free. After that, get out of here."

She disappeared up the stairs. Arno collapsed into the closest seat.

"You okay?" Thalia asked.

"I'm just tired," Arno said. "It's been a really long day."

"And all for nothing," Phoenix said. Not only had Angel not known anything about the contract, she killed every single lead that had stormed into the bar, and Arno didn't have the supplies or energy for a resurrection.

"You said yourself Angel wasn't a guarantee," Arno reminded him.

"Yeah." Phoenix sighed. "But I'd be less frustrated if she wasn't so happy to be unhelpful."

"She's upset," Arno defended.

"She's always upset."

Arno's eyes narrowed. There was a time in his life where he wouldn't have said anything when he thought Phoenix was wrong. But that was then. Now, he was a leader and a teacher, and his friend needed correcting.

"Do you know why she's upset with us?" Arno asked.

"Because she's Angel?"

"Because we made her feel exactly like everyone else in her life did," Arno corrected. "All her life, people only cared about what she did or didn't do for them, and that's exactly what we reminded her of."

"We were together for years," Phoenix said defensively. "When she went to war with Saint Ricard's Order, we were right beside her."

"And then Relgen happened."

Phoenix's eyes went wide. For a while, he'd thought he and Arno had a mutual, silent agreement not to mention Relgen. Now, he realized Arno had just been waiting for the right time to use it against him.

"We got an entire city killed. We almost killed each other," he continued. "And we all traded blame for it. What we said, what we tried to pin on each other . . . That was what we left her with, and we haven't done anything to make it right since. Even if you've forgiven yourself, are you really surprised she hasn't?"

"We are being hunted by every dirk in Corsar. I would have thought that took priority over hurt feelings," Phoenix protested. "I figured maybe you and she could focus on the actual problem in front of us, but you're both just fixated on what happened back then. That's not now. This is."

Arno held back a frustrated groan. "This is what I meant when I said I was hoping you'd changed. Arman—" he took a second to bury his face in his hands and regain his composure. "You were always a good person, but you got distracted. You would find a problem to solve and fixate on it and forget that the people around you are *people*, not puzzle pieces. You know what Angel is like, what she went through, and if you thought about that for even a second, the first thing you would have done when we got here was apologize."

"She didn't apologize to us!"

"We came to her!"

Arno drew in a sharp breath and slowly let it out to calm himself down. He hadn't meant to raise his voice, but arguing with Phoenix like this brought bad memories . . . and worse instincts.

He needed some space. Actually, maybe they both did.

"I'm going back to Aenerwin," Arno said, standing up.

"What?"

"I am tired. And I need to think about what I'm signing up for by working with you again," Arno said. "And you need to think about what I said."

"So, you're going to walk back to Aenerwin, in the middle of the night?"

"No."

Realization dawned on Phoenix. "Oh."

"Come find me when you've figured out what you want to do next," Arno said.

He took his talisman in his hand. Then, with a single word and a brilliant flash of light, he was gone. Thalia, who up to this point had been trying to mind her own business, stared in awe and confusion at the space where Arno had been a second ago.

"Where did he go?"

"Home," Phoenix said.

Arno knew dozens of prayers. Some simple, some incredibly powerful. But he had one prayer specifically meant to take him home. The prayer of recall worked like teleportation with caveats. All Arno had to do was say the one word prayer, and he and anyone else he wanted to bring would be instantly transported back to the closest church dedicated to his saint.

Arno had used it on them all, to get them clear of Relgen before it fell. In the obsessive years that had followed, Phoenix had gone out of his way to learn exactly how this prayer worked, to find out if there was anything he could have done to stop it.

"Are you going to do something like that?" asked Thalia.

"No."

"Well. If you want a place to sleep, it's on me. Just don't tell the boss. I think I still like this job."

Phoenix stared at the ground, and he stayed quiet for a long time. He could still vividly remember the last time Arno had used that prayer and how angry he'd gotten at the priest for it. And he knew if Arno hadn't, he wouldn't be alive, or have found his way to Elizabeth, or done anything that he'd done in the years since Relgen that had made life feel good and worth living again.

He felt trapped. For all the pushback he gave Arno, he couldn't actually say he was wrong. Phoenix knew what a double-edged sword his focus could be. It brought clarity, let him figure things out that nobody else could. It kept doubt and hesitation out of his mind, and that made for snap decisions that usually meant the difference between life and death. But it rendered things into so many variables—their role in the solution to whatever problem he was picking apart. He could miss things when thinking like that. Like how people felt.

But that didn't change the fact that he was neck deep in danger, miles from home, and still with no clear path to fixing things. When he let himself think past that problem and out to the effects it must be having on his family, his city, his friends, the weight and scope of it was crushing. Too many problems. Too many variables. Too many things to protect. All interlocked so that he couldn't think of one without considering the others. One miscalculation, one move out of order—

He just wanted things to be simple and clear again. He knew what to do with that.

But the priest had gone and planted the seed in his mind. Think about what he said. What Angel must have been feeling. How things had ended. How poorly he'd handled it. How poorly they all must have handled it.

"Are you okay?"

Arman took his wand out of its holster and turned the device over in his hands. It was his crowning achievement as a spellforger. Sleekly designed, intricately machined, modularly enchanted. He could shoot fire, create electricity, repair objects, spew smoke, weave spider silk. But he had nothing in the wand for fixing the past.

"I don't know," he admitted.

He hated not knowing things.

33

SURVIVOR

R uby woke up in a bed with silk sheets dressed in a nightgown. The sheets carried a light scent of perfume, and the gown was softer than any fabric she'd ever worn. She was in a spacious room with a full wardrobe and a window that took up nearly an entire wall, though curtains had been pulled over it.

It was the nicest place Ruby had ever woken up in. And she had no idea where she was or how she'd gotten there.

There was a short-haired woman in the room with her, sitting off to the side of the bed. She was wearing silk robes adorned with softly illuminated glyphs stitched into the sleeves and was staring into a small, handheld mirror while tracing patterns in the air with a glowing fingertip.

Every time her finger paused, her hair shifted colors from blue to red to black to blonde.

Ruby had never met a mage before, but she couldn't think of what else the woman could be. Slowly, feeling stiff and sore, she sat up.

"Um." Her voice came out hoarser than she'd expected. Her throat was dry.

Ink looked up. The mirror in her hand disintegrated into scattering particles of light, and her hair returned to a vibrant blue that matched her eyes. "Oh, good, you're awake."

"Who are you?" Ruby asked.

"You sound awful," Ink said. "Hold that thought."

The mage crooked a finger twice as if beckoning someone over, and a serving tray resting on a nightstand floated across the room into her lap. A kettle and a set of cups sat on the tray. She poured out two cups of tea from the kettle and handed one to Ruby.

"Drink this."

Ruby stared down at her cup for a second. She was suspicious, and the way this woman casually threw around literal magic left her uneasy. But thirst overrode her suspicions. The tea was warm and tasted faintly of raspberry. More important, it eased her throat almost instantly.

"Now, you have questions." Ink offered a tight-lipped smile as she pressed her fingertips together. "So let's get that part out of the way first."

Ruby cleared her throat. "Who are you? Where am I? How did I get here?"

The mage held up a hand. "Stopping you there before we're here all night. My name is Kira Arakawa, High Inquisitive of the Academy. You're in a guest room in the castellan's keep in Olwin. And I brought you here because I have some questions for you."

"What?"

The High Inquisitive's thin smile dropped. "Oh dear. This is going to be difficult."

Ink set aside her tea and serving tray and sat up a little straighter, preparing for a long haul of a conversation. Ruby bristled at the condescending look on her face.

"Last night the Crimson Lilac went up in flames that couldn't be put out without magic," Ink said. "Just about everyone who was inside when it went up is dead. But not you."

Ruby struggled to process what Ink had said. Almost everyone who was inside was dead. Did that include the other escorts, the guards, Vera? Just about everyone she knew in Olwin had been in that hotel. Gone. She fell back against the headboard of the bed, reeling. It was as if the world had fallen out from underneath her.

Ink watched all this and sighed. "I'm sure this is a lot," she said. "Take a second to process if you need it, but I—"

"What the fuck is going on?" Ruby snapped.

Ink leaned back in her chair. "All right. Done processing then."

First Pitch, now this woman. Ruby was out of patience for people talking down at her. Her mind dragged her back to the room in the Lilac, surrounded by flames as Pitch loomed over her with that look of smug superiority, and her blood boiled. "What do you want?"

Ink looked the girl over, reevaluating her. She didn't seem any less out of her depth, but there was a fire to her that Ink hadn't picked up on. Defiance in the face of power and a demand to be taken seriously. Whatever had resulted in her being caught in the middle of a burning building, Ink would have expected it to have left the girl broken and terrified. Instead it just seemed to have made her angry. She gave the girl a nod of acknowledgment.

"The fire at the Lilac isn't the first. I'm trying to get to the bottom of them, and you might be the first eyewitness of one that I can actually talk to without calling in a grave speaker," Ink said. "Assuming you saw what caused the fire."

Ruby's gaze hardened. "I did."

Ink raised an eyebrow, and with some coaxing Ruby explained how Pitch had attacked, questioned her, set the Lilac alight by touching it, and left her to die. Ink put some of Ruby's worst fears aside—Vera was alive. So was Brandy. Knowing they'd made it out helped her calm down enough to talk.

Partway through Ruby's recounting, Ink produced a book and quill seemingly from nowhere, and began jotting down notes.

"All of this over finding Brass and Phoenix." Ink rubbed her chin. "What have those two gotten themselves into?"

"Wait," Ruby had a sudden realization. "Brass and his friend. I told him where to find them. Are they—?"

"There haven't been any more fires in Olwin or the surrounding homesteads, so I would wager they're fine," Ink said.

"Then they're in danger," Ruby said. "I have to warn them."

Ruby started to sit up, but Ink held a hand up to stop her.

"Those two are more than used to a little danger. You can go *after* we're done."

Ruby's hands balled into fists. One person with magic pushing her around had been bad enough. Another right off the bat was making her blood boil. But she recognized that playing along was the path of least resistance.

And at least this mage wasn't a murderous psychopath—just incredibly full of herself.

"Fine."

"Thank you," Ink responded. "Now. The man who set the fire. Describe him."

When Ruby described Pitch, she could tell from Ink's reaction that the mage knew him. It was her turn to ask a question.

"Who was he?"

"His name is Ronan Highwater, though he goes by Pitch. He was a freelancer until his company finally dropped him for being more trouble than he was worth. Switched to straight contract killing afterward," Ink explained. "Although I never knew him to be a fire mage."

Ink flipped through pages in her book, skimming as she went.

"You know him?"

"Knew. Once. We used to work together, back when the Cord of Aenwyn could afford me and hadn't kicked him out," Ink looked up from her book, noting the shock on Ruby's face. "Relax, I'm not going to hurt you or hand you back to him. We're not affiliated anymore. Actually, I was the one who—ah! I thought so."

She stopped flipping through her book. She bit her lip as her eyes scanned the pages. Ruby felt annoyed. She was being ignored.

"What?" Ruby asked.

"Hm?" Ink looked up, remembering Ruby was there. "Well, as I said, Pitch was never one for magic. But at the first fire, there was an artifact that was destroyed. I had to double-check some old notes, but I was right. If Pitch had been at the site of the first fire when it was destroyed, it would explain where he picked up an affinity for pyromancy so fast."

"What artifact?"

Ink closed her book and offered another condescending smile. "I'm afraid that's need to know. It's all very private, sensitive information. Suffice to say, an incredibly powerful, incredibly dangerous one."

Ruby's annoyance was fast bubbling back into anger. Ink didn't seem to notice. In actuality, she did notice; she just had more important things on her mind. She was much more focused on the new developments in the investigation. Pitch was involved. And he'd been changed by the artifact's energy. It was a fascinating and dangerous situation. Her favorite combination.

Ruby was less enthused. "Can I leave now?"

"You can," Ink said. "If I need you again, I can find you."

"Great," Ruby got out of bed, before glancing at the gown she was wearing. "Where are my clothes?"

"Scorched to shit from the fire," Ink said. "If you just need something to wear, there's plenty of options in the wardrobe."

"Thanks." Ruby opened the wardrobe. There was a nearly overwhelming array of options, ranging from elegant dresses to simple traveler's clothes. Ruby grabbed a skirt, bodice, shirt, and a pair of boots and immediately started changing.

Ink's eyes widened in brief surprise at the girl's lack of modesty but quickly got over it. The sight reminded Ink of something she'd noted when she'd first found Ruby in the Lilac's smoldering remains.

No burns.

Surviving the fire was a miracle in and of itself, but without any sign of ever being in it? That question alone had kept Ink busy while she'd waited for Ruby to wake up. A detection spell revealed Ruby was giving off a magical aura, but it wasn't arcane like the artifact that had changed Pitch. Whatever was going on with the girl, it was something else.

If she weren't so busy with cleaning up the artifact's mess, she might have asked the girl to stay so she could study her. But if Pitch was the one who'd ended up with its power, her job was going to be considerably harder than she'd anticipated. And in all likelihood, considerably messier as well.

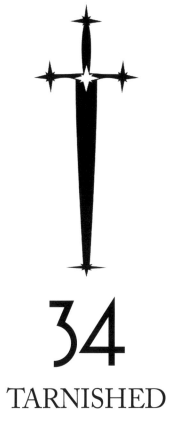

34

TARNISHED

I t was midday when Brass got to Olwin, and business was in full swing. Shops were open, restaurants and taverns were catering the lunch rush, and runners were making deliveries all over town.

He had to get back to the house and Wings at some point, which meant he couldn't do anything that would get him trashed or require an overnight stay. That ruled out all of the most fun activities, but it still left him with plenty of options.

While he pondered the question, his footsteps carried him in the direction of the Pale, and the Lilac. It had been a minute since he'd seen Ruby. Now was as good a time as any to catch up. Maybe go clothes shopping. He had taken a crossbow bolt through the jacket back when they'd escaped from Clocktower, and that was excuse enough for him to buy a new one.

This was assuming she was free. He figured she was more of a night-shift girl, but there was only one way to know for sure.

As he got closer to the Pale, however, he noticed a shift in the atmosphere. People seemed to gravitate toward each other. Cast nervous glances at one another. The kind of lingering fear experienced by people who were new to the sensation and didn't quite know what to do with it hung in the air. The presence of the watch grew, well beyond anything there should have been in this part of the city. Then he saw smoke.

Brass picked up his pace to the Lilac, though gut instinct told him what he would find before he arrived. Getting there only confirmed it.

Where the Lilac should have been standing, there were only charred remains. White smoke still curled from it, and bits of blackened wood flickered orange. An acrid smell choked the air, and ash littered the ground around the ruin. A loose rope barricade had been set up around the building's husk, and several members of the watch were posted around the perimeter. Even at a distance, charred bodies were visible among the wreckage.

Brass stared at the smoking remains, trying to process the questions running through his mind. How? Why?

Who?

The perimeter gave the remains a wide berth. When Brass got closer, he understood why. The Lilac's remains still radiated heat, like they were still on fire. The watch guarding it were sweating.

"What happened?" Brass asked the closest one.

The watchwoman stood a little straighter and gripped her weapon a little tighter. She was on edge. "There was a fire."

"Fair enough, I walked into that one," Brass said, pinching the bridge of his nose. "How did it happen? Did anyone make it out?"

Brass never got a response. A familiar voice shouted, "You!"

Dressed in a robe, Vera stormed toward him with fury in their eyes. Fury, and quite a bit of red. They looked like they hadn't slept a wink and spent the morning sobbing. And all of that now drilled into Brass as they jammed a finger into his chest.

"You did this," they hissed.

"Beg your pardon?"

"Don't. Don't you dare say a damn thing," Vera spat, shoving him. "This is your fault!"

Brass barely budged, but his concern only grew. He was prepared to handle this sort of thing. Fourteen years on the job had given him plenty of experience with people blaming him for things that weren't his fault. But this was Vera, and the Lilac. This was a friend, and something they'd put their soul into.

"How is this my fault?"

"Two dirks come in looking for you, torture two of my girls, and then my hotel burns down," Vera said. "You tell me."

Brass felt unsteady as Vera's words sunk in. He wasn't sure whether to be embarrassed or impressed that someone had tracked him down to the Lilac. He wondered if the price on his head had anything to do with it, but that wouldn't explain the fire. No decent professional would burn down a luxury hotel to cover up an interrogation. That was just petty and putting a lot of good people out of a job.

Oh shit.

"Did Ruby make it out?" Brass asked.

"We can't tell. Nobody's seen her, but we can't get to the bodies," Vera said, their voice bitter and hollow. "Everything I've ever worked for is gone, and I don't even know who to mourn."

"Vera . . ."

"If I ever see you again," Vera warned, "I will kill you myself."

Brass opened his mouth but for once decided not to say anything. Instead he simply nodded and backed away. He slunk from the scene, feeling disoriented. Every time he thought he'd managed to get the furious look in Vera's eyes out of his head, it came back with a vengeance. And Ruby. The poor girl. There was no guarantee that Ruby had been in the Lilac when it went up. There was also no guarantee she wasn't. He forgot about clothes shopping. Brass needed to find a tavern, or really just some booze, and toast Ruby and either her incredible luck or unfortunate passing.

On the way to find a tavern, he passed through one of the dozens of miniature marketplaces that dotted Olwin. Small spaces cleared out where no buildings were erected and roads converged. Here, people of every creed and credential in the city intersected, and the most enterprising and desperate of them peddled simple wares from carts and wagons. The markets of the city had never not been busy, but these days they were almost suffocatingly packed and more colorful than ever as local and immigrant populations blended together.

An older man with one arm and the telltale pointed ears of elvish descent was selling bottles of wine from a small stand. He displayed four bottles in front of him, each with a different label. Brass thought it over. It wasn't a tavern, but right now the idea of skipping a social setting appealed to him. And he could pick up an extra bottle to give to Wings as a belated housewarming gift. And wedding present. And any other occasions he'd missed.

He took a breath, put on a smile to hide his shock, and gently elbowed his way to the stand.

"My good man, how much for two bottles?" Brass asked.

The man offered no response. He didn't even acknowledge Brass standing in front of him. Instead he just stared at the ground. Brass cocked his head and cleared his throat. No response.

"Sir?" he raised his voice. The man didn't look at him. "Excuse me!"

He was yelling now, but the man still didn't say anything.

A woman approached the man's stand and walked past Brass.

Instantly the man looked up and gave the woman a smile. She returned it. "Dalgo. Did you manage to get ahold of any more Riodante?"

"I saved a bottle especially for you," the man said. With his one arm, he began rifling through the storage bin built into his side of the stand.

Brass stared, jaw slack. He turned his attention to the woman. "Does he just like you more than me?"

The woman said nothing. She just stood there, smiling and waiting patiently for Dalgo to produce the wine she'd ordered. She didn't just act like she couldn't hear Brass. She acted like he wasn't there at all.

"Hello?" Brass waved.

Dalgo found the bottle, and the woman thanked him. They exchanged a few more pleasantries while she dug through a coin purse.

Grief and frustration mixed into a cocktail that left Brass's head spinning. Right now, he didn't have the patience for whatever this was.

"What is wrong with you people?"

"They can't hear you."

A voice, slick and oddly melodic, wormed through the crowd into Brass's ear. He felt a shiver go down his spine. Standing behind Brass was a short man with long, greasy hair. He wore an oversized gray tunic that covered his arms and came down to his thighs. An ornamental dagger depicting some kind of saint's iconography glinted in his hand, but Brass didn't recognize it.

"No one can," the greasy cleric said. His mouth hung ever so slightly agape, the corners pulled up. Not quite a smile. Close, but off.

Brass glanced around him, careful never to take his eyes off this man for too long. It took Brass a few glances to understand what he was looking for. Then he noticed. No one was looking at him.

Brass dressed in bright colors, walked like he could always hear music playing, and half of the time openly carried a sword despite it supposedly being a crime for a civilian in Olwin. He was used to having eyes on him. More than that, he'd honed the skill of becoming the center of attention in every room he walked into. Now, in a crowded marketplace, there was not a single pair of eyes on him, and it felt unnatural. Like he didn't exist.

"All right, whoever you are. You have my attention," Brass said.

"I am the Jury of Saint Adresta," the cleric said.

"Good to know. I'm Brass. Never heard of you," Brass said. "Hey, am I dead?"

"Not yet," the Jury said.

There was a cruelty to his voice that set Brass on edge. It wasn't malicious or vindictive. In fact, there was a twinge of enjoyment to it. Brass's skin crawled. He took another look at the Jury, at his sunken eyes and weathered skin, and he decided whoever Saint Adresta was, their Jury was probably closer to an executioner.

Son of a bitch. I hate Betrayer priests.

With a flourish, Brass summoned his sword from his wrist-pocket and lunged. Dagger in hand, the Jury finished a prayer he'd already started, and Brass's thrust halted inches from the Jury's eye.

Brass's entire body turned to lead. His arms, his legs, his chest, his head, all felt heavy and unresponsive. It wasn't just his body. His thoughts slowed to a crawl. Everything around him was suddenly moving faster. Too fast.

The Jury's mouth hung open in that same not quite a smile. He circled Brass, moving faster than Brass's eyes could track.

"No easy feat, moving with a leaden mind," the Jury said. Brass heard the words, but processed their meaning on a delay, like he had to manually translate it into a language he understood. "What an interesting mind you must have."

Brass lost sight of him and felt a warm sensation on the back of his neck. It took a moment to realize the Jury was behind him. Only after that did he think to turn around.

It was like moving in molasses. Everything felt stuck. Lethargic. His body responded with painstaking delay. By the time Brass turned around, the Jury was already walking out of view again, and Brass was too slow on the uptake to figure out where he'd gone.

Somewhere in the back of Brass's memories, he recognized this feeling. Church had used this prayer on him before. Several times, actually. There was a way to end it. He had to remember. Think. That was so hard now. So slow.

"When the dead and the wronged cry out for retribution, Adresta hears them," the Jury said.

More words Brass was thinking too slowly to understand. He didn't bother trying. He blocked them out. Focused on the prayer. On Church. There was a way to break this; he was sure of it.

"My work allows Adresta to guide me to the subjects of that retribution," the Jury continued. Brass ignored him.

Was this one of the prayers that needed concentration to maintain? Did it matter?

"In all my years in her service, I have never felt so many calls for someone's blood as the ones I've heard for you and your companions."

No. It didn't matter. He could barely move. There was nothing Brass could do to the Jury that he wouldn't see coming from a mile away. He'd never be able to touch him.

The Jury was in his face again, inspecting him. "What did you do to wrong so many?" He searched Brass's face. Supposedly Brass and the others from his company were important. But now, as he looked Brass over, the Jury struggled to find anything remarkable about him. Perhaps that was just the prayer's work, muddling the man to nothing. But the Betrayer priest saw nothing in his target's eyes that marked him as anything exceptional.

Brass grit his teeth. There had to be another way. There was. He knew there was. He'd gotten out of this before.

Brass strained to pull up memories of times long gone. Church running out of patience and shutting him down. Angel clocking him while he couldn't move. Phoenix being too busy with Snow to break up the ensuing brawl.

Wait.

Angel had hit him. Angel hit him, and it had snapped him out of the prayer's hold. That beautiful, violent misplacement of divine favor. Brass could have kissed her then and there.

He needed someone to hit him. Easy. He made people do that all the time. He searched around for the closest person besides the Jury. They were still standing right next to the wine stand. The woman and Dalgo were still chatting away, oblivious to the assassin and his helpless victim standing literally right next to them.

In his addled state, it didn't even occur to Brass that the prayer might stop his plan from working. He simply went for it. Slowly, with incredible delay, Brass reached out. The Jury, having seen the movement coming, had already taken a step back, assuming it was another attempt to attack.

Instead Brass's hand found the rear of the woman talking to Dalgo, and squeezed.

The woman whirled around in a blur too fast for Brass to track, and the next thing he was aware of, his head was facing ninety degrees to his right, and his face hurt. But the world had snapped back into focus. He could see. Hear. Think. Move.

The woman he'd just groped shoved him hard, and Brass tumbled to the ground. "Pig!"

He deserved that.

"Sorry! Someone's trying to kill me!"

The Jury was confused and stunned. He berated himself for not realizing what Brass was trying before it was too late. He began to say another prayer, intent on not making the same mistake again. Brass didn't give him the chance.

With a sweep of his leg, he dropped the Jury to the ground and used the momentum to leap to his feet.

With a swipe of his sword, he knocked the Jury's dagger aside and into the crowd. It disappeared into a sea of boots. Brass held the point of his sword to the Jury's neck.

"You know, you're lucky I remembered I need to ask you some questions," Brass said. The Jury's eyes were wide and his jaw was slack. All around them, people were calling out, gawking, and backing away. The prayer was broken. The Jury's talisman lost. He'd been outmaneuvered.

Before Brass could ask any questions though, something collided with him and sent him flying off of his feet and into Dalgo's wine stand. Now people in the crowd scattered. As they fled in every direction and called out for the watch, Cull stepped forward. Nearly seven feet of steel and muscle loomed over Brass.

"Oh crap," Brass muttered.

Cull raised a metal-clad boot and stomped. Brass only barely rolled out of the way. Scooping up his sword, he leaped to his feet and attacked. He was faster, but Cull's armor was well-made, and Brass's attacks left little more than scratches and dents. It would take Brass dozens of prodding stabs to slip past a weak spot. By the look of him and his sword, Cull would only need one to end this. The first time Brass dodged, Dalgo's wine stand got cleaved in two in his place. Cull was a big man, but the sword's force was inhumanly overwhelming. Brass was certain it was enchanted. Exactly what the enchantment did, he was still figuring out.

"That was a waste of perfectly good wine!" Brass yelled.

Brass finally landed a counter, producing a gash in Cull's cheek. He used the opening to leap away and get some breathing room. "Have we met before? Strangest thing, I know I recognize that face."

Cull didn't answer; all focus. He leaped forward with more speed than Brass expected from a man his size and swung his sword down as it began to glow bright white. Brass moved with unmatched precision, sidestepping and deflecting the attack. Cull's blade skid across Brass's, redirected rather than outright blocked, and struck the ground.

A shockwave rippled out from the blade along the ground, scattering cobblestones and cracking the wall of a nearby building. Brass marveled at the destruction. *So that's what it does.*

"Wait, I remember you," Brass said. "You're the big guy from Clocktower's old barber-shop hideout. I never got your name."

Cull lunged and Brass jumped away. Charnel cut through an entire apple cart and sent the two halves of it flying in either direction. Brass had to duck to avoid getting hit by one.

"You know, I prefer a proper introduction with the people I fight to the death. I'll even go first," he continued in between moves and counters. "I'm Brass. But you already knew that."

The glintchaser lunged at Cull, getting close to avoid his sword and to get inside his guard. It half worked. He was too close for the dirk to use his weapon's blade but in the perfect range to take an armored elbow to the face and a pommel strike to the ribs. On that second one, Brass felt something crack. Pain shooting through his abdomen, Brass was only just able to dodge another swing from Cull's sword, and the ensuing shockwave pulverized the ground around them.

". . . fair enough." Brass stood up tall, sword held at the ready. "If you're not going to tell me your name, can I at least have my knife back?"

Cull was confused for a second, until he noticed the sharp pain in his side. A knife was embedded between two plates in his armor, buried to the hilt. Blood began to leak from the gap in the armor, and Brass smirked. Nothing distracted an opponent quite like running his mouth. He almost felt bad for the brute.

"Drop the swords!"

The watch had arrived on scene. Half a dozen men and women in chainmail brandishing spears. They advanced in a line, weapons pointed at Brass and Cull. Brass waved them back.

"Stay back, he's dangerous!" Brass yelled.

"Drop it! Now!"

"Him first!" Brass pointed his blade at Cull, who was clutching his side.

The watch yelled again for them both to surrender. Brass was about to try and explain the situation when he saw another figure walking up behind the watch. Brass recognized Pitch on sight, but he was different from what he remembered. For one, his hands were on fire.

While that was certainly new, when Pitch raised a burning hand, Brass immediately understood what was about to happen. "Behind you!"

Only one of the watch even looked back and saw what was coming. Pitch grinned. The watchman yelled for Pitch to stop, and Pitch responded by sweeping his hand.

A wall of fire erupted from the streets, engulfing the entire line in flames that Brass could feel from across the market. Screams filled the air as the watch dropped their weapons and scrambled in all directions; all of them hideously burned, and some of them still on fire. A moment later, Pitch stepped through the flames, unscathed. His eyes were orbs of pure glowing orange. With a wall of fire roaring behind him, he looked like a demon.

For the first time in seven years, Brass was afraid. Dying didn't scare him. But for a moment, he imagined the monster in front of him with free reign of the city. Of the people who would die. And then the wheels started to turn as Vera's story replayed in his head. Dirks looking for him at the Lilac. The whole place going up in flames.

His heart was pounding, but instead of sending blood and adrenaline, it carried ice. He forgot to breathe, forgot to move. Cull seized the opportunity, enveloping Brass in a bear hug, lifting him up off his feet and body-slamming him.

The impact was enough to shake Brass out of it. Now wasn't the time to piss himself—he had done that a second ago—now was the time to fight.

"Cull, move!" Pitch yelled, drawing both of his swords. "I want a piece of this."

Brass grunted. He clicked his heels together, and a blade extended from the toe of his right boot. The way Cull was hunched over him, he couldn't just kick him with it, but with a bit of contorting, he managed to press the edge of the blade to the side of Cull's ankle and dragged. It didn't cut deep, but between the pain and the ongoing blood loss, Cull's strength wavered enough for Brass to shove himself free and wriggle away.

Pitch roared and surged forward. Brass lost track of everything else as his sword met Pitch's. Immediately, they began to trade blows, their blades dancing across each other. Brass had to parry twice as many attacks as Pitch, and yet he kept up. He was faster than Pitch and probably better with a sword.

But he was already hurt, and he was getting tired. Just standing next to Pitch was making Brass sweat, and he could feel his skin and hair slowly being scalded. The air around Pitch hurt to breathe. Cull was keeping his distance, still clutching at his side and looking for an opening, but the giant of a man was unsteady on his feet, and more to the point, not spewing fire with every swing.

Brass knew who to prioritize.

Brass drove his sword through Pitch's chest, and the assassin seized up. Brass thought he had him. He should have had him. But for some reason, instead of dying like a considerate piece of garbage, Pitch just got angry, yanked himself off of Brass's sword and roared as fire cascaded off him. Brass was forced back, taking multiple burns while he did.

Brass and Pitch locked blades again. But this time was different. Pitch's sword, heated and glowing, cleaved Brass's in two.

Brass glanced at his broken sword, then at Pitch. Then he kicked Pitch in the groin with the blade in his boot.

Pitch screamed and staggered, and Brass ran in the opposite direction, kicking Cull in the face when the brute dove for him. He didn't kill him, but he did put a hole in his cheek and cleared his escape route. He tore through the streets, darting through alleys, doubling back, and cutting through any place that had an open door or window. Always, as he ran, he could hear fires breaking out behind him and people screaming.

Brass yanked off his jacket and threw it aside. He grabbed anything he thought he could wear. When he passed by someone's home, he grabbed a rag they'd hung out to dry. When he ducked into a tavern, he snagged a coat someone had left on a hook, dropped a few glint behind him, and ran out the back door. He passed a blacksmith walking to work and tore his apron off of him without breaking stride.

By the time Brass made it a block away from the fight, he'd thrown together a makeshift disguise. He could still hear Pitch. Still track him from where crowds of people scattered. He was close. Too close.

If this chaos kept up, sooner or later knights would get involved. Hopefully several. Brass had seen power like Pitch's before. He couldn't take him. No amount of watch could. But four or five good knights might stand a chance. Maybe Ink would help. She was still in town looking into something about a fire, and he was pretty sure this qualified.

Or maybe Pitch would just get bored.

One thing was certain. Brass was exhausted. Whole parts of his body screamed in pain from burns, and the situation with his ribs was unclear but not promising. His run quickly began to slow to a limp. Columns of smoke rose up throughout the Stays. People were dashing through the streets. Some of them ran toward the fires to help fight them or to try and save the few possessions they had. Others ran for safety.

Brass was just trying to get away.

He limped off for the city gates. He needed to get to Akers, or a church, or just to anyone who knew anything about healing. The adrenaline was wearing off, and real pain was starting to set in.

A hand reached out from an alleyway, grabbed him by the arm, and pulled him off the street. Brass stumbled, but for a split second where the hand touched his skin, he felt relief from the pain of his burns. Then he found himself face-to-face with a dark haired masked woman dressed in black. Brass wondered if his pain was starting to make him delirious, because when he looked at her eyes, he saw that they were solid white. What skin was exposed almost seemed to match.

The woman drew a dagger on him.

"You've got to be kidding me," Brass groaned.

The woman disappeared from in front of him. A thief's blink. Brass spun completely around, just in time to see the woman in mid-swing. He caught her wrist in his hand, stopping her strike short.

"Hi, I'm Brass," he said. His arm was shaking with the effort of holding the woman. She spun her arm, breaking his grip, and blinked again.

Brass turned around again, expecting another backstab. But she wasn't there. Too late, he realized he'd been feinted. The woman reappeared exactly where she'd been a moment ago, only now, Brass's back was to her.

She brought the pommel of her dagger down on him, and he dropped.

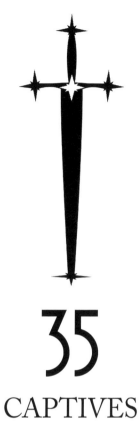

35

CAPTIVES

I n an abandoned house at the southeast end of the Stays, Snow sat in a chair in an otherwise empty room. Everything from the bare stone floor to the windowsills was covered in dust, and cobwebs clung to the corners of the ceiling. A few faded sheets, once used to protect unused furniture, were scattered across the floor in crumpled, stiff heaps. The late-afternoon sun sifted through dirty windows, giving most of the air a hot, dry quality. Everywhere except immediately surrounding Snow. That, as always, was cold.

She'd been waiting for almost an hour. She fiddled with a dagger while she waited, twirling it, catching it, all while keeping her eyes trained on the door.

Finally it opened. Cull staggered in, doing his best to stand tall and keep a neutral expression. It was a convincing front, but there was a slight wince in his step, and he was paler than normal. Brass had gotten in a good shot. Pitch was back under control. His eyes were back down to a muted orange, but his face was set in an annoyed frown. The Jury was expressionless.

Snow stood up. She stopped messing with her dagger but kept it in hand.

Pitch sized her up, almost surprised to see her.

"So, did you actually get him?" he asked.

Snow said nothing. Instead, she walked away. She found the only other door in the house. Hot, stale air grew briefly cool as Snow descended the staircase to the basement, and it heated back up as Pitch followed her.

At the bottom of the stairs was a surprisingly spacious but barren room. Burn marks scarred the floor in the center. On the left were rusted, floor-to-ceiling iron bars that formed a holding cell. In it sat Brass, battered, burned, and tied to a chair with a bag over his head.

"Well, looks like you did," Pitch said. He walked past Snow to get a closer look. He noticed Brass was barefoot, with his boots resting just outside the jail cell along with his belt pouch and wrist-pocket.

A smart move, stripping Brass of his tricks. Pitch would have thought of that too, obviously. If he'd been the one to catch him.

"No thanks to any of you," Snow said.

When she spoke, her voice sounded like her vocal cords were made of glass—hollow and shattering. She'd learned to use her powers to alter her voice. Pitch thought she was doing it to be intimidating.

His eyes became a little bit brighter. "The hells are you talking about? We did all the work."

"You call that shitshow you pulled out there 'work'?" Snow asked. "Blind the crowd, lock him down, get him out. That was the plan. Instead you tore up half the Stays and set the other half on fire!"

Snow's eyes were shifting rapidly from pale to bright blue. "Do you want them to send knights? Because that's how you get them to send knights."

"There aren't enough knights in Olwin to take me," Pitch said.

"Thanks for dragging us all with you to test that theory," Snow said.

Snow could feel her heartbeat, which was the only reason she stopped shouting. She couldn't let herself get too angry. If Pitch wanted to start something, she needed absolute focus. With a single breath, she grounded herself, and the blue of her eyes grew pale and icy once again.

"Not to mention you nearly killed him," she said more calmly.

"We're assassins," Pitch said.

"Who will get paid a lot more to bring him in alive," Snow replied. She kept her voice measured. Stern, but passionless. "When we agreed to work together, I assumed you wouldn't screw up my paycheck. But you did it with the Shield, and you almost did it again." Snow glared at Cull. "Both of you."

Cull grunted. Pitch threw his arms out. "Will you quit bitching? It worked out in the end, didn't it? Besides, you wanna blame somebody, blame Courthouse over here." Pitch jerked a thumb at the Jury. "He was the one who was supposed to keep eyes off us and Brass on lock."

"His finding a way to break the prayer was unexpected," the Jury said.

"Because you underestimated him," Snow said. "All of you did."

Pitch was about to retort, but Cull beat him to the punch.

"She's right."

Pitch gave Cull an incredulous look. "Really, big guy? I thought we were friends."

Cull grunted. He'd known Pitch personally less than a month. His reputation from his days in the Cord of Aenwyn was mixed. What he'd seen of him before the incident with the Shield had not impressed him. What he'd seen since then only gave him cause for concern and no small amount of contempt.

"I'm with the lady and big bald guy," Brass said. "You guys completely shat the bed on this one."

Cull gave a low grumble. Pitch threw his head back. "Saints. He's awake."

"You especially, Pitch," Brass said. "The big man at least went down swinging, and Jury Duty actually had me for a second, but you just made yourself look bad. I'm not mad. I'm just disappointed."

"I seem to remember kicking your ass," Pitch said.

"Pitch, we're friends. Well, not really. More like peers who always used to fight before one of us clearly outclassed the other," Brass said. "My point is, I want to be honest with you. I played you like a viol."

Pitch's eyes began to glow, and his fists clenched.

"You know, you always had dog-cart brain, but I think whatever fire magic you snorted burned away the last bits of your sense."

"I'm gonna kill him," Pitch said.

Underneath the bag, Brass smiled. There was something uniquely satisfying about puppeteering people with nothing but a few well-chosen barbs. Even when it was as easy as it was with Pitch.

That satisfaction alone kept the pain from his wounds at bay, and there were a good amount of them. Some of his burns were minor, but there was at least one that felt bad in the way the worst burns did—in that he couldn't feel it at all. His ribs were, at the minimum, bruised, and his head was still swimming from the hit he took.

Escaping was going to be a bit of challenge . . . that is, if Pitch didn't make good on his threat right now.

Pitch stepped forward, smoke beginning to curl off of him. Snow put a hand on his chest, stopping him. An audible *hiss* came from where they touched. Anyone else would have been burned, but Snow only felt a sensation of warmth on her palm.

"Out of my way," Pitch demanded.

"You're not screwing up another target on this list," Snow said.

Pitch tried to shrug her off, but Snow held firm. Their eyes locked. Embers began to flick and trail off of his hands. Ice crawled across Snow's features. The Jury stood back, a gaping smile slowly spreading across his face.

Pitch relented, backing away from Brass's cell. "Fine."

Snow gripped her dagger tight in her hand, but otherwise relaxed.

"You seem like a woman with her head on straight," Brass said. "Why work with these idiots at all? I'm pretty sure you could have just taken me in yourself and kept all the money."

"She wouldn't," Pitch said. He glared at Snow.

Snow said nothing, only narrowed her eyes at him. She could tell he was trying to threaten her. It wasn't working.

Cull fidgeted slightly in his armor. He'd thought he'd grown used to wearing it so often, learned to be comfortable with it in any climate. But with Snow and Pitch in the same room, the temperature was alternating too fast to keep up with.

"So, now what?" Brass asked. "Because I'm hungry. Is anyone else hungry?"

"Can we at least shut him up?" Pitch said. "Break his jaw, or something?"

"Or we could not do that," Brass said. "I vote no."

"You've done enough with him," Snow said. "If you want to be actually useful, get word to the Handler, and tell him to get the money ready."

"Who put you in charge?" Pitch said.

"I did," Snow said. "What's wrong? Afraid you'll cock up delivering a message?"

Pitch growled but stomped toward the stairs. "Bitch."

Snow watched him go, folding her arms. "Prick."

Cull nudged the Jury. "Heal me."

"Hmm?" the Jury glanced down at Cull's side, where there was still blood on his armor. "I can't. I need a new talisman."

"How do you get one?" Cull asked.

"Ideally, I'd have one forged from devoted metal," the Jury said. "But as I doubt we have the time, I can make do by modifying another cleric's talisman."

"Go get one then," Snow said. "Brass is going to need healing too if he's going to survive long enough to be delivered alive."

"I'm doing all right," Brass lied. He was starting to think his ribs might actually be broken. "Don't trouble yourself on my account."

The Jury raised his eyebrows slightly, but nodded. "Very well." Leaving this place was all well and good for him. It was difficult to suppress the urge to kill Snow. Even without his talisman, he still possessed the senses bestowed on him by Adresta. Demands for vengeance against the ice woman were even more deafening than those for Brass. What interesting bloody individuals the Starbreakers were turning out to be.

"Cull, go with him," Snow said. "Sooner you're back in fighting shape, the better."

"And you?" Cull asked.

Snow rolled her eyes. "I'm not trying to steal him. If I was, we wouldn't have been waiting for you here to begin with."

Cull didn't say anything, but the look he gave her was clear. *If you're lying to me, you'll regret it.* Snow gave no reaction, her blue eyes so pale they bordered on white. With a nod, Cull left up the stairs.

Brass waited to hear the door close, and for them to be alone.

"It's good to see you, Snow."

"How long have you known?" Snow dropped her voice disguise.

"Well, you had me fooled back in the alley," Brass said. "But I can count the number of people who could stand up to Pitch like that on one hand."

Snow sighed. All the extra effort to make sure he didn't see her face and couldn't recognize her voice, and it didn't even work. How he knew made it worse. If it had been Phoenix, he'd have laid out the chain of logic that all but proved it was her. But Brass did it with barely more to go on than a gut feeling.

"So, can you get this sack off of me? It's kind of itching on my neck."

Snow rolled her eyes, but she opened the cell doors and pulled the sack off of Brass's head.

"Better?" Snow asked, like she was talking to an annoying child.

For the first time since waking up, Brass got a look at his surroundings . . . and at Snow. Her arms were folded, and she had a familiar impatient look on her face. She still wore her hair basically the same way as before, though it looked a little shorter. Her armor was new, but still the same dark blues and blacks she liked before. There was a new scar on the corner of her lip. It was a small thing, but it made him wonder how much he'd missed.

Snow bristled at his staring. "What?"

"Snow . . ." Brass shook his head. "What are you doing?"

"There's a price on your head. A big one," Snow said. "This is what I do."

"Fair enough. We all have to make money somehow. No hard feelings," Brass said. "But what are you doing with *them*?"

"What I have to," Snow said. "I was on the list too."

She hadn't told any of the others that. Even lied to Phoenix about it. But she hadn't needed to come for them yet. She'd taken down Brass. He deserved to know why. With a heavy sigh, and blue coming back to her eyes, she sat down in the cell with him.

"A lot of the targets on the list aren't pushovers. Knights. Freelancer companies. Us. It convinced people who were normally solo acts to team up to take marks down. I got backed into a corner, and I had a choice to make," Snow said. "Hunt or be hunted."

Brass felt a sharp pain in his chest. It wasn't his ribs. "Why didn't you ask for help?"

"There was no one for me to ask."

"What about us?"

Snow scoffed. "We've all had years to make up, and we haven't. There's a reason for that. No one would have helped if I'd asked."

"I would have."

Snow shook her head. "You'd have been the only one."

"It's been just me and you before," Brass said. Not the old days, but the old, old days. Before the Starbreakers, before Phoenix had ever picked them up at that tavern in Aenerwin as glorified bodyguards, when they were just a pair of kids trying to get rich and see the world.

"It wouldn't be enough." Snow found it hard to look at him for too long. She kept finding excuses to look at the floor or the bars of the cell.

"What about Phoenix?"

Snow folded her arms. "I think we both know that bridge was burned even before Relgen."

"Give the man some credit," Brass said. "Just because you two don't fuck anymore doesn't mean he doesn't care what happens to you. He can be up his own ass at times, but he's a decent guy. Deep down. If you really needed help, he wouldn't leave you hanging."

"It doesn't matter," Snow said. She stood up and prepared to leave. She justified herself enough already. "I don't need help. This, me working with them, is me helping myself. Surviving. Like you taught me."

Brass's shoulders sagged. He didn't begrudge Snow for doing what it took to survive. Life was something to fight for, every day, any way you could. It's not like they were still companions. They hadn't even spoken in years. If she had to hunt him down and sell him out to save herself, he understood that.

He just hated that she was doing all of this for nothing.

"They're gonna stab you in the back," Brass said.

Snow shook her head, but her grip tightened on her dagger. Brass recognized it. The blade was engraved, and though Brass didn't read Arcania, he knew what it translated to. *Companion Piece.* The first thing Phoenix had ever enchanted.

"We have a deal." She sounded like she was trying to convince herself rather than him.

"Someone is willing to pay for you to get killed or caught. A deal with the people doing the catching doesn't change that," Brass warned her. "And dirks will do anything for money. They're like trulls, except they make new holes instead of using the ones that are already there."

"This is what I'm doing," Snow said. "You can't change my mind. Sorry."

She put the bag back over his head and left the cell, shutting the door behind her. She gripped the bars for a moment, trying to steel herself. *This is the only way.*

"So," Brass said from under the bag. "What really happens now?"

"Now, we turn you over to the Handler and get paid."

"What about the others?"

"There's two guys gunning for Church," Snow said. "They left town a while ago, so they've probably made their move by now. There's rumors of where to find Angel, but she's out of the way. She's got a while before anyone serious gets to her."

Snow stopped herself. For just a moment, she felt exactly like she had the day she'd woken up with her powers. Surprised at just how cold she sounded. She pushed the feeling down. That cold was an armor. She needed to wear it, not feel bad about it.

"We'll probably go after Phoenix next."

"Wings and Robyn?"

So that's what they named the baby. "Wings isn't on the list. I'll do what I can to make sure they don't get dragged into this."

"You really think that's a line you can avoid crossing?" Brass asked. "They're married."

"I said I'll do what I can," Snow said. "Phoenix isn't with her right now. If the others think he's exposed enough, they'll target him and leave Wings and the kid alone."

It wasn't perfect. It still meant the kid was probably going to grow up without a father. But that was the business.

"I would never tell you not to do what you had to," Brass said. "But you don't have to do this."

Snow couldn't bring herself to say that, no, she did. That felt too much like admitting that she was bending to threats. That she was being controlled.

Instead she just said, "Well, I'm going to."

36

BACKSTAB

A canopied carriage made its way through the streets of Olwin, headed for a mansion at the north end of the Pale. Inside it, Snow, Cull, Pitch, and Jury sat on benches, opposite each other. At their feet in between them was a long, lumpy drawstring bag.

Pitch absentmindedly bounced his leg, arms folded. His attention was mostly focused on the bag, but every so often he'd catch Snow's eyes and offer a smirk. Cull remained motionless, hands resting in his lap over Charnel. It was the only way the sword would fit in with everyone else. Jury sat quietly, staring intently at his new stolen talisman and the fresh scratches he'd carved into it. The dagger was a crude replacement, but it would serve his purposes for the time being.

Snow had her dagger out, twirling it in her hand or tapping it against the carriage door. Space in the carriage was tight with the four of them and the bag. Pitch at least had enough of a handle on his abilities to avoid burning anyone, but with the two of them sitting at opposite ends, the temperature was at war with itself.

Pitch's silence unnerved her. He'd come back after an hour or so to confirm the message was sent, and he'd said little since. Nothing since they'd gotten into the carriage. More than once, Snow glanced out the carriage window to make sure they were still traveling in the right direction.

So far everything was still going as planned.

The house was surrounded by a massive yard fenced off from the rest of the city by stone walls and an iron gate. It loomed in the distance, three stories tall, with opal-blue clay tiles across its roof. The carriage pulled to a halt outside the gate.

The four of them piled out. Cull was last, slinging Charnel onto his back and the bag over one shoulder. A muffled grunt came from the bag as it smacked against Cull's shoulder, and before long, it was squirming in Cull's grasp.

The carriage driver stared, not sure what to make of it. "Is your . . . bag all right?"

"Hey. Mind your own business," Pitch said.

The carriage driver wasted no time pulling away after that. He'd been a driver in the Pale for a number of years now. Met a lot of strange people doing a lot of strange things. He'd learned not to start trouble if he could help it.

The gates opened of their own accord, ushering them in. Pitch gestured for Snow to lead on. "Ladies first."

Snow narrowed her eyes, but preceded them. When Jury, bringing up the rear, stepped through the gates, they swung shut again. There were no operators of the gate in sight.

The path that led to the house was long and winding, flanked by shrubbery, trees, and statues. Hedges were trimmed in tight geometric shapes. Halfway to the house was a wide fountain with a statue of a faceless human figure holding a mask in each hand. Water streamed from the eyes of one mask as if it were crying. The other mask bore an eerie, ear-to-ear grin.

They passed another statue, a lifelike rendition of a knight in armor. He was recoiling from something, arms up to shield himself, and his face was twisted with panic and desperation. The detail was stunningly precise.

The front doors of the mansion opened when they approached. This time, at the very least, there was a person waiting for them. Beyond the door stood a tall, thin butler dressed in black formal wear. He wore a white porcelain mask contoured to mimic a human face that left only his eyes exposed—his pupilless, dull gray eyes.

When Snow had first seen a Faceless, she'd assumed they were demons. Apparently they weren't, but that didn't make them any less unpleasant. They could look however they wanted but preferred their natural form whenever possible: slick, sinewy, gray skin. A smoothed-over face with no mouth or nose. Their hair was only blond, silver, or white. Just in case their looks didn't make being around them uncomfortable enough, they could also read minds.

Between the hair, the mask, and gloves, most of the creature's inhuman visage was obscured, but the masks left a bit of gray flesh visible. Snow tried not to look at it.

The Faceless stood rigidly with his hands folded behind his back. "Are you the contractors who reached out earlier today?"

"That's us," Pitch said.

The mask swiveled to inspect them all, one by one. Its eyes lingered on Snow, and she immediately wondered if it was listening to her thoughts. Just when she was about to confront him, the Faceless nodded. "I understand. Come with me. The Handler is expecting you."

The assassins followed the Faceless butler inside. The foyer was extravagantly decorated, with brilliant red tapestries rolling down from vaulted ceilings, alcoves housing suits of ornate, jeweled armor, and lush carpets over polished white floors. On the walls hung paintings depicting historical and mythological scenes. Everything was almost unnaturally clean and polished, and the stench of ammonia hung in the air.

A pair of spear-wielding guards flanked the central stairwell. Each of them wore a full suit of plate armor, with a helmet in the exact same shape as the butler's mask. A cleaning woman in a black dress walked past on her way to another part of the house, and she too wore the same mask.

"This is never not creepy," Pitch said in a not-so-quiet whisper.

Cull grunted.

If the butler took offense, nothing in his body language gave it away. He led them up the stairs and through the lavishly decorated hallways, their footsteps echoing in the otherwise silent house. Finally they reached their destination and were let into a large carpeted study.

The room was lit by a roaring fireplace that bathed the interior in deep orange light. The flames started to shrink when Snow first entered, but returned to normal strength when Pitch followed a second later. More guards were waiting in the room with the same masked helmets as the guards in the foyer. They stood at attention, flanking the door.

Sitting at a desk with a clear view was a caramel-skinned man dressed in a luxurious, deep red suit with a wide collar and golden trim that glinted in the firelight. Like everyone else in the mansion he wore a mask, though his was cut off at the nose and left his mouth and jaw exposed.

"Sir," the butler said, "these are the contractors who confirmed their acquisition of one of the targets."

"Thank you." The man spoke in a deep, honeyed voice. "That will be all."

The butler bowed deeply and exited the study, shutting the door behind him. At his desk, the Handler folded his hands in front of him, and leaned forward. "Do you have him?"

Cull threw the bag he'd been carrying to the floor and loosened the drawstring. Immediately, Brass began to wriggle out of the bag. He blinked as the light hit his eyes, blinding him after so long in darkness. He was gagged, with his wrists and ankles bound by manacles. He was still barefoot. Cull grabbed him by the shoulders and forced him down to his knees. Brass struggled and mumbled something into his gag, but failed to break free.

With a bit more squirming, he did get his gag out. He'd been working on that since waking up. With a defiant spark in his eyes, he craned his neck to glare over his shoulder at the assassins.

"I've got a pretty long list of complaints, but I think I'll start with the gag," Brass said. He smacked his tongue a few times, then spit. "Wool? Really? You couldn't have used silk?"

"Oh saints," Pitch muttered.

"Alive. Good," the Handler said, standing up. "Of course, I'll have to make sure that it's him."

"What's that supposed to mean?" Pitch asked. "He's right in front of you, what proof do you need?"

"As someone who's done business with *us* in the past, you should know firsthand that appearances can be deceiving," the Handler said.

Jury stepped forward. "Would you accept a testimony given under a prayer of truth?"

"That will not be necessary, god botherer," the Handler said. "It would only prove that you think it's really him. Or that he thinks so."

"Is there a reason I wouldn't think I'm me?" Brass asked.

Cull leaned over and socked Brass in the stomach, knocking the wind out of him. He doubled over, groaning. The Handler, unconcerned, addressed one of his guards.

"Bring the revealer."

The guard left and came back a minute later with an ivory rod a little more than a foot long, with the shape of an eye carved into the tip. The material had the same sheen to it as the skin of the Faceless themselves. The Handler took the rod gingerly and pointed it at Brass.

"What's that do?" Brass coughed.

A beam of white light shot from the eye at the tip of the rod, striking Brass in the chest. He lurched, his back arching involuntarily, and he let out a scream. Cull held him in place as he writhed until smoke started to curl off of his chest.

Snow remained motionless as she watched; didn't blink as Brass screamed in pain. She let the cold heart inside her take hold, let her emotions freeze over as she had dozens of times before. It always helped to clear her mind, helped her to focus or make a kill that much easier. Her eyes became almost pure white.

And so did her knuckles as she gripped her dagger.

Finally the Handler stopped pointing the rod, and the beam faded. Brass collapsed face-first on the floor, panting. Cull left him there. The Handler smiled and handed the rod back to the guard.

"We're satisfied. I apologize if you took any offense. The client has specifically requested the utmost certainty in these acquisitions," the Handler said. "So nice to see you, Brass."

"I'm sorry." Brass forced himself back up onto his knees. "I think my recent head trauma's made my memory a bit fuzzy. Do we know each other?"

The Handler smiled. "I suppose we've never officially met. I am the Handler."

"Well, that actually explains a lot then," Brass said. "Guess whoever organized this whole party is a little shy?"

"Shy and inexperienced," the Handler said. "The criminal underworld is an alien landscape to the client, so naturally we were employed to facilitate the details of your retrieval."

"Did you ever think about maybe just sending an invitation in the mail?" Brass asked. "I'm not a particularly expensive act to book these days."

"I'm afraid the client's business is too important to rely on your consent," the Handler said.

"Did you have to phrase it like that?"

Cull kicked Brass, and he collapsed again onto the floor, groaning. That seemed to shut him up for a moment. The Handler nodded.

"Well, you were true to your word. Two targets delivered."

Snow felt her stomach drop. They'd only brought one target. In an instant, she realized what was about to happen. Brass was right.

Snow drew both daggers and swept her leg in an arc across the floor. Ice spread out from her, rooting everyone to the spot. The doors of the study burst open, and more guards came rushing in.

Snow threw Companion Piece, embedding it straight into the eye socket of one guard's helmet. She held out her hand, and a moment later, the dagger tore itself free from the now dead guard's head and flew back to her hand. At the same time the dagger hit her palm, she felt a stabbing pain shoot up her back. A burning sensation filled her abdomen as a glowing hot blade came jutting out of her stomach. Standing behind her, readying his other sword, Pitch grinned.

"I've been waiting for this."

Snow elbowed Pitch in the stomach and stabbed behind her, forcing him back. His sword tore into her as he pulled it free, but almost immediately the wound froze over. If she were anyone else, she would have been dead.

Cull drove Charnel into the floor, and a shock wave rippled out from the blade, shattering the ice. Snow blinked out of sight, reappearing behind Cull. She slashed with the ferocity of a cornered animal. Everywhere her daggers hit, a thick layer of ice formed, slowly encasing him.

Then Jury finished saying a prayer.

All at once Snow felt her legs give out. She dropped to her hands and knees as an oppressive weight came down on top of her. It felt like her very sense of self was being crushed.

A thousand memories played over in her mind. Parents killed in front of their children. A lonely, pained creature talked into taking its own life.

The worst argument she'd ever had with Phoenix. Angel, lying bleeding in a barn because of her. The flash of white that wiped Relgen off the map.

Tears streamed down her face and froze on her cheeks. She couldn't breathe. Everything seemed like it was spinning and closing in on her. Deafening voices that all sounded like her shouted in her mind. They called her weak. They called her a monster. They called her spoiled. Pathetic. Lying. Murderer.

They mounted in number and volume until they became an incoherent din that drowned out everything else.

"Stop," she whimpered. "Please."

Jury wavered unsteadily on his feet, his own strength drained from calling on one of the deepest and most cutting prayers Adresta had entrusted him with. It reached deep into the soul of a person and buried them in the weight of their every regret. He had seen this prayer bring men and women to their knees, but Snow's response was a new low point for the victims of Adresta's judgment. The Jury reveled in it.

He was so preoccupied he forgot about Brass.

Still bound, Brass swung his legs around and took Jury's out from under him. As the cleric fell to the floor, Brass leapt to his feet and jumped on Jury's stomach. The cleric had the wind knocked out of him, and his concentration on the prayer dissipated.

Snow felt the weight lift off her, and the voices died down, but she was still disoriented and slow in getting up. Cull lunged for Brass, who dove down between his legs and slid across the ice to get away. He made it across the room to Pitch, who he promptly kicked in exactly the same spot he'd stabbed with his boot earlier.

Snow staggered to her feet. In that moment, everyone was focused on Brass. More guards were running down the hallway. Her head was still reeling from whatever Jury had done to her, and pain shot through her body from the sword wound her powers had yet to heal.

Brass locked eyes with her as Pitch and Cull closed in on him.

Snow grit her teeth, picked up her daggers and herself, and ran straight for the nearest window.

A layer of protective frost formed over her. Using the ice to shield herself from the glass, she dove through, shattering it. She blinked out of the air, reappearing some distance from the Handler's mansion. And then she kept running, not daring to look back. Before anyone had time to run to the window, she was gone.

Cull grabbed Brass by the shirt, lifted him into the air, and slammed him on the floor. His ears rang from the impact, and everything went fuzzy for a moment. He winced as Cull grabbed him by the hair and lifted his head up, but he didn't take his eyes off of the window Snow had jumped through.

There wasn't an ounce of resentment in his heart. After all, he probably would have done the same thing if he were in her shoes.

He'd taught her well.

"Run like hell, Snowflake," he whispered.

37

CHURCH

Arno materialized in the nave of the Church of the Guiding Saint in a flash of light. Even as the sight of the familiar walls brought a bit of relief, doubt crept into his mind. *Did I just do the right thing?* He stared down at his amulet, hoping that just maybe Beneger would be willing to offer input again.

He felt a pair of eyes on him, patiently watching, but the Guiding Saint didn't manifest, nor did he offer an answer. Arno half chuckled to himself despite the day he'd had. Leaving Phoenix by himself to figure things out on his own for a bit was certainly the Beneger thing to do, if nothing else. At any rate, the decision had been made, and he didn't have a way to go back on it. Whatever happened next was up to Phoenix.

Grappling with uncertainty, he expected to have trouble falling asleep. But he was more exhausted than he realized. As soon as he hit his bed, he was out. For a few blissful hours he rested, and the magic that suffused the church did its work. Worry melted away, tension in his muscles evaporated, and scrapes and bruises mended themselves.

Then, just a few hours into his sleep, Arno jerked as if he were slapped awake. He sat up, already brandishing his amulet in hand, and then blinked as he stared at the dark interior of his room. Nobody was around. The sun wasn't up yet. His heart pounded like he'd just had a nightmare, but he didn't remember having one. He stared at his amulet in bewilderment.

He could have sworn he'd left it on his desk before he'd gone to bed.

He sat in bed for a few minutes, collecting himself. His heart slowly returned to a normal pace, but a sense of unease remained, even when he made a conscious effort to quiet and clear his mind. After a moment he realized it was because he was feeling Beneger's unease, not his.

Slowly Arno made his way through the rest of the church, one hand clutching his amulet, the other resting on the hilt of Zealot. He heard something, a sound like someone rifling through cupboards, and followed it, doing his best to stay quiet. He navigated the dark halls by memory and the occasional light that came from underneath a door, not daring to use a prayer for light in case it gave him away.

The sound led him in the direction of the kitchen, and with every step he took, the feeling of Beneger's unease grew. Whatever was setting the saint off, Arno was getting closer to it. Candlelight leaked out from the kitchen as he approached, and Arno could clearly hear someone now. Bracing himself for anything, he rounded the corner.

"Bart?"

"Vicar?"

The young acolyte stood in the kitchen, bowl of dried fruit in one hand, candle in the other, looking confused and embarrassed. Arno released his grip on the sword.

"What are you doing awake?" he asked the boy.

"I couldn't sleep," Bart said sheepishly. "Then I got hungry. But Vicar, when did you get back?"

Arno briefly wondered if it was more appropriate to say, "late last night" or "early this morning," before he gave up and went with, "A few hours ago."

"Did something happen?"

"No. Well, not exactly. I just needed a rest, and I was able to make it back here for one."

"Did you fly back on that sail thing?"

"No—" Arno stopped, noting the look in Bart's eye. "Bart, were you spying on us when we left?"

Bart knew better than to try to lie to a vicar of the Guiding Saint, so he just changed the subject. "What about the freelancer? Is he here too?"

"No. He'll be back . . ." Arno considered his answer. ". . . later."

Bart nodded, not in understanding so much as in trust that whatever was happening, Arno knew best and was handling it.

Arno did his best to offer Bart a comforting smile, but he could still feel something was wrong. And it felt even closer now.

"Vicar? Is everything all right?"

Before Arno could answer, a woman skulked into the doorway dressed in piecemeal armor and wielding a mace. As soon as she spotted them, she yelled, "Found him!"

Arno gripped his amulet, ran forward, and shouted in the language of the gods, *"Fall, you who stands in my way!"* He grabbed the woman's shoulder with his free hand, and fatigue and pain tore through her body. Her eyes rolled back as she dropped to the floor, unconscious. Bart looked horrified.

"Did you just—"

"No," Arno interrupted, knowing what that looked like. "But we need to move, now."

Bounty hunters were here, in the church. They were here for him, but Brother Michael was a grim reminder that anyone in the vicinity was in danger. He needed to get Bart somewhere safe. Sending him off on his own might send him right into a bounty hunter's path.

"For Atreus," he spoke into his amulet.

The amulet vanished in a flash of light, and Arno's traveling clothes were replaced with a breastplate and chainmail, the amulet itself now embedded in the breastplate. Bart stared, awestruck. Knowing time was short, Arno grabbed the boy by the wrist and started running.

They ran into more intruders in the nave. There were at least half a dozen, though Arno didn't stop to try and count them. Their eyes were hungry, but their stances were uncertain. Amateurs. Inexperienced, but still plenty dangerous if underestimated.

He doubled back, trying to go the way they came. In the doorway, shadows coalesced into the shape of a man, then solidified into a familiar visage—the Fell user from before.

The Fellblade stood blocking their escape path. He rubbed his hands together, and when he pulled them apart, ink-black tendrils formed, hardened, and shaped themselves into a single object—a wicked sword made of pure shadow.

"Just the man I wanted to see," he said.

"I don't want to fight," Arno offered. "Let him leave, and we can talk about this."

One of the intruders laughed, sparks dancing across his fingers. "I wouldn't want to fight me either. But come on. You should try."

"Fight implies it's fair," the Fellblade said. "This won't be."

Arno could feel his blood rushing in his ears. Adrenaline burned in his veins. For the last seven years, he'd used Renalt's power exclusively to heal and guide others. But that was not all Beneger had empowered him to do.

If they wouldn't listen to reason, he was going to have to do this the old-fashioned way.

Elijah Menchaca

"Take him," the Fellblade ordered.

Before most of them could take a step, Arno reached into their minds and, with a prayer, took hold of them. Instantly, every bounty hunter in the room froze in place. Slowly, the Fellblade's face curled into a glare. Everything felt so slow. Cripplingly, maddeningly slow.

For his part, Arno's head was splitting with pain. The prayer was meant to hold one person. Using it on so many at once was so taxing, it was all he could do to maintain it.

"Bart, run!"

Bart did not argue, but bolted deeper into the church. As soon as he was out of sight, Arno dropped the holding prayer. Immediately, the bounty hunters collapsed in on him. With two words his skin became as hard as stone, and the blows his armor didn't catch skipped harmlessly off of him.

He grabbed a man's arm mid-swing and drained his strength until the man fell to the floor, too weak to stand. He shouted, "Get back!" in a booming voice, and everyone backed away, supernaturally compelled.

With more space, Arno drew Zealot from its sheath. The blade was a pure white, impossibly smooth material, and it shone like the sun in the dim light of the nave. The sword hummed in his hand, spreading warmth through every muscle in his body. Released from its scabbard, the sword's mind awakened, taking in the world through Arno's eyes and quickly understanding the situation. It felt particular disgust at the sight of the Fellblade, and it spoke in Arno's mind with an almost gleeful rage.

For years I have waited! Leave this to me!

The bounty hunters charged again, and Arno, sharing control of his body with Zealot, proceeded to take them apart. The sword used his senses, but its perception was unbound from his, letting it catch things he missed. Arno deflected attacks from one side while Zealot steered him to parry anything coming from the other. The attacks they didn't block bounced harmlessly off of Arno's skin.

In between deft moves with Zealot, Arno lashed out with prayers, draining his opponents until they collapsed from pain and fatigue. As he fought, a golden, translucent duplicate of Zealot materialized in the air and began attacking anyone Arno wasn't focused on.

When the hunters formed a tight-enough circle to actually have a chance at overwhelming him, Arno channeled a new prayer, and wisps of white light poured out of the eye sockets of all his opponents and concentrated into the amulet in his breastplate.

"What happened?"

"I can't see!"

The bounty hunters stumbled and swung blindly, and between Arno, Zealot, and its spectral copy, they went down, quick and easy. Only the Fellblade moved undaunted, even though Arno knew he'd taken his sight too.

Fell magic is darkness incarnate! He does not need to see to fight!

Once Zealot pointed this out, Arno almost felt stupid for not realizing it sooner. Blind, the Fellblade's skill was still a match for Arno and Zealot. He moved like liquid, melting into the shadows and reforming to launch his attacks. But Arno held a clear advantage. Every time their swords clashed, the Fellblade's would flicker and sputter in his hands. The Fell magic struggled to maintain itself under Zealot's divine light, and the sword relished its encroaching victory over a power it despised.

Be purged, foul devotion! Feel the wrath of the noblest gods!

"Skip, tag in!" Fellblade shouted as he dissolved into a shadow again.

"Finally!"

Arno barely turned around in time to see the sparking bounty hunter leap from cover. He raised Zealot just as Skip unleashed a bolt of lightning from his hands. The bolt arced off Zealot, and the sword sang in Arno's hands. He reeled from the hit, even though he'd blocked it. His mouth tasted like copper, and the air reeked of ozone. Tendrils of electricity rolled across Skip's body as he rushed forward, throwing another bolt of lightning. Arno blocked with Zealot again, feeling his whole arm go numb.

He needed to end this before one of those actually hit him. Seeing as Skip was coming at him from the other side of the room, Arno took a chance on a particular long prayer, all while he kept Zealot raised to block any incoming lightning.

The closer Skip got, the harder the lightning hit. The air crackled, and hairs on Arno's body stood on end. He kept talking. Another lightning bolt blocked, and Arno felt his tongue go numb. He hoped a prayer still counted if he didn't pronounce the words quite right.

Just before Skip got close enough to touch him, Arno finished the prayer.

The altar to Renalt at the front of the nave lit up as if it were a sun, and beams of light shot down from the ceiling directly on every bounty hunter in the nave. It only lasted a second, but that was all it took. Skip dropped to the floor, smoking. He let out a whimper. Small sparks still danced across his body, but he stayed down.

Glory to Renalt! Victory is ours again!

"Did you actually think you could attack a cleric in his own church?" Arno berated him.

"I liked our chances."

The Fellblade staggered back into the nave, looking haggard but still standing. And in his arms, struggling but unable to break free, was Bart. The Fellblade held a dagger made of shadow to the boy's throat.

"Drop the sword and the amulet," he ordered.

"Don't!" Bart pleaded.

Do not! He is weak, and I can strike him down from where we stand!

"Or try something. Summon that ghost sword, say a prayer. See if it's faster than me."

Arno clenched his jaw as he weighed his options. A prayer was out of the question. Zealot made him fast. Maybe even fast enough to cut the

Fellblade down. But if he was wrong, Bart was dead, and he didn't know if Fell magic would block a resurrection.

Do not yield to this abomination! Attack!

The arm holding *Zealot* shook as the sword fought for control. Before it could take it, Arno released his grip, and it clattered to the floor. Bart's eyes filled with shame as he watched, too terrified to do anything.

"The amulet too."

Arno complied, pulling the amulet free from his breastplate. In a flash, his armor vanished, replaced by his normal clothes. Arno used it one last time, reaching out with his soul to find Bart's.

Everything's going to be okay. I promise.

Vicar? Is that you?

Arno let the amulet fall to the ground, severing the connection. "Now let him go. It's me you want."

"You holy devoted are so predictable," the Fellblade said.

He released Bart and threw his shadow dagger straight into Arno's chest. The dagger remained there for a moment before it seemed to melt into him. Arno felt something inside him pop, and everything suddenly felt cold. The world seemed to pull itself out from underneath him. He dropped to his knees, suddenly finding it hard to breathe.

"Vicar!"

38

RELGEN

B rass had always wondered what it would feel like to be on a sinking skyship. If he accomplished nothing else today, he would at least be able to check that off his bucket list. *Rogue Imperia* was the crown jewel of the Corsan navy—the largest Old World skyship ever recovered.

And it was falling out of the sky.

Brass stumbled down the stairs to the ship's lower deck, doing his best to keep his footing as it listed and groaned beneath his boots. The sounds of fighting had stopped, which either meant all of the cultists were dead, or his company was. The lightstone illuminating the sky-blue wooden interior of the ship flickered again as the ship lurched, and Brass finally lost his balance, tumbling the rest of the way down the steps.

Thankfully, as he reached the cargo hold, the only bodies he saw on the floor belonged to people he didn't care about. The other Starbreakers were all still standing, gathered around Phoenix as he hunched over an angrily sparking artifact shaped like a giant ceramic lotus flower.

"I'm here!" Brass announced, picking himself off the floor. "Did we win?"

"They armed it," Phoenix said, not looking up from his work.

The spellforger's hands were moving furiously, tugging and prodding the tendrils of white light that curled off the artifact as his bracers threw glyphs in his face that only he knew how to read. The others watched, not moving, not speaking. Nobody else even acknowledged Brass.

"Can you fix it?" Angel asked.

"Dispel discs didn't work," Phoenix said, not stopping. "I'm trying to dismantle its magic, but it's rebuilding everything I try to take apart."

"Phoenix," Church said. "What's the radius of this thing?"

Phoenix didn't answer as he continued struggling with the artifact. His eyes were hidden behind his goggles, but the desperation on his face was still plain to see in his scrunched brow and frantic movements. He muttered incomprehensibly to himself as he worked, pausing only to growl in frustration or slap one of his tools.

The artifact he was fighting against was the Ending, an Old World weapon Phoenix had tracked through the historical records to the mountains outside of Relgen. The chance to examine an unmatched piece of Old World technology had been too good to pass up for the spellforger. Despite some recent disagreements and misgivings among the company, things might have gone smoothly, if the weapon hadn't been stolen by the one group the Starbreakers had never expected to worry about again: the Cult of Stars. But evidently, however many the company had killed the day they earned their name, they had missed some. And everything had spiraled out of control from there.

"Phoenix?"

"The city, Church," Phoenix barked. "This thing could take out the entire city, now shut up and let me focus!"

The color drained from Church's face, and he clutched his amulet for comfort. "We need to get to the control room, steer the ship away from Relgen."

Brass bit his lip. "Uh. One problem with that plan."

"What?"

"I sort of blew up the control room."

"You what?!" came a chorus of voices from his companions.

Brass threw up his hands. "Hey, it was me or the room and every cultist in it. It seemed like a pretty obvious call at the time!"

"I said shut up!" Phoenix shouted over his shoulder.

A labored, wet chuckle caught their ears from the corner of the room.

Sitting propped against a wall, shirt bloody from a stab wound, was a single cultist yet to breathe his last. The star carving on his forehead seemed to be splitting open, like it was still fresh. He flashed the Starbreakers a bright red smile.

"I suppose you really should have found better help," he taunted.

The words froze Phoenix in place. His mutterings went silent. Jaw slack, he turned around, finally trying to get a good look at the cultist. He was a young pasty-skinned man with a shock of red hair and cruel green eyes. None of the Starbreakers had ever met this man in their lives. And yet, there was recognition in the cultist's eyes.

"What?" Phoenix asked, dazed.

Those words. They were last thing Phoenix said to the Cult of Stars' leader before Snow had killed him.

How did he know those words?

The dying cultist cackled, his laughter quickly decaying into a choking fit. The rings and tendrils of energy coming off the Ending grew brighter and larger, making it difficult to even look at the thing. Church was no expert on the workings of Old World weaponry, but he knew a bad sign when he saw one.

"Phoenix!"

The cleric's voice snapped Phoenix out of his trance, and he turned his attention back to the artifact. His hands started working even faster now, but his movements were different. Before, they'd been precise, fluid, purposeful. Now, Phoenix was working in fits and starts, his hands constantly freezing with uncertainty. His mutterings had turned to whimpers.

"I can fix this," Phoenix said, more to himself than anyone else. "I . . ." The more he worked, the brighter the artifact got. The temperature in the cargo hold climbed upward at a steady pace, as the whole room began to be swallowed by white light.

"Phoenix?"

"Come on . . . come on!" the spellforger was ignoring them all again. It was impossible to see him, but they could all hear it. Whatever fight he was having with the artifact, he was losing. And they were running out of time. The heat became sweltering for everyone but Snow, and the Ending let out a high-pitched whine.

Then, Church grabbed his amulet and spoke a single word of prayer.

The heat vanished in an instant, replaced with a shock of freezing cold. The cargo hold of Rogue Imperia was gone, replaced by mountain air and a snowy ridge beneath their feet. The others looked around, briefly disoriented.

Church's prayer had deposited them on a mountain ridge overlooking the city of Relgen from the north, just outside a tiny rundown shack that bore the sun disk symbol of Saint Beneger above its door. Even from this distance, the fortress city's walls towered above the cliffside it had been built into. The heraldry of the kingdom was still clearly distinct on the banners that waved from its turrets. And hovering above the city, slowly drifting down toward it, was Rogue Imperia herself.

Phoenix remained hunched over, his fingers groping empty air. With shaky hands, he tore his goggles off his face, and stared straight at Church.

"What did you do?" His voice was hollow.

Church shook his head. "I'm sorry."

"What did you do?!" Phoenix roared, finding his voice and with it a burning fury.

He shot to his feet, stormed toward Church, and grabbed him by the shirt collar. Before either man could do anything else, a sound like shrieking, high-

pitched thunder tore through the air, loud enough for them all to feel it in their chests. Rogue Imperia was completely enveloped in a blinding ball of white light that spread out to engulf the entire city of Relgen and the terrace farms of the surrounding mountainsides. For several seconds, the only thing any of them could hear was ringing in their ears, and the only thing they could see was white.

The world slowly came back into focus, and from their position on the ridge, they had a prime view of what had become of the city.

The color of every terrace farm surrounding the city had changed from verdant green to burnt umber. What few alpine trees had managed to take root at the city's elevation had turned amber. Rogue Imperia, still listing in the air, finally collided with part of the city's walls, cracking itself in half before detonating in another explosion that sent a pillar of smoke and debris into the air. Dozens of black dots fell from the sky. After a second, Brass realized they were birds, dropping dead over the city.

"What . . . did it do?" Brass asked.

"It's dead," Phoenix stated, never taking his eyes off the city. "Every single living thing in that city is dead."

Brass's eyes told him Phoenix had to be wrong. Except for where Rogue Imperia had crashed and the dead crops, Relgen looked fine. It was all still standing, right there, walls and buildings intact. Banners still proudly displayed. It looked pristine. At least until he really started to look at the city, and realized it was too pristine. The entire city was perfectly still. No carts moving in the streets. No movement of crowds milling outside the gates. Nothing. The entire city had gone motionless in a flash of light. Any sign of life was gone.

When it finally, really sank in that he was looking at a dead city, his first reaction was that there had to be something they could do. The Ending was magic. Magic always had a loophole, or reset, or do over. And they always figured it out or found it right when they needed it.

They were the Starbreakers. They'd been freelancing since they were teenagers. They'd rediscovered entire fields of magical study. Founded churches. Killed things that weren't supposed to exist. They were the heroes of more places than he could remember the names of. This wasn't how things were supposed to go.

Except this was supposed to be the part where Phoenix pulled a daring, impossible plan to reverse the Ending's effects out of his ass and they rushed off to save the day, and he wasn't doing that. He was just standing there, anguish in his eyes.

Brass's stomach churned as he watched the mouths of his companions hang open. Tears welled in Church's eyes, and Snow had to look away from the city. One by one, it finally dawned on each of them.

They'd lost.

"Oh my gods," Church whispered.

"I could have stopped it," Phoenix said.

Angel shook her head. "Phoenix . . ."

"I could have stopped it!" He whirled back around, jabbing a finger into Church's chest. "You pulled me away before I could!"

"I got us out of there!" Church defended. "You weren't going to stop it in time, and I wasn't going to let you die trying."

"Oh, so you're an artifact expert now?"

"No, but I am an expert on you," Church retorted. There was an edge to his voice that Brass had never heard before. Brought on by pain and grief. "I know what you look like when you have things under control, and you didn't."

"I had that!" Phoenix bellowed. "I could have stopped the Ending. You stopped me. Every death in that city is on your head!"

"I'm not the one who wanted to dig up the Ending in the first place!" Church snapped.

Brass was starting to get nervous. He knew what this was. Church and Phoenix were both too golden-hearted to take this many dead people lying down. They needed something, someone to be angry at. But the Cult of Stars was already dead. Gone in the same blast that killed Relgen. He knew firsthand that Phoenix could snap if he was pushed too hard. But now it was looking like even Church had found a breaking point.

"You're right. You didn't want to be here," Phoenix said. "You haven't wanted to be here for months. You want to quit freelancing and go be a knight or bishop so you can sit around and judge the rest of us. Your head's not in the game, your heart's not in this company, and that's why people are dead."

"Hey, back off!" Angel yelled. "You wanna be mad at someone, start with the dumbass who blew the control room of a ship that was flying over a city!"

"Hey, at I least I got my bad guys!" Brass defended himself. He may have understood what the others were feeling, but he wasn't about to take more than his fair share of blame. "You were the one who let the guy with the damn thing get away and steal the ship!"

"They never would have been able to steal it if Snow hadn't killed the one guy who could've grounded it!" Angel redirected.

"How was I supposed to know who their hostage was? He had a bag over his head!"

"You could keep your message coil on when you disappear on us," Phoenix said.

Snow's eyebrows shot up as Phoenix jumped in to pile on accusations. Angel or Church giving her crap, she was used to. But Phoenix was different. Or, he had been.

"Oh, I get it," Snow said. "You always had my back when I was still sleeping with you. But now that that's done, you're fine blaming your mistakes on me."

"Okay!" Brass stepped between all of them before this could get any worse. "He fucked up, you fucked up, how about we just admit we all fucked up and be a pile of fuckups? Wow, that's an image."

"Is this a fucking joke to you?" Angel asked.

"No. Barring maybe a touch of morbid irony?"

That was the wrong thing to say. With a growl, Angel shoved him in the chest, sending him flying through the air and straight for the edge of the ridge. Snow reached out, and the frozen powder around them responded, whipping itself into a wall that stopped him from going over. With another flourish, more of the ice swirled around her body before lashing out to encase Angel.

Angel stared at the ice encasing her body for a moment before leveling a glare at the assassin. "Snow. Let me go. Now."

"Calm down first," Snow ordered.

"Both of you—all of you need to calm down," Church interrupted. "We are missing the bigger picture here."

Church said something else, but Brass wasn't paying attention to him. Lying in the snow, he was watching two powder kegs about to explode. Only barely restrained in ice, Angel's eyes had already begun to glow. And standing next to Church, Phoenix was fuming. For all the cleric's wisdom, he had made a colossal mistake—it was never a good idea to tell an angry person to calm down.

A look of cold, misdirected fury set into Phoenix's face, and he cracked Church across the face as hard as he could with the back of his hand, cutting him off mid-admonishment. In the same breath, he drew his wand from its holster, doubled the cleric over with a low-powered blast to the stomach, and cycled it to strike him in the back of the head with the lightning-stunner setting. At the same time, particles of ice rained down as Angel burst out of Snow's encasing ice and charged.

The hells broke loose as the Starbreakers turned on each other. Snow moved like a whirlwind, her eyes pure white as her ice danced across Angel's skin. Church met Phoenix with Zealot in one hand and his amulet in the other. Brass darted between them all, trying to keep anyone from landing a hit they wouldn't be able to take back.

After getting yelled at or attacked for his troubles, restraint gave out, and even Brass decided the best solution to the mess was just to leave everyone so wounded they couldn't keep fighting.

They fought, all of them, until they forgot what they were even fighting about. Just that they were angry and in pain and needed to let it out.

Everything came out. Every argument, every misunderstanding, every failure. They threw out whatever words they thought would hurt the most. Murderer. Coward. Scum. Whore. They used fists. They used weapons. They drew blood.

It all came to a head as Snow was dropped to the ground by Angel driving her axe's handle into the side of her knee. Her eyes blazed, and her halo burned with unchecked fury as she raised her axe into the air.

Maybe she was going to embed it in the ground to prove a point. Maybe she was going to throw it to the side. Maybe she was about to take Snow's head off.

Whatever she would have done, she never got the chance because Phoenix saw it and, without thinking, turned his wand on her. A low-powered blast wouldn't have stopped Angel. So he let loose with every ounce of power his wand's cells had.

The blast tore into Angel's clavicle in a spray of blood, and she scattered snow in every direction as she fell to the ground, staining everything around her red. And for a moment, as she lay motionless, everyone froze. As ugly as the fight had gotten, seeing one of them actually lying bleeding and broken on the ground was enough to shock the rest of them to their senses.

Phoenix was horrified. His wand clattered to the ground at his feet, and his face went ashen.

Then Angel started glowing again. Brighter than she had for the whole fight. Steam coiled off her body as the snow around her liquified, and she forced herself to her feet. Her eyes had been completely replaced with burning orbs of divine rage. All traces of rationality were gone from her face. In that moment, she was pure, righteous fury.

"Angel, don't!" Church shouted a moment too late.

She roared with twin voices, and beams of light fired out from her eyes straight toward Phoenix. He threw up a force shield from his bracer, only to be knocked off his feet by Angel's sheer power. The beams scattered across Phoenix's shield, carving deep gashes in the surrounding granite. One of the deflected beams struck Church dead in the chest, and he screamed.

His cries did for Angel what her fall had done for everyone else, and the light coming off her immediately extinguished as Church fell back into the snow, smoke and steam curling off his chest. A huge portion of the front of his breastplate was gone, its edges still glowing orange, all armor beneath it had been burned away, exposing his angry red, burned, and blistering chest. If he hadn't been wearing enchanted armor, he would have been dead.

"Oh my gods, Church!"

She raced toward him, only for Church to throw a hand up before she could reach him.

"Stop!" he grunted through clenched teeth. "Just stop."

With a trembling hand, he reached out to scoop his fallen amulet out of the snow and spoke a healing prayer, knitting his flesh back together even as his nerves still remembered the pain. His breaths came out in shaky, ragged fits as he tried to fight off going into shock.

". . . Church?" Angel's voice cracked as she pleaded for him to look at her.

But when he did, there was nothing but fear and pain in his eyes. Everyone else was wearing a similar expression.

"I . . . I didn't mean to . . ." she stammered.

"What did you mean to?" Phoenix demanded. That blast had been meant for him.

"I . . ." For a single moment, Angel was utterly mortified. But as her own chest ached and screamed in pain, that feeling was quickly replaced by indignation. "No, fuck off. You don't get to fucking put this on me when you shot first."

"You were going to kill someone!"

"So you tried to kill me?" Angel demanded. "The fuck was I supposed—no."

She cut through the air with her hand. She refused to have this conversation. She had nothing to defend. Nothing to apologize for. She had gotten too much judgment and fear from her life before the Starbreakers. She would not take it from them too.

"No," she repeated. "Fuck this. Fuck all of you. I'm done."

"What?" Brass asked.

She turned her back to them instead of answering, grabbed her axe off the ground, and without another word walked away.

"Angel! Hey, where are you going? The closest city just got exterminated! Angel?" Brass called after her. She didn't respond.

Snow stared at her feet for a few seconds before shaking her head. "I can't believe I'm agreeing with her."

Brass spun around, all thoughts of Angel gone from his mind. "What?"

"Don't look for me," she warned them, before blinking out of sight—gone.

"Snow?"

Brass looked around, knowing that she couldn't have gotten far with just a blink. But for the life of him, he couldn't see her. He never could . . . when she didn't want to be found. He kicked the snow at his feet.

"Damn it," he said. "Okay, well, we've got to go after both of them, I guess. Who wants which girl?"

Phoenix and Church both stared at him, neither saying anything.

"Guys?" Brass prompted. "We can't just let them leave, right?"

"Just shut up, Brass," Phoenix said.

The duelist's shoulders sagged as Phoenix and Church both wordlessly hauled themselves out of the snow. With a sullen, bitter look on his face, Phoenix dug his sky surfer out of his bag and mounted it. He cast his glance back on the men one last time, his eyes a storm of pain and regret, and then he flew off. Church limped into the tiny shack on the ridge, angry tears rolling down his face. Brass remained where he was, looking in turn in the direction that each of his companions had left in.

The sun was going down, and it was getting cold.

39
PAIN

B rass woke up exhausted and aching in every part of his body. His arms felt like they were going numb, and his mouth tasted like copper. His bare feet scraped against a rough stone floor, and when he stirred, chains rattled. Shackles around his wrists held his arms above his head.

He couldn't see anything. He wasn't sure if it was pitch-black from lack of light or if he'd been blinded. He'd heard stories that a severe-enough beating could do that. So could being stabbed in the eyes, but for all the injuries he could feel, it didn't feel like anyone had done that to him. Yet.

The sound of his chains didn't travel far. Which meant it was a small room, mostly if not completely bare. Walls were stone too. At least the one he was anchored to was.

A dungeon. I haven't been in a dungeon in years.

"Anybody else around?" Brass called out.

No response. He tried a few more times just to be sure, without any change in results. On one hand, it was disappointing. He got lonely easily, and bored even easier. Someone to talk to would have been great. Someone who knew where they were and what was going to happen to them now would have been even better.

No such luck, it would seem.

Well. Not getting any younger.

Brass wriggled against the wall, trying to figure out which, if any, of his tools were still on his person. He couldn't feel any of them, which was a problem. He could always break a few bones to slip out, but he wanted to avoid that if he could.

He decided to play the waiting game. Sooner or later someone was bound to come check on him. They'd gone to all the trouble of having him brought in alive. Presumably it was because they wanted something from him.

When they came to get it, he just might get a chance to escape.

Or maybe they just wanted the satisfaction of knowing he was rotting in their basement and nobody was coming to check on him.

He'd give it a few hours.

He drummed his knuckles on the stone wall behind him for a bit. Scratched the back of his leg with his foot. Chewed his tongue. Tried to count to sixty and got bored at thirty-five.

It was eerily quiet. His chains rattled when he moved. His feet scuffed at the dirt on the floor. His clothes wrinkled when he shifted. He counted heartbeats until he realized he was just counting to sixty again.

He tried humming, and it put him in a musical mood. Within a few minutes, he'd started singing to himself, working his way through his library of drinking songs and half-remembered operas. There was one show he actually still had a pretty good memory of. A show about a human who fell in love with a forest elf that he saw about thirty times while the Starbreakers worked security at an opera house.

He was pretty sure he could sing that show from memory. Not having anything else to do, he gave it a shot.

Three songs in, he finally heard footsteps, and he snapped back to reality. He did his best to stand up straight, even as his stiff muscles protested. Metal hinges creaked, and he was blinded by a sudden flood of light.

There was nothing but white, then spots, and then finally his eyes adjusted enough to see in front of him.

Oh good. Those still work.

A short man in sleeveless chain mail stood in the doorway, holding a backpack in one hand and a lantern in the other. Two shortswords were sheathed on his right side. The lantern was harshly bright, revealing Brass's prison.

It was small, like he'd expected. The door of the cell was solid iron, which just seemed like overkill. There were bits of straw scattered around the floor that he hadn't noticed before. There were also multiple very old bloodstains.

"I don't suppose you're here to break me out?" Brass asked.

"No."

"Well, didn't hurt to ask. Interrogation then?"

The man set the lantern and backpack down and cracked his knuckles. Toned arms crisscrossed with scars rippled as he flexed. If the circumstances were different, Brass might have been turned on.

"Yes."

"Well, all right," Brass said, as if he were conceding a game of cards. "Full disclosure, my memory is not what it should be for a man my age. I may have over-experimented with mind-altering substances in my youth."

The man said nothing for a moment, just eyed him up and down. "They said you'd be difficult."

"I guess my reputation precedes me." Brass smirked. "I don't believe we've had the pleasure of being introduced, though. Who might you be?"

"I'm asking questions. Not you."

"Oh sure, ask away. I'm not trying to pry, just after your name."

"Why?"

"Well, interrogation is a lot like fighting. It's an intimate thing. Hate to have to do it with a stranger."

The man considered Brass, who gave the most disarming smile he could muster. Eventually, the man grunted. "Silas."

"Pleasure to meet you, Silas."

"Were you a member of the freelancer company called the Starbreakers?"

Brass stared up at the ceiling for a few minutes, pretending to think. "That's a very good question. Who's to say, really?"

Silas grumbled something, and Brass chuckled.

"You don't need to resist questioning," Silas said. "We are not villains. We simply need information."

"A thousand apologies then," Brass said. "You'll forgive the misconception. I think I got confused when you hired a pack of killers to hunt down me, my friends, and a bunch of other people I don't care about."

He shook his wrists, which were still shackled above his head. "Also this whole thing. Seriously, I think I'm starting to chafe."

"It had to be done. Time is short."

"Time for what?"

Silas narrowed his eyes, realizing he was allowing Brass to ask questions again. Brass felt a twinge of respect and frustration. Silas was clever. Paid attention.

"If you make this harder than it has to be, I'll have to be more forceful," Silas warned.

"Don't threaten me with a good time."

Silas kneeled down and rummaged through his backpack, producing a series of tools and jars, one by one.

After setting aside a few of them, he selected a short, jagged-edged blade.

"If you don't answer my next question, I will hurt you," Silas said. There was no malice in his voice. No anger or frustration. Only resolute focus. "I will hurt you every time you don't answer, and I will make it worse every time I do."

A wicked grin spread across Brass's face.

"During your time with the Starbreakers, you encountered artifacts known as Servitor Hearts. How many times did you encounter these artifacts?"

"When you've stolen as many hearts as I have, you tend to lose count."

Silas swiped his blade across Brass's chest. The jagged edges bit, caught, and tore as the blade dragged across the skin, leaving a ragged wound. Brass howled and threw his head back, and his breathing turned to panting as he struggled to recover from the sudden burst of pain.

Silas's expression hardened. He took no pleasure in this. "This will only get worse."

Brass clenched his teeth and sucked a breath in. His chest burned with pain as he did. "This was one of my favorite shirts."

"How did Phoenix know how to drain the Hearts from the Servitor at Loraine?"

"A wizard did it."

Another cut, just below the first one. Brass screamed again, and his body gave out from underneath him. If not for the chains holding him by the arms, he'd have collapsed to the floor. He let out a whoop as he struggled to catch his breath.

"I tell you, there's nothing like being tortured to get the blood flowing." Brass laughed until the laugh broke down into a grimace. "Oh. No, but really, that's a lot of blood. I've only got so much of that."

Silas set aside the jagged blade and picked up a ceramic jar. He took off the jar's lid and held it for Brass to see its contents. Iron filings. Brass glanced at them and then down at the open wounds on his chest. He gave Silas a nod of understanding.

"How did Snow receive her powers from the Heart of Ice?"

"Hang on." Brass struggled to get his legs back underneath him to stand under his own strength. "I'm so sorry, I can usually last longer than this, but there were three guys before you who completely wore me out. What was your question?"

"Your companion Snow absorbed the power of the Heart of Ice," Silas said. "How did this happen? Where? Was it intentional?"

Brass stood as straight as he could, chest out, head held high. "She won it in a card game."

Silas reached with a gloved hand into the jar of iron filings, took a large pinch of them, and threw them into the open wounds on Brass's chest. Brass's scream filled the room and echoed out into the hallway beyond. His whole body shook. The worst part was that the pain didn't stop. Not really. It just kept burning, and stinging, and every shiver of pain only seemed to agitate everything, and cause the filings to burrow deeper into his flesh.

"Oh yeah!" Brass shouted. "Now we're cooking with grease! Fuck! You know, maybe it's the blood loss talking, but you, sir, are a credit to your craft. I can't actually think straight, and I'm pretty sure if I stop talking, I'll start crying. Oh, damn you, damn, shit, sound a rusted corkscrew, ow!"

Silas waited for Brass to quiet down. It took a few minutes. And he was right. He did cry. No sobbing to his credit, but tears ran down his face in streams.

"If you answer, I can make this stop," Silas said. "I was a battlefield doctor once. I can heal what I've done. Make the pain go away. Release you. Just answer the questions."

"Rim a chuck."

"This information is needed to save lives. More than you could ever count."

"Okay. You know what? I think I see the problem." Brass planted his feet again. He hadn't even noticed them giving out on him this time. "You're missing the point. I don't care . . . if you're trying to bring Renalt to climax. I'm not telling you a damn thing about any of my old companions. So, if you're having fun right now, then by all means, torture away." Brass's friendly smile hardened into a glare of grim determination. "But if you're actually hoping to get anything out of me, save us both some time and either kill me or let me go."

Silas shook his head. A part of him was frustrated. It was difficult to reason with Brass without discussing things he had been sworn to never reveal. Even barring that, Brass's behavior irritated him. Making this into a game. Resisting for the sake of resisting.

But he had a job to do. And Brass had left him no choice but to do it. He reached for the next tool.

40

ON THE
RUN

R uby felt like the world was ending. She'd been getting directions to Akers when she spotted Brass hovering over a man. He'd appeared so suddenly, like he'd been there the whole time and she'd only just noticed them. But before she could say a word to him, the seven hells broke loose. First, Cull showed up and seemed to destroy something with every swing. Then Pitch arrived, and quickly went to work setting the entire Stays on fire.

That was when she ran, and she barely slowed down all the way to Akers.

The Lilac was gone, Olwin was on fire, and she had no idea if Brass had made it out in one piece. She was out of her depth and alone. All she knew was that a murderous pyromaniac was on the loose and out for blood, and there was at least one other person on his shit list. Brass's friend needed to know what was happening, what was coming for him. He might even know what to do about it.

Everything she'd ever heard about glintchasers said that it was a bad idea to get mixed up with them, but at this point, she was pretty sure she was already in too deep. And at any rate, she didn't have any better ideas.

There weren't many houses in Akers, but there were just enough that checking each of them one by one was going to take too long. But there was a place near the center of it all that looked like a tavern, and taverns were always a decent place to learn about the neighborhood. If anybody was going to be able to point her toward Phoenix, they'd be there.

She turned a few heads on the way in. Even at a distance, she looked like a mess. Soot clung to her clothes, her hair was a tangle of frizz and dirt, and her face was red from exertion. By now, the smoke rising from the city was visible, which only fueled people's curiosity and imaginations when they saw her. She didn't see Phoenix though, and everybody seemed more keen to give her space than approach her, so she continued her beeline for the tavern.

She finally paused to catch her breath once she barged through the doors. As soon as she did, the adrenaline that had been propelling her the last several miles gave out, and she collapsed onto the closest chair she could see. It was almost deathly quiet inside, but it took her several labored breaths before she realized that everyone inside was staring slack-jawed at her.

"Does anyone know," she panted, "where I can find Phoenix?"

The big-bellied Gypic man behind the counter looked concerned at the question, but before he could say anything, a woman carrying a small infant stepped forward.

"Why are you looking for him?"

The woman looked Ruby up and down, trying to get a sense of her while Ruby did the same to her. The questioning look in her eye, the baby on her chest, the way her interest piqued the moment Ruby said Phoenix's name. She knew a suspicious spouse when she saw one. Normally when she met them, it was when they came to Lilac to ask pointed questions about what their partners had been doing behind their backs, but Ruby didn't get that sense from this one. She was looking for something else.

"There are these guys in the city," Ruby tried to explain, still short of breath. "They came after Brass, and there was fire, and I think they're coming here—"

"You saw Brass?" the woman interrupted. "He was at the fire in the city?"

Ruby nodded.

The woman's gaze darted around the room, to the baby she was holding, to the door, and back to Ruby. She looked like she was suddenly in a much bigger hurry than she'd been a second ago, and Ruby swore she saw the green of her eyes begin to swirl like storm clouds. When the woman fixed her stare back on Ruby, her eyes were downright crackling, and growing brighter green by the second.

"You're coming with me."

41

COMEBACK

Shooting pain gripped Arno's chest as he desperately took stock of the situation. The Fellblade loomed over him, grinning victoriously. Bart wasn't being held anymore, but he was still here, still in danger. Desperate to keep him safe, Arno lunged for his amulet, and spoke the words of a prayer to hold the Fellblade's mind again.

The Fellblade laughed.

Something was wrong. Arno could feel it. It was like being naked. Something was missing from him, something vital. His amulet, which usually gave him comfort, felt like cold, dead metal in his hands. Sweat formed on his brow, and his chest tightened. It was getting even harder to breathe.

"What's the matter, god botherer? No one answering?"

Arno said a healing prayer, like he had a thousand times before. Nothing happened. No feeling of Renalt's power restoring him. No hint of Beneger's presence. The dagger had severed his connection to his saint.

For the first time since he was a child, Arno felt completely alone.

Tears in his eyes, Bart balled his hands into fists. He was about to do something stupid.

"Bart . . ." Arno shook his head. "No."

The acolyte didn't listen but charged the Fellblade with a yell. Barely bothering to turn around, the Fellblade planted a boot in the boy's stomach and knocked him to the floor, coughing. Arno looked on in horror, but the Fellblade shook his head.

"Don't worry about him. Like I told you before, this isn't personal. Just business."

The Fellblade staggered forward, pausing once to lean against a pew and to catch his breath. The last prayer had done a number on him, but he was confident that he could handle a priest without a saint.

Then the front doors burst open, and Phoenix came in with his wand already drawn.

Phoenix missed his first shot at the Fellblade as the exhausted assassin narrowly dove out of the way, but it was all the distraction Arno needed. Propelled by adrenaline and righteous indignation, he forced himself to his feet and delivered the uppercut of his life to dislocate the Fellblade's jaw. Not giving him any time to react, Arno grabbed the man by the scruff of his neck and slammed his head into the nearest pew, knocking him out.

Phoenix lowered his wand, equal parts surprised and impressed. "Nice move."

Arno didn't answer, wavering on his feet. His chest still ached, and the room was spinning. Cold sweat beaded on his forehead, and it hurt to breathe. He tried his best to prop himself up on the nearest pew, but even that felt like a strain.

Whatever the Fellblade had done to him, it wasn't stopping. It was getting worse.

Phoenix realized something was off and frowned. "Church?"

"Bart," the vicar gasped. "Get the watchman."

And then he collapsed.

"Vicar!"

Arno wasn't moving, and all of the color had gone from his face. Phoenix checked him over and didn't see any sign of bleeding. That ruled out physical injury. But that didn't exactly narrow it down much. Then he got under his shirt, and he saw it. An ink-black stain covering most of the left side of Arno's chest, the edges of it seeming to move and shift. And it was spreading.

Phoenix looked to the boy who'd been hovering since Arno collapsed. "What happened?"

"I . . . he got hit by something. It was . . . I don't know," Bart stammered.

"Is there anybody here who knows healing prayers?"

"No. There was, but—" Bart's voice failed him. The only other person besides the vicar who could call on Saint Beneger for power had been Brother Michael. But he was dead. And now Vicar Arno was lying on the ground, looking like he was halfway to joining him. The Church of the Guiding Saint was the only family Bart had known since he was eleven. He couldn't lose another teacher and friend, and not less than a day after the first.

Phoenix waited for more details, which never came from the boy. He was panicking. Maybe in shock. Either way, Phoenix was on his own. He ran an identification spell over the stain, praying it actually was magic and not just a very animated poison.

He got lucky, and the spell came back with something. The mark was magic being drawn from the Fell, cutting off the flow of life in Arno's body. He latched on to the most useful information and ran with it, immediately forming a plan and digging through his pockets for the tools he'd need.

The problem was magic. He knew magic.

Please don't be a curse.

Curses latched on to the soul, and only divine power could touch that. But other magic affecting the body was more exposed. If he was dealing with something like that, his dispelling disks would be enough. If it was a curse—well, he didn't have anything for curses.

He arranged the discs around the mark on Arno's chest, traced the activation pattern on his gauntlet, and prayed. The discs pulsed, and Arno's body spasmed. After a moment, thick black smoke wafted off of him, and the stain dissolved from his chest.

But he still wasn't breathing.

"Is he . . . ?" Bart was too terrified to finish the sentence.

"No."

Technically Phoenix was lying when he said that, but there was a surprising amount of wiggle room when it came to death. Arno was only technically dead. Which meant he had a few seconds before he was actually dead. And he was going to take every one of those seconds he could get.

Phoenix drew his wand and cycled through its settings until the shock cell clicked into place and the tip of the wand began to spark. With more than a little desperation, he smacked the wand against the priest's chest, sending a surge of lightning through his body. His chest lurched, and Phoenix held his breath.

Seconds stretched out into what felt like an eternity while he waited for a response, until finally, mercifully, Arno started wheezing, then coughing, then finally started drawing in a few ragged breaths. With each one, he got a little more steady, and his eyes fluttered open. Phoenix fell back as relief washed through him, along with no small amount of satisfaction.

"Phoenix?"

The spellforger snapped out of his own stupor as the priest slowly sat up. "Hey. Still with us?"

"I think so," he groaned.

Bart immediately threw his arms around Arno, hugging him like it was the only way to keep him alive. The best Arno could manage was to return the embrace with one arm while he propped himself up with the other.

"Hey, it's all right," Arno assured him. "I'm okay."

"Vicar . . ." Bart gave up trying to say anything else as tears overtook him.

It took a minute before Bart calmed down enough to let him go, and in the end it took reminding him that there were several dangerous individuals that needed to be rounded up for him to get a grip. The young acolyte left to get the town watchman while the two former companions got a head start on restraining the intruders.

Arno retrieved his amulet from the floor while they worked, and said a quick healing prayer for himself. At his request, a wave of energy and strength filled his body, restoring him. The real relief though, was just in feeling his connection to Beneger. The feeling of a firm, guiding hand on his shoulder returned. He was whole again.

"Thank you." Arno was genuinely grateful to Phoenix. But he couldn't shake a nagging question that had hung in his mind since the doors had burst open. "How did you know I was in trouble?"

"Magic," Phoenix answered. When he realized it might be hard to tell that wasn't sarcasm, he clarified his answer. "I set up a few alarm wards before we left. The second that shadow guy came back into town, I knew, so I came back."

"What?"

Phoenix tilted his head. He knew he'd explained these to Arno before. "Alarm wards. I can set them to monitor an area, and they tell me if—"

"No, I know what they are," Arno interrupted. "I meant . . . why?"

"Interrogating someone working the contract is the best shot at getting to the bottom of this," Phoenix said. "I didn't think anyone would come for the town while you were gone, but you seemed pretty worried, so I figured it wouldn't hurt to be thorough."

Arno found himself fixated on a tiny part of Phoenix's explanation. *You seemed pretty worried.* It could have been nothing. Him reading compassion into a purely pragmatic action, but there was just enough ambiguity to make the priest wonder.

"Right," he said, keeping the musing to himself for now. "Well, we've got a few people working the contract. And I didn't kill some of them."

Phoenix nodded, noting the *we* in that sentence. "Does this town have a jail?"

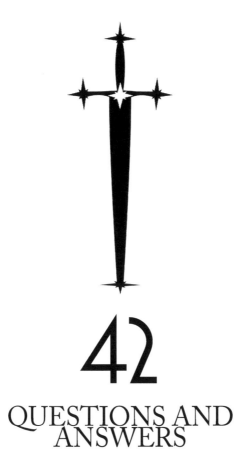

42
QUESTIONS AND ANSWERS

The people of Aenerwin were an immense help in securing the bounty hunters and hauling them off to Aenerwin's jail. It was a bit cramped, since besides the Fellblade, they had another four bounty hunters, and the solitary jail cell wasn't made to do much more than hold a few trouble-makers overnight while the watchman figured out what to do with them. But it would do.

Phoenix was honestly impressed. The whole town hung on Arno's every word and were eager to help him with anything he needed.

"When did you become so popular?" Phoenix asked once they were left alone with the unconscious prisoners.

"It just sort of happened the more I helped people."

"I refurbished a tavern with enchanted appliances, and the best I got was being left alone."

Arno shrugged before turning his attention to the bounty hunters. The Fellblade was skilled and powerful, and the other one, Skip, seemed to have a decent grasp of lightning magic. But the others were a motley bunch. Younger, far less equipped. Amateur tagalongs, if he had to guess, but they'd know for sure soon. With a healing prayer, he mended their injuries and restored their stamina. He didn't do enough to get them back in fighting shape, but it was enough to wake them up.

All of them began to groan. The biggest of the three amateurs shook his head, trying to rouse himself. The woman to his left cursed. The lightning mage, Skip, jerked awake, sending sparks dancing across himself as he did. As soon as the Fellblade saw the two of them, his dark eyes narrowed, but he said nothing.

"What happened?" one of the amateurs asked.

"You tried to bag a friend of mine, and now you're in jail," Phoenix said. "Everybody's anxious to get you out of their town, and you're probably anxious to leave. But we're going to ask you a few questions first."

"Save your breath," the Fellblade said. "There's nothing you can do to get anything out of me."

"Or me," Skip was quick to add. "Won't talk. Not a word. Not a syllable. Nothing!"

Phoenix rolled his eyes and looked at Arno expectantly. Arno spoke, and Beneger's presence descended into the room. A sudden clarity took the air, as if it had just rained. The hairs stood up on the back of everyone's neck, and they were all met with the sensation of being watched, and a firm, formless hand on their shoulder. The prisoners and Phoenix both shifted in place. If Arno felt the effect of the prayer, he didn't react to it.

"What was that?" the big amateur asked.

"I used a prayer to purge this room of falsehood," Arno said. "Everyone here will speak the truth, the whole truth, and nothing but the truth."

Phoenix felt a pressure build in his chest, and the invisible hand at his shoulder squeezed. "You weren't supposed to use it on us!"

Arno pointedly did not look at him. "An undisciplined mind will even be compelled to think out loud."

"Are you calling me undisciplined?"

To avoid speaking the truth, Arno chose to remain silent. In the cell, the bounty hunters were having a bit more trouble.

"This feels weird," the big man said. "I wanted to be a jester, but nobody thought I was funny."

Everyone in the cell looked at him with confused expressions. Skip cocked his head a full ninety degrees. "What?"

The man shook his head. "I never told anyone that."

"Also you might do that," Arno said.

"Keep your mouths shut," the Fellblade ordered. "Don't give them anything." He sent a look of pure contempt Arno's way. "Do you think this is my first time being questioned by a cleric? I know how you work. I can't lie, but you can't force me to answer. All I have to do is sit here and wait for you to give up."

"One problem with that plan," Phoenix said.

"What?"

Phoenix turned to the big man, who was fidgeting. "Who hired you?"

"The sparky guy!"

The woman next to him kicked him in the shin, but the man kept talking. "I don't even know any of these people."

Another kick.

"I've never done this before, I just needed the money."

"Shut up!" the Fellblade yelled.

Fear of the Fellblade was enough for the man to get himself under control. He bit his tongue and rocked himself back and forth, trying to stay silent. Phoenix turned his attention to Skip.

"All right, who hired—"

"I got a tip that the Handler was in Olwin looking for dirks willing to go after some big game, so I checked it out. He had a list of names with descriptions, locations, and prices. Grab a name on the list, bring 'em back to the Handler dead or alive, instant payday! If you couldn't make the trip, you could send word to them and they would pick the mark up, but that's a pay cut. So is bringing in a corpse. Met some real interesting folks on the job. The Butcher of Black Bay; the Jury of Adresta; Mr. Grim, Dark, and Gruesome over there. We got in each other's way for a bit, but then we hit on the idea of working together to bring down the really big names, like you guys!"

Skip breathed a sigh of relief as he finished. He'd talked so fast, Phoenix had caught, at most, three quarters of what he'd just said.

"Hey, nobody judge the first timer over there for blurting out his clown fantasies; this shit is hard!" Skip said, a smile on his face.

The Fellblade glared daggers at Skip, who didn't seem to mind that he'd given them everything they wanted and more. Phoenix was dumbstruck. He figured the prayer was going to streamline the process, but this was almost too easy.

"Where's the Handler now?"

Skip opened his mouth, but the Fellblade tackled him. For a second, Phoenix thought it was funny. Then he realized the both of them were melting into the shadows in the jail cell, and he drew his wand. He fired off three blasts, all of which seemed to be swallowed into shadows without hitting anything, and then both of them were gone. Phoenix cursed himself for not thinking that might happen. Again.

"I'm an idiot," he said, his mouth moving without his consent.

He and Arno rushed outside, searching. Phoenix looked with every setting his goggles had but saw nothing. Arno tried reaching out with his soul to find theirs. For a moment, he felt two presences he thought were them—a ball of barely contained energy and a sinking, endless void. Then they were gone.

The watchman came running out after them. "Vicar? What happened?"

"Two of them got away through the shadows," Phoenix answered for him.

The watchman looked like he wasn't sure how to process that information. "Through the . . . shadows?"

"Black magic," Phoenix tried again.

The watchman understood that. "I can get a search party together. We'll find them."

"Don't," Arno said. "Those two are wounded animals on the run. They're not dangerous unless we try to corner them."

"But what if they come back?"

"They'll come to us," Arno said. "And I think we're headed to Olwin?"

Hearing Arno use the word *we* again lit a spark of hope in Phoenix. He couldn't tell for sure on his own, and he was too self-conscious to ask, but it felt like an olive branch. For the first time since he'd come to Aenerwin, he dared to hope that the rift between them was shrinking.

"Yeah. Olwin."

The Handler was a professional middleman in the criminal underworld who was always on the move and always seemed to have a staff consisting entirely of Faceless. It was a guarantee that he was hiring the dirks on behalf of someone else. Still not the person they were looking for, but a lead they could follow.

An incredibly dangerous one.

43

AN EXCHANGE

The castellan's keep in Olwin wasn't the largest building Phoenix had ever been in. But it did have over a dozen guest rooms, which meant that more than once he frantically burst into the wrong room while looking for his wife and child. But finally on the fourth try he threw open a door and felt instant relief of his anxiety when he saw Elizabeth and Robyn, safe and sound.

He didn't waste a second, pulling her into the tightest hug he could manage. She hugged him back even tighter.

"When you weren't at the house, I—"

"Did you not get the note?"

"Yeah, but—"

Phoenix didn't even bother trying to rationalize the rush of fear that had gripped him when he'd walked into the house and his family wasn't there, so he didn't try. But as his panic started to subside, he began to notice that some things were off with Elizabeth. The smell of smoke clung to her hair, and her face was streaked with soot.

"What happened?" he asked, his concern mounting again.

"Pitch attacked Brass and set half the city on fire. I couldn't stay in the house anymore. I had to do something."

"Did you—"

"I just helped with the fires," Elizabeth reassured him. "I didn't find him, he didn't find me."

Arno cleared his throat to remind them both that there were other people present.

"Church," Elizabeth greeted. "Well . . . hi. This is a surprise."

"Hi . . ." Church was uncertain what terms they were on. "Wings."

Phoenix saved him by cutting back in. "Wait. If you didn't find Pitch, how did you know he attacked Brass?"

Elizabeth jerked her head toward another person in the room that Phoenix had been too distracted to notice.

"Ruby?" Phoenix helped Brass track the girl down after the mess with the ocre, and he hadn't seen her since. "What are you doing here?"

"I ran into her in Akers," Elizabeth explained. "She saw everything."

Ruby gave them the full story, from the Lilac to Brass's fight in the city.

Phoenix's mind was racing. He'd been hoping to get Brass's help tracking down the Handler. This threw several wrenches into that plan. Brass was captured, and either with the Handler or already handed off to whoever the Handler was working for.

"We need to find the Handler, soon."

"Well, it's a good thing I know where to find him," Ink said, announcing her presence as she materialized in the doorway.

"Ink?"

"Oh, don't act so surprised, I'm staying two rooms down the hall," she said, sauntering in like she owned the place. She was about to keep talking, but got distracted when she saw Robyn, who was transfixed by the new woman, who seemed to defy her fledgling object permanence. She smiled and pointed to the child. "That is adorable."

"What do you want?" Phoenix asked.

"Lots of things," she said. "A raise. A spell to create clothing that lasts longer than an hour. But right now, I want to help."

"I don't believe you."

"Believe whatever you like, but it's true."

Arno was reminded of how conversations between Phoenix and Ink tended to go, and decided to interrupt. "You know where the Handler is?"

"I can give you his address."

"How?"

"The Academy and the Handler have an . . . arrangement."

"Why am I not surprised?" Phoenix said with contempt.

"Do you want my help or not?"

"We do," Arno cut in. "What's the address?"

Ink held up a finger. "Aha. That's not how this works, and you know it. You want the Handler, bring me back my autostruct. In working order."

"Are you serious?" Phoenix asked. "You're extorting us, now?"

"I extort everyone, all the time. Don't act like you're special."

"Brass is captured, and the longer we take, the worse our odds of finding him get," Arno said, trying to appeal to Ink's decency.

"Well then you'd better get to work."

Gamma's head was back at the house, still inert because Phoenix had been a bit too busy to work on it. He didn't even know how long it would take him to fix it.

"What if we gave you the head and a Tavian Wheel?" Elizabeth asked. "You'd have the head and you could fix it yourself."

Ink's eyes lit up in exactly the sort of way that reminded Phoenix why he didn't like the Academy. "You have a Tavian?"

"Yes," Phoenix said, "but it—"

"Is collecting dust in the basement," Elizabeth finished. "You never use it, and Brass doesn't have time for you two to argue."

Arno and Elizabeth both stared at Phoenix, reminding him with their eyes that he needed to choose between Brass and an Old World artifact. A very nice one, that he had specifically avoided selling to the Academy, but still just an artifact. He knew what the right answer was. But he still didn't like it.

"Fine. The head and the wheel for the Handler."

"Deal." Ink smiled. The Headmaster was going to love this.

"So, where is he?"

"Where's my autostruct?"

"Ink!"

"If I tell you now, you'll run off to go save your friend. And if you die going up against the Handler, which I'm inclined to think you will, I don't get anything. Except you dead, which I have . . . mixed thoughts on."

"How about you tell us where the Handler is, and I go get the head now?" Elizabeth asked, trying to find a compromise as quickly as she could.

Ink made a show of considering this, tapping her chin and staring up at the ceiling. "All right. I suppose that'll do. Time is of the essence."

She gave them the address and wished them luck before returning to her room. When the High Inquisitive was gone, Phoenix and Elizabeth exchanged looks.

"The Tavian Wheel? I kept one of those on purpose."

"All I ever hear you say about those things is they're cheating, and a real spellforger can fix things himself," Elizabeth countered.

"Can you at least grab the rest of my old gear from the basement when you go back? And not immediately sell it to Ink?"

Elizabeth rolled her eyes. "Go save Brass."

"About that," Arno asked. "Do we have a plan for getting information from the Handler? Or even getting close to him?"

"Now that I know where he is? Yeah, we do," Phoenix said. "I'll explain on the way."

Phoenix cast one last look at Elizabeth and Robyn and realized the last thing he'd said to her had been in argument. He didn't think he was going to die anytime soon. But just in case, he kissed them.

"I love you both."

Afraid that if he didn't leave now, he never would, Phoenix turned and marched for the door, calling for Church to follow. The cleric lingered behind, held up by Elizabeth's grip on his arm.

"Take care of him," she pleaded.

For a moment Church was surprised. Considering how he'd left things with her husband, he'd expected Elizabeth to have a low opinion of him. Of all the Starbreakers, really. But not only was there no resentment from her, there was trust in her voice. He wondered where that came from.

"I will," he promised.

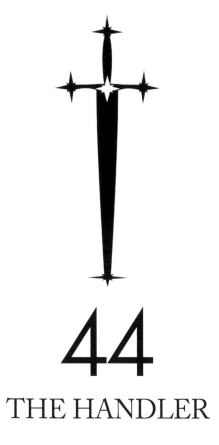

44

THE HANDLER

The Handler sat in front of the fireplace in his office, nursing a glass of pale wine as he watched the flames. It was a calm evening, a rare thing for his business, and he was taking the opportunity to indulge in the simple joy of inactivity.

He took a cool, refreshing sip, savoring the wine's floral notes. He employed an Academy dropout to chill all his drinks before they were served.

To his palate, it was an investment that paid off several times over.

His guards stood motionless in the room, flanking the doors or hovering close at his side. Though outwardly at rigid attention, they were not prohibited the same luxuries as their employer. Far from it, their

Faceless minds could take in his own experiences as he indulged in them. As he drank, they could taste the wine in their minds if they so wished.

A dull thud reverberated through the walls of the estate, causing the crystal decanter on the table next to him to rattle. The guards shuffled nervously, tightening their grips on their weapons. They all sensed something was wrong.

Guessing his leisure time was coming to an end, the Handler finished his glass of wine and stood up. His evening robe thickened and split into layers, morphing into a formal suit. The soles of his slippers hardened as they transformed into more practical shoes. The Handler smiled, indulging one last pause to take a moment to appreciate the utility of the garment. The clothing of the Faceless was as phenomenal as the people themselves.

A moment later, his intuition proved well-founded, as someone knocked on the office door. He signaled his guards to open it.

The doors parted, and the masked butler stepped in.

"I am sorry for the intrusion, sir. The estate appears to be under attack. Guards are working to rout the attackers, but they are employing arcane measures."

The Handler raised an eyebrow. This was an intriguing development. "The Inquisitive?"

He was aware of the High Inquisitive Arakawa's presence in the city and her fixation on one of the dirks currently under his employ. It wasn't outside the realm of possibility that she'd managed to track him here, but a direct assault seemed a bit brazen. He would have expected her to be smarter than that.

"Unknown," the butler reported. "The situation is currently out of hand, and guards are struggling to get a visual. Mental probes have proven equally unsuccessful at identifying them."

That implied the attackers were using some form of mental shielding. Which meant they knew who they were dealing with and what they were doing.

"Given current circumstances, I would recommend relocation, sir."

The Handler nodded and began to follow his guards to a predetermined escape route. Others would be directed to run diversions, empty carriages fleeing the estate along convincingly secured roads. Meanwhile, he would depart through a tunnel that led off-site.

The mental shielding was still bothering him. That kind of precaution didn't align with the bullheadedness of a direct assault.

Unless it wasn't a direct assault.

The Handler smiled. He still wasn't sure who was behind this attack, but he was at least sure that it would be entertaining. And, if he was lucky, even profitable.

Along with four guards, he made his way through the mansion, through the secret door behind a bookcase in the library, and down through the escape tunnel. The tunnel was polished stone with carpets adorning the floor and artwork lining the walls. Passages like this crisscrossed the mansion and estate grounds, ensuring that no matter where in the mansion he was, a secure escape was close and available.

The Faceless guards marched in supernatural synchronization, their spears casting a faint glow in the dim light of the tunnel. As they approached an intersection in the tunnel network, a small clay ball rolled out into the hallway in front of them. The guards halted, wary but confused.

Thick dark-gray smoke erupted from holes in the sphere, filling the tunnel and blinding everyone. Mentally connected, the Faceless remained aware of each other's presence and the Handler's, but their surroundings were obscured.

Flashes of light burst from beyond the smoke, and blasts of force slammed into the guards, dissipating on their armor but still knocking them off balance. Arno burst through the smoke, wearing a breastplate and brandishing Zealot as he spoke the words of a prayer to harden his skin. One of their spears scraped his hand. A blow that should have skipped off instead left a thin red line. The Handler's guards were well-equipped with magical devices. But that wasn't only an advantage to *them*. With his goggles set to highlight magic, the guards and their enchanted armor and weapons made easy targets for Phoenix in the smoke. He fired off another volley of blasts, tripping them up, and Arno deftly cleared a path with Zealot.

In just a few seconds, the guards were scattered and disoriented, and Phoenix had his wand leveled at the Handler. Arno moved to cover him from behind, sword at the ready.

"Any of you move, I blast the mask right off his face," Phoenix warned. Energy crackled and sparked at the tip of his wand.

The guards gripped their spears tightly but hesitated. The Handler held up a hand to signal them to hold. They didn't relax, but they didn't charge either.

"I must say, I'm genuinely impressed," the Handler said. "Using an attack to try and flush me out is one thing, but infiltrating the tunnels to intercept me is quite another. Well-executed. But I suppose I shouldn't expect any less from the . . . *former* leader of the Starbreakers."

The Handler cast a glance at Church. "Or maybe not so former anymore. You both look well."

"You look different," Phoenix noted. The last time he'd been face-to-face with the Handler, it had been white skin under the mask, not dark. He'd often wondered if the Handler was a position rather than a person, or if he did more than just employ Faceless.

"That should hardly surprise you by now," the Handler said. "You know, most people who would like a meeting just send a letter."

"Given there's a contract on our heads that you're running, I didn't trust that you wouldn't stab us in the back. So we figured we could have a meeting on our terms instead," Phoenix said.

The Handler shrugged. "Sound judgment. So. You went to all the trouble. Is there something I can help you with?"

"Where's Brass?" Phoenix asked.

"Ah, I see," the Handler said. "Well, he's not here. You've missed him by a few days."

"I asked where he is, not where he isn't." Phoenix stepped closer to the Handler. The arcane sparks from his wand were landing on the Handler's shirt now. His mask was illuminated in the wand's angry glow, as was his wide, unperturbed grin.

"And I'm afraid I can't tell you," the Handler said. "Among other things, people come to me for discretion and security. I can't divulge information a client wishes kept secret. It would be bad for business."

"You know what else is bad for business?" Phoenix asked. He actually touched the wand to the forehead of the Handler's mask, producing a shower of angry sparks. "A hole in your head."

"All right! No need to get testy."

"Church," Phoenix prompted. The cleric nodded and once again purged the immediate area of falsehood. The Handler's smile only grew.

"Now, there's the kind of precaution that separates the novices from the experts. I must say, I have missed people of your caliber. The new generation's so . . . easy," the Handler said.

"Where's Brass?" Phoenix repeated.

"Your friend was moved to the Petrov Estate. Thirty miles east of Olwin, in the mountains."

"Who owns the estate?"

"Lots of people have, over the years. A noble family did once. The Petrovs, naturally. Paranoid bunch. Didn't like the idea of living in a city surrounded by other people, so they headed for the hills. Then, of course, they all died when the hills fought back, but that's what you get for living in the wilderness. A freelancer company took over at one point; used it as their little base of operations. Not any friends of yours, before you ask. It was before your time."

Both glintchasers narrowed their eyes, and the Handler sensed he'd reached the limits of their patience.

He chuckled. "But these days, it's owned by Sir Silas Lamark."

"Is he the one who put out the contract?"

"Indeed he is."

After weeks of trying to figure out who was after them, they had a name. Phoenix and Church exchanged glances, silently asking each other if either recognized it. Neither of them did.

Phoenix had more questions. But the longer they stayed, the greater the chance that something would go wrong. They had what they came for. Brass's location. The identity of the person after them. They could figure out the rest later.

"Thanks for the information," Phoenix said. "We'll be on our way."

Carefully, with Phoenix keeping his wand trained on the Handler, they started to retreat. The guards all began to close ranks around their boss.

"A word on Silas that might interest you," the Handler offered as they left. "As I understand it, he's a former knight. From Relgen."

Church stopped dead in his tracks. Phoenix felt an uneasiness stir in his stomach.

"Is that what this is about?" Church asked.

"You know, I'm actually not sure," the Handler said, naked anticipation dripping from his voice. The Handler was always delighted to encounter something he didn't already know "He's played that rather close to his chest. According to him, all of this is for a search of some set of artifacts."

Phoenix wanted to believe that it wasn't about Relgen. The Starbreakers weren't the only targets on the list. But the coincidence unsettled him. And it distracted him.

"He's putting up enough money to buy a title over some artifacts?" Phoenix asked.

"Strange, isn't it?" the Handler said, smiling even wider now. "He's quite certain the people on the list are the key to finding them, and he's very desperate to do so."

"What artifacts?"

"He didn't say. But I have a theory."

"What?"

"It wouldn't be any fun if I just told you. You're a smart man. I'm sure if you put your mind to it, you can figure it out."

Phoenix resisted the urge to blast the smug grin off the Handler's face and found himself taken in by the challenge. This knight, Silas Lamark, was after artifacts and people he thought could lead him to it. That tracked with all the known targets being freelancers. When it came to long-lost relics of unfathomable power, there wasn't a profession more acquainted with recovering them. There were still the questions of which artifacts and why.

There had to be a common thread between targets, but Phoenix only had two specific ones to go on: the Golden Shield and the Starbreakers.

The more he thought about it, the more his thoughts drifted to Gamma's story about how the Golden Shield members had been killed. That explosion should have killed Pitch. Instead he was running around with fire magic.

His eyes widened as he realized what the Shield had found, and what they had in common with the Starbreakers.

"He's after the Servitor Hearts," Phoenix said.

The Handler laughed, barely restraining himself. "A man from the city you ruined, chasing the artifacts you helped save the kingdom from. Even if this isn't about you, isn't the irony of it all just delicious?"

Church watched the exchange with a sense of anxiety that only grew the longer it went on. The Handler was too relaxed, giving them too much too freely. Too late, he realized what was happening. The criminal middle man had dangled information in front of Phoenix like a worm on a hook, and he'd taken the bait. As soon as he made the realization, the Handler made eye contact with him, and winked. The cleric's ears picked up the sound of footsteps. Lots of footsteps. "Phoenix. We need to go."

"Oh dear me," the Handler said, hand over his heart with mock embarrassment. "I didn't mean to keep you gentlemen. You must think I've been stalling."

Phoenix and Church ran. The metal clank of armored footsteps echoed through the halls, getting louder by the second.

"Tell me you've got another fire bomb in that belt," Church said.

"Down to one," Phoenix said. "And in a space this tight, it'd just take us with it."

They rounded a corner and came face-to-face with a squad of Faceless guards.

There were a lot of them. Maybe not more than they could handle, but a fight would slow them down. Give reinforcements time to arrive. They tried looking for a different way out, but they didn't make it far before they ran into another squad.

They were pinned.

"Don't kill them."

The sound of a slow, casual gait echoed through the halls. Phoenix craned his neck to see the Handler stride into the corridor, a victorious smirk smeared on his lips.

"They're worth substantially more alive."

45

THE GOOD OLD DAYS

Angel rolled out a kink in her neck as she descended the stairs of the Rusted Star. Normally she got up a lot earlier than this, but it had been a long night. The lingering smell of lemon and cooked fish hung in the air, but she could hear no sizzle from the kitchen, which meant she'd slept through the lunch rush.

She stepped into the main hall of the inn, where she found a scattered assortment of late comers still at tables, finishing food or holding idle conversation. Fishing season would be starting soon, and business had been slowly ramping up in the lead up to it. The perks of setting up shop in a lakeside town.

She left the service side of the business to her hired hands.

Waiting on people was not her strong suit. But there was always something heavy that needed lifting. Stock to be checked on. An entitled asshole who needed to be put in their place. Owner stuff.

She was about halfway to the kitchen before it really sank in that people were here. There was no hole in the wall. Windows were intact. The door was on its hinges.

It was like last night's fight had never happened.

"You look lost."

Sitting at a small window table by herself, Thalia waved her boss over. Now Angel really knew she'd overslept. Thalia's shift was through the night. If she was up and moving, it was late in the day.

Angel tried to gauge the expression on Thalia's face. Until last night, as far as Thalia had known, Angel had been an unusually strong but otherwise perfectly normal woman with a bit of a temper. The burning halo, murderous rampage, and beams of light would have all been news to her. But if that was on her mind, she didn't show it.

Angel sat down opposite her, still glancing around at the pristine condition of the inn. "Correct me if I'm wrong, but didn't this place look like shit last night?"

"It did," Thalia nodded. She glanced down at her drink. "You really did a number on the place. And those people."

Angel glanced at the spot in the floorboards she'd broken when she'd slammed a man into them. There was no trace of the damage. But it had happened. The look on Thalia's face was proof of it.

Angel folded her arms. "So, are you quitting?"

Thalia looked confused. "No."

"Told anyone else?"

"No."

"Are you afraid?"

Thalia hesitated. She wanted to say no. Last night, she would have said yes. Instead she said, "I have questions."

Angel finally looked at Thalia after going out of her way not to. The last time she'd given staff a light show, every one of them who'd seen it had resigned and fled. She'd had to relocate after that.

She didn't like talking, but she was eager not to have a repeat of that incident. "What questions?"

"Well, I don't have a way to say this that isn't rude," Thalia said. "What are you?"

Straight to the point. Angel was surprised but also impressed. *Well. Here we go.*

There was a book name for what she was, she knew. Father Ortega, Sir Richard, Church, and Phoenix had all used it, explained it to her multiple times. She thought it was pretentious to give it a fancy title, so she skipped that bit.

"Know how angels are like the gods' soldiers?"

"Sure," Thalia lied.

"Well some of them are really into the job, and the world's full of things they really want to fight. Cults, monsters, demons, ghosts, whatever," Angel said. "But for reasons, they usually can't come here, so they normally can't fight all that stuff. So, sometimes, when they just can't get rid of their justice hard-on, they decide to be born as a human, and grow up and fight all the monsters they were eyeing while they were up in heaven."

"So, you're . . . ?"

"Apparently." Angel shrugged. "People made a big deal of it when I was younger, so these days, I keep it to myself. When I can."

"Okay." Thalia leaned back in her seat, trying to absorb this. She'd grown up with stories of angels in church. She had a vague concept of a world beyond this one, where souls went after people died and gods lived. But it had all seemed so distant. The business of clergy and people at death's door. This was different. In her face. "You aren't like what I pictured angels to be like as a kid."

Angel grunted. "I get that a lot. A lot, a lot. Don't really understand the details. People kept explaining it to me, and I kept ignoring them. When an angel's born as a human it . . . forgets being an angel? I don't know. Point is, I'm not a saint, I'm just me. And most people were disappointed with that."

"I mean, I'm not complaining." Thalia hastened to clarify. "They always sounded kind of stuck-up."

A small smirk flickered across Angel's lips, and relief flooded through her. She'd lost count of the number of times people had looked down on her for being her and not some paragon of virtue and justice they figured she should be.

When she'd first started freelancing and needed a name, she'd chosen Angel just to give a great big middle finger to everyone and their expectations. It was nice to talk to someone who got the joke. It had been a long time since she'd met anyone who did.

"Oh, they are, trust me," Angel said.

"You've talked to them?"

"Well, one. Once."

"Really?"

"It's a long story."

"I've got long shifts."

Thalia gave her a smile, and genuine curiosity sparkled in her eyes. Angel pictured staying up with Thalia through her shift, telling her stories from her freelancer days and watching her smile and stare at her with rapt attention. Her stomach fluttered.

"That how this place fixed itself up?" Angel asked, changing the subject. "Because I didn't know you were a carpenter."

"I'm not," Thalia said, taking in the restored inn. She gestured to their surroundings with a finger. "This was all one of your old friends. The brown one."

"What?"

"He had some magic wand," Thalia said. "Started poking everything that was broken with it, and things would fix themselves. It was super slow though. He kept having to hold things in place while he put them back together. He didn't get a wink of sleep. Worked through the whole night."

It was Angel's turn to lean back in her seat. As apologies went, repairing her inn was . . . still not an apology, really. But a nice gesture. And more of one than she would have expected from Phoenix, especially after telling him, in so many words, to go fuck himself.

"Hope you don't mind, but I gave him a coffee on the house while he was working," Thalia said. "He seemed like he needed it."

Angel took another look around, recalling just how much damage there had been the night before. "That's fine."

Thalia stirred her drink with a spoon, though it didn't need it. "So, you're really not gonna help those guys?"

"Nope."

Thalia shrugged. Now she looked disappointed.

Angel sighed. "Go ahead, say it."

"You're the boss," Thalia said. "I don't tell you what to do."

"You're not working now, are you?"

That seemed to be all the excuse Thalia needed. "Well, I always used to hear about how freelancer companies are basically families. And me and my family don't really get along, but if people were trying to kill them, I don't think I would turn them down if they asked me for help."

"That 'companies are families' stuff's bullshit and survivor's bias. Most freelancer companies are a bunch of strangers who hate each other, and they break up or all get killed before anybody has ever heard of them. The ones that get along and last are rare. But they're the ones who actually make money and get shit done, so that's all anyone hears about."

"How long did you guys last?"

Angel realized her mistake too late. She had an idea where Thalia was going with this, and a part of her didn't want to give her any ammunition.

But she was a shit liar.

"Seven years."

Thalia nodded. "Sounds like you guys were pretty rare."

Against Angel's will, memories of better days came to her. Nights spent around a campfire, lost in the woods. Spending the last money they had from a job getting plastered in a tavern. Feeling like she'd found people who liked her for her.

No. I'm not falling for that trap again.

"It doesn't matter either way," Angel said. "They left already, to who knows where, and I've got no way to find them."

Thalia shrugged again. Angel came up with an excuse to leave and went about her day. Eventually, she found herself chopping firewood for the evening. She didn't need to. They had plenty of logs split and ready to use, but she liked the opportunity to hit something with an axe.

She'd spent the better part of the day trying to put Phoenix and Church out of her mind. To remind herself that anything she thought was there was just wishful thinking. When that failed, she rationalized that she didn't know how to find them and they didn't need her help regardless.

But she couldn't rationalize the disappointed look on Thalia's face. It was different from the kind of disappointment she normally resented and was used to getting from people. That wasn't someone thrusting expectations on her because of how she'd been born.

Those were the eyes of someone who genuinely believed in her.

Then she heard them. Voices. Young, bickering, and headed her way. It only took a second of searching to spot them. Five teenagers—kids—wandering through the woods, just outside town. They had armor and weapons, though almost all of them looked handed down or scavenged. Two of them were fighting over a map, while the others trailed behind them, their faces a combination of exhaustion and amusement.

Angel recognized their type almost instantly. Freelancers. Just starting out, by the look of them.

"See! There's the town! I told you we weren't lost."

"Are you sure this is the *right* town?"

"I know how to read a map," Phoenix said defensively, burying his nose deeper into it as if it somehow proved his expertise. Not Phoenix as Angel knew him now, but young, with the smooth face he'd had before he'd been able to grow a beard.

"You say that," Snow retorted, swiping it from his hands. Her old self, before the cold. With normal, healthy skin and bright brown eyes. "But we should have made it to Brightben like two days ago."

"So now you're an expert navigator?"

"No, but I can count."

"Oh my god, will you two just fuck and get it over with? This trip is unbearable enough without having to listen to this all day." Angel lost count of how many times she'd told those two that before they finally went through with it. And nobody in the Starbreakers got a peaceful night's sleep for a week after.

"Oh come on, where's your spirit of adventure?" Brass chimed in, hopping from one stone to the next as they walked through the woods. "Half the fun in a job's getting there!"

"Right, fun," Church mumbled. "Does it have to involve this much walking?"

"Well, since somebody set our cart on fire, yes," Brass said.

"You mean since you did?" Snow retorted.

As long as she lived, Angel would never be able to forget the image of the idiot surfing their cart, on fire, straight into the wooden barricade of the Cord of Aenwyn's base camp.

Or how that stupid stunt had gotten them back everything the Cord had stolen from them.

"Look, someone we can ask for directions!" Brass deflected, pointing at Angel as she stared dumbstruck at them all. "Excuse me. Miss?"

Angel blinked, and the Starbreakers were gone.

It wasn't Brass talking to her, but a teenage girl with curly hair and a pair of almost impossibly well-made shoes.

"Boots, you can't just walk up to people in the forest!" one of the girl's companions scolded.

"I'm just being friendly!" the girl replied. "Sorry about them. I was just hoping you could tell us if this was Brightben?"

Angel blinked several more times to make sure what she was seeing was real before shaking her head. "Brightben's half a day north of here."

"Fucking called it!" the girl who'd swiped the map declared.

Angel watched the young company turn on its heels, continuing to bicker as they made their way northward. She wanted to yell at the kids to pack up their stuff, disband, and go home before they ruined their lives. To warn them that whatever they thought they would find out in the world, they were going to be disappointed.

But the only thing that came out was a wistful "Good luck."

She stared until she couldn't see them anymore before she let out a frustrated sigh and swung her axe again. She cleaved a log in two and split the stump underneath she'd been using as a platform. The axe lodged itself, immobile. She was angry, but not at Church, or Thalia, or even Phoenix.

She was angry at herself.

"Fuck it."

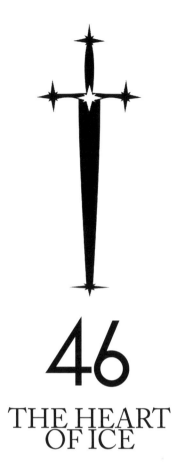

46
THE HEART OF ICE

F or not the first time in his life, Phoenix wondered if he was going to live to see twenty-three.

As he dove for cover behind the weathered remains of a stone pillar, the wind howled, and a layer of ice coated everything around him. Even with his armor set to protect him from the cold, the air stung. He'd completely lost track of the others, and the cells in his wand were running out of charges.

A week ago, the Starbreakers had heard a story about an old mining town that had frozen in the middle of summer. They'd figured that whatever monster or artifact was behind it had to be worth something and started digging. Now they were deep in an abandoned mine shaft, facing down a lunatic with an artifact more powerful than anything they'd ever seen. And they were losing.

Snow blinked into cover next to Phoenix, trying to catch her breath. The cold had left her cheeks bright red, and she was shivering.

"This could be going better," she noted. "Ideas?"

"Everything he's thrown at us has come from that rod," Phoenix observed. "If we can get it away from him, it should shut him down."

"Perfect," Snow said, risking a peek out from behind cover to get a look at her target. "So, you distract him, and I'll go for the thing?"

"Everything I've got left either doesn't work on him or would bring the whole mine down on top of us. How am I supposed to distract him?" Phoenix asked.

"No clue. Use that brain of yours," Snow said.

Before he could protest further, she darted in, kissing him. Even with everything around them below freezing, her lips sent a shiver of warmth down his spine, and for just a second, he forgot that they were all going to die. Then, as quickly as she started the kiss, she broke it off and blinked out of sight again.

Phoenix shook his head in disbelief, even as he smiled and returned his mind to the problem at hand. The problem was standing confidently at the center of the ruins the mine had led them to. Frost covered his clothes and skin, but he felt no discomfort. In his hand, a rod made of ice and bronze pulsed with pale blue light. Wherever he pointed it, freezing winds and ice surged forward.

"You had your chance to walk away!" the mage shouted. "But now, your frozen corpses will serve as a warning to the next fools who try to challenge me!"

"Gotta give him points for originality!" Brass's voice echoed from somewhere else in the ruins. "No one's ever threatened to freeze us to death before. Hey, has anyone else lost feeling in their toes, or is that just me?"

"Shut up and take him!" Angel yelled.

Angel vaulted over the crumbled wall she'd been hiding behind, and Brass leaped into action right after, as they both rushed to close the distance.

"I got him!"

With a stomp of his foot, the mage sent ice crawling across the floor to intercept Brass, and the swordsman tripped, sliding across the floor. Immediately, ice crept across his body, pinning him.

"Don't got him!" Brass corrected himself. "A little help?"

"Hang on!" Church yelled after him, shielding himself from freezing winds as best he could with his arms. "Cover me!"

Before the mage could target Church, Angel charged, axe in hand and her entire body burning with golden light. Ice shot toward her, spreading across the floor before growing and rising into a wall of spikes. With a roar, she swung her axe, shattering the ice. For an instant, she came within swinging distance, but the ice kept coming. After a few more swings to keep it at bay, she was finally overwhelmed. It completely engulfed her until she was only a glowing light somewhere inside a frozen mound. With her down, the mage turned his attention to Church and promptly froze him to a wall.

There was no more time to plan. Phoenix stepped out of cover to get a clear shot at the mage. The cylinder of his wand rotated, and the fire cell clicked into place. By the time the mage saw him, he was already unleashing a torrent of flames straight into him. He didn't take any chances, pouring the heat on until the cell was spent and the flames fizzled out. Steam curled off of the mage, but he was otherwise untouched. Phoenix felt a knot form in his stomach.

"I'm almost amused you thought that would work," the mage taunted, aiming his rod. "See what a real artifact can do."

Phoenix raised his arm and threw up a force shield, but after only a few seconds of keeping the freezing blast at bay, it gave out. In another second, he was pinned to a pillar. His armor was the only thing that saved him from cold shock, and even then he felt the chill in his bones.

With the four Starbreakers immobilized, the mage relaxed, striding slowly and deliberately toward Phoenix. For a moment, the glintchaser wondered why the mage didn't just kill them and get it over with. Then, in a flash of realization, he remembered the one weakness every mage seemed to share without fail. One that he might just be able to exploit.

"What is that thing?" Phoenix asked, layering fear and awe into his voice. Given how much of the feelings were genuine, it was an easy sell. And the mage bought it.

With a smile, the mage stopped, taking a moment to examine the rod in his hands. "This? This, you simple fool, is the Heart of a Servitor. The power that fueled the greatest weapons the Old World ever produced. And now it's mine."

"And you're going to do what with it? Freeze more towns?" Phoenix asked.

"Whatever I want," the mage said. "With this power, I will bend cities to my will."

Phoenix glanced around the cavern, looking for any sign of Snow. He didn't see her, but knew from experience that it didn't mean she wasn't around. And there was something else. The mound of ice holding Angel was starting to crack.

"Unless we stop you," Phoenix said, trying to keep the mage's attention.

The mage chuckled darkly. "No one can stop me."

"You know, you remind me of the last mage we fought," Phoenix said. More cracks were forming on the ice. A chunk fell off. Phoenix gave it another second. "He couldn't stop talking either."

A look of irritation crossed the mage's face, but before he could decide how to kill Phoenix, Angel burst out of the ice in a glittering flash of light. At the same time, Snow blinked into range, stabbed the mage in the back, and lunged for the rod.

As soon as Snow's hand gripped it, a cold so intense it burned spread across her skin, and she screamed. She powered through the pain, yanking as hard as she could. The mage pulled back, and the two entered a tug of war over the artifact, stumbling back and forth. While Snow had him distracted, Angel reared back and threw her axe with everything she had. She was aiming for the mage, but at the last second, his footing shifted, and the axe smashed into the rod instead.

There was an explosion, and Angel was blown off her feet. For a moment, everything went white.

And then silence.

Slowly everyone's vision started to return as snowflakes gently fluttered through the air. The cavern was already blanketed. Still stuck frozen to the floor, Brass tried to look around.

"What happened? Did we win?"

Angel looked around for the mage. She found him suspended a few feet off the ground, impaled on an ice spike. Dead.

"Oh gods," Angel muttered. "Yeah, we won."

"Everyone okay?" Phoenix asked.

"One second," Brass said. After taking a few breaths, he managed to pull himself free from the floor, but he lost a bit of skin doing it. "Ow! Ow! Church!"

"Coming," Church said through chattering teeth. With a prayer enhancing his strength, he broke free of the ice and quickly made his way over to Brass.

Snow remained silent.

"Snow?" Phoenix called out. When she didn't respond, he got worried. "Snow?"

Angel looked around, spotting the thief lying face down in the snow. Now she was worried. She rushed to Snow's side, turning her over. Angel recoiled at what she saw.

Snow was violently shivering as frost spread across her body. She was cold to the touch, and the color had drained from her skin, leaving her unnaturally pale. And her eyes. Instead of their normal brown, they were pure white.

"Snow?!"

47
BETTER ANGELS

Phoenix woke up to the sound of horse hooves and the feeling of a cart bouncing down a hard dirt road. Chains rattled, and after he started to move, he realized they were his. His wrists and ankles were both shackled. A burlap bag was over his head, leaving him in the dark.

Doing his best to sit up, he tried to piece together what he could without sight. His coat and armor were gone, along with his belt, his wand, and his goggles. The cart interior was bare wood. Probably made for carrying cargo rather than people.

From the way the air felt, he guessed it was covered, and blind fumbling eventually confirmed it.

There was a flap of canvas and a voice. "Sit down!"

Phoenix's head whipped instinctually in its direction and caught a brief tint of torchlight through the bag before whatever flap had been opened in the cart cover was closed again. Torchlight, not sunlight. Traveling at night.

With his vision limited, he focused on his other senses. Whoever was driving the cart wasn't talking, but there were other sounds he could use. The sound of another cart, somewhere close. It didn't get closer or farther as they went on, which meant it was traveling with them. A caravan.

Information. Even if he didn't know what to do with it, it was all he had now. He had to make the most of it. He had to figure a way out of this. Somehow. Without any equipment. Or weapons. With multiple wounds from the fight he and Arno had tried to put up.

Gods and saints, I'm in trouble.

With nowhere to go and nothing else to do, Phoenix decided to think. He tried to figure out an escape plan, but after a few minutes of not being able to come up with anything that didn't end with him dead, his thoughts drifted.

He thought about a lot of things. Elizabeth and Robyn. His old companions. A possible way to synthesize rubber. And he thought about what the Handler had said.

Silas was after the Hearts of the Servitor. Phoenix was sure of it. He didn't know exactly what a former knight would want with them, but in all his years dealing with the things, Phoenix had never met anyone who had a good reason for wanting one. The fact that Silas was willing to employ people like Pitch or the bounty hunters who attacked Aenerwin only made Phoenix more worried.

"Hello?"

The sound of Arno's voice dragged him out of his own head, and relief flooded him. He wasn't alone, and Arno was alive.

"Church?"

"Phoenix!"

"Shut up!" a voice at the front of the cart barked.

Phoenix crawled in the direction of Arno's voice until he bumped into a leg and sat down next to its owner. He spoke again, leaning in so he could keep his voice low.

"What's the damage?"

Arno shifted in place next to him, groaning. "I took two spears back at the mansion. Bandaged but not healed. My amulet is gone. Zealot too. You?"

"Back, calf, and wrist. And they took my stuff."

"We're really in trouble, aren't we?"

"Yeah," Phoenix said. "But, don't worry. I'll think of something."

"Like what?"

"Well, I was at a loss before, but now that I know there's two of us, we could try fighting our way out."

"We're injured, in chains, with bags over our heads."

"It's not ideal."

"Do you have another option?"

"The only other cart traveling with us is in front of us. If we can find or make an opening in the back of the cart cover, we can try and slip out without them noticing. We'll have to be careful about the noise from the chains, but if we do it right, it's the cleanest, safest option."

"Won't we be stuck in the middle of Renalt knows where, still in chains?"

"Do you have something helpful to contribute?" Phoenix snapped.

"Sorry."

Phoenix sighed. He wasn't mad at Arno. Not really. "No. I am. This is my fault."

Arno had helped people through enough confessions and breakdowns to be able to hear one coming. Something about getting outmaneuvered by the Handler, getting captured, had broken a barrier in Phoenix. And whatever it was holding back was about to come out.

"I thought I could get us in and out of there, no problem. I thought I was smart enough to beat the Handler with just us, and I was wrong," Arman said. And it was Arman, not Phoenix talking now. "And I wouldn't have even needed to try if Angel had come with us, but I fucked that up even worse than before so of course she told us to screw ourselves. I'm supposed to be the leader of the Starbreakers, and I couldn't even convince her to help for one mission."

He remembered this feeling. Like the floor had been pulled out from under him and the world was weighing down on him.

"Arman?"

"Yeah?"

"Why are you trying so hard to live up to yourself?"

Arman was surprised by the question, but he was even more surprised that he had an answer. "Because I miss it. I miss . . . feeling like I had all the answers. Like there was nothing I couldn't handle."

"Like you could do no wrong?"

Arman felt a brief wave of shame as the question brought back terrible memories of the exact same accusation. That he thought he could do no wrong. He'd been younger then. Fresh off what felt like a lifetime of successes and minor setbacks they always overcame. It had been easy not to think he could really mess things up.

Then Relgen showed him what failure felt like, and he'd learned that even the self-proclaimed smartest man in Corsar could be wrong. It was only thanks to Elizabeth he'd managed to learn that failure didn't make him worthless.

"I'm guessing you don't miss it?"

"Of course I do," Arno said, and somehow he made it sound like he was scolding him. "The Starbreakers were the first family I ever had. Even Snow and Brass, Renalt help them. And we did a lot of good in those days. But it was almost always an accident. We weren't freelancers to do good, we were freelancers to get rich, avoid problems, and show up people we didn't like. Our priorities were all wrong. And it got a lot of people hurt. Too many."

"There were things Phoenix couldn't handle," Arno reminded him. "You never knew how to take failure. You never entertained the idea that you were wrong, and you couldn't stand it when you were."

Arman couldn't argue with anything Arno said. It didn't even feel like he was the one saying it. More like the cleric was simply holding up a mirror and letting him argue with everything he should already know by now.

"I still don't know what to do with it," Arman said. "Every time I even try to think about it, it just piles up, and everything that could happen and everyone that could get hurt goes through my head, and I can't move. I can't breathe. I don't know what to do when I fail."

"Yes you do," Arno said. "You failed at Relgen. We all did. But you came out the other side. You put your life back together. You started a family. And you changed. The Phoenix I knew never would have listened to an idea he didn't think of, but you warded Aenerwin. Not because you thought you should, but because *I* was worried. That's what you do with failure. You rebuild, and you change."

The priest sighed. "We've all got a lot of complicated feelings about the old days. But you need to stop trying to be the person you used to be. It's time to be better than him."

It was like a dozen disparate chunks of a puzzle finally came together, and everything made sense again. Arno was right. He'd spent this whole time leaning in to old instincts and ignoring new ones he'd formed over the years. Things Elizabeth had taught him about people. Things Akers had taught him about giving back to the world. Things he'd learned about moving on.

"Arno?"

"Yes?"

Arman drew a deep breath, and said something he should have said the day he showed up in Aenerwin. "I'm sorry."

"You already apologized."

"No, I mean . . . I'm *sorry*. For Relgen. What I said. What I did. It wasn't your fault. You didn't murder anyone. You saved my life. And now I have a family because of you. So . . . I'm sorry. And thank you."

Arno was silent. For a moment, Arman was left agonizing over his potential reaction. He cursed the bag on his head. Talking was hard enough when he could see the other person's face. This was torture.

"See? You never apologized back in the day," Arno said.

Arman swore he heard a tinge of a taunt in the cleric's voice, not that he had any way to confirm it. Though he did seem to remember Arno being fond of saying "I told you so." Despite the pain from his wounds and the mess they were in, despite everything that had happened not just these last few days but for the last seven years—or maybe because of all of it—Arman chuckled. Arno ribbing him without dredging any feelings of ill will felt good. Like they were really comfortable with each other again. He'd been hoping and seeing traces of it since saving the cleric's life, but for the first time it felt like something had genuinely healed between them. He felt renewed.

Phoenix. He picked the name from a book of myths he'd grown up reading. A fitting name for a library steward embarking on a new life of adventure and discovery. It was time for him to live up to the name again. Just thinking it, setting that mission out in his mind, he felt better. More sure of himself.

Then he remembered that personal growth couldn't break chains.

"You are really good at this," he said. "But how is being a better person supposed to get us out of this?"

"I'm a priest, not an escape artist."

Before Phoenix could come up with a retort, the cart jerked to a halt, and the drivers outside started yelling.

"What's the hold up?"

Phoenix cocked his head.

"Out of the way, woman!"

Arno felt the hairs on the back of his neck stand up, and his heart fluttered. There was something here, something that colored the very air with its presence. And it was making the cart drivers just a little bit uneasy.

"Has that inn always been on this road?" one of the drivers of their cart muttered.

Someone further up the road yelled. "Hey! I said get out of the—"

The man's words were cut off by his own scream and a slew of curses from multiple people. The sounds of a struggle ensued.

Horses whinnied, and swords were drawn. Shouts and screams came from outside. Someone tore the canvas on the cart up ahead. The crack of wood snapping into splinters reverberated through their own cart.

"We've got trouble," Phoenix said.

It sounded like the caravan was under attack. Unsurprising. At a certain distance from major settlements, roads belonged to the bandits. Doubly so at night.

"Isn't this good?"

"Maybe," Phoenix said. "It's a chance. But we might just be moving out of the frying pan and—"

Their cart started moving again, erratically. A feral shout rang out that seemed to shake the air, and suddenly the cart tumbled over on its side, tossing around Phoenix and Arno as it crashed.

Phoenix groaned. He was pretty sure he'd broken something in the crash. Arno sounded worse than he felt. The canvas covering their own cart was torn open.

"I swear to Renalt, it better be you two," came a familiar voice.

A strong hand gripped the bag on each of their head, and tore them off, bringing them face-to-face with Angel.

"Was starting to think I jumped the wrong caravan," she said.

"Where did you come from?" Phoenix asked.

"Heaven," Angel said, deadpan. "Also, you're welcome."

Angel hauled Phoenix to his feet over the protests of his battered body. When he tried to stand on his own, he almost collapsed, and she had to catch him.

Angel was giving off more light than the torches, which were lying in the road, sputtering out. Men were sprawled across the road, their weapons discarded or broken. The horses who pulled the carriages were gone, the tattered remains of harnesses mixed in the wreckage of both carts. The cart farther down the road had its front smashed and its cover torn off. The one that had carried them had an axle destroyed and a wheel missing.

She grabbed hold of the shackles around his wrists.

"Hold still."

Her fingertips began to glow as she gripped the metal, and Phoenix felt the metal begin to heat up. It burned a little, but he forced himself to stay quiet. Her muscles tensed, and after a moment of pulling, she popped the shackle off. The metal glowed where it had broken.

"Thanks."

Angel nodded. Within a few minutes, she had them both out of their chains and propped against the overturned cart. She told them to wait there and went rummaging through the debris of the wreck she'd caused. She came back hauling a sizable wood chest.

"I brought presents," she said, throwing it open to reveal everything that had been taken off of them. "Found it in the first cart instead of you guys."

His holy symbol back in hand, Church used a prayer to heal Phoenix, then himself, treating them all to the sound of bones unbreaking and skin knitting itself back together. It was an odd sensation, but when it was over, they were almost as good as new.

The injuries from the fight with the Faceless healed more slowly, and Phoenix could tell just from the feeling that at least one of them was going to scar. When it came to healing magic, the older the wound, the messier the healing process.

"Come on," Angel said, jerking her head up the road. "Let's get out of here."

Just a few paces up the road was an inn, and Phoenix did a double take when he saw it. It was the Rusted Star. He'd seen too much to consider anything impossible, but it was still surprising to see Angel's inn just off the road as if it had been built there.

"Just to clarify, is that your inn?" he asked.

"Yep."

"Where are we?"

"Little bit east of Olwin," Angel said.

"How is your inn here?"

Angel glanced over her shoulder and—with no humor in her voice—said, "I moved it."

Phoenix blinked, waiting for an explanation he didn't get. Just to sate his curiosity, he pulled down his goggles and cycled through the filters. The whole inn was suffused with divine magic.

"How did you find us?" Church asked.

"Wasn't fucking easy," Angel said. "Took a few days to track you guys back to Olwin. Got there, figured the castellan was my best bet to find you. Then fucking *Wings* showed up at the castellan's keep and told me you were going after the Handler. By the time I got to his place, carts were leaving."

"How did you know that we were in the carts?" the priest asked.

Angel shrugged. "Dumb luck. Took a guess."

Angel went inside, and Arno hurried after her, intent on scolding her for attacking carts on the road on a hunch. He got distracted for a second when he walked in and saw the inn in pristine condition again. After a second of wondering if this was just something else the inn could do, he remembered his concerns.

"What if you had gotten it wrong?" Arno asked.

"It was a couple of carts from a crime lord's mansion. Even if it wasn't you, it wasn't gonna be anyone who didn't deserve a beatdown," Angel said, annoyed by the judgment she heard in his voice. She jabbed a finger at him. "You know, I liked it better when you were being grateful."

"We are." Phoenix walked in, rubbing the back of his neck.

Angel lowered her finger and shrugged. "Well, you're welcome."

"So, that's how you found us," he said. "But I still have one question."

Angel folded her arms, waiting expectantly.

"Why?"

Angel thought about lying. She could play it like payback for fixing her inn. It would keep things simple. The way they were. Even give her an out, if she felt like getting out now.

But she didn't want to get out.

Not yet.

So she told the truth.

"A friend helped me remember that you weren't always a piece of shit," Angel said. She paused, considering her words. The more she thought about them, the more she realized they might not have been appropriate. "Okay, that was wrong. You were always a piece of shit. All of you, for different reasons. But so was I, and we were all shit together."

Her eyes drifted to the floor as she muttered, "And however much I'm still pissed at you, I don't actually want either of you to die."

This was as close as Angel came to being sentimental, and it still tasted unpleasant in her mouth. More than once while talking, she came tantalizingly close to abandoning the effort, telling the two of them to fuck off then and there and washing her hands of the whole mess.

"And as apologies go, cleaning up my mess in the inn . . . it's still not an apology, but it wasn't the worst thing you could have done. Look, whatever the plan is to deal with this whole dead-or-alive manhunt shitstorm, I'm in. Okay?"

There, I said it. Too late to back out now. She waited for them to say they didn't want her around. Or to accept it in some condescending, asshole-ish way.

Instead Phoenix just nodded. "It's really good to have you."

"Yeah, I know. Your lives just got a hell of a lot easier. My turn to ask a question," Angel said, pointedly eyeing the both of them. "What exactly is the plan?"

Arno and Phoenix exchanged glances, and Arno gestured for Phoenix to go ahead. "We've got a lead to the possible location of the person who put out the contract."

"Great." Angel threw her hands in the air. "Let's go kill them."

"We're also going to have to rescue Brass."

Angel stared at Phoenix. "You're joking."

"Afraid not."

Angel groaned. She rubbed her temples between her thumb and middle finger for a few seconds before slapping the countertop of the bar. "Fine. Whatever. Where's the lead?"

"An estate in the mountains. But we should go back to Olwin first."

"Why?"

"I could use a resupply," Phoenix said. "And I want to tell my wife where I'm going, in case this goes south. Again."

"Fine, fine," Angel said, placing both her hands on the counter. She glanced between the two of them. "Do me a favor, one of you go make sure the front door is shut, and then hold on to something. This is gonna get weird."

Arno went to check the door. Phoenix looked around for something anchored to hold on to, but came up short.

"Weird how?" Phoenix asked.

"You remember that dwarf we found in the mountains?"

"The one we moved to Allhammer?"

"Yeah. I went to him for help building this place, since he was the only person I could think of who'd take a magic axe as payment," Angel said. "Anyway. He went a little overboard. Turns out, really special dwarf buildings all have this neat trick. And he passed it on to this place."

There was a rumbling sound, and the inn's floor began to shake. Glasses and tankards rattled against each other. The windows vibrated. Arno and Phoenix both found it difficult to keep their footing.

Outside, the dirt surrounding the inn began to loosen and kick up. It built up around the inn's walls, and the entire building began to sink, inch by inch. Then, as if a sinkhole had opened up underneath it, the inn plummeted into the ground, and was swallowed up by the earth, leaving only a disturbed patch of dirt in its wake.

48

FRICTION

In a well-furnished sitting room that sat downstairs from the guest rooms of the keep, Ink and Elizabeth watched the Tavian Wheel work. The wheel was two feet across and made of segmented blue-gray metal with gold inlays. As soon as Wings had come back with it, Ink had placed Gamma's head on the wheel and set it to work. The pieces of the wheel unfolded into articulated arms tipped with tools that immediately set to work repairing Gamma's head, piece by piece.

Ink was fascinated by the process, making dozens of notes as she watched the wheel work. Elizabeth took a passing interest in it, but most of her attention was dedicated to keeping an eye on Robyn, lest the girl crawl away and get herself into trouble while her mother wasn't looking.

All the while, she kept throwing glances back at the stairs, wondering if the newest occupant of the keep was going to come down. She had a few hours to think about it before Phoenix, Arno, and now Angel came into the keep's guest wing. Brass still wasn't with them, she noticed.

"What happened?"

"I saved their asses," Angel said.

"And we know where Brass is," Phoenix added.

"Good."

Angel glanced between Phoenix and Elizabeth and the baby currently gnawing on the wing of a stuffed owl and processed what she was seeing. "Holy Renalt, you two got hitched."

"Unfortunately," Elizabeth joked. "Thanks for bringing him home."

"We're not staying just yet," Phoenix said. "Did you grab the rest of my stuff?"

"In the room," Elizabeth said, jerking her head to the guest room. "But maybe I should go get it."

Elizabeth ignored the questioning look on her husband's face, and, after picking up Robyn, disappeared upstairs for a few minutes. Then everyone felt the room cool as Elizabeth came back—with Snow.

The assassin recoiled just a bit at the sight of them.

Phoenix blinked and tried to think of something to say. He came up short, only able to get out a confused, "Snow?"

Angel did a bit better. "The fuck are you doing here?"

Snow glared in response. The temperature in the room dropped, and Arno and Phoenix both grimaced. Before Snow could retort, however, Elizabeth stepped in. "She was in Akers for a while, keeping us safe."

She cast a glance at Snow, who offered a confused and annoyed look in return. She didn't need defending. But if Elizabeth got that message, she ignored it. "I didn't know for sure until after you left," she said. "She kept her distance, but she was looking out for us. And then she got hurt. I found her at the house when I went back for the head."

Snow felt a twinge of frustration but gestured to the hole in her armor left by Pitch's sword when he ran her through. She felt like she was on trial.

"What happened?" Arno asked.

Snow considered her next words carefully. The moment she'd decided to come to Elizabeth, she'd been thinking through her story. She was a damn good liar when she needed to be. But Arno and Elizabeth were both damn good at telling when people were lying.

"I was there when they took Brass," she said. "I couldn't stop it."

Both statements were technically true, but she knew that wouldn't serve as a defense if the truth came out. She wasn't really paying attention to their faces. Looking at the ground made it easier to lie, and it sold the regret she found surprisingly easy to layer into her voice.

She almost believed it herself that she'd gotten hurt trying to fight to stop them from taking Brass, even when she knew the opposite was true. She'd abandoned him after he'd tried to warn her and she'd ignored him. And then he saved her anyway. Somehow, that gnawed at her more than turning him over in the first place.

"We know where Brass is," Phoenix said.

Snow looked up. "What?"

Phoenix brought Snow up to speed on everything that had happened and everything they'd learned from the Handler. When the story was over, Phoenix laid out their next step: go to the estate in the mountains, save Brass, and, if they could, find Silas Lamark and get him to end this.

When it was all over, Snow nodded. "Okay. I'm in."

"Really?" Phoenix asked. "What happened to before?"

"Do you want my help or not?" Snow asked.

"Well . . ." Angel mused.

"I'm coming," Snow said. "Let's do this."

"Arman?" a metallic voice spoke up.

Phoenix turned his attention to the Tavian Wheel. The arms on the device folded back up, revealing the light that had returned to Gamma's eyes.

"Gamma! You're awake."

"I am." Gamma's golden eyes shifted to examine its surroundings, including the others. "High Inquisitive Arakawa. Greetings."

"Hello, Gamma." Ink waved.

Snow stared at the head and felt a flicker of dread. She did her best to stay calm. It was a massive coincidence. That was the only thing it could be.

"I do not recognize this location or these individuals. Explain and identify."

"You're in the castellan's keep. The High Inquisitive has been using a Tavian Wheel to repair you," Phoenix said. "And these are old companions of mine."

"Are they the company you spoke of previously?"

"Yeah."

"Congratulations. I surmise you are happy to see them," Gamma stated. He spoke in the same monotone as ever, and yet Phoenix could have sworn he heard a pang of some emotion. Grief? Jealousy?

"Well, this has been fun, but Gamma and I have things to discuss," Ink said.

Gamma's eyes took in Phoenix's company as Ink lifted him off the wheel. They were all approximately the same age as Phoenix. The dark-skinned woman was the largest and eldest, and the young white man dressed in a cleric's attire the youngest. One of the other women carried herself like a thief. It was not uncommon for such people to join freelancer companies, where their skills could be leveraged into slightly more legal uses.

But there was cause for concern. On further study of Phoenix's company, Gamma determined what it was.

"Warning. You are in danger," Gamma reported.

Ink froze, looking down at the head. "Why?"

Angel looked around. Arno gripped his amulet. Snow felt her sense of dread grow. She recognized the autostruct now.

"Your female thief companion is one of the assailants who attacked and killed the Golden Shield," Gamma said.

Phoenix was in disbelief, while Ink looked over at Snow with renewed interest, and Angel was glaring murder.

All eyes were on Snow, who looked indignant.

"That thing is lying," Snow said. "Or confused. You said it yourself, it's broken."

"Height, build, hair, and eye color are a match. Her attire and equipment indicate the skill set of a thief, consistent with one of the assailants," Gamma said. "I am certain. She is the one who decapitated me, assaulted my company, and caused the destruction of our home."

49
EXPOSED

Snow looked around at everyone staring at her. Instinctually she took a half step back but managed to suppress the reflex to grab a dagger.

Arno eyed her and everyone else in the room warily. Angel looked ready to lunge if anything she didn't like happened. Phoenix didn't look angry, but the thousand-yard stare on his face told him he wouldn't be much use defusing the conflict.

It was up to the cleric.

He cleared his throat. "Snow? I think maybe for everyone's sake you should explain what that thing's talking about."

"I told you, it's lying or it's wrong," Snow said. "I don't know what it's talking about."

"The Golden Shield were other freelancers on the list of targets, like us."
Phoenix spoke up, never taking his eyes off Snow. His voice rang hollow,
like he could barely believe the words coming out of his own mouth. "Pitch
went after them. And he had someone with him when he did."

"It wasn't me," Snow said.

"Okay." Church nodded slowly, trying to let the calm in his voice
keep everyone else from doing anything they'd all regret for the next seven
years. He took hold of his amulet and used the truth prayer again. This
time, he targeted everyone in the room. "I need you to repeat that."

Angel watched Snow intently, fists already clenched. Snow glared at
her and at Arno. She recognized the sensation of the prayer and only just
kept the look of panic off her face. Her body tensed, and for the first time
in years, she felt real heat behind her face.

She only had to say three words, and she'd be completely exonerated.
It wasn't me. Three words. But her mouth didn't move. Her lips shifted,
but she couldn't even bring herself to part them. Pressure was building in
her throat, words trying to force their way out, but nothing came. Her jaw
was wired shut.

And while she stood there in silence, her guilt mounted in everyone
else's eyes. Phoenix's disbelief. Arno's fear. Angel's fury. It grew by the
second, and she hated it. She hated this prayer for exposing her like this.
Hated that damn autostruct head.

Her rage fueled her determination to beat Arno's prayer. With effort
that made her whole body burn, she willed her mouth open and forced out
a single word.

"It."

Arno's eyes widened. There was a flicker of hope in Phoenix's. Snow
barely noticed. Her fury turned inward. How could she be so stupid to get
cornered like this? She hated herself for not recognizing the autostruct
head sooner. She hated herself for not swiping Arno's amulet before trying
to convince them of her innocence.

"Wasn't."

The effort was making her feel physically ill. Her body felt like it was burning; a sensation she'd gone so long without feeling that it was almost alien to her. She hated that she was taking so long.

She hated herself for being guilty.

She agreed to work with the other bounty hunters to save her own skin. She attacked the Golden Shield. She brought Brass down and handed him over. And she was an idiot for thinking she could make that go away by trying to team up with a bunch of people who hated her.

Her eyes were bright blue, and tears welled in them. Any will to get the last word out drained from her. The heat vanished, she gasped for breath.

"Fuck."

Angel's fists started to glow. Arno pleaded with his eyes for her not to attack. She almost didn't listen.

Snow willed herself to go cold, to let the Heart of Ice freeze everything over so she wouldn't have to feel anything she didn't want to. Her eyes snapped from blue to pure white in a blink, and Phoenix winced. He'd never seen her eyes shift that much, that fast.

"I did what I had to do," Snow said defensively. Her voice was like glass shattering.

Phoenix shook his head. "Why?"

"I was a target too!" Snow said. It was exposing another lie, but she didn't care anymore. This bridge was already burning. She might as well take an axe to it and get some things off her chest. "I had a choice. I could help them, or they could take me."

"You're working with the people out to get us?" Angel growled.

"I was alone! It was that or end up caught or dead. What would you have done?"

"Told them to go fuck themselves! Fought!" Angel said, advancing toward Snow.

"You'd lose! Probably die."

"At least I wouldn't have died a backstabbing bitch like you!"

Angel swung for Snow, who blinked out of the way of the punch and reappeared behind her. Snow brought a dagger down into Angel's back. The blade barely broke skin, but ice spread out from the wound, freezing Angel's arm and shoulder in place. Angel threw her free elbow, knocking Snow back.

With an enraged flex of her arm, she managed to break the ice.

Phoenix drew his wand and aimed it at Angel. Arno hardened his own skin with a prayer, preparing to throw himself between everyone. Snow drew her second dagger just as Angel's eyes began to glow.

"Stop!"

A gust of wind whipped through the room. Everyone froze, turning their attention to the stairs. Elizabeth stood partway down them, looming over all of them with fury and disbelief etched into her face. Robyn's cries echoed through the halls from the guest room upstairs.

"You are not doing this here! You are not doing this, *period*!" she said.

Angel glared at her and Phoenix. "Why are you defending her? She sold us out! She probably came to your place to kill you!"

"I didn't!" Snow shouted.

"Liar!"

"I can't lie right now, you idiot!"

"You're both idiots!" Elizabeth shouted, silencing them again. "There are actual people who are actually trying to hurt you. They already have Brass, and they killed everyone Ruby knew to get to him. They've killed Church's friend, they killed Kaitlyn's team, and they tore up Angel's inn. They are still coming for all of you, and they are going to keep tearing all of our lives apart until you can stop this. You have more important things to do than try to do their jobs for them!"

Everyone fell silent. Phoenix was the first to react, putting his wand back in his holster. "She's right."

Arno dropped his prayer. Angel's burning glow began to die back down.

Snow sheathed her daggers in disgust. "Forget it. Coming here was a mistake." She stormed out.

Angel glowered at her the entire time, then scoffed when she was finally gone. "Good riddance."

Elizabeth shot her a disappointed look, but Angel held her glare. Phoenix ran after Snow while Arno just sighed. At the very least, that went better than the last time they'd all been together.

Ink surveyed the chaos everyone else had fallen into and smiled. It had been a long time since she'd been with a freelancer company. She'd forgotten how entertaining they could be.

"Well, Gamma, I think everyone could use a bit of privacy to sort this out," Ink said. She traced a pattern and disappeared into thin air.

Phoenix caught up to Snow in a hallway that overlooked the courtyard. To his surprise, she'd stopped trying to walk away. Everything immediately around her was covered in a thin layer of frost, but it was quickly melting. Snow was staring at her left wrist. At the tattoo of a constellation of five stars.

Their company tattoo.

She covered the tattoo up when she heard Phoenix coming and didn't turn to face him. If she was going to have to look at that confused, betrayed look on his face again; she was going to have to brace herself for it first.

"Come to get a few more shots in?" she asked.

"Do you actually think I would do that?"

Snow finally turned around. Her eyes had faded from pure white to an icy blue. Going cold was her shield, her escape, but it was failing her with Phoenix. It always had. It was one of the reasons things had ended between them. He cut through every defense she had.

"Why didn't you say anything?" Phoenix asked.

"About what?"

"About the other assassins," Phoenix said. "You didn't have to fight them alone. I would have helped. The whole reason we're all here is to help each other with this."

"I didn't think you would."

"Why not?"

"Because if things had been reversed, I wouldn't have helped you."

Phoenix winced at that. Snow was surprised she said it out loud. For a moment she blamed Church. But the prayer's magic had already disappeared. She'd made that confession all on her own.

Too late to take it back. "If you came to me with that story, I'd figure you were setting me up. And that's exactly how I thought you'd take it. I didn't think you would trust me enough to help me, so I didn't bother asking."

Phoenix shook his head. "But you helped *me*?"

Snow rolled her eyes. "I gave you a half-baked warning and then left before you could ask too many questions."

"And you kept an eye on my family."

"Pitch was eventually going to try to drag them into this. I was trying to make sure he didn't," Snow said, rationalizing. "They weren't part of the contract. They didn't have anything to do with this. But that didn't change anything. I helped bring down Brass, and I would have helped bring you down too."

Despite the number of lies she'd told him, Phoenix believed her when she said that.

"I have been on my own for the last seven years," Snow said. "The only reason I am still alive is because I have been willing to do whatever it takes to survive."

"Except ask for help."

"I don't deserve help!"

Snow's chest heaved. Her eyes were back to a piercing, bright blue. She could feel everything, almost as fully as before she'd ever gotten the

Heart of Ice. She felt scared, and ashamed, and desperate. More than anything though, she felt alone. And she wanted more than anything not to be.

"Chloe."

Her breath caught in her throat when he used her name. If it had been anyone else, or any other time, she'd have drawn a dagger and corrected him. Now, it just made her feel vulnerable. And it gave her just a sliver of hope, which she tried desperately to quash.

"You don't have to be alone. We're all in this together."

Snow scoffed. "Look me in the eye and tell me Angel or Church want anything to do with me."

At that moment, all she wanted was for Phoenix to say that he would talk to them, tell them to give her a chance or at least ignore how much they hated her and let her help them rescue Brass. And in another second, he might have. But at the prospect of having to talk to everyone, to try and smooth things over and work out a peace, he faltered. He hadn't been able to do something like that the last time they needed it.

But he wanted to try. He opened his mouth, but before he could say anything, Angel joined them in the hall.

"Hey. We going after Brass and Silas or not?"

Phoenix looked from Angel to Snow, but Snow's eyes were already going white again.

"Forget it," she said. "Just go."

"I—"

"Go."

Angel waited impatiently, and Snow had thrown up her walls again. Shoulders hanging, Phoenix sighed in defeat and left to join the others.

Snow turned back around so neither of them could see the tears that froze on her cheeks.

50
BETTER OR WORSE

Elizabeth stood in the sitting room rocking Robyn to calm her down. It had been a stressful day for the girl. First she had to leave the house for a completely new environment, then there was a shouting match just as she was thinking about going to sleep. Ruby had come downstairs to sit with her and had taken to staring at the floor. Elizabeth frowned.

They were going to have to figure out what to do with Ruby at some point. The girl was young. She'd been interrogated, tortured even. Almost everyone she knew was dead or missing, her job had been burned down, and she had no family to turn to.

Elizabeth knew firsthand what it was like for the Starbreakers to come crashing into your life, upend it, and leave you feeling completely out of place in your own world. She felt for the girl, wanted to help her, even if she wasn't exactly sure how.

"So, they were all Brass's company?" Ruby asked.

Elizabeth nodded. "They all met when they were kids, accidentally saved a town from a cult, and decided to stick together."

"Were you with them?"

Elizabeth chuckled. "No. I had a few run-ins with them back then, and Ar—Phoenix and I became close right before they broke up."

"What really happened?" Ruby asked. "I've heard about Relgen, but everyone has a different story to go with it. The . . . wrath of the gods. A plague. And everyone says it's cursed now?"

"We dug something up that should have stayed buried." Ruby jumped at the sound of Snow's voice in the doorway. "And we couldn't put it back in the ground fast enough."

Every word Snow spoke had a cold edge to it, so it was hard to tell when she was trying to be intimidating. Still, Ruby got the sense that she shouldn't pry into it any further.

"Sorry," Ruby apologized.

"Sure."

Elizabeth cast a disappointed look at Snow. "You really didn't go with them?"

"I think they made it pretty clear they didn't want me around." Snow waved a hand.

"That is not what that was about, and you know it."

Snow shot her a glare. "Really? Then tell me, what was that about if not telling me to fuck off?"

"You betrayed their trust," Elizabeth said. "But instead of trying to earn it back, you dug your heels in and tried to pretend you weren't at fault."

"I'm not."

"And you're lying to yourself."

Snow had absolutely no idea how Elizabeth was able to do that. She was a better lie detector than Church. "Is that just some warden thing? You can tell whenever people are lying?"

"No, it's an Elizabeth thing." She paused, lowering her voice once she realized Robyn was drifting off to sleep. "You still care about them. Even after the Heart changed how you felt about everything, even after Relgen, you care about your company."

"You don't know anything about how I feel."

Elizabeth glared and gestured with her eyes to the now sleeping baby in her arms.

Snow rolled her eyes but lowered her voice. "They're not my company anymore."

"Then why do you still have your tattoo?"

Snow tried to think of another defense to retort with, but nothing came. Tattoos were permanent to a point, but there were ways to be rid of them. Cover up jobs or magical removal in Sasel. The Starbreaker tattoo was just a five-star constellation loosely shaped like a sword. It could have been worked into anything. As for removal, it wasn't cheap, but money was no object for her.

She could have erased the reminder of her companions anytime she wanted to.

And she hadn't.

"Arman still has his too," Elizabeth said. "He thought about getting rid of it a few times, but he could never do it."

Snow shook her head. "Shut up."

"If you didn't care, you never would have warned Arman. But you gave him a fighting chance, and you knew he could give the others one too."

"Stop it."

"They need you. And you need them. And that's okay."

"I will stab you," Snow said, but her voice was devoid of any threat. If Elizabeth had been talking out of her ass, Snow could have ignored her without a second thought. But there wasn't a thing she'd said that Snow hadn't already tried to admit to herself a dozen times over.

She was so tired.

"It doesn't matter either way," Snow said. "They're already gone in Angel's burrow bar, or whatever it is. I couldn't go after them if I wanted to."

Fighting back the slight fear she still felt around Snow, Ruby spoke up. "Isn't there a wizard literally upstairs?"

Snow cocked her head. "What about her?"

"Brass told me that she can teleport people. Couldn't she get you to them?"

"I helped kill her errand squad. The only place she wants to teleport me to is a cell in Oblivion."

"While you're not wrong"—Ink materialized, sitting on the couch next to Ruby, who all but fell out of her seat—"I could theoretically be persuaded otherwise."

"I thought you went upstairs," Ruby said.

Ink rolled her eyes in amusement. It was almost too easy to spy on people when nobody knew the difference between a teleportation and an invisibility spell.

"I wasn't actually about to let an assassin connected to my investigation out of my sight," Ink said, her gaze fixed on Snow. "I wanted to see what you'd do while you thought I was distracted. I'm honestly surprised you didn't run away."

"Why not just arrest me?"

"Short of Oblivion, I can't think of any place that could hold you," Ink said. "And rotting in a cell there is a waste for a woman of your talents. If you tried to run, I'd have to send you there. But seeing as you haven't yet . . ."

Elizabeth looked at Snow. She didn't say anything now. The moment spoke for itself, and the choice in front of Snow was clear. If she was willing to put in the effort, she had a shot at getting her company back.

She was running out of excuses not to try. Elizabeth wasn't saying anything, but she was waiting for an answer. Companion Piece somehow felt heavier than normal on her hip.

"Fine," Snow relented. She looked at Ink. "What do you want?"

"You know, that might be one of my favorite things to hear people say," Ink mused.

Despite herself and the circumstances of the last weeks, Elizabeth smiled. But just as Snow was warming up to this, the smile suddenly vanished. Snow felt a fresh twinge of annoyance. "What? You got what you wanted, I'm going after them."

Elizabeth looked around at the windows. She could feel that somebody else was close by, someone she thought she recognized. But it wasn't any of the others. "Someone's here."

Snow's hands were hovering over her daggers. "In the keep?"

"I'm not sure. Maybe, maybe outside."

Snow looked at the window. A faint orange glow began to emanate from outside, getting brighter and brighter. Her eyes widened.

"Get down!"

She dove for Elizabeth and dragged her and Robyn to the floor as Elizabeth instinctively wrapped her daughter tightly in her arms. Snow hovered over them, shielding them both with her body. Meanwhile, after seeing the same glow, Ink rapidly worked through the motions of a spell to shield herself. Ruby didn't have the reflexes or instincts the other women had and stayed standing, confused.

Before Snow could repeat herself, the entire living room erupted in a ball of fire.

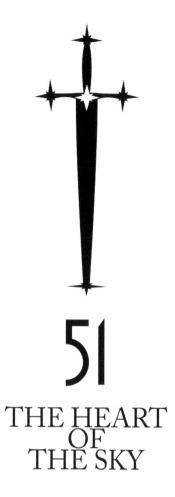

51
THE HEART OF THE SKY

Scorching heat and flame rolled through the room, and everything went orange. The only sound any of them could hear over the roar of the fire was Robyn screaming her lungs out. Smoke was rapidly filling the area, billowing out of the room through the gaping hole that had been blown in the wall.

The space immediately around Snow was spared from the blast, leaving Elizabeth and Robyn mercifully unscathed. The heat from the surrounding inferno was oppressive, but without Snow hovering over them, it would have been far worse.

To Snow, the room felt like a particularly warm summer's day. Uncomfortable but tolerable for now. She was more concerned with Elizabeth and Robyn, but they seemed all right. She stood up, and with a wave of her hand sent out an icy gust of wind that extinguished the flames immediately around them.

Elizabeth hugged Robyn as tight as she could against her chest as she staggered to her feet. "Ruby? Ink?"

"I'm okay!"

Ruby stumbled out of a column of flames, her clothes burning. Elizabeth and Snow both stared in shock, but Ruby seemed completely oblivious to the flames licking at her back and the hem of her shirt. Snow threw out another gust, putting the flames out.

"What happened?" Ruby asked.

"One guess," Snow said.

With the fire partially put out, they could hear now. An angry, arrogant voice bellowed from outside.

"Did you really think you were going to get away?"

Pitch had come. Probably for her, Snow guessed. *I brought him right to them. Stupid, stupid, stupid!* Snow drew both of her daggers, preparing for a fight.

From outside the gaping hole where one of the room's windows used to be, the sound of guards shouting and rushing out carried through, followed quickly by screams. The watch were brave, and those assigned to guard the keep were among the best, but they weren't a match for Pitch.

"Where's Ink?" Elizabeth asked.

The High Inquisitive of the Academy lay slumped in the corner, dazed and half conscious. She hadn't quite managed to get the shield spell up in time. Her combat magic was rustier than she thought.

"Just get out of here," Snow ordered. "I'll deal with him."

Elizabeth grabbed a dumbstruck Ruby's hand, and dragged her away. They slowed down only to haul Ink to her feet and then kept running. With them clear, Snow turned her attention in front of her and leaped from the window to see what was going on outside.

Just past a molten hole in the keep's outer walls and surrounded by dead and wounded members of the watch was Pitch. Flames licked his sleeves and his eyes burned solid orange. With every step, he set fire to the grass underfoot. A wicked grin spread across his face.

"Get tired of running?"

"I'm tired of you." Snow scanned the immediate surroundings, searching for the other assassins and seeing none of them. "Where're your friends?"

"Picking their next target," Pitch said. "I wanted to settle this score myself."

Frost rapidly spread across Snow, creeping over her armor, her face, and the blades of her daggers. Under her feet, the ground froze.

"You could never beat me before."

"Times change."

Pitch shot forward, flames trailing behind him. Snow blinked to meet him.

Meanwhile, Elizabeth ran, cradling Robyn in her arms while Ruby half supported, half dragged Ink. Elizabeth led them deeper into the keep, until they finally passed a small group of watch members running in the direction they'd come from.

Elizabeth halted and grabbed one of them by the arm. Kaitlyn, moving at a near sprint, jerked to a stop and would have fallen if Elizabeth hadn't held her up.

"Sergeant!" Elizabeth barked.

"Ma'am, you need to—" Kaitlyn stopped when she realized who she was talking to. "Elizabeth? I thought you were still on leave."

"Long story. I need you to take my daughter and these two and get them somewhere safe."

Elizabeth handed Robyn over to her gently, not letting go until she was absolutely sure that Kaitlyn had her.

"What are you going to do?" Ruby asked.

"I'm going to help Snow."

"What?!"

Elizabeth stared at Robyn, who was still crying. She felt like her heart was being ripped in two. But between Ruby, Kaitlyn, and even Ink, she had to trust that her daughter would be safe. Right now, there was nobody keeping Snow safe.

"Go!"

Elizabeth sprinted off in a different direction, moving at a speed that surprised Ruby. The young woman turned to Kaitlyn, confused. "Is she crazy?"

Kaitlyn gave Ruby a look that said Elizabeth was going to be fine and started shoving them in the direction of safe haven.

The fight between Pitch and Snow had carved a path of destruction through the keep and now spilled out into the courtyard. Some members of the watch had tried to follow after them, but anyone who'd gotten close had been quickly dropped by Pitch. All that remained were a few archers who'd taken positions in balconies or behind pillars and were taking shots at both of the assassins dueling in the courtyard.

Pitch swung his swords in wide arcs, producing wreathes of fire that raced out toward Snow and several members of the watch. She blinked out of the way of some and parried others out of the air with a cloud of frost. When they got close, their blades danced across each other.

Screaming as his eyes burned solid orange, Pitch swung with both swords, forcing Snow to parry with both of her daggers. Companion Piece held, but the unenchanted dagger in her off hand was cleaved at the hilt, and Pitch's sword carried through to tear a wound across her face. She screamed from the searing pain of the blade's white-hot edge, and for a second she lost focus.

Pitch threw an elbow to her face, followed by a slam of his sword hilt to her temple. She tried to parry his next attack, but he took the opportunity to disarm her, sending Companion Piece tumbling through the air. He stabbed at her heart, and she only just managed to blink out of the way.

She reappeared a short distance away, taking cover behind a pillar. It wasn't enough to escape, but it gave her a reprieve. She touched a hand to the fresh cut on her cheek, freezing it over to treat the burn and stop the bleeding. She'd been burned. She hadn't thought that was possible anymore.

"Not so easy when you're not the only one with power, is it?" Pitch taunted, throwing his arms open wide. When a watch archer tried to loose a crossbow bolt into him, he dodged, and answered with a fireball. Nobody else tried to shoot him after that.

"Congratulations," Snow spat. "You finally found a crutch big enough to prop you up."

Pitch dragged his swords across the ground, leaving trails of fire in his wake. "I'm going to enjoy this."

Snow grimaced. Despite her bravado, she wasn't sure about this fight. But she couldn't run. Not anymore. Let him come at her. Let him kill her, if he actually had it in him. Angel's words rang in her mind.

I'd have told them to go fuck themselves! Fought!

Snow held out her hand. Companion Piece whistled through the air, returning to her waiting hand. She gripped the dagger for dear life and prepared to meet Pitch's advance. She didn't have to.

The wind picked up to a howl that extinguished every flame in the courtyard and whipped Snow's hair into her face. She almost didn't see what came next.

In a blur of movement, Elizabeth came tearing through the air toward Pitch. The clothes she'd been wearing earlier were gone, replaced by hunter green leather armor and a silver circlet keeping her hair back. The emblem of a knight of Corsar, a three-pointed crown resting atop a sword, was emblazoned on her shoulder. In her hands, she wielded a polished, birch-white hunting bow with golden filigree along its grip. Most striking of all though was the massive, glowing, ethereal image of a pair of feathered wings that extended out from her back and propelled her through the air.

She came in fast and low, moving like a falcon in full dive. At the last second, she spun around, bringing both of her feet slamming into Pitch. A second after her boots connected with his chest, wind gusted out from her soles with enough force to send him flying backward. She backflipped away without ever touching the ground before finally coming to a stop, hovering a few feet in the air. Snow staggered out to meet her.

"Everyone, fall back!" she yelled to the members of the watch still present. "I'll handle this."

"Wings." Snow greeted her.

"Sorry I took so long," Wings said. She jerked her head at Pitch, who was forcing himself back onto his feet. "Is this guy bothering you?"

"Actually, yeah," Snow nodded. She almost didn't say anything else, because she knew it would give Wings satisfaction, but she was feeling generous. "I could use some help."

Wings reached into the quiver of arrows on her back. "Happy to."

Pitch glared up at her, pointing a sword. "Who the fuck are you?"

"Remember the Broken Spear? I was with them when you took the Crown of Daggers from us," Wings called out. "You broke my favorite bow."

Pitch cocked his head, vaguely recalling a company of pushovers and a stupid girl who could decently use a bow but otherwise couldn't fight worth a damn. "What?"

"You know what? Forget it. You're under arrest in the name of the castellan and the crown of Corsar."

"You think you scare me?" Pitch shouted, readying his swords. "I'll kill you both!"

"You go high, I'll go low," Snow said.

Wings shot up into the sky, and Snow sprinted forward. Pitch roared in fury, stabbing his swords into the ground. A line of fire shot out from him, forcing Snow to dodge. Up above, Wings nocked three arrows at once and fired. The wind took over their flight, scattering them in different directions before they each turned and homed in on Pitch.

The arrows came in from three different angles. He dodged one, sliced another out of the air, but the third struck him in the back. He growled but barely had a second to register the pain before Snow blinked into position in front of him and stabbed him in the leg.

He swung to counter, only for another arrow to pierce his hand and force him to drop one of his blades.

He lashed out in a fury, sending a jet of flame each at Snow and Wings. The heat was searing and turned the arrows embedded in him to ash, but his split attention made for poor aim. Wings looped through the air to avoid the blast, and Snow was able to blink out of its path.

Snow threw Companion Piece straight at Pitch's face. He batted the knife out of the air, only to regret it an instant later. As soon as his sword touched the dagger, ice spread across the blade, weighing it down.

Wings dove down from the air to deliver another kick, this time to the back of his head. Snow recalled Companion Piece and blinked in, stabbing Pitch again. He deflected it from his heart with an open hand, but it still struck him in the shoulder.

He rolled with the momentum of the strike, which spun him around to face Wings while she was still within striking distance. He struck her with his still frozen sword, knocking her out of the sky. Keeping his movement going, he transitioned into a spinning kick that knocked Snow back.

"Burn, you bitch!" he screamed.

He threw out both hands to unleash more fire, this time just toward Snow. Wings moved like a blur, speeding past Pitch to get between him and Snow. Her wings flapped once, and a wall of wind rushed out to meet the flames, scattering them.

"Why the fuck does this always happen!" Pitch shouted, desperate to kill Snow now. "How the fuck does someone always save you?!"

"Somebody's whiny," Wings noted.

"And stubborn," Snow added, looking at the number of freshly cauterized wounds they'd made across Pitch's body.

Wings shot forward, gripping her bow in both hands and pulling it apart at the center. In a flash, instead of a bow, she was holding two short, curved swords. Pitch and Wings crossed blades, sending sparks flying. Pitch grinned. Wings was fast, but he was better.

"You should have stayed in the air where I couldn't touch you," he taunted, as his lips curled into a snarl.

But, just when he thought he had an opening, the wind picked up, lifting Snow off of the ground and launching her into the air. She flew up and over Wings and him, disappearing into his blind spot. He tried to track her, exposing his back to Wings.

At the same time, Wings and Snow stabbed their blades into him. Snow landed on her feet and placed a hand on Pitch's chest. Ice crawled across his body, holding him in place, and Wings lifted into the sky before delivering another kick that sent him flying up into a wall. Weakened by the fire, it collapsed on top of him.

Both women panted, finally able to catch their breath.

"What was that?" Snow asked, gesturing to where Pitch had landed.

"What? You set him up, so I hit him," Wings said.

"I had him frozen in place, and you have *swords*. Why didn't you just take his head off?" Snow demanded, pointing her dagger at Wings now.

"I'm not usually a decapitation person! And did you miss the whole under arrest part?"

"Maybe the wall killed him," Snow said, hoping.

Wings combined her swords back into a bow and loosed an arrow. The winds traveled with it, blowing away some of the fires Pitch had ignited in the fight.

The section of wall that had collapsed onto Pitch was broken into pieces by the force of the winds, revealing Pitch, in pain, barely conscious, but very much alive.

"Well, on the bright side, I think we've got something you can trade to Ink for that teleport."

52
GLINTCHASER

B rass was barely able to raise his head when his cell door opened again. He'd lost track of how long he'd been locked up here. Days? Hours? He couldn't keep it straight. Pain and blackouts had robbed him of any real sense of time. There was only what was right in front of him.

He'd always been one for living in the moment, but this felt a bit extreme, even for him.

Sometimes it was Silas who came to him in his cell.

Sometimes it was other people; all of them generally less interesting but also easier to frustrate. Sometimes it was one of his old companions, just stopping by to reminisce about the old days, but he was pretty sure those weren't real.

Fading in and out of consciousness, Brass was vaguely aware that people were opening his cell door and half dragging, half carrying him somewhere, in chains. He saw stone walls, long hallways, other people, but it was mostly a blur. When the world finally came back into focus, he found himself sitting on one side of a desk, opposite Silas in a sparsely furnished office. An aroma of incense hung in the air here, at war with a lingering scent of tobacco.

"Silas?" Brass just managed to see the man. There wasn't much light in the room, just a dying fireplace and a single lightstone lamp, but it was enough to make his head hurt. "It's been a while. How've you been?"

Silas shook his head. "You aren't the first person we've questioned. Not the first person to resist questioning. But the amount of pain you've inflicted on yourself, for no other reason than to spite us, is utterly without sense."

He waited for a response, but for a few seconds, all Brass did was slump in his chair and struggle to breathe. He supposed he should have expected as much. Even with some minor attention and healing magic, Brass was in poor shape.

Eventually, Brass collected himself enough to ask a question. "Do you know what freelancing is?"

Silas raised an eyebrow. Of course he thought he knew what freelancing was. Everyone thought they did. But as far as Brass was concerned, nobody but another freelancer really understood the game.

"Being a freelancer is leaving your nice quiet life behind and trading it in for a worse one. Almost everybody you meet is someone trying to kill you, and the ones who aren't still don't like you very much. And that's the only constant you'll have. You never sleep in the same place for longer than it takes to run a job. You meet too many people to keep track of if you don't write it down. Your work changes every week—and the work you do?

"You're fighting monsters, tracking criminals, committing crimes, crawling underground, digging up ruins, running deliveries, and trying to keep a bunch of inept rich people with no survival instincts alive.

"And for all your trouble? You get to travel. Sometimes to places that don't exist. You'll see things nobody else alive has seen. Everywhere you go, you coming to town is the only thing anyone will talk about for years.

"And if you're damn good at what you do, smart about where you look for work, and *inconceivably* lucky, you survive longer than a season and end up making more glint than you know what to do with. But maybe you're good and smart and lucky and you still get killed, because that's the life.

"Does any of that sound like something that would attract a lot of *sensible* people?"

Silas narrowed his eyes. "You take *pride* in it?"

"If you don't embrace who you are, no one else will."

Ragged and covered in his own blood, Brass still managed to force a smile onto his face. It would have been a charming one, if it hadn't been so disfigured. "What's this about, Si? Don't tell me you actually think that the two hundredth time's the charm."

"You may have convinced several of the men you can't be broken, but I won't be so easily deterred," Silas warned.

"People say I can't be broken?" Brass asked, his voice thick with sentiment. "That's so sweet of them. Hey, tell them I said hi. Especially that one Iandran with the cleft chin? He was cute."

Brass looked Silas over, trying to see what torture was in store for him, but he didn't see anything that looked intended to extract information from him. He sincerely hoped that Silas didn't intend to simply beat answers out of him. Even with the change of scenery, it would be boring. And it still wouldn't work.

"I'll pass along the message," a new, gruff baritone spoke up from behind him.

Brass craned his neck, wondering how he'd missed somebody standing behind him. It was a man in his later years. He had blond hair, though it had started to go gray, and steely blue eyes. Age had done nothing to dull his soldier's physique. He was tall with broad shoulders and a muscular body. He wore simple, finely tailored clothes, but he had the rigid posture and confident bearing of a professional soldier.

"Oh. You're new. Hey Silas, who's your friend? Somebody else who wants a turn with me?"

"There won't be any torture today." The man answered for Silas, confirming what Brass had already suspected.

The way Silas looked to the man with equal parts deference and a desire for approval, the way he stood when he showed up, Brass knew—this was the real man in charge.

"To break a man," Silas's boss intoned, "you must first understand him."

Brass chuckled, even as his ribs punished him for it. "Good luck with that."

"You think you're beyond comprehension. But you're not," he said. "There are things that defy understanding. You are not one."

The way he said it, he sounded like he had seen those things. Brass wondered what they were and just what seeing those things had made this man into.

"Well then, what's your read so far?" Brass asked.

"You're insufferable."

"I'm told."

"But not without respectable qualities," he continued. "You have skill. A tolerance for pain. And though you play the fool, your mind is sharp."

"Now you're giving me mixed signals."

"Ultimately though, you are impulsive, undisciplined, and full of bravado. I find it little wonder that a trail of destruction and chaos follows you and your kind." His expression was stern. Disciplinary, but not angry. "You are useful for what knowledge you can provide, and nothing more."

"Right," Brass said. Through blood and a swollen face, he saw an opportunity. "Job to do. Lives to save. All very important. How's that going?"

Silas's face twitched, and his hands balled into fists, but the man in charge held up a hand. "So callous towards the plight of so many," he said.

"Can you blame me?" Brass gave a weak shrug. "I've never met them."

"You are exactly the sort of scoundrel people imagine when they use the word glintchaser," he said. "You care nothing for the lives ruined in the wake of your own selfish pursuits."

"And you—" Brass tried to stand up from his chair, only for his body to give out from underneath him the instant he attempted it. This wasn't like his first conversation with Silas. He was at the end of his rope. "Fuck." He paused to catch his breath, swallowed, and settled for just looking the man in charge in the eye. "You are everything everyone hates about knights."

Both Silas and his master's eyes widened. Brass was even more clever than they'd given him credit for. The glintchaser smirked.

"Did you actually think you were doing a good job of hiding it?" Brass asked. "Walking around without fancy symbols doesn't change what you are."

"No," Silas's master said. His voice almost sounded like he took solace in that.

"I wouldn't normally disparage a person's career choice, but I think you and your friends might have gotten into the wrong one," Brass said.

"You dare—" Silas snapped.

"Hey, last I checked, knights were supposed to help people. Not hire out assassins to hunt them down so they can torture them." If he could still feel his arms, he might have held a hand up. "Don't tell me. The greater good?"

"The enemies we face make no considerations for niceties. We can afford no less."

"So you make deals with crime lords and assassins. And torture people for information. All so you can chase after some magic powers," Brass said. "I've been paying attention." He swung his head around to gesture at their surroundings. "All of this. Over a bunch of magic sticks some fossils used to make big angry statues shoot fire. Remind me what's so great about this good?"

"If you knew what we were up against, you would not be so quick to judge," Silas said.

"Then enlighten me."

Brass stared them both down as best he could with one of his eyes swollen shut. It was more pathetic than intimidating. Silas met his stare with contempt, but his master was bemused. Despite every reason there was to hate glintchasers, their recklessness and selfish profiteering, it was impossible not to recognize the fight in Brass's spirit.

For Brass's part, he was at a crossroads of enervation and elation. On one hand, he had been in so much pain for so long that paradoxically it hurt less now, as pain simply became his new normal. Not a single movement or breath didn't sting or ache, and he was so very tired. But on the other, he was very close to cracking this whole thing wide open. Silas's master was fixated on him. On glintchasers as a whole. And that fixation was making him chatty. Just a little more prodding, and Brass would have him.

But before either knight could give anything else away, or Brass could ask more questions, the door of the office opened, and a man who walked like a soldier but dressed like a civilian came in.

"Sirs!" he barked, holding out a sealed envelope. "A letter from the Handler. Marked urgent."

Silas read it first, and Brass did his best to read Silas. Whatever the letter said, it had him worried. After a few moments staring at the paper, he passed it to his master, looking for guidance. He was harder to read for Brass, his reaction stoic.

"Inform the men we're moving to high alert," the master ordered. "And get this man back in his cell."

Brass cursed his luck as he was dragged out of the office. Unable to struggle or even hold up his head, he could only weakly call out as he was dragged away: "Okay, this was fun. Same time tomorrow?"

When Brass was gone, Silas turned to his commander. "Sir, if the Starbreakers are coming here . . ."

"We will need support," the commander stated. "Hold this place until I return."

"Sir? Where are you going?"

The commander's face hardened. "To get support."

53

REUNION

Back in his cell, Brass sulked. So far, this plan of letting himself get captured to get information on the bad guys—which he hadn't come up with until after he'd already *been* captured—was going poorly. After working Silas for he didn't even know how long in interrogation, he had some information, but still nothing he could act on. And then, just when he had the head honcho himself running his mouth like a river, he was cut off. Somebody or something had Silas's boss scared enough to make him do some very un-knightly things, and he needed to know who or what. That was the real key to ending this.

If only he wasn't in a constant fog of agony, he might be able to think straight long enough to figure it out.

Maybe the next time they talked, he'd get more out of them. Next time. It could be hours until then. Or days. Or minutes. Or maybe never. Maybe today was finally the day they caved and killed Brass. A sudden, loud ping of metal snapped him out of his own thoughts. The spots on the door where the hinges would be were glowing red hot. A second later, the door fell to the floor with a clang that echoed through the stone cell and hallway beyond.

A flood of light from the hall blinded Brass, and it took him several seconds to adjust. When he did, he wondered if he'd already died when he wasn't paying attention, or if he was close enough to death to start seeing things.

Standing in the door of his cell was a tall, well-muscled, dark-skinned woman with glowing fists and eyes.

"Angel?" he asked.

Angel turned and called down the hallway. "Found him!"

His skin was swollen from cuts, bruises, and burns. Dried blood streaked with sweat covered his face, matted his hair, and stained his clothes. Wounds covered his body, several of which looked infected.

"You look like shit."

"I figured I'd try a new stylist, but I don't think the look works for me."

"Oh good. You can still talk."

More footsteps came from the hallway. Phoenix and Church appeared in the doorway, and Brass's face broke out into a massive, bloody smile. When Phoenix saw Brass, he winced. Church gagged.

"Gods and saints, Brass," Phoenix whispered.

"I know," Brass lamented. "They took my shoes."

"Church," Phoenix said, "can you do something about this?"

Church kneeled down in front of Brass. "It'll probably be the last big prayer I can manage today, but yes."

Church touched a hand to Brass's chest and spoke. The amulet embedded in his breastplate began to glow as he neared the end of the prayer.

Then, Brass's head jerked up, and he involuntarily gasped for air. His whole body began to glow from inside, and light poured out of his eyes and mouth. A feeling like fire tore through his veins, pulling the torn fibers and broken bones back together. The aches in his muscles vanished. His exhaustion dissolved as if he'd just snorted a week of sleep. Every second of torture and pain burned away over the span of a few seconds. He let out a mad cackle.

The light subsided, leaving behind a rejuvenated Brass, who perceived the faint taste of wine. Brass's cackle faded to a light chuckle, and he got to his feet. His body was healed, and his company—his friends—were back together. He felt on top of the world.

"Oh yeah! That is good stuff!" Brass laughed. "I could kiss you right now."

"Please don't."

"Should've just carried him out," Angel muttered to herself.

"Saints, it's good to see all of you." Brass's eyes scanned them for a moment, and his smile shrank. "Hey, where's Snow?"

The other three exchanged looks. Church spoke first. "Snow?"

"You know. Super pale. Makes ice. Likes to stab people. Is she here? Did she get away?"

Phoenix cleared his throat. "Brass. I don't know how to tell you this but—"

"The bitch is a traitor," Angel interrupted. Phoenix shot her a glare.

"Snow was the one who put you here," he said.

Brass rolled his eyes. "I know that."

"You do?"

"Yeah." Brass looked around as if he'd just stated the obvious. "Figured it out a while ago. After she and the other dirks turned me over to the Handler, the rest of them turned on her and tried to turn her in too. I told her they would, but you know how that song and dance goes. Nobody ever listens to me." An annoyed expression crossed his face for a second, but with a shrug, it was gone. "I tried to buy her time to get away, but I wasn't sure if it worked."

Angel gave him a look of utter disbelief but said nothing, opting to just shake her head.

"She ended up at my place. She's safe," Phoenix assured him.

"She went to you?" Brass sighed in relief, only to then look at all of them with questioning eyes. "Well then why isn't she here?"

"Because we didn't want a backstabbing dirk for back up?" Angel offered.

"Well, way to ruin a perfectly good reunion, everyone," Brass huffed. "It's fine. I can say hi when we get out of here."

"Not yet," Phoenix said.

"Not to sound ungrateful, but *why?*" Brass asked, cocking his head. It wasn't that he didn't enjoy being locked in a dungeon, but he was starting to miss the sun.

"The person who put out the contract on us is a man named Silas Lamark. If he's here, and we can find him, we can end this whole thing."

"And him," Angel added.

"You know what? Perfect. I've been meaning to have another chat with him," Brass said.

"You've met him?"

"Met him? I've been interrogating him since I got here," Brass said. When nobody believed him, he sighed, and gestured to his chains. "Is someone going to get me out of these?"

All gazes fell on Angel, who groaned in annoyance.

After Brass stole a pair of shoes off one of the guards, Angel tossed the men that were still breathing into a cell. The rest of the dungeon was empty, though there were signs of recent occupants. While she tried to figure out which of the eight keys she'd stolen were used to lock the cell doors, Phoenix dug into his bottomless bag and produced a sword for Brass.

"Ooh!" He admired the intricate, sweeping design of the handguard. "What's this one do?"

"It's the one we got from the sunken playhouse," Phoenix explained.

Brass smiled as he recalled the trip and unsheathed the blade. It glided out of the sheath as if it wasn't even there, revealing a thin silver blade with an impossibly fine edge. Fountaine, the unbreakable sword whose blade never dulled.

"You just had this sitting around?" Brass asked.

"The Academy still pesters me for something every so often," Phoenix said. "Selling them a few artifacts from the old days usually shuts them up, so I keep a bunch in reserve. I'm actually starting to run out."

"Guess I can give it back when I'm done with it," Brass lamented. He gave the blade a test flourish. He tried to send it into his wrist-pocket, before remembering that was gone now, and settled for resheathing the sword.

"So, where to?"

54

THE
KNIGHT

The estate's exterior grounds were well-patrolled, but inside was another story. There were people around, but almost all of them were servants and cooks. The busiest place was the kitchen, but it was also easily avoided and not exactly surrounded by high security.

The decor was barren to an almost unsettling degree. In some places, there were sparse inclusions for comfort, like benches and carpets, but entire halls and rooms were empty, with the smell of dust clinging to the bare walls and floors.

Which isn't to say it wasn't well-supplied.

On the way out of the dungeon, they passed massive storerooms that were full of provisions. Silas was keeping the small army guarding this place fed. There just wasn't anything in the massive house that didn't serve a basic function.

The few times they did run into actual armed guards, it was a nonissue. They were well equipped and disciplined, but not a single one was quick enough to do anything more than look startled before Angel punched them or Church put them to sleep.

It left a question in all of their minds though. *Who are these people?* Everything Brass passed along seemed to indicate knights or soldiers, but those they saw all lacked any kind of heraldry those sorts would normally wear. No shared colors, no symbols, no device. But all the behaviors.

Whoever these people were, they didn't want anyone else to know.

They managed to get to the door of Silas's office without alerting the entire mansion to their presence, though there were maybe a dozen unconscious people who would wake up in the next hour and be able to do just that.

Considering the only one of them who'd had any practice at sneaking around in the last seven years was Brass, Phoenix considered that an acceptable performance.

"When we get in there, don't just kill him," Phoenix said, staring directly at Angel. He spoke in a hushed whisper, careful not to give them away. "We still need answers."

She grunted and cracked her knuckles. "No promises."

She approached the door and rolled out her shoulders. Then, almost casually, she kicked the door clean off its hinges.

The four of them moved in.

Silas wasn't there. In his stead, sitting calmly as if waiting for an appointment, was the man Silas took his orders from. He stood up before any of them could say anything but otherwise held his ground. Phoenix aimed his wand, Brass and Church readied their swords, and Angel's hands began to glow.

"Don't move," Phoenix ordered.

The man didn't so much as flinch. After an initial look of surprise when they'd burst in, his expression had remained even and unmoving.

"The Starbreakers," the man said. It was less a greeting and more a statement that he knew who they were.

"Call for help and Angel puts you through your desk," Brass said.

"I'll put the desk through him," Angel corrected.

"Even better. Hey, where's Silas?"

Phoenix looked from Brass to the man. "This isn't him?"

Brass shook his head. "Nah, this is his boss."

"You've met him?"

"Yeah, a while ago."

"And you didn't think to mention it earlier?"

"It slipped my mind! Cut me some slack, I've suffered a serious trauma."

Phoenix groaned but dropped it. Bickering in front of the enemy always got embarrassing, fast. Instead he turned to Church and gestured with his head to the man. Church nodded and used his truth prayer.

The man raised an eyebrow but said nothing.

"Who are you?" Phoenix asked. He kept his wand trained on the man. Even though they had him outnumbered four to one, there was something about him that made Phoenix uneasy.

The man's piercing gaze zeroed in on Phoenix, and judgment burned in the blue of his eyes.

"Sir Haegan of Whiteborough."

"Are you the one who put out a contract on us?"

"I ordered Silas to arrange it."

"Did anyone order you to do that?"

"No."

It seemed like they had their man, but Phoenix wanted to be absolutely certain that this was the top of the chain. If they were even a link off, this wasn't over. Truth prayers could be talked around with enough discipline.

That was something Haegan seemed to have plenty of.

"Do you work for anyone else?"

"Not anymore."

Phoenix cocked his head. *Gotcha.* "Who *did* you work for before?"

"The castellan of Relgen, under the Knights of the Purple Rose." Haegan looked them in the eye in turn, and it felt like he was looking through their lives and daring them to look through his. The raw force behind his eyes rooted them to the spot.

Church was the first to figure out who they were dealing with.

"You were at Loraine."

"I was at Relgen. I could see you boarding *Rogue Imperia* from a farm at its outskirts. And I watched the light swallow the city whole and the life leave every living thing," Haegan said. "It was my home. And it died in front of me."

There was no malice in his voice, as there had been every other time someone had said those words to Phoenix. In its place was sadness, profound and raw.

"So this was revenge?"

"Of course you'd think that," Haegan said, sounding almost disappointed. "But no, glintchaser. However hard it may be for you to imagine, this isn't about you or your failure." He paused to stare into the distance, briefly lost in a memory. "When I walked what was left of Relgen, and I saw the bodies lining every street and home, I was angry. But even then, I knew you were symptoms, not the disease."

With hollow eyes, he stared at each of them in turn. "This kingdom is in ruins. It was even before Relgen fell. Wars. Monsters. Crime. Calamity. It's all the crown and their castellans can do to keep people safe within their walls. And beyond them? Chaos. The knightly orders were made to change things, but there are so few of them and so many dangers, they can only be deployed for the most dire missions. And in their absence . . . we turn to you. Thieves and profiteers, who care only for themselves and their own ends. The kingdom's suffering is your opportunity. The threats to its existence are your curiosity. No, you are not the disease. Relgen is what happens when we rely on glintchasers to protect us." Haegan shook his head. "And I said never again. Never again would Corsar depend on the selfish and the cowardly to defend her. I would find power, and allies, and I would use them to save us from all the evils you abandoned us to. Whatever the cost.

"I saw the power of the Hearts firsthand when you stopped the Servitor at Loraine. They have the power I need to end this nightmare. To resolve the unfinished business of you and every other company who scours the bones of this land without a care for what they dredge to the surface in the process," Haegan said. "All of you, and all the other names in the contract, are the keys to finding them."

He picked a silver-and-gold amulet up off the desk, running his thumb along its face. "I assume you came here to end the contract. Surrender now, and that will be the end of it. Resist, and what I did to Brass, I will do to all of you."

"You can't want to do this," Church said. "You're a knight. You want to help people. This isn't the way to do it."

"I'm not interested in what *you* think the right way is," Haegan said. For just a moment, his composure cracked, and Church saw through to Haegan's core. One of pain and grief and righteous indignation. In that moment, the cleric understood, there was nothing he could say or do that would make Haegan back down. "Every second I spend gathering strength, so does every source of darkness in this world. Every moment I spend persuading people to give me what I need, people are dying. I tried the 'right' way. I served my king, worked with people like you. The results speak for themselves."

"Okay." Angel had heard enough. "Fuck this."

She lunged, grabbing Haegan by the throat and dragging him up and over his desk. She slammed him into the floor and kneeled down over him. The light cascading off her filled the room. She raised a fist, even as Phoenix and Church yelled for her not to kill him.

Then Haegan's eyes changed from blue to purple.

As if pulled by ropes, Angel flew off of Haegan and shot straight up into the air, not stopping until she collided with the ceiling. Everyone else jumped back in surprise. He slowly rose to his feet and picked his amulet up off the floor.

He spoke a command phrase into it. "For Atreus."

The amulet vanished in a flash of light, and in a blink, Haegan was encased in ornate, golden-plate armor, complete with a winged helmet. Brass reacted first, lunging with *Fountaine*. Haegan held up a hand, and the sword skipped off the air in front of his palm as if it had struck an invisible wall. Church tried to use a prayer to hold him, only to feel the prayer blocked as it tried to latch on to his mind. Phoenix fired a blast from his wand that splashed harmlessly against the knight's armor.

Haegan threw out a hand, and Brass, Church, and Phoenix were thrown backward into the walls of the room. Phoenix set his goggles to detect magic. Haegan's armor lit up, but through the visor in the helmet, Phoenix could see that the knight himself was lighting up, even brighter than his armor.

For a second Phoenix was utterly confused. Then he made the connection. Haegan wasn't just searching for the Hearts. He'd already found one.

Angel had barely fallen back down to the ground before she shoved herself to her feet and launched herself at Haegan. Before she could touch him, Haegan's eyes changed from purple to silver, and a cloud of crackling smoke appeared behind him. He disappeared into it, the smoke vanishing with him. Angel passed through the space he'd been a second ago, catching nothing but air and the taste of ozone.

A sudden stillness fell over the room. Brass looked around, frantically waving his sword in case he saw anything that needed stabbing.

"Where did he go?" he asked.

"Phoenix?" Church prompted.

Phoenix looked around, still with goggles set to detect magic, but there was no sign of Haegan in the room.

"He's gone," Phoenix said.

"With as many tricks as he has, I'm starting to wonder why he didn't come after us himself," Brass said.

"Anonymity," Phoenix guessed, thinking back to the knights without any colors. "There's someone he doesn't want knowing this operation exists."

"So can we kill him or not?" Angel asked.

"Everyone," Church interrupted. "I think we've got company."

Several more smoke clouds appeared in the room, surrounding them. Instinctually, the four of them began to close ranks in the center of the room, arranging themselves back to back. One by one, figures began to step out of the smoke, until a small crowd of armed men and women encircled them. At the vanguard on one side stood Cull. Opposite him, the Fellblade.

Cull looked around and grunted.

The Fellblade took in the situation with a grin. "It looks like the madman wasn't lying."

"He brought them right to us," Phoenix realized.

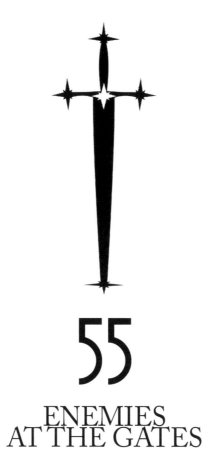

55

ENEMIES
AT THE GATES

n an entirely different part of the estate, Silas waited. He didn't like any
of this.

A crackling smoke cloud signaled Haegan's arrival in the room.

He walked right past Silas, who immediately fell into step alongside
him.

"Sir."

"I want you to order a full evacuation of our people. Burn whatever
they can't carry," Haegan said, not slowing down.

"But sir, we have them cornered. The bounty hunters alone outnumber
them six to one."

"It won't be enough," Haegan said.

Silas was incredulous. "Sir, everyone has their limits. And if the mercenaries aren't enough, our men and women could support them."

Haegan stopped and finally turned to face Silas. A loyal soldier. A skilled knight. But a young man. Too young to know just what the Starbreakers had been capable of in their prime. Haegan needed to make sure he was understood. "No." The weight in his voice made Silas shrink back. "I know the Starbreakers. I've seen them fight with my own eyes. For whatever their deficiencies, they excel at death. And they are cornered. They will fight with everything they have, and they will destroy everything in front of them. I won't sacrifice our blood to that."

"We are more than willing to die."

"Then die when it matters." Haegan's brow furrowed. Silas had always been eager to martyr himself. Too eager. "There will be other ways to find the Hearts. But if this order is compromised, it's the end of everything."

Silas nodded his understanding.

"Do a thorough search of the grounds, starting with the dungeons," Haegan added. "If the Starbreakers got in, they likely left some of our own in their wake."

Silas nodded again, but he didn't leave yet. "What will you do?"

"I can't teleport all of us to safety," Haegan said. "So I'm going to make sure you have enough time to leave."

Silas's eyes went wide. He wanted to protest, but he choked it down. He had his orders.

Steeling himself, he saluted Haegan and left to begin the evacuation.

Haegan walked as briskly as he could to the mansion's armory. Teleporting would have been faster. But he wanted to conserve as much of his strength as he could. He suspected he was going to need it.

56
THE STARBREAKERS

B rass scanned the faces of everyone around them. Some of them were still trying to get their bearings. Others were already staring, recognition on their faces. If this many dirks collapsed on them at once, they were in trouble.

"All right, nobody move!" Brass shouted, waving his sword.

Through sheer confidence in his voice and the mad look in his eyes, Brass had everyone rooted to the spot. Everyone except for Cull, who had seen this trick before and was having none of it.

As Brass opened his mouth to start rambling, Cull charged, brandishing Charnel. Angel shoved Brass aside and raised a hand. The sword struck, and a shock wave ripped through the room, kicking up debris and pushing everyone a half step away from the epicenter. Blood ran down from the hand Angel had used to catch the blade.

"Nice sword," she said, clenching a fist.

She threw a punch, and the room exploded into chaos.

Brass lunged and *Fountaine* became a blur, cutting down three men before anyone could react and parrying the first man to actually attack him. He danced through the crowd, deflecting blows and expertly countering. Church followed his lead, Zealot flashing as he stole the sight of the people closest to him and started swinging, alternating between sword and prayer.

Hanging back, Phoenix cycled his wand and pointed it straight down, obscuring himself in a cloud of smoke. While people searched for him, he cycled the wand again and blanketed every dirk in front of him in fire. For a few seconds he had them in retreat, and several of them on fire. Then a bolt of lightning cut through the smoke, striking Phoenix dead in the chest.

His vision went white, and he was flung off of his feet and across the floor. Smoke curled off him, and every part of his body felt numb. If not for his enchanted armor, he wasn't sure he'd still be awake.

Skip chuckled. He had to give the glintchaser credit. The smoke had been a neat trick. But Skip didn't need to see someone to feel the electricity inside them, and that was all he needed to aim.

Brass became lost in the crowd of cutthroats, fending off attacks on all sides. He disarmed one person and used their weapon to stab someone else. He parried an attack at the same time that he ducked under another. He kicked, stabbed, even pulled somebody's hair at one point and dragged them around to use as a human shield. Then, Brass crossed his sword against one made of shadow, and found himself face-to-face with the Fellblade.

"Ooh. That's neat." Brass eyed the weapon. "Where'd you get it?"

"Do you ever shut up?" the Fellblade asked.

"Nope."

Brass kicked the Fellblade back, giving him space to deal with the two other attackers closing in on him. Annoyed, the Fellblade sank back into the shadows, reappearing in Brass's blind spot and lunging. As if he had eyes in the back of his head, Brass neatly stepped around the attack, came up behind the Fellblade, and slashed, raking Fountaine across the Fellblade's back. It didn't kill him, but it sent him reeling.

Brass smirked. "You'll have to do better than that."

Nearby, Church was calling on prayer after prayer as he fought, healing himself, enhancing his strength, and weakening his enemies. But as he finished another one, all he felt was a pop and a queasy feeling in the pit of his stomach as something undid his prayer.

Zealot took over defending as Church sorted through his confusion. He'd used several prayers, but he knew he hadn't overreached yet.

Everything made sense when he spotted the Jury, who stood back from the mob. The priest of the black saint made eye contact with Church and nodded. With a prayer of his own, he doubled the strength of one of the people attacking Church.

Church broke the prayer with a counter and dropped the man with a deft swing of Zealot. The sword raged at the Jury's presence.

A servant of the Betrayer! Slay him where he stands!

Each cleric tried to hold the other's mind, and neither of them succeeded. But while Church and Zealot were both distracted, another dirk got in close enough to bury an axe in Church's back. His armor saved him, but pain shot out from the wound. Zealot moved his arm for him, dropping the attacker, but that only made everything hurt more.

On instinct, Church tried to heal himself, forgetting to pay attention to the Jury. Instead of healing him, Church's prayer made the wound open even more as the Jury reversed it. His vision swam, and he dropped to his knees.

On the floor, still seeing spots, Phoenix quickly set his armor to resist electricity. Skip, annoyed Phoenix was still moving, let a shower of lightning arc off him and onto Phoenix. It made him feel like his entire body was covered in pins and needles, and he was pretty sure his heart skipped a beat, but he stayed awake.

His whole body was shaking too much to aim his wand properly, so Phoenix dug into his belt and pulled out a fire sphere. He threw it in Skip's general direction and then threw up a shield. Skip was confused for a moment as the sphere rolled across the floor, but once it started to glow bright orange, he realized what was about to happen.

"Incoming!" the bounty hunter screamed.

The ensuing ball of fire engulfed half of the room. Skip managed to clear the epicenter of the blast and avoid being incinerated. Several other dirks weren't as lucky. The Fellblade heard Skip's warning and melted into the shadows. Brass improvised a human shield out of the closest bounty hunter.

Flames licked at Cull and Angel, who were at the edge of the blast. Cull recoiled from the heat, but Angel barely noticed. While the pain threw Cull off balance, Angel finally landed a solid hit, and the flash of light that came off her was even brighter than the one from the fire sphere. Cull was lifted off his feet and sent flying through a window of the study. The Fellblade tumbled to the floor, spat out by a dark corner that had been illuminated in the flash.

Brass leveled *Fountaine* at the Fellblade's throat, tipping his chin up with the tip of the sword. His eyes dared the Fellblade to make a move.

At this point the dirks who were still standing began to rethink their odds of success, and whether any reward was worth this. Most of them decided it wasn't and began running.

The blast and Angel also distracted the Jury long enough for Church to actually heal himself. Gripping Zealot tightly he jumped to his feet and rushed forward. Jury prayed for stone skin. Church broke the prayer with a counter and drove Zealot through the Jury's chest.

"Counter that," he spat, Zealot's fury leaking into him.

Phoenix smiled through his pain as he staggered to his feet, still tingling all over from the bath of lightning he'd gotten. They were winning.

The smile disappeared when another cloud of crackling smoke formed in the center of the room and Haegan returned, now wielding a sizeable war hammer.

Angel glared as he appeared, her eyes burning. With a growl, she fired beams of light from her eyes straight at Haegan's face. At the same time, he gestured with a hand, and Phoenix was lifted off his feet and catapulted into the path of Angel's beams.

Phoenix screamed before falling to the floor, smoking. His pockmarked armor sizzled at its edges, and his chest was covered in burns.

As she saw Phoenix lying motionless on the ground, Angel froze. And for an instant, she was back on the ridge, looking at Church bleeding in the snow, as her stomach sank into her feet. In the moment that she faltered, lightning surged through her body, and she dropped to her knees.

Skip chuckled to himself in a corner as he put everything he had into frying Angel. After almost getting burned to a crisp, Skip had been planning on running. But when the shiny man who'd teleported him here in the first place showed up again and started kicking ass, he figured he had a chance.

He'd wanted to run with the others until he saw things turn back in their favor. In a way, this was even better—now there were fewer people to split the reward with.

"Guys!" Brass shouted.

Before he could run to either of his friends' aid, the room immediately around him grew impossibly dark. Too late, he realized the Fellblade had taken his dare. With a yelp from Brass, he and the Fellblade were swallowed by shadows and disappeared from the room.

To Brass's eyes, everything had been replaced by an empty, black void. Nothingness stretched out in from him in every direction. And it was cold. Impossibly, painfully cold.

Shapes began to materialize in the void. Like bodies but twisted, bloated, and stretched out all wrong. Some of them wore the faces of people he knew. Others didn't seem to have faces at all. They ambled toward him, coming from all sides. A chorus of hollowed, tortured moans emanated from them as they drew nearer.

Brass chuckled nervously to himself. "Oh, this isn't good."

Across the room, Church's eyes went wide as he watched Phoenix and Angel fall and Brass vanish, all in rapid succession, only to have his attention pulled back to the Jury when he felt stabbing pain shoot across his neck. By a combination of divine favor and sheer will, the Jury was still alive and was using all his strength to bury his dagger in Church's clavicle. Blood dripped down his chin as he said another curse. Church immediately felt his legs go weak, even as he watched the light return to the Jury's eyes. With a word from his bloodstained lips, the Jury stood up farther, and Church's own strength drained away. He recited his own prayer to keep himself healed and standing. They entered a stalemate—the Jury unable to kill Church faster than Church could heal himself—but Church too busy keeping himself alive to fend off the Jury's attack. With his free hand, Jury made a grab for Church's amulet, trying to pry it from his armor. Church grabbed at Jury's wrist, trying to stop him.

Slumped in a corner, Phoenix coughed. His armor was ruined. His chest screamed in pain, and his friends were down. In a desperate attempt to turn the tide back in their favor, he aimed his wand at Skip. If they could get Angel back in the fight, they still stood a chance. He hoped.

He fired once, missing. Haegan, realizing Phoenix was still fighting, closed his fist. Phoenix's wand was yanked from his hand and flew across the room. Then he was lifted off the ground and pulled close enough for Haegan to swing his hammer. Phoenix turned his head to avoid the blow, but it caught his goggles, turning one of the lenses into a spiderweb of cracks.

"I'm beginning to wonder if I overestimated you," Haegan said.

Phoenix flailed and kicked in midair to no avail. As he struggled, Haegan slowly closed his fingers. Phoenix felt his whole body constricted until he could barely move. Then it started getting hard to breathe.

"Silas believed Brass couldn't be broken," Haegan said. "I hope for your sake, you put up significantly less resistance."

Phoenix's goggles were on the fritz, straining his eyes as they flickered between settings. It became impossible to make sense of any of it. For a moment, as Haegan slowly crushed him to death, he thought he saw a second figure covered head to toe in magic as bright as the reading he got off Haegan, only for it to disappear as soon as he saw it. Everything started to feel cold, and his head felt lighter than it should.

At the hole in the wall Cull climbed back into the study, a massive dent in his armor and blood dripping down his chin. He took stock of the situation, decided that Skip was having more problems than the Jury, and made his way over to Angel until he loomed over her.

He readied Charnel, preparing to put everything the sword had into one blow. And then a dagger struck him in the back, and ice rippled across his body, covering his head.

Skip was so confused and exhausted, he stopped releasing lightning to look for whoever had thrown the blade. He spotted them just as another dagger sank into his eye socket and was dead before he hit the ground.

The dagger pulled itself from Skip's head and sailed across the room—straight into to Snow's waiting hand as she blinked into the center.

Angel, finally able to breathe, shoved herself to her feet and delivered an uppercut to Cull's head hard enough to shatter the ice still on him. This time when he hit the ground, he stayed down.

"How the fuck did you get here?" Angel asked Snow.

"Do you really care right now?"

Angel shrugged, and the two women turned their sights on Haegan. He was the only person in the room Snow didn't recognize, but given the circumstances, she felt pretty safe assuming he wasn't on their side. Angel charging him and screaming bloody murder was just confirmation.

Taking the initiative, Haegan flung Phoenix off to the side like a rag doll and threw his hammer out to meet them. Phoenix's head swam with pain as he tumbled across the floor. He was too hurt to stand, but he refused to be out of the fight just yet. Crawling, he managed to prop himself up against a wall and turned to examine the battlefield. Of everyone, Church was having the most trouble, but Snow and Angel weren't in good shape either. And there was still no sign of Brass.

The Fellblade had him. Somewhere. But there was a way to draw him back from wherever he was hiding. He'd seen Angel do it completely by accident. All he needed was a bright enough flash of light. With one hand, he dug into his belt pouch to find a lightstone. With the other, he summoned his wand back to his waiting palm.

He rolled the lightstone to the part of the room he'd last seen Brass in, aimed his wand, and fired. The blast shattered the lightstone, bathing the study in a burst of light. As the light banished most of the shadows in the room, the Fellblade coalesced back into existence, followed a moment later by Brass, who was covered in black blood.

Brass pointed his sword accusingly at the Fellblade. "That was cheating!"

The Fellblade looked at him in utter disbelief. The freelancer shouldn't still be alive, and yet there he was. He readied his sword to meet Brass's, only to be blasted off his feet as Phoenix emptied the rest of his wand's charge into him. Brass turned to him, briefly offended that Phoenix had stolen his bad guy, until he saw the state Church was in.

Brass rushed in their direction. The Jury shoved Church aside to meet him. Of all the Starbreakers, none of them had more souls crying for revenge against them than Brass. The Betrayer priest was going to enjoy this.

With a wicked grin, he spoke a curse against Brass—one to bury him in all his regrets. The very same one he'd used to cripple Snow.

This would be delicious.

His anticipation turned to confusion as the curse failed to take hold. No, it did. He could feel it. Brass was experiencing his every regret in life, all at once. But instead of bringing him to his knees, it did little more than produce a frown.

Shock turned to blinding rage. Of all the insolent, unrepentant, disgusting displays of arrogance he'd ever seen, this filled him with more anger than any other. The voices baying for Brass's blood were innumerable, and Brass walked around without a care. So consumed by indignation, he didn't have time to wield another curse, and Brass stabbed.

The Jury of Saint Adresta stared at the blade in his chest. Although it didn't kill him, he knew that his time in this world was at an end. But he had been given a chance. He could make sure revenge was served, one last time. With the ferocity of a man with nothing left to lose, the Jury grabbed onto Brass's arm and said another prayer. If he could not break the freelancer's spirit, he would break his body.

But something went wrong. Partway through the prayer, his lungs stopped drawing air correctly, and a sharp pain raced up his side. His insides grew cold and numb.

Snow twisted the knife in the Jury's back while covering his mouth, just in case he thought he could manage to get some words out with freezing lungs. Memories of the prayer he'd used on her, everything she'd felt, came rushing back as she held him. She leaned in, her voice cold against his ear. "Got you."

Jury hadn't noticed that Angel had taken over the fight with Haegan, and Snow had come for him. As the numbness spread to his whole body, Jury felt an odd moment of comfort that it would be Snow, out of all of them, to finish him off. He got to serve revenge one last time after all.

"Thanks," Brass said.

"Shut up and fight," Snow said before blinking away to rejoin Angel.

Brass didn't bother trying to hide the grin on his face as he took in the chaos around him. They were all together again. Fighting for their lives against a bunch of murderers and magic lunatics. There was blood everywhere, and everything was smashed, burnt, or frozen.

He hadn't felt this at home in years.

Picking Zealot up off the floor, he held out the hilt of the weapon to its rightful wielder. "How about it, Church? Got anything left in the tank?"

Church held up a hand. "One second. Please."

"Sure, sure," Brass said, nodding in understanding. He bit his lip while he waited and scrunched his face. "Could you take the sword though? It's starting to burn."

Rolling his eyes, Church grabbed Zealot by the hilt and used the weapon to prop himself up. Brass shook out his already blistering hand before blowing on it.

"Gah, that thing does not like me."

"Can't imagine why."

57

FALL

As Snow and Angel continued to try to bring down Haegan, their fight spilled out of the study and into the halls of the manor. What little furniture could be found in the halls, he threw at them. And when there was none, he threw his hammer or tossed them into each other. Every time one of them managed to get close, they were launched backward or into the air. But between the two of them, they were able to keep pressure on him.

Angel was knocked through a wall in a shower of brick and mortar, crashing to the floor in a massive dining hall filled with tables of half-eaten food. A moment later, Snow blinked into the room after her, trying to steer clear of Haegan's flying hammer. Getting back to her feet, Angel picked up the closest table and flung it at Haegan, who stopped it in midair, turned it around, and propelled it back toward her along with every loose bit of debris she'd created going through the wall.

Snow blinked in close, only to be lifted off her feet and suspended in midair. Haegan stared at her, judgment in his eyes.

"One of the greatest powers ever forged by the Old World, and you squander it on selfish gain."

Snow spat at him, and it froze on his cheek. Before he could say anything else, someone threw a goblet that pinged off of his armor. Confused, Haegan turned around.

Standing a ways behind him was Brass, Fountaine in one hand, dinner plate in the other. He readied his arm to throw the plate. "Let her go."

The actual doors of the room burst open, and Church strode in, Zealot at the ready. Limping in behind him came Phoenix. Angel shoved the table off of her and got to her feet. They had him surrounded.

Haegan scanned the room, weighing his options as he tried to determine how long the fight had taken. He reminded himself not to forget what this fight was really about. Time. He had to give Silas time.

"Another step, and she dies," he warned, tightening his telekinetic grip on Snow.

"Fuck. That," Snow grunted.

She didn't have much mobility left, but she had just enough to flick her wrist and throw Companion Piece into the floor. As soon as the blade hit, ice spread across the floor and up Haegan's body. It broke his concentration, and she blinked away.

At the same time, Phoenix aimed his wand.

The fire cell was out. Spider silk wouldn't do him any good. He couldn't get close enough to use the stunner, and he doubted a force blast from the wand would feel like much more than a strong breeze to Haegan's armor. But he'd been paying attention to how Haegan fought. And he had one trick left.

Smoke billowed from the wand, blanketing Haegan and completely obscuring his vision—he couldn't control what he couldn't see.

Haegan realized what Phoenix was doing and sent out a force wave to disperse the smoke. He was too late. It had given the Starbreakers the cover they'd needed to get close.

As the smoke parted, Snow blinked forward and dragged her fingers across Haegan's face. Ice spread where she touched, blinding him again. Angel came in and slammed a fist into Haegan's stomach before grabbing his hammer. They fought over it until Church came in with Zealot, batting aside Haegan's hand and letting Angel take his weapon. Brass, right behind him, drove Fontaine under a gap in the knight's armor and straight into his chest.

Haegan coughed up blood, and another wave of force tore from him. The others were blown back, but Angel dug her heels in, pulled back a fist, and punched, breaking the ice on Haegan's face. She kept punching, eventually having to grab him by the collar of his armor so she could hold him up and keep punching. Haegan's resistance crumbled under the assault until he was limp and bleeding. Angel pulled her fist back one more time, ready to deliver the killing blow, only for it to freeze inches from Haegan's face.

Through clenched, crimson teeth, Haegan snarled, "You are in my way!"

His eyes flashed a purple bright enough to match Angel's burning gaze and her grip on his collar broke as she was forced back. Arms shaking, he lifted both hands to the sky and pulled. The ceiling above began to rumble, then crack, as he pulled the building itself apart to create weapons to crush her with.

He turned his back to the others.

The Starbreakers moved in perfect sync. Phoenix tossed out a small lightstone with one hand, and took aim with his wand. With the last of his blast cell's power, he fired, shattering the stone directly in front of

Haegan's face and creating a dazzling flare of light. At the same time, Snow slid her foot forward, spreading a slick surface of ice across the floor that Brass immediately took advantage of as he slid forward on it until he collided with Haegan's legs and swept them out from under him. Standing back, Church gripped Zealot in both hands and wound his arms back. For just an instant as Haegan tumbled through the air, he made eye contact with the cleric.

The knight's eyes held the same righteous indignation that had propelled Church's own sword on that snowy ridge all those years ago. The desperate, painful need to fix what was wrong in the world. And the impotent frustration of realizing you couldn't. In that moment, Church finally understood him. Haegan had seen the same horror that all of them had. Broken the same way they had. They had turned their pain on each other. Haegan had turned his on the world.

"I'm sorry," Church whispered.

The servant of the Guiding Saint slashed through the air with Zealot, and a spectral copy of the angelic sword materialized beside Haegan to mimic the strike. Before the knight could hit the ground, the magical extension of the sword's power cleaved into the side of his throat with a flash of divine radiance. Haegan went limp in the air, and crumpled to the floor with a wet thud.

He didn't get back up.

With a heavy heart, Church lowered his sword, the deed done. In spite of everything Haegan had done and all the pain he'd caused them, Church only pitied him. And now the number of people who had died because of their failure had climbed by one more. He prayed it would be the last.

The Starbreakers stared at the body. The source of all their troubles, a magical powerhouse, and maybe a monster of their own making, was now just a man. And a dead one at that.

"So . . . is it over?" Brass asked.

A second later, Haegan's lifeless eyes and mouth flashed with a blazing purple glow, and the debris around the room was scattered into the air as the ground around his body cracked and the estate itself was rocked by a final wave of invisible force ripping out from Haegan's body. The cracks Haegan had made in the ceiling rapidly expanded, and everything began to collapse.

"Right! Shouldn't have said anything!" Brass cried.

"This place is unstable!" Phoenix shouted. "We need to move, now!"

He tried to force himself up, only for his arms to fail him. The minor healing Church had been able to give him had kept him alive, but he was still too weak to move as fast as he needed. Brass and Church both scrambled to help him up, even as the quaking floor threw them off balance.

Debris rained down as the ceiling began to collapse above them. Phoenix threw up a force shield above his head, but everyone else was exposed, and none of them were moving as fast as they needed to. Snow looked for a way out, and spotted a window. She had the balance to move in a place this unstable. If she blinked and hauled ass, she could get away.

But the others couldn't.

Instead of running, she slammed her hands into the ground, and ice exploded out from around her. A dome of ice rapidly solidified around the Starbreakers, just as a massive portion of the ceiling broke apart and rained down on them. The dome cracked, very nearly giving out until Snow refroze it. She lost feeling in her hands. What little color remained in her skin vanished. But she kept going. As more of the building collapsed onto them, she willed the ice to freeze it in place, turning it into more structure for the dome, until finally the impacts against the dome stopped.

The ice around them crackled and popped as it settled under its own weight, but it held. Snow panted, her whole body shaking from the exertion. But she'd done it. Everyone was safe.

Brass looked up at the dome above them, beaming. "Nice save, Snow!"

She collapsed.

58
A NEW DAY

Snow woke up on the softest mattress she'd slept on in years, and she was immediately unsettled by it. She sat up with a start. She was in a room at an inn. A nice one too, going off the bedding. Her armor was gone, replaced by a tunic and pants. It was blue, but it wasn't hers, which immediately left her with questions.

Brass was at her bedside, sleeping upright in a chair with a fresh set of clothes and a new pair of thigh-high leather boots. When she stirred, one of his eyes cracked open. A smile spread across his face, and he sprang out of his chair.

"You're awake!"

"How long was I out?"

A somber expression came over Brass, and he stopped looking at her. Worry lines creased his forehead.

"Snow, I don't know how to tell you this. It's . . . been almost two years."

"*What?*"

Brass burst out laughing, almost falling out of his chair. Tears welled in his eyes as Snow's scowl deepened.

"But no, it's been a day and change," Brass said when he finally calmed down.

"Why are you here?" Snow asked. "Also, where is here?"

Brass brought Snow up to speed. Angel dug them out of the remains of the estate, and managed to drag everyone who couldn't walk back to the Rusted Star. The next day, while Snow had still been asleep, recovering from overexertion, Phoenix went to Ink with everything they had, and the High Inquisitive was currently digging through the remains of the estate. She'd found plenty of bodies so far, including Haegan and the bounty hunters he'd tried to sic on them, but so far there was no sign of anyone matching Silas's description. In light of Snow's help capturing Pitch and killing several names on Corsar's most wanted list, Ink was willing to overlook the rumors that the Cold-Blooded Killer had been involved in the deaths of the Golden Shield.

Snow chafed at the last part. She knew Ink well enough to know that this wasn't simple forgiveness. She owed the High Inquisitive a favor now. And Ink always called those in.

But Brass saved the best news for last. This morning, Ink passed along a message from the Handler: In light of his client disappearing and his client's financier meeting "an untimely end," the contract had been canceled.

Nobody seemed to care about the why so much as the results—there was no longer a price on their heads.

As for the change of clothes, Brass assured Snow that Wings had been the one to handle that while she was healing her. Her things were in the trunk at the foot of the bed.

"So then why are you here?"

"Someone had to make sure you didn't run off the second you woke up." Brass gave her a knowing wink. "Think you can stand?"

Snow hopped out of bed to test her legs. Everything still felt sore, but she was steady enough. Brass beamed. "Come on downstairs then. The place across the street has a damn fine cook."

Brass dragged her downstairs. The Rusted Star itself was empty, but just outside, a small crowd had gathered to marvel at the new inn that had quite literally sprung up overnight. As Snow got a good look outside, she realized that they weren't in Olwin anymore. They were in Akers.

The crowd's eyes shifted from the building to Snow and Brass as they exited. A few were bold enough to ask questions. Others waved at them from their porches as they walked past.

Everyone seemed excited or intrigued, and yet, for a place that had been visited by a tavern that came out of the ground, it all seemed so surprisingly normal.

These people were surprised and interested in the recent events, but they were taking it in stride. No paranoid mobs demanding for the mysterious building to be destroyed. Nobody running off to find a watchman or an appraiser.

How did Phoenix find this place?

Across the street was Carp's, the inn Akers was used to having around. Brass threw open the doors to announce their arrival.

"Guess who's alive?" he called out.

Angel, Church, Ruby, Phoenix, and Elizabeth all sat around two tables that had been pushed together. Even Robyn was there, sitting in a specially made high chair next to her mother.

Conversation at the table faded, and the room got quiet except for Robyn's burbling. Snow considered turning around and walking out. Then Angel stood up and sauntered over. Now Snow wanted to hold her ground just to spite her. "What?" Snow demanded.

Brass nervously glanced from one to the other. Angel nodded to Snow. "Thanks for the save at Haegan's."

Snow's eyes widened, and they only got wider when she looked past Angel to the others and saw everyone else smiling at her. No anger. No pity. Just a bunch of people having lunch, some of them even looking genuinely pleased she was there.

She thought about leaving again.

A large man burst into the dining room from the kitchen, carrying a stack of plates, and his eyes lit up when he saw Brass and Snow. "Do I need to bring two more?"

Before Snow could protest, Elizabeth spoke up. "Yes."

She turned to Snow with a smile and told her to sit with her eyes. Brass was already pulling up chairs. With a groan, Snow sat down to lunch. It was only after the food was brought out that she realized how hungry she was. Brass hadn't been kidding about the cook at this place.

It was a few minutes before Snow got around to asking the question that had been hanging in her mind since Brass had told her the contract was rescinded.

"So, what now?"

"Well, now that you're not crashing in my inn, I can finally get out of here," Angel said. "Was gonna take off after lunch."

Phoenix's brow furrowed. "You're leaving?"

"You sound surprised. The whole contract mess is done. I said I was in for that. I didn't say I was sticking around after."

"Right." Phoenix's heart sank, even as he understood. This incident had brought them back together, but that wasn't the same thing as repairing what had been broken. Truthfully, he didn't even know what repairing it would look like. "Angel, I want you to know—"

"Save it. What happened, happened," she interrupted. For a moment, Phoenix expected a very colorful metaphor about where he could stick his wand. Instead her expression softened. Not much, but enough for him to notice. "But, the next time something like this goes down . . . don't be a complete stranger. Like I said, I don't want any of you dead. Yet."

Phoenix nodded. That was better than they'd left things last time. "Right."

Church cleared his throat. "I'm leaving too."

Phoenix wasn't surprised about this one, but Brass was. Especially after Ruby added, "And I'm going with him."

"Did I miss something?" Brass said. "Did you discover religion?"

"I don't actually know," she said.

Phoenix explained. "Ink thought there might be something off with Ruby after she found her in what was left of the Lilac, so Church and I looked into it. And there's something there."

Brass looked at Ruby, who was uncomfortably drumming her fingers on the table. He raised an eyebrow in question.

"Well, didn't really think about it before, when everything was happening so fast, but . . ."

Ruby held out her hand to Phoenix, who created a small flame at the tip of his wand and held it under her hand for several seconds. The flame licked at her skin, but she gave no reaction. When she pulled her hand away, there was no burn.

"Well that's a neat trick," Brass said.

"There's more," Phoenix said. He pulled the demon detection rod from his belt and held it up to Ruby. The rod gave off a blood-red glow.

Brass blinked. "Oh."

"It's *never* demons," Phoenix said. "Until it is."

"This is sort of my thing, but a lot of what I'd need to look into this is back home in Aenerwin," Church said.

"And I'd really like to know what's going on with me, so . . ." Ruby let the sentence hang for a few seconds before smiling sadly. "Besides. My job got burned down. I don't exactly have anywhere else to go."

"Can I come?" Brass asked.

Church suddenly looked very worried. Brass kept talking before either of them could voice a protest.

"I did sort of get you mixed up in all of this in the first place," he said. "I'd like to help you put your life back together. If you want the help."

Ruby smiled and shrugged. "I wouldn't mind the familiar face, but you'll have to ask my ride." She jerked a thumb toward Church, who now looked doubly concerned. Brass gave him an expectant smile.

"Sure . . . you can come," Church said. He could feel the color draining from his face, as he imagined Brass loose in Aenerwin. Staying in the church dormitory. "Beneger, help me."

Snow sat silently, watching and listening as plans were announced and being made. Then she realized all eyes had fallen on her.

"What about you?" Phoenix asked Snow.

Snow looked around at everyone at the table. At Church trying to hide his growing horror at the thought of having Brass around. Elizabeth passing tiny bits of mashed potatoes for Robyn to try. Angel warning Ruby about all of Brass's more annoying habits, and Brass alternately defending them and claiming them with pride.

This whole place felt so normal, so safe, and so very alien to her. But when she thought about how they probably weren't ever going to get another moment like this, she felt sad.

She missed having a family. She could admit that now, if only to herself.

"I don't know," she answered Phoenix. "I'll think it over."

Brass raised someone else's glass.

"I'm probably not going to get another chance to say this. So, I just want you all to know. These last few weeks have been the best time I've had in years."

"Brass, people have died," Church said.

"Well, way to kill the mood, Church." Brass's shoulders sagged. "I'm going to miss having the rest of you around to balance him out."

He tipped his glass to Robyn. "And I'm especially going to miss you, little bird."

"Aw ho!" Robyn exclaimed with glee, pointing at Brass.

Elizabeth turned to her daughter, surprised. "Wait, did she say something?"

"Owl?" Phoenix guessed.

"Uncle?" Church ventured.

Brass smirked in absolute victory. "No, I'm pretty sure she just said *asshole*."

The whole table balked at Brass, save for Snow, who had to cover her smile. Elizabeth stared at her child, at Phoenix, and then at the ceiling.

"Fuck."

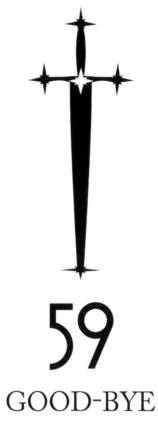

59
GOOD-BYE

After lunch, Angel decided it was time for her to go. She didn't hug anyone when she got up, though not for Brass's lack of trying. But she did let them walk her out, and she didn't decline a handshake from Phoenix.

"Thank you again. We wouldn't be alive without you," Phoenix said.

"I know."

She released her grip, and Phoenix thought he did a good job of hiding the fact that he couldn't feel that hand anymore.

"See you the next time somebody tries to kill us," she told him.

"Or maybe without the threat of death hanging over us?"

Angel considered Phoenix and the others. Forgiveness wasn't her forte.

Even if she didn't hate any of her old companions anymore, she wasn't there yet.

"Maybe."

Angel gestured with her head for Snow to follow her. "Come and get your stuff. I'm burning daylight."

Snow followed Angel inside the bar and collected her things from the room she'd woken up in. Angel intercepted her at the bottom of the stairs.

"Hey."

There was anger in Angel's voice. Snow thought she saw the tips of her fingers glowing, but that might have just been the sun. Snow's hands were full, but she maneuvered them to touch her daggers. If it came to it, she was ready to do this.

"Turning on us to save your own skin was a shit thing to do," Angel said.

"I know."

Snow tried to walk past Angel. Angel grabbed her by the arm. With all the restraint she could muster, Snow held off on stabbing her.

"You don't." Angel's grip tightened. "You weren't there when we found Brass. You didn't see the fucking mess they turned him into. That was what you were planning to do to all of us, and the only reason you didn't screw us was because you found out it was going to happen to you too."

"Make your point." Snow's skin grew colder to the touch.

"Brass doesn't hold a grudge over it. Nothing that bad happened to the others because of you, so *they're* all letting it slide too. But you don't get to just forget what you did," Angel said.

"What happened to 'thanks for the save'?"

"You did a good thing. Not the same thing as being a good person," Angel said. She frowned. "Not that any of us are good people."

Snow surprised herself by disagreeing with Angel. They had their faults, they'd certainly pissed her off and made her feel unwelcome, but Snow didn't think of the other Starbreakers as bad people.

"They want to forgive you," Angel said. "Earn it."

Snow said nothing, yanking herself free from Angel's grip. The two women exchanged a glare, and Snow left, feeling proud of them both. A few days ago, that conversation would have ended violently.

When she left, the ground around the Rusted Star began to shake, and the whole of the inn began to sink into the ground. First a few feet, and then all at once, as if a hole had opened up underneath it. It dropped down, and the earth closed up above it, leaving no sign that it had ever been there except for a patch of disturbed earth.

"That is absolutely fascinating," Phoenix said, staring at the dirt.

"I kind of wish it grew legs and walked," Brass said.

After a pause, Brass clapped his hands and told Church and Ruby to get their things. Church opted not to point out that he was the one who decided when they left and went along with it. More good-byes were said, and this time hugging was involved at Brass's continued insistence. Then, with a prayer, Church transported the three of them back to Aenerwin in a flash of light.

Seeing Church use that prayer still bothered Phoenix. He wondered if it ever wouldn't.

It was just Phoenix, Elizabeth, Robyn, and Snow now. Eyes fell on the assassin.

"So, figure anything out yet?" Phoenix asked.

Snow nodded. "Yeah, actually. The Handler was willing to put a hit out on me, and Clocktower was willing to pass that on. I need to put the fear of hell back in some people."

"Do I want to know how?"

"Nope."

"And after that?"

Snow paused. Something had been eating her about what Brass had told her, and she knew Phoenix well enough to know it was eating him too. "Silas is a loose end. And the one who tortured Brass. I'm gonna kill him."

"It doesn't have to be just you," Phoenix said.

"I know," Snow said. She repeated it, just to make sure she heard herself. "I know. But you've got enough on your plate. Plus, I can go places where you'd be killed on sight."

Phoenix started to protest, but Snow cut him off. "If something comes up or I need some extra hands—or *wings*—I know who to go to. I'll be fine. You've got a beautiful daughter and a damn good woman for a wife," Snow reminded him, jabbing a finger into his chest. "Don't fuck it up. Or I will steal her from you."

Phoenix, too stunned to speak, just nodded.

Snow looked around and threw her arms up. "Welp. I'm gonna head into town and find a place to crash that's more my speed."

"Take care of yourself," Elizabeth said.

"Always," Snow called back, already walking away.

Elizabeth sidled up to Phoenix as they both watched her leave. Robyn made some indistinct noise and fidgeted as if she were waving good-bye. Elizabeth glanced at her husband, not surprised by the wistful look on his face.

"What is it?" she asked.

"Nothing," he said. "I think I just realized how much I missed them."

A palpable weight lifted off of Phoenix's shoulders when he made the discovery. As happy as Elizabeth and Robyn both made him, something had always felt wrong about his life. It felt good just knowing what was missing.

The last time the Starbreakers had gone their separate ways, they'd hated each other. What they had now was fine. Better than fine, it was good. For the first time in seven years, things with his old companions were good.

And in a twisted way, he had Haegan to thank for that.

But the more he thought about the knight, the more his accusations echoed in his mind.

Abandoned the world.

He'd never thought of it like that before.

He'd spent too long hiding in his workshop—from his grief, from his guilt, from his fear.

It was time to get back to work.

ACKNOWLEDGMENTS

As a person, I often find myself ruminating on the nature of legacy and the impact each of us can have on each other's lives. Sometimes, when I feel like my life hasn't had much meaning or weight, I remember all the people whose lives I have had the privilege to be a part of and help shape. And this part of the book is where I get to give a little bit of that back.

It might be my name on the cover but there are so many people I owe the existence of this book to. I want to take this time and these pages not just to say thank you to them but to tell them that *you* did this. This book would not have happened without you and your part in my life, and I hope you are as proud of that as I am.

First and foremost, I want to thank my family. My parents, my sister, and of course the love of my life. Your belief in me and support of my passions and weirdness weren't just uplifting, they were motivating. You made me want to be that person you saw when you looked at me with pride already in your eyes.

I want to thank God, for giving me a gift and the opportunity to share it with the world. It is because of Him that I strive to be a positive force in every life I touch, and regardless of whether I was just a popcorn read or spoke to something in my audience's lives, I hope I was at least that.

I want to thank my editor, Bridget McFadden. Working with you was nothing short of an absolute pleasure. You know your stuff, and you are the standard by which I will probably judge every editor I work with for the rest of my life.

Thank you to Pitch Wars, for organizing an event that gave me the poke I needed to start putting *They Met in a Tavern* out there, and thank you to Sue Arroyo and the rest of the team at CamCat Books for seeing something special in *Tavern* like I did.

Rick Riordan, Karen Travis, Adam Carnavale, Matt Mercer, Matt Colville, Jenna Moreci—all of you inspired me to create and to tell fantasy stories that stick with people the same way yours stuck with me.

Thank you to Mrs. Eiffert, for putting the first "book" I ever wrote on the classroom's bookshelf, giving me my first audience, and sparking a love of writing that hasn't gone out since, and to Mrs. Glazer, for teaching me how to really answer the question of what a story is about.

Thank you to all of my beta readers: Christy Gasner, Maureen McSherry, Aya McGuire, Alivia Haven, C.W. Spalding, Katie Kalinyak, Megan McCarter, Lauren Birge, and Megan Chernosky. Your eyes saw things which mine could not, and this book is all the better for it.

All of you mean the world to this book and to me. From the bottom of my heart, thank you.

FOR FURTHER DISCUSSION

1. What do the lives of each of the Starbreakers after their disbandment say about them, and why might they have gone down the paths they did?

2. How does Elizabeth, Ink, Ruby, Bart, and Thalia not being former members of the Starbreakers affect their relationship and interactions with them?

3. This story is framed as a sequel to a previous series of adventures the characters had when they were younger despite these adventures largely never being written or shown. Does this story convey a sense of continuation, and if so, how does it achieve this?

4. All of the freelancer characters (The Starbreakers, Ink/Kira, and Wings/Elizabeth) have aliases which they use at various times. What do these aliases say about each character based on how and when they are used? What does it say about Brass being the only freelancer whose real name is never revealed?

5. In what moments or lines of dialogue do you think each of the main characters' worldviews are most evident? Where on an alignment chart would you place each of the characters?

6. Does basing the story around a group of heroes rather than a single individual enhance or detract from the story and its themes? Can any of the Starbreakers be said to be the main character?

7. Does the Starbreakers' relationship with each other make sense given their last experience together at the fall of Relgen? Why?

8. If you had been a member of the Starbreakers, how would you have reacted to the Fall of Relgen?

9. What does the story say about people's relationships to their pasts? How do the Starbreakers' feelings of their past compare to your feelings of your own? Are you the person you thought you would be seven years ago?

10. What similarities, parallels, and/or inspirations can you draw between this book and other stories and properties? How does it fit into the larger landscape of its genre?

ABOUT THE AUTHOR

E lijah Menchaca was born and raised in Bakersfield, California and has been writing and telling stories since he was five. After seeing his first short stories on his grade school classroom's bookshelf, he knew he was destined for greatness.

To chase that greatness (and a girl), he attended the University of Louisville where he minored in Creative Writing, discovered a love for Dungeons and Dragons, and got engaged. When the group of friends he'd made began to go their separate ways and the adventures they told around the table reached their conclusion, Elijah sought to explore his relationship to his past, which eventually gave birth to the story of *They Met in a Tavern*, his debut novel.

Now, based in Ohio, when he isn't exploring the world he's created with more stories, he's making new memories around the virtual table with his old friends, pondering the worlds of fantasy and superheroes on his YouTube channel, and playing the role of devoted partner to a woman far too good for him.

If you enjoyed
They Met in a Tavern by Elijah Menchaca,
try this excerpt from,
So You Had to Build a Time Machine, by Jason Offutt.

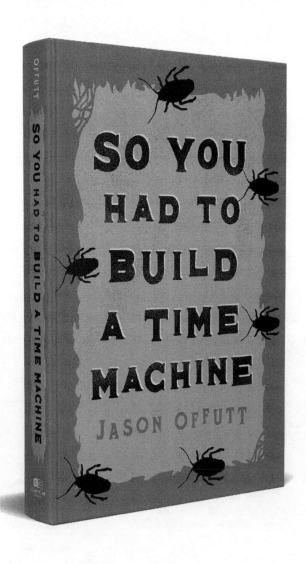

CHAPTER ONE
SEPTEMBER 1

1

IT WAS A WARM, PLEASANT Kansas City evening, the sun dropping below the skyline as Skid walked home from work. A drink in a friendly quiet place to unwind, she thought, would be nice. Slap Happy's Dance Club was not that place. It was crowded, loud, and for whatever reason Skid liked it. Sitting at the bar, she ordered a vodka tonic, smiling at the people on the dance floor. People she had no interest in talking to. That was a headache she could do without, not that anyone would bother her tonight. She hadn't washed her hair in two days, and she was sporting a sweat-stained T-shirt.

Then some moron sat next to her.

"Hey," he said, startling Skid. That barstool had been empty a second ago. The guy was about forty and dressed in Dockers. A whiff of ozone hung in the air around him. *I hope that's not his cologne.*

Skid nodded. "Hey."

He looked nice enough, but lots of people looked nice. Her father Randall wouldn't approve of him, but Randall didn't approve of anyone.

"I'm Dave," Dockers guy said. "Let me buy you a drink."

Skid froze. *Let me buy you a drink* wouldn't fly tonight. No, sir.

Her plans were: Drink. Relax. Go home. Do not repeat. *I shouldn't have come in here.*

"I'm Skid and thanks, but no th—" The bartender set a Bud Light in front of her. "—anks."

"You're welcome," Dave said through the neck of his bottle, and Skid knew this conversation wasn't going to end well.

A frown pulled on the corners of her mouth as she turned away from Dave and looked across the dance floor. A big hairy guy in red flannel stood next to the bathrooms. He could have stepped off the side of a Brawny Paper Towel package. Yikes.

"Is Skid your Christian name?" Dave asked, laughing, "The Book of Marks, right?"

Don't do it. Don't talk to him. Her last relationship ended two months ago when a thirty-two-year-old fool who acted like a teenager thought dating a nineteen-year-old behind Skid's back was a good idea. Spoiler alert, it wasn't. She'd successfully avoided men in her life since that one *(Guy? Jerk? Loser?)* and planned to keep it that way. She wanted a quiet life of watering plants, reading, and sitting in coffee shops ignoring everyone, especially those pretentious types who thought they were poets. She also wanted to find a couple of women who liked to binge watch online baking shows and didn't make her want to jump out a window. Of course, that would mean getting close to someone.

Now there was this guy.

She turned to him. Dave who drank Bud Light grinned at her like he'd just won twenty bucks on a scratchers ticket. Skid never bought scratchers tickets.

"I had a wreck when I was a kid," she said, pausing for a drink.

"Russian dancing bear, clown car, motorcycle, and tire skids. The usual. Now, if you—"

"Your last name's Roe, isn't it?" Bud Light Dave said.

"Maybe." Skid cut him a side look then elaborately looked around the bar for someone, anyone else, to talk to besides Bud Light Dave. There were no good prospects, so she decided to finish her drink, leave, and pick up Thai food on the way home. Stopping at Slap Happy's Dance Club was looking like a bad idea. Her eyes briefly met those of Brawny Man, who quickly turned away. The giant stood scanning the room with his back to the wall.

She sucked the last bit of vodka tonic from her highball glass, slurping around the ice. The bartender set down his lemon-cutting knife (absolutely the wrong knife for the job, Skid noted) and motioned to her empty glass. She shook her head.

"I'm a doctor," Bud Light Dave suddenly said, which seemed as likely as him being Mr. Spock from *Star Trek*.

She squinted at him. "Sorry. I don't have any pain. Unless I count you."

Bud Light Dave took a long suck off his bottle. "I'm not that kind of doctor. I'm a theoretical physicist. I spend most of my day postulating space-time."

Maybe, she considered, he actually thought he was Spock. She'd dated worse.

"Where?" Skid asked.

Bud Light Dave gazed at a beer poster, the guy holding a can of cheap brew and way too old for the bikini model next to him. "A little place south of town. Probably never heard of it."

"Try me."

"Lemaître Labs," he said, turning to face her. "But I probably shouldn't have mentioned that," his voice suddenly a whisper lost in the music.

She had heard of the place, a government weapons lab. Skid lifted her empty glass and swirled, ice clanking the sides. *Leave. Leave, Skid. Go home.*

But Skid couldn't resist two things: one, knee-jerk self-defense, and, two, proving someone wrong.

"Okay, science boy," she said, setting down the glass. "What's the underlying problem with the Schrödinger's cat scenario nobody talks about?"

A smile broke across Bud Light Dave's face. He smiled a lot. "I knew there was a reason I sat by you." He leaned back on his bar stool. "It's not so much of a problem as it is an ethical dilemma. We don't know if the cat inside the box is alive or dead, but we do know looking inside will kill it if it still is alive. At this point, the cat isn't alive, and it isn't dead. It's alive *and* dead. The would-be observer has to ask himself a question: should I, or should I not open the box, therefore preventing, or perhaps causing, the zombie catpocalypse?"

For a moment, just a moment, Skid considered she may have misjudged this guy. "Yes, but I was going more for chastising Erwin Schrödinger for being a bad pet owner."

This brought out a laugh, and Skid realized Bud Light Dave's smile was kind of nice, and, maybe the way his eyes looked in the dim bar light was kind of nice, too.

She shook her head. *No. Go home, now.*

"What about you?" he said. "What was all that about the Russian dancing bear and the clown car? You don't look like the type."

"Excuse me?" Her eyes flashed. She'd dealt with this kind of bullshit all her life and hated it. "What do you mean by 'type'?"

He took a drink and shrugged. "If I may perpetuate a probably unrealistic stereotype: four teeth, gang tattoos, rap sheet, the usual. You seem too well-educated to be a carney."

Standing, she jammed her glass onto the bar coaster. "My father had a master's degree in chemical engineering and worked at Los Alamos National Laboratory before he ran the family business."

Bud Light Dave nodded. "Los Alamos? Daddy was not a lightweight. What's the family business?"

Skid stretched over the bar and plucked the knife from its citrus-stained cutting board. "Hey," the bartender barked. She ignored him.

"A circus," she said. "I grew up in a fucking circus." Skid took a deep breath and drew the knife behind her ear, holding it by the tip of the blade.

Bud Light Dave was motionless. Someone behind Skid shouted, and Brawny Man took a step toward her but stopped. Skid lined up the too-attractive fake-boob model in the Dos Equis poster at the end of the bar.

"Skid," someone said. Bud Light Dave probably, but she couldn't be distracted. *Why are you doing this, idiot? Just walk away.*

But it was too late, she'd put herself in The Zone. Skid's arm shot forward and the knife flew from her fingertips. A blink later the knife was buried an inch into the wood paneling behind the poster, the blade pinned between Fake-Boob's baby blues.

Skid uncurled her hands toward Bud Light Dave and wiggled her fingers. "Ta-da."

A couple nearby clapped, but she didn't notice. She was proving some kind of point.

"So, you were raised in a circus, huh?" Bud Light Dave said, still grinning. "What's your rap sheet look like?"

Good people worked in the circus. Nice people. Sometimes even honest people. Family worked in the circus. Randall's mantra ran through her head—*If something needs done, do it*—and before Skid knew what was happening, she'd pulled her right hand back in a fist and let it fly at Bud Light Dave's stupid face.

The connection was solid. He fell backward in slow motion, the best way to fall, like Dumbledore from the Astronomy Tower, or Martin Riggs from the freeway. Blood splattered from Bud Light Dave's nose as if he'd caught a red cold. A smell, like a doctor's office, flooded Skid's nostrils as he dropped. She twisted her shoulders for a follow-through with her left if she needed it, just like Carlito the strongman had taught her, but she didn't need it. Bud Light Dave was there, on his way down, falling through air that suddenly felt thick and heavy.

He was right there. But he never hit the floor; he simply vanished.

2

THE GIRL WAS HOT. Problem was, her boyfriend was hot, too. He worked out, a lot, or was just naturally ripped like those TV vampires. Maybe the guy was a vampire. Damn it, vampires are so hot. Cord hated good-looking couples. He was in this business for the money, sure, but he flirted with the cute women as a bonus. A pretty boyfriend complicated matters.

"Why's it so hot in here?" asked a man built like the Muppets' Telly Monster.

Cord didn't stop at the question. He held up his left hand, his eyes focused on the EMF meter in his right.

EMF meters were useless. These devices measure AC electromagnetic fields, which are everywhere, even in nature, but especially in the kind of wiring in houses and definitely the Sanderson Murder House Cord bought because it was haunted. Supposedly. He'd installed a few extra devices in the walls to make the EMF meters ghost hunters brought with them light up like they'd discovered something. "Ghosts create electromagnetic fields," he told the skeptical ones who sometimes come through. If someone doubted him, it always made Cord smile. "You forget the Law of Conservation of Energy. Energy can neither be created nor destroyed; it can only be transformed. So, if ghosts exist, they're made of invisible energy, such as, oh, I don't know, a magnetic field. You can prove me wrong, if you'd like."

This would garner some "oohs" from the crowd, and the skeptic usually shut up.

VISIT US ONLINE FOR
MORE BOOKS TO LIVE IN:
CAMCATBOOKS.COM

FOLLOW US

CamCatBooks   @CamCatBooks   @CamCat_Books